SINFUL DESIRES

WILD ONE PUBLISHING

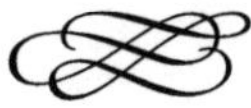

KATYA ENSMORE MIRANDA MAY BRE ROSE

IRIS JAMES ROSA LEE M. BONNET

KEEPING OUR SECRETS

KATYA ENSMORE

ABOUT KEEPING OUR SECRETS

One weekend fling was all it took for my life to be turned upside down. Or at least I thought that was all it took.

Two pink lines...

I tried to contact the father, but got no response. A day after I found out I was pregnant, I learned my mom got remarried and we were moving to another country.

But that wasn't the kicker.

Not even close.

Turns out the fling isn't a fling any longer. When my mother and I arrive at our new house, and I meet my new stepbrother, he turns out to be the guy who blew me off a month earlier.

And now he was going to be right across the hall.

Which made everything even more complicated.

Especially when things heat up between up, and we have to tell our parents the truth.

CONTENT WARNING

Due to some of the content of this fictional story, it is recommended for mature readers of eighteen years old and above.

Topics may include, but are not limited to: death of a family member, flashback to motor vehicle accident, teenage pregnancy, and underage drinking.

If you are unsure of the content and would like to contact me for more specifics, please feel free to email me (Katya.Ensmore@gmail.com).

CHAPTER 1

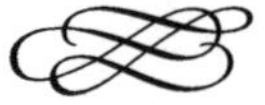

MAIRI

I hit the snooze button and stared up at the ceiling.

A kaleidoscope of stars stared back at me. It didn't surprise me I was in Michael's room again. It didn't matter which room I went to sleep in, most mornings this was where I woke up.

I rolled over to glance at the clock.

The movement was just enough to make my stomach turn again.

I was up and out of the bed so fast my head spun, barely making it into the Jack and Jill bathroom that connected his bedroom to mine.

A familiar dull ache in my chest reminded me that Michael wouldn't be pounding on the door for me to hurry.

My brother wouldn't be banging on that door. Not today, or tomorrow. Never again would we bicker about the timing of our showers, or how much hot water was left. No matter how many years passed, this ache would be a constant reminder of him being gone.

Especially on days like today where I really could have guilted him into holding my hair as I emptied the contents of my stomach for the fiftieth time this week.

Tears sprung to my eyes as I used my elbows to brace myself over the porcelain bowl. I closed my eyes, hoping the feeling would pass.

Both feelings.

If only grief was a person, so I could smack the shit out of them.

I pushed myself back from the toilet bowl just enough to situate my body so that my back was against the cool bathtub. Then I pulled my knees up to my chest and rested my head there while I thought back to how I got here.

This whole mess all started a year ago.

The night I almost died.

The truth was, at times, I still felt like I was dying. It took some time for me to stop wishing I had died the day I lost my other half, my twin. It was getting better day by day, even if a chunk of me was forever gone.

A million different scenarios ran through my head on almost a daily basis since the accident.

Why did we go have to go out that night?

Could we have done anything different?

Michael and I left my best friend Jen's house just after midnight on a school night.

The roads were clear.

There was no rain, sleet or snow.

Neither of us had been drinking.

It was only a night of movies and popcorn. With Jen's parents in the other room, none of us could have gotten away with sneaking a drink. Even if we'd been drinking, Michael would have stayed sober. Every time Jen and I drank at parties, Michael was the self-appointed designated driver.

What we hadn't counted on was someone without the same sense of self preservation. A middle-aged man who thought he could drive home with a blood alcohol level two times the legal limit. A drunk driver who less than two blocks away from the pub ran a red light and broadsided our vehicle.

Maybe we would have been okay if he hadn't have been driving eighty kilometres per hour.

The only thing I knew for sure these days was that I sure as hell wasn't going to blame my best friend for the reason Michael was with us that night.

My brother and I had always been close, but we had our own set of friends. Lately, he had been tagging along with me because he had a thing for Jen. Unlike most sisters, I didn't care that he wanted to crash our girl time. I actually wanted them to get together because if everything worked out, then Jen would be my sister for real.

To this day, I hadn't told Jen about my brother's true feelings.

Maybe I would someday, but not now.

It was hard enough for her to lose a friend, but I didn't want her to have the added guilt of being part of the reason he was there that night. Michael was so head over heels for her that he wouldn't have wanted to leave her with that pain.

After the accident, I spent a week in the hospital, in and out of unconsciousness. The only thing I remembered were snippets of me asking for Michael. They refused to tell me what happened to him until I was out of the woods.

Michael was unresponsive when they removed him from the mangled wreckage that was our shared car.

They weren't able to resuscitate him in the ambulance on the way to the hospital. For an entire month after the funeral, I didn't leave the house. I could barely stomach any food, but when I couldn't handle it anymore, that was the only reason I left his room.

I did all of my coursework for school online. The only reason I made it through this last year was because of Jen.

The only thing I wouldn't admit to my mom or Jen was that most nights, I slept in Michael's bedroom. My mom refused to go in there, which was just fine by me.

As close as I had been with my mom before everything happened, now we were just a couple of strangers passing in the hallway of our house. Halfway through my self-isolation stint, she had acted disinterested in me, and everything around her. She threw herself into work so much that I barely saw her and I threw myself into school. At least with all of my hard work, I would get to be the valedictorian of our class when I graduated.

~

"I'm late," I told my best friend as she drove down the road from the mall.

After I had dragged my ass off the bathroom floor, I took the bus to the mall, where I wandered around until I got up the nerve to buy something I never thought I'd be buying while I was still in high school.

Jen took her eyes off the road and looked at me funny. "Are you grounded or something? It's only five o'clock. Your curfew is eleven. Do you want me to speed up? I'm already going ten over the limit."

"I don't want you to go any faster, you speed demon." I rolled my eyes. "I'm not grounded, and mom didn't change my curfew yet. I'm late, late, if you know what I mean." I took a deep breath. "So you know, she might just change it to some time after never when she finds out why I needed this excursion."

She took her eyes off the road again. "You're preggers?"

The car swerved, so I instinctively reached for the wheel.

"I got it," she told me.

"You know how I am."

The only reason I was riding in her car was because after what happened to my brother, mom didn't want me to drive anymore. After what we both went through this past year, I didn't blame her. She probably wouldn't have wanted me driving with Jen either if she knew how bad she was when she was behind the wheel. She had a tendency to take her eyes off the road and gesture with her hands when she talked. With her, both had the possibility of ending up in a ditch.

"Sorry," she responded. "I shouldn't be so insensitive." She eased her foot off the accelerator and allowed the vehicle to slow down closer to the speed limit. "You didn't answer my question."

I sighed. "It's the only explanation I can come up with."

"I don't know. Maybe you're just worried about finals and graduation. Studies have shown that stress can cause you to miss or be late."

"I've never been late."

"There's a first time for everything."

"That there is," I responded.

"Is that why you wanted me to pick you up at the drugstore?"

"Mom is out on another date with James, and I didn't want to risk her seeing the box."

"Where do you have it stashed? I didn't even see it."

I reached into the inside pocket of my jacket and pulled out the package.

"Is that one of those early ones?" she asked.

"I don't think I need an early one. Easter was a couple months ago."

She nodded her head. "Oh yeah, that's right. Hard to believe it's been that long."

It had been the one-year anniversary of Michael's death during Easter break and, of course, my mom was conveniently out of town with her new boyfriend, James. So Jen talked me into something crazy to keep me from dwelling on the memory of his death.

It didn't take much for her to convince me.

We packed enough clothes for the week, took a taxi to the airport and used her dad's credit card to buy two tickets to the cheapest place.

Which just so happened to be Paris.

Spending one week in the city of love was all it took for my life to change forever.

Well, there were a couple of wrong turns somewhere too. Losing my twin, not wanting to attend college before losing my virginity, alcohol and a gorgeous hunk of a man, contributed to the delinquency of this girl. Yes, I was eighteen, but it was my last year of high school. The death of my brother fuelled my desire to change into the perfect daughter.

Maybe then I would garner a bit of my mom's attention?

Unlikely story.

I transformed into little Miss perfect, an honour roll student who never dated, and never did anything wrong. Maybe people would have called me a control freak, and until my trip, I would have concurred.

"Are your parents home?" I asked her.

"Tonight's date night, so they won't be home until after midnight."

"What about your brother?"

"Josh is going through an emo phase, so he won't leave his room."

"He probably found your dad's porn stash," I teased.

"Ew." She made a face. "I don't need that visual."

"Do you think he'd leave us alone long enough to do this stupid test I don't want to do?"

"Wanna spend the night?" she asked. "Just like old times?"

"I don't have extra clothes with me."

"Don't be a dingbat. You can borrow some of mine," she told me. "Just not my underwear, cause that's gross."

"Don't worry. I don't want to wear any of your granny panties anyway."

"I don't wear granny panties." Her cheeks turned red. "I'll have you know I went shopping the other day and got some nice lacey ones."

"I'm not going to borrow any of your butt floss ones either."

"I'm not even going to dignify that with an answer."

"You just did," I told her.

"Whatever." She rolled her eyes. "Are you staying over or not?"

"I could use a night away from home."

"One night away from home coming right up," she replied as she took the next exit and headed in the direction of her neighborhood.

Within twenty minutes, we were pulling into her garage.

"Josh," she called into the empty house. "I'm home."

No response.

"See, emo phase."

"I still stand by my original statement," I teased her. She deserved it after all the times she told me my brother's extended showers were because he was jacking off.

"We should do this downstairs. Less chance of the little punk overhearing our conversation," she told me as she opened the door next to the garage that led into her basement.

The small package weighed a ton as I followed her down the stairs.

Talk about the ultimate punishment for caving into peer pressure.

A few moments later, I found myself locked in her downstairs bathroom, while I peed on a stick, to see if two pink lines would be the consequence of my one week of letting go.

The road to hell was paved with good intentions, or a crazy weekend in Paris, as it were.

I would have gone home to do the test, but I left the house before my mom returned from her business trip. After a couple of weeks away, she would be tired, so I knew she'd be at home.

I wanted to avoid any possibility of her knowing anything was going on until I knew more. I didn't have to imagine what her reaction would be to finding out what we were up to.

Even the mere mention of a possibility of me being pregnant would probably send her over the edge.

She would be devastated because she had better hopes and dreams for me than she did for herself at my age. My mom married my father when she was eighteen, got pregnant a month later, and their marriage lasted a whopping year after that. We were three months old when our parents separated and she emigrated from Scotland to Canada. Dad remained in Edinburgh and had since remarried, but he visited when he could and we went there twice.

Our mom did what she could, but being a single parent had

always weighed on her. Not that our dad wasn't in our life, but she had no other family where we moved. Also, he couldn't just drop by to pick us up for the weekend or to give her a break.

She had travelled a lot over the years for business, and since she started dating again, she was gone more. Unfortunately, that left me alone most of the time, but being the model daughter, until now, of course, she trusted me without question.

However, I knew if I was pregnant, she'd find a way to blame herself.

The last thing I wanted to do was disappoint her.

Yet, sitting here in the bathroom with Jen holding my hand as we waited two minutes, as directed on the box, I knew deep down I would be.

CHAPTER 2

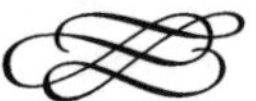

LIAM

One of my friends was getting married in a week, so a bunch of us flew to London to celebrate one last weekend with him before he got hitched.

We were almost at the pub when my phone rang. Seeing it was my dad, I said, "Sorry guys, I'll be a minute, then I stepped to the side and answered before it went to voicemail.

"Hi Dad."

"I'm not bothering you, am I? Do you have a minute?"

"Yeah," I responded. "We're just going out for drinks."

"I know you're on a trip, but I was hoping I could ask you a question."

"Okay?"

"You know that since Alana and I reconnected that we've been dating for the past half year."

"Yeah."

"Being back here where we found each other for a second time and after everything we went through with your mom made me realize I didn't want to let her go. So last night, I asked her to marry me and she said yes."

"Congratulations," I told him. "When's the wedding?" He was back in Las Vegas for another hotel convention, so it didn't surprise me that he got carried away with the nostalgic moment.

"That's actually the reason I'm calling you," he replied. Then he paused for a moment, as if he was trying to consider his next words. "What would you think if I told you that neither of us wants to wait any longer?"

"You're asking for my permission to get married now?"

"More like I'm asking you if it would bother you if you weren't here for it?" he responded. "I understand if you want us to wait, and if it's that important to you, we will."

"If you want to elope, go ahead," I answered.

"Thank you, son. You don't know how happy it makes me that you're on board with this."

I didn't begrudge him his happiness because he had been a widower and hadn't dated at all since Mom died. It wasn't like I was still a small child having to deal with a new mom; I was an adult living away from home. Her presence wouldn't affect my life in the grand scheme of things.

My dad had been sad for so long, it was great to see him getting out of the funk. He was too young to be a widower. I couldn't fathom expecting him to remain alone for the rest of his life. Running into Alana at a convention in Las Vegas just before Christmas last year had been the best thing for him. It had been a complete fluke they even reconnected after so many years.

They dated for a couple of years when they were in high school, but went their separate ways when they got into different universities. That was where my dad met my mom, and they were married shortly after. My parents were together and blissfully in love until my mom lost her fight with cancer five years ago.

"Have you guys decided where you're going to live after?" Considering Alana lived on a completely different continent, it was a relevant question.

"I'm hoping Alana and her daughter will come to live with me," he responded. "I'm sure you'll like her."

If I didn't, I wouldn't be there long enough for it to matter. This was my last summer vacation before I entered the workforce. At that point, I would live wherever my new career would take me. Which, for all I knew, could be on the other side of the country.

"When do you think you'll be back?"

"I'll be back next weekend."

"And are they moving in with us right away?"

"If everything works out the way Alana and I want, they'll be at the house within a month. She still needs to give notice at work and her daughter has to finish school for the year. Then they'll organize whatever they need to for relocating and then pack their house up."

Mulling that over, I still had one more month until everything changed.

"Look, I know it will be an adjustment, but you'll be back at school in the fall."

"As long as you're not expecting me to look after her all the time."

"Not at all."

"Great. I'll see you when you get home."

"Thanks again, son."

"No problem, Dad." I ended the call.

I glanced up at the guys, who all looked at me with matching expressions.

"Your dad's getting married again?" Rick asked.

I sighed. "Yeah." No one was a fan of change, and this was a big one.

"Is he moving?"

"Nah, she is. Apparently she's got a daughter too."

Darren chuckled. "Good luck with that."

"Hope you're not stuck babysitting for the entire summer while they're on their honeymoon," Rick added. "Ashley's mom remarried someone close to her age and they're gonna have a baby. They roped her into looking after her step-sister for a couple of weeks while they go on a baby moon or whatever the fuck it's called."

Fuck.

I didn't even think about that being a possibility. I didn't know anything about Alana's daughter. Hell, I didn't even know she had one until tonight.

"Maybe I'll just be conveniently gone for most of the summer," I laughed. "At least I'll be returning to uni in the fall."

"There's that," Rick replied as he pushed open the door to enter the pub.

The pub wasn't packed, but it wasn't empty either. There were no booths available, so we sat next to each other at the bar. In a way, it was the perfect place to sit because the bartender was right there and drinks were at our fingertips.

Rick elbowed me. "She totally wants you."

"Not feeling it tonight, man." It was hard to miss the leggy brunette on the other side of the bar, but lately I had no interest in starting anything with anyone.

"That's what you've been saying for months."

I shrugged, then took a swig of my beer.

"It's not like she's going to suddenly walk in the door and see you. She lives on the other side of the planet," Darren interjected.

"This has nothing to do with her."

"Like hell it doesn't."

"It doesn't."

"Whatever you say, man. I'm gonna go see if she wants to spend some time with the Rickmeister."

I rolled my eyes. "No woman wants the Rickmeister, especially when he speaks in the third person."

"The ladies like me just fine," he replied as he picked up his drink and moved to the end of the bar.

Darren and I watched and waited for the usual response. Rick sat down next to the brunette, whispered in her ear, and was rewarded with a fruity daiquiri shower. The woman was on her feet and had marched away in a huff before he even knew what had happened.

"Looks like we're ending early," Darren chuckled.

"Looks like," I agreed, shaking my head. "Rick's gotta be Rick."

"You'd think he'd learn. What do you think he said to her?"

"Who knows?"

We finished our drinks in record time while we waited for Rick to saunter his way back to us.

"Sorry guys," he said as he approached.

"It was worth the laugh," Darren responded.

We meandered through the ever-growing crowd and made our way onto the street. We walked a couple blocks before we agreed to take the last transit boat back to our hostel in Greenwich.

My phone buzzed in my pocket.

Paris girl: Hey, how's London?

Paris girl: I wish I could have been there with you.

Paris girl: School's almost over!

I lifted the phone to snap a photo for a response. With my eyes glued to the screen, I wasn't paying attention to my surroundings. Which was why I didn't see the drunkard ambling in my direction. Just as I put my thumb on the screen, someone suddenly nudged me in the side, which was when the phone slipped out of my hand.

It was almost like everything went in slow motion as I watched it drop, hit the edge of the boat and drop over the edge into the water.

Fuck me... was my last thought as I watched the surface of the water, willing the phone to magically return to me.

CHAPTER 3

MAIRI

I made a mistake.

A slight error in judgement that I would have to live with for the rest of my life. It wasn't like I was dying or anything... That was, unless my mom killed me when she found out.

"I'm here for you, no matter what happens," Jen assured me as she squeezed my hand.

I stared at the stick, willing it to have different results than all the other previous times I'd taken the test. Jen's watch beeped, making us both jump. I took a deep breath and looked in the window for the result.

My stomach lurched at the sight of two pink lines. "Are we sure we know what two lines mean?" I asked her, even though I knew deep down what it meant.

"We read the directions five times before you peed on the stick. I'm pretty sure it still means what it meant the first time we read them."

"Well, I guess that's that," I sighed. Obviously, they all showed I was indeed pregnant. "This can't be happening," I squeaked.

I was positively fucked.

"Are you going to tell your mom?"

"What am I supposed to say? 'Hey mom, remember when Jen and I promised we wouldn't do anything crazy while you were away... well, we did. Oh, and by the way, I lost my virginity to some random stranger in Paris and I don't mean Ontario. I have no idea what his last name is, but you're gonna be a grandma.' Something like that?" I scoffed.

"Well, obviously you're not going to say that," she agreed. "Besides, that's not entirely true. Aren't you guys still texting?"

"Yeah."

"Are you going to keep it?"

"I don't know yet. Aborting... just doesn't feel right for me, and I'm not sure I could give up my baby. Knowing its out there—"

"Okay, that's your choice. So take time to figure out what you're gonna say to your mom. There is a timeline, but if you're gonna have the baby either way, you have time," she hugged me, as I sobbed on her shoulder.

"This isn't the end," she told me again. "You have options."

On our way out of the bathroom, I almost tossed the results in the garbage, but then reconsidered. This thing needed to go in the outside receptacle so her parents didn't find it and start asking questions before I was ready to tell my mom.

This was already enough of a clusterfuck.

The last thing we both needed was for Jen to get accused of being the one who was pregnant instead of me.

"What do you want to do tonight?" she asked.

"Let's watch a movie to keep my mind off things."

As much as I tried to focus on the random rom-com she put on, I couldn't stop thinking about the future.

I sure as hell wasn't ready to have a baby.

I didn't know if I was ready to be a mother.

"Are you ready to text him yet?"

"Not yet," I told her. "I'll do it tomorrow."

~

JEN DROVE me back home the next morning.

The entire ride home from Jen's house was silent. I didn't really know what to say. When I was shopping for the test, I had already decided if it was positive I would have the baby. I just didn't know until this morning if I would keep it and now I wasn't sure if I could say it out loud. I just didn't know how I was going to do it all on my own.

I still hadn't decided how I was going to tell my mom, but it wasn't like I could stay away forever.

When we pulled up outside my house, Jen put the car into park and turned to face me. "I know your life has just been blown all to hell, but I wanted you to know that whatever you decide, I'll be here for you."

I took a deep breath.

"I think I'm going to keep it."

"Really?"

I nodded my head.

"I'll be an awesome auntie," she told me. "He would have been there for you too, I know it."

She pulled me into a hug when my eyes welled up. "I know," I mumbled into her shoulder.

"Now dry those eyes before you go inside," she released me. "Cause it looks like your mom's here."

"Great."

"You don't have to tell her right away. You're also allowed to change your mind anytime. Why not just take a week to think about it?"

"I might do that," I responded.

"If you need to talk, you call me day or night. I don't care."

I got out of the car and waved as she drove away.

"I'm home," I called out, knowing my mom was somewhere in the house.

"We're in here, honey," Mom yelled from the kitchen.

My mom's boyfriend, James, was sitting at the head of the table when I entered the kitchen. He had broad, muscular shoulders and stood a little over six feet tall. He looked distinctive, with his salt and pepper hair. They'd been in a long distance relationship for six months, and lived in Edinburgh, which coincidentally was the same city my dad lived in.

"Hi guys," I greeted them.

"Hi, honey. How has everything been going while I was gone?" Mom asked, hugging me.

"It was good." I paused, but reconsidered telling her about the baby.

"Where'd you stay last night?"

"I stayed with Jen."

"Are you ready for your graduation?" James asked.

"Totally."

"What are your plans for next year?"

"I think I'm going to take a gap year," I responded.

Originally, I planned to go to university, but with the pregnancy, I needed another option. I'd already received several acceptance letters for university and had narrowed it down to two choices. In the future, I might regret not going to university right away, but right now it wasn't in the cards. Once things settled down, I'd revisit the decision to see if they would reconsider my application.

The only thing I was sure of right at this moment was that I wasn't ready to tell my mom and James I was going to have a baby. So telling them I wanted to take a year off from school seemed like the best option with the least amount of questions.

"That's perfect," she beamed.

"What do you mean, mom?"

"Well, honey," she started, and then glanced at James lovingly. "There's something that we wanted to tell you."

I looked back and forth between them. They both had huge smiles on their face, and I knew immediately where this was going.

"James and I got married in Vegas last weekend," my mom told me as she held out her hand, showing me her diamond engagement ring and wedding band.

"What does that have to do with my gap year?" I asked, unsure of how I felt about their quickie nuptials. I thought she was just going to tell me they were engaged, not married.

"You and your mom are going to move back to Scotland with me," James answered.

"Really?" I was truly excited.

With the pregnancy, there was no other option for me. But I'd be close to dad who I hadn't seen in almost a year.

"Yes, really," my mom answered with a smile. "We are going to leave the day after graduation. James has to fly back tomorrow."

"Are you sure you're okay with this?" James asked.

"Of course," I smiled. "I just wish that I could have been there."

"I know, honey. It was a last-minute decision. We got wrapped up in the moment and just did it."

"It's okay, I've just been thinking about finals," I responded.

"You'll be fine. You always do," my mom assured me.

"It has been a while since I visited Scotland," I told James.

"My son will be home for the summer. Maybe he can show you around."

"Oh, honey, isn't that great? I know you miss Michael, but maybe having another brother to hang out with will help ease the pain. Besides, you've always talked about having more siblings."

Did she really think James' son should be a replacement brother? I didn't know where she came up with that asinine idea, but as pissed off as I was, I was too tired to argue.

When I got upstairs that night, I picked up my cell, took a deep breath and texted the father of my baby. He deserved to know what was going on.

Me: Hey, how's London?

Me: I wish I could have been there with you.

Me: School's almost over!

The next day, when I hadn't heard from him I texted again.

Me: Hi! What sights are you seeing today?

A couple days later...

Me: Hi! Is everything okay? I haven't heard from you in a while.

A week later.

Me: We need to talk.

A week later, when I couldn't handle the radio silence, I sent him one last message.

Me: I'm moving.

That night, when he didn't respond, I blocked his number.

CHAPTER 4

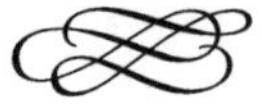

LIAM

A couple of months had passed since my week in Paris, yet I still couldn't get my mind off the woman I spent the last weekend of it with. Hooking up with a stranger hadn't even been at the top of my list when we planned our trip. It wasn't like I needed to travel to another country to find a one-nighter. Yet the moment I spotted her walking into the nightclub wearing a skin-tight dress, all bets were off.

While her friend was touring the sights, we were exploring each other between the sheets. My dad worked for a large hotel chain that owned one of the Paris properties, so I got my friends and me a deal for the week. Each of us had our own rooms and until the weekend I met her, we had done everything together.

Until she entered my orbit.

After that, nothing else mattered.

She was also there with a couple of friends who didn't mind at all when she disappeared.

One night of mind-blowing sex was followed by another because I just couldn't seem to get enough of her. It wasn't just my dick talking because I had been with more than a few women, but there was something about her that kept me coming back for more. Besides being physically compatible, we also had some great conversations when we weren't sleeping or screwing.

On the last morning, I woke up alone. The only reminder that she had been there was the sweet scent of her perfume on the pillow beside me. It had been the first time I wasn't the first one to leave in the morning. Hell, most of the time I didn't spend the night.

If they weren't my girlfriend, there wasn't an obligation.

But it was different with her.

From the moment I saw her, we just clicked. When she left, a part of me had been thankful we didn't have to deal with the awkward goodbyes. It disappointed a tiny part of me when she didn't get my number, but at the same time, it worked out perfectly.

On the last night we were there, I had almost left it alone. But then I remembered my connections, so I conned her friend's phone number out of the main desk. Since then, we'd been texting back and forth with a couple of video calls when we could. It was going good, until last month when she sort of dropped off the planet. I chalked it up to her moving on with her life, so after my last unanswered text, I did, too.

After all, we were from two different countries.

Besides, I had a five-year plan that didn't include the distractions of a romantic entanglement.

For the past couple of days, I had busied myself with cleaning out the spare room for my new stepsister. My dad had been dating his high school sweetheart for the past six months, so I wasn't that surprised he took it to the next level. What I hadn't expected was getting a little ankle biter out of the deal. When I said as much to him, he told me she just graduated high school and was planning on taking a gap year.

That was all he told me about her, and I wasn't sure how I felt about sharing the house for the summer with a girl so close to my age. Then again, it could have been worse. She could have been a bratty ten-year-old hell bent on ruining my summer vacation. Hopefully, he didn't expect me to chauffeur her around.

My life as an only child was ending, but thankfully I was only at home for the summer vacation. I wouldn't be around to deal with all the changes beyond that. In a couple months, I would pack up to leave for uni in Glasgow. One more year left of school before I graduated and then I could start my career in business.

No clue where I would live after that, but I was itching to get on with my life and start making some money.

Unfortunately, I didn't have time to think about any of that right now because they would be here in a couple of days and I wanted to hang with my friends tonight before my dad roped me into showing the new women in his life around.

Later that night, I hopped off the bus and headed into a pub on Princes Street, where my friends had told me they would be. I usually spent my summer vacation hanging out with them because I knew once we graduated we would go our own direction. Who knew where we would be after that, so I wanted to hang with them as much as I could while we had the freedom to do so? We might even end up on opposite sides of the country or even the world. Who knew what the next chapter of our lives would contain?

Only one of them would head to Glasgow with me at the end of the summer.

There weren't many people in the pub, which was a nice change of pace from the way it usually was. All I needed was a night of drinking before everything in our house changed. Before I could make it to the table where the guys were, Miranda, my ex-girlfriend, approached me. After the way I had ended things, I thought I wouldn't be seeing her again for a while.

Maybe she just needed a couple days to think about it.

She had blown up when I ended things for good. After we broke up at the beginning of this year, there hadn't been a friend with benefits agreement. However, I had a couple moments of weakness that I regretted.

The most recent one being a little over a week ago when we slept together at a party. Looking back, we never should have gone beyond friendship because no matter how hard I tried to see something more in what Miranda and had, it was never anything more than lust between us.

"Liam, I'm so happy you're staying home this summer and spending time with all of our friends before you go back to uni," she gushed as she pulled me into an unwelcome, tight embrace.

She even went as far as to push her breasts further into my chest to accentuate her cleavage. She was a pretty woman, but for the sake of our friendship, I knew we couldn't go back to the way things were. I glanced over at the guys, who were conveniently staring into their drinks.

Before we dated, we had never been the type of friends to be affectionate.

So, her sudden invasion of my personal space threw me.

"I thought you went back to Glasgow?" I asked her when we arrived at our table shortly after she let me go.

"That didn't work out. I'm here now."

"Are you living with your parents right now?"

"Yeah," she sighed. "At least until I get another job and a new flat, or convince Rick or Darren to let me live in their spare room."

"Not likely," Rick told her.

"Awe, Ricky—" she pouted, jutting out her bottom lip.

"Nope," Rick responded.

For the next hour, we talked about anything and everything. With Miranda being with us, I didn't want to broach the subject of me getting a stepsister. The last thing I needed was for the two of them to become friends.

An hour later, when Miranda finally got up and headed to the bathroom, I asked the guys, "Do either of you have any idea what that was all about?"

Both of them smirked into their beers, which made me all that more suspicious.

"Seriously though, what's with Miranda?"

Darren, who had been my best bud since we were kids, finally piped up. "She might have overheard us talking about your weekend fling in Paris."

Since he was one of the guys who had joined me on my trip, it was most likely his big mouth that had clued Miranda into what I had been up to.

I ran my hands through my hair in frustration. "I thought we agreed that what happened in Paris stayed in Paris?" I told him.

"I think that's Vegas."

"Neither of us knew she was behind us. Rick told her we were coming tonight because she was back in town and missing her friends," he told me.

"Last I heard, you guys were trying to patch up your friendship, so I didn't see the harm," Rick defended himself, even though there was no reason to.

"I honestly wanted to be friends again, but I didn't expect her to smother me to death by squeezing her breasts through my chest."

Rick guffawed.

"Yeah, yeah, laugh it up, chuckles. This whole feckin' mess is all your fault."

CHAPTER 5

MAIRI

The next month flew by fast, and my graduation was over in a matter of minutes. I had a tearful goodbye with Jen, who promised video calls with me every chance we got. She also added a brief visit with me at the end of summer to kick off her backpacking trip around Europe. With everything we could possibly fit in our suitcases, my mom and I boarded our plane to Edinburgh. I took the window seat so I could stare outside and avoid the serious conversation I'd been dodging for a month.

Little did she know, I had been keeping a secret of my own. The real reason I didn't argue about uprooting my life and leaving my friends to cross the pond. After all, I don't know if I can do this alone. I was only eighteen, and I was going to make her a grandmother. I had planned to tell her the day after graduation, but her own news made me lose my nerve. I promised myself I would tell her in a week. If I waited any longer, I would start to show. I had already exchanged my usual clothes for some more loose fitting ones.

One step at a time since I was still trying to get used to my mom being married. James spent a couple of weeks with us to help pack all of our things, but he had to go back to work a week ago. There was no way I could say I wasn't happy to see him go. Their lovey dovey honeymooner phase was grating on my nerves. I only hoped our new house would have my bedroom far away from theirs because playing my music full blast probably wouldn't be kosher with my stepbrother.

I sat back in the seat, staring out the window, and thought back to the week that changed my life. I think back to that trip often. That trip of firsts forever changed my life. One last hurrah before we all go off to university is what Jen said as we boarded the plane to Paris.

The only thing left on my bucket list before I went off was to lose my virginity. I had a fake ID and not a care in the world. We checked into the hotel and immediately hit the bar.

The night Liam and I met, I'd succumbed to peer pressure when Jen talked me into wearing some of her skimpy clothes to the bar. So I grabbed one of her smallest red dresses. It was so short on me it barely covered my ass, but she thought it was awesome, so I caved. She said we were in another country, so I should pretend to be someone else for the night.

With the way I was turning heads, the men made me feel desired. It was something I'd never noticed before. She pulled me onto the dance floor, and that's when I spotted him in the corner with a group of guys. They were all standing at a table drinking beer. I almost stopped dancing when our eyes met. I blushed and looked away, but kept dancing.

The next song was slower. I turned to leave, saw Jen's eyes go wide and felt two extremely warm hands tighten on my hips. My heart raced, but I didn't move away. Jen winked, then left the dance floor. Strong hands spun me around and pulled me close. We spent the next hour between dancing to any and every song that came on and talking at the table with him and his friends. Jen and another one of our friends had gone to sit with a couple of other guys they had met the night before, so they were occupied.

I spent the next seventy-two hours learning anything and everything about what it was like to be pleasured by a man. The entire experience made me glad I hadn't done the whole fumbling in the back seat of a car at prom with some teenage boy who would either come prematurely or not have a clue where to put it.

The next morning when I met Jen and another one of our friends at the airport, both of them eyed me knowing that something had changed, even if neither of them knew exactly what had happened.

Or they didn't until we were on the plane ride home.

Cause what else would we do during a fourteen hour connecting flight.

Little did we know, that would be the weekend I got pregnant and forced everything to change. Even now, I didn't regret the experience. Every day, I was closer to accepting the consequences. If only I could get up enough courage to confess my secrets to my mom.

When we landed, we went through customs and then retrieved our bags and walked toward the exits. James promised to meet us at the airport. He was true to his word. I saw him standing off to the side with a huge smile on his face and a poster with our names written in black marker. I nudged my mom's arm and nodded my head in his direction. She bounced like a schoolgirl and picked up the pace.

They embraced and kissed long enough for me to be uncomfortable. I stood back and averted my eyes, glancing around at the bustling crowd. It had been ten years since I visited Edinburgh, even though my dad lived here. He brought me back with him after a business trip. We aren't close, but that trip meant the world to me.

When they finished kissing, James gave me a hug and directed us toward where he parked. Once we were in the car, we drove to our new home. I drowned out the sound of them chattering as I watched the buildings fly by. It had been several years since I'd visited so I couldn't wait to sightsee. I vibrated with excitement as we pulled into the driveway of a new home, a two story red brick building. James parked the vehicle and helped unload our luggage. I trailed behind them to enter the house.

"We parked the car at the curb outside. My son is waiting for us."

"That's wonderful, James," my mom responded.

For a moment, I actually forgot I'd be getting a new sibling. I wondered what he would be like and whether we'd get along, or completely hate each other. I figured as long as we stayed out of each other's way, we would be fine. James opened the door and pushed his way inside while we followed.

"You guys can leave your bags by the door and deal with them later," James smiled.

When we walked into the living room, I looked past James and my mom into a set of familiar eyes.

Eyes that belonged to the man I thought I would never see again.

CHAPTER 6

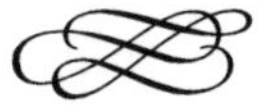

LIAM

Shit.

It had to be her.

The gorgeous, leggy blonde from Paris that had starred in many dreams over the past few months. She looked so different with her sweat pants and loose shirt. Still smoking hot, but not at all how she was when we met in Paris. It was halfway through my vacation when I spotted her dancing in the club. Normally I don't dance, but seeing her swaying her hips was like a siren's call I had to answer. We lasted a couple of songs until I asked her to my room. She hesitated at first, but when she noticed her friend with a guy on the other side of the club, she nodded.

The way she moved on the dance floor exuded confidence, but when we got back to my room, she became shy. I could tell she'd never done anything like that before. We took things slow and talked for a while, but once I kissed her, there was no turning back. I had to have her, and she was asking for me to. I couldn't believe she was still a virgin at twenty-one. Normally, I had avoided virgins like the plague because they were clingy. Something about her made it impossible to stay away; this time it was different.

How could I turn down a gorgeous woman I'd never see again?

A chick had never gotten under my skin before. For the last four months, she'd been on my thoughts and in my dreams. We spent every moment of that weekend together before I left. The last night in the hot tub was the most memorable. We used a condom every time, except that night. She said she was on the pill, and she was just too hot in that red bikini. I'd be back in Scotland and never see her again. Or so I thought. Never in a million years did I expect to see her again, let alone have her move in.

Lucky me, now she's going to be my stepsister.

The key question weighing on my mind right now was to do with how old she actually was. She told me she was twenty-one in Paris, but from everything my dad had explained was that she had just graduated high school. So either she was lying or she went back to upgrade her credits to get into a better college.

I eyed her once again.

Everything about the way she dressed set me on edge. From the lack of makeup, to the baggy sweatpants and loose shirt she was wearing.

Fuck me.

Every. Single. Thing. About her, screamed she was under eighteen or on the cusp of adulthood.

"This is my son, Liam," Dad introduced us. "Don't just stand there, son. Say hello to Alana and Mairi."

"Nice to meet you." I held out my hand and shook her mom's hand, then turned to Mairi. "Mairi?"

"Mairi." Alana nudged her arm. "Stop being so weird."

"Sorry," Mairi replied, then shook her head as if she was trying to clear the fuzz.

"Liam, why don't you show your new sister to her room?" my dad told me.

"Sure, dad," I replied, then turned to Mairi. "Which bag is yours?"

"It's the purple one in the corner, but you don't have to take it. I can carry it myself," she told me as we both started for it.

"No worries, I got it," I said as I reached her back first and picked it up. "All the bedrooms are upstairs."

As far as I knew, my dad had helped them pack up most of their items to ship over here, so I doubted her bag was going to be very heavy. Also, I wouldn't be a dick. A man was supposed to be a gentleman and help a woman with her bags. Besides, our parents would have totally known something was up if I would have acted like an ass. Even if there was absolutely no way they knew about us meeting in Paris.

At least, I hoped they didn't know.

"Okay," she replied timidly. No doubt she was feeling the same shock as I was at our sudden reintroduction.

She followed close behind me in complete silence as I walked toward the stairs. Once we reached the top of the stairs, we went to the room across the hall from mine. If I would have known my new stepsister was going to be the girl who had been burned into my memory, I would have pushed harder for me to move my stuff into the office my dad barely uses on the main floor.

Having her so close and not being able to touch her was going to be sheer torture. It was bad enough wanting her, but not being close to her. Now she was within reach, but since she hadn't responded to any of the texts I had sent over the past month, I had effectively given up on her.

"Where would you like me to put this?" I asked her.

"You can just set it over by the closet. Thank you for bringing it up for me. You really didn't have to do that."

"You're acting as if you don't know me at all. I'm not an asshole."

She glanced down at her hands. "I know you aren't."

"Good. I also don't want to be an asshole, but my next statement is going to piss you the fuck off."

She needed to know that what happened between us, most definitely couldn't happen again and our parents could never know. Who knew what either of them would do with that news?

"Okay?" she half responded, half questioned in confusion.

"Our parents can never know what happened between us," I told her.

"Do you think I'm an idiot?" she snapped back, her eyes narrowing in anger.

"Good, I'm glad that's settled," I told her. "I'll leave you to get settled."

"Don't worry, Liam. I'm not here to rock the boat, and I'm definitely not going to upset the delicate balance. Just remember I had no choice in where I lived when we moved here. The last thing I expected was to see you again."

I nodded and closed the door when I left.

She was getting the last word this time. Only because I didn't know what to follow that up with. All I knew was that my life as I knew it was fucked all to hell and right up the arse.

I still didn't know why she never responded to any of my texts.

This was going to be one hell of a long summer.

CHAPTER 7

MAIRI

Another week into my pregnancy, I continued to struggle with morning sickness and stress induced insomnia. If zombies were real, I would have resembled their second cousin, twice removed. There wasn't a moment when I didn't feel like utter shit. James and my mom thought I was still trying to acclimate myself to the new time zone.

Some days I wished that was the case.

Mom and James were still up in the clouds with their new lives, and I was up late at night worried about the future. Still unsure of what to say to them, or to Liam, I kept mostly to myself. Which was easy, since he had consistently avoided being anywhere near me since our conversation the night we moved in.

Which worked perfectly until this morning.

Our parents, upon emerging from their cocoon of love, were convinced that we all needed to sit down to have breakfast like a *real family*. Which was what they told both of us before we went to bed the night before. Apparently they were tired of us not spending any time together as a family. So when I rolled out of bed and walked downstairs, it didn't surprise me to see Liam seated at the table.

When I glanced down at what I was wearing, I crossed my arms over my chest in an effort to hide a possible perky nipple.

What had I been thinking?

I wasn't even wearing a bra!

Which had been something I hadn't even considered until I saw the heated expression in his gaze. Why the fuck didn't I take one second to worry about my appearance? Then I thought back to the moment I woke up from yet another fitful sleep. I was too fucking worn out to care. My head was so fogged up that I couldn't seem to think straight.

"Hey honey, how was your sleep?" my mom asked, snapping me out of my minor freak out.

"Um, it was okay." I glanced between the two of them. "Do I have enough time to go get dressed?"

"What's wrong with what you're wearing?" she asked from her tasks the stove, completely clueless to Liam's perusal.

Surprisingly, even though we slept across the hall from each other, he hadn't seen me in anything but my regular clothes. It was hard enough being around him in the house, but now he was in my room with the door closed.

"Do you need any help with breakfast?"

"I'm almost done. Liam already set the table when he came down, so why don't you take the chair across from him?"

"Okay," I responded and sat down.

James came out of his downstairs office, walked into the kitchen, said, "good morning." Then he kissed my mom on the cheek and took a seat at the end of the table. He used to do the same thing when he would stay with us in our old home.

A few moments after we all sat at the table, mom placed breakfast in the centre of the table and we all started filling our plates.

"What are the two of you up to today?" James asked.

I shrugged my shoulders in response, stomach rolling as I watched him dip his toast in his runny eggs.

Maybe breakfast was a bad idea.

"Do you want to go shopping with us this afternoon, honey?"

"No, that's okay mom."

"Are you sure?"

"Yeah. I don't really need anything right now."

"You could come with us just to get out of the house," James added.

"I've got a book that I've been wanting to read, so I might just do that today."

"If you're sure."

"I'm sure."

"What about you Liam? Do you want to go shopping with us?"

"I appreciate the offer Alana, but I'm good."

"Okay. I just didn't want you to feel left out."

"I'm a little too old to go shopping with my parents," Liam responded.

"You're never too old to spend time with your parents," my mom argued. "But I understand how you might think we'd cramp your style."

I glanced back and forth between them, wondering where the conversation would lead.

"Don't mind him, sweetheart. Liam and I haven't gone shopping together since he got his license."

Liam and I spent the rest of the meal mostly in silence as we listened to Mom and James.

"Wasn't this nice?" my mom asked aloud.

Neither Liam nor I answered back, but James was quick to respond, "I think so, love. We should do this a couple times a week while both the kids are still at home."

"We should," she agreed. "What do you think kids?"

Kids? Yeah, we were still toddlers.

"I think that's a great idea, Alana," Liam finally answered. "It will give Mairi and a chance to get to know each other better." Mom beamed at James, completely missing the predatory look from Liam. "Don't you think so, *sis*?"

~

LATER THAT AFTERNOON, both of our parents had left the house to go shopping, when Liam cornered me in the kitchen.

"I still can't believe you didn't tell me you were moving here."

"I tried to tell you."

"When?"

"So many times."

"Hard to believe, considering you never answered my texts."

"I didn't get any of your texts."

"Why not?"

"Probably because I blocked your number."

"Why would you do that?"

"I texted you straight for a week without a reply. I thought maybe you met someone in London and had stopped talking to me."

"I didn't."

"Then why didn't you answer any of my texts?" I glanced to the side because staring into his eyes was too difficult. I didn't know if I could handle his response.

What if he told me that he stopped texting because he didn't want anything to do with me?

"A couple days into the trip, I lost my phone in the Thames," he replied.

"That's such a cop out. You seriously expect me to believe that?"

"What reason would I have to lie to you?"

"I don't know. It just felt like that was the end."

"So you blocked me?"

I nodded. "It hurt too much to think about what you were going to say to me when you finally responded, so I decided to just cut the connection."

"I thought we had some good conversations."

"We did, but you were literally an ocean away, entering your last year of university and I was still finishing high school, without a plan."

"What happened to going to uni?"

"I took a gap year."

"You did?"

"Yeah," I responded. "And the day I decided to, mom told me she was moving here, and she wanted me to come with her. So I jumped at the chance to be closer to both of my parents for the first time in my life."

"And closer to me?"

"Maybe, but now it doesn't matter."

He shook his head in disbelief as he walked out of the kitchen. Just as he got to the bottom of the stairs he looked back and said, "I still can't believe you're really here." Then just as quickly as he cornered me, he was out of sight.

"Neither can I," I replied to the empty room.

Neither can I.

The rest of the evening I avoided everyone, holed up in my room. I couldn't handle another confrontation with him. When I closed my eyes for the last time that night, I didn't know how much more my heart could take.

CHAPTER 8

LIAM

"I can't handle much more of this," I told Darren.

For the past week, I'd tried my damndest to avoid Mairi, but it was nearly impossible since her bedroom was across from mine. She hadn't made any friends here yet, so she was always around.

"You could crash on my couch for a while," he offered.

"If it gets any worse, I might take you up on that."

"Blue balls getting to you?" he busted up laughing.

Since the family breakfast they had forced us to attend, she'd given up on worrying about what she wore around the house, which usually consisted of tank tops and shorts. I still couldn't believe she was here, after all these months.

Under the same roof.

Talk about forced proximity.

The months we had been apart had brought on some physical changes in her. Sometimes I thought I was going crazy because she was even more gorgeous now than she was when we first met. Her hips were fuller and I could have sworn her breasts were bigger.

"With the amount of time I spend taking cold showers, I could have been preparing for an Arctic challenge."

"Are you sure your balls haven't shrivelled up by now?"

"Enough about my balls, they're just fine," I responded.

"So are you coming out tonight then?"

I glanced at my closed door, wondering what Mairi was doing on the other side of the hall.

"Yeah, I'm coming out," I agreed and then ended the call. I quickly got ready and walked out into the hall. Mairi stepped out the moment I got there, dressed for bed. Yet another reason for me to flee.

"You're going out?" she asked.

"Yup." I knew I was being short, but I didn't care. Hopefully, I'd find someone else to occupy my thoughts tonight.

"Oh, okay then. Have fun."

"That's the plan." With that, I bounded down the steps and was out in the car before she could respond. Finding someone other than the off-limits newly appointed step-sister across the hall. She was everything I wanted and shouldn't touch rolled up into one smoking hot package.

I was fucked if I didn't find something to take my mind off of her. If our parents ever found out just how much fun we had in Paris, we would both be fucked.

Which was exactly why we needed a little separation.

The problem was that I would rather curl up on the couch beside her and watch a movie. The truth of the matter was that until Miranda, I hadn't dated at all. I was a nerd and a loner in high school. Top that up with my mom dying from cancer and my dad being gone on business trips.

I could have gone the other way and turned into a wild child, but I wanted my mom to be proud so I threw myself into school.

Studying instead of dates.

Studying instead of patties.

Studying instead of having sex.

That was until I went away for uni and Miranda convinced me

we should date. She wasn't my first, but there hadn't been many girls before her. In between her and Mairi, there had been a couple one-night stands and several failed attempts at dating.

After Mairi blocked me, it was easy to return to what or rather who I knew.

Miranda.

It wasn't because I loved her; I never developed feelings for her beyond a platonic friendship. I was ashamed to say it went on so long because she was willing. Believing that cheapened her somehow, and somewhere between school and meeting Mairi, our friendship suffered.

It wasn't because of Mairi, regardless of what Miranda believed. It had everything to do with her inability to accept that our sexual relationship was over and that we had never been more than friends.

And now my actions had placed me between a rock and a hard place.

"So it's getting crowded at home?" Darren asked as soon as we got our beers..

The drinks were flowing, and the music was pumping. Darren and Rick showed up just as they promised, and without Miranda.

"Yeah." I took another swig of my beer and glanced around the pub.

"So what you're saying is you need to find someone else to get under?"

"Not sure if I need the added complication in my life, but yeah, I would welcome the distraction."

"Take your pick," Rick told me as he surveyed the crowd.

A few moments later, he waggled his eyebrows just as a manicured hand gently caressed my forearm. I glanced over to find a tall brunette, with a cute, girl next door look.

"Hey baby, wanna buy me a drink?"

"Sure," I told her. "What are you drinking tonight?"

She licked her lips before responding, "I'd really like a sex on the beach." Then her eyes got brighter. "Or maybe a fuzzy navel."

Okay.

Maybe she wanted the girl next door look to work like a flytrap. A little sweet, at least until the stickiness of the trap made it impossible to leave.

A little like the one I left at home.

Then I knew I was completely fucked when I breathed in her perfume and the first thing that came to mind was how much she didn't smell like the vixen across the hall.

So I did what any other insane guy would do, I ordered her a drink, and tried to let her down easily. By asking if I could order her friends' drinks too.

"You're not interested in me at all are you?" she pouted.

"Sorry."

She shrugged her shoulders. "Well, at least we got some free drinks."

"Have a nice night ladies," I told them, then went in search of my friends.

"Guys, I think I'm gonna head out of here."

"But you just got here, and they packed this place with girls, prime for the picking."

"You're an ass."

"Everyone wants a piece of the Rickmeister."

"No, they don't," Darren piped in.

"I'll try a piece."

"You'll never be able to stop at one."

"Get a room," Darren booed.

"Let's get out of here, sweetheart. D here is just jealous of what I've got."

The woman examined Darren and I from head to toe and said, "I could do all three of you."

Darren's eyes widened, but he didn't say a thing. Before I could respond, Rick took her hand and guided her away, whispering in her ear.

I watched as she giggled at his antics.

"Now that they're both gone, what are you going to do?"

"I'll find someone or something to occupy my time," he responded.

At that, I left.

So much for a night out to avoid the distraction at home.

All the lights in the house were off when I pulled into the driveway. I turned off the car and made my way inside as quietly as possible. Dad never cared when I was out late, even in high school, but I needed to be concerned about disrupting the ladies of the house.

Mainly one in particular that I couldn't seem to get my mind off of.

I made it through the house, had a shower and crawled into bed. My head had just hit the pillow when I heard Mairi call out another guy's name.

Did she already meet someone else?

Is he in there with her right now?

CHAPTER 9

MAIRI

Bright lights blinded me.

Glass shattered and rained all around me. The world started tilting and I couldn't do anything to stop it. I was just along for the ride. No wait, that was the car.

I reached for Michael's arm, but he was too far away. No matter how hard I tried, I couldn't get to him. Something or someone was taking him away from me.

"Michael," I screamed into the darkness. "Don't leave me!"

Then the car was rocking, and I struggled against hands as they grabbed for me. "Wake up," whispered a male voice. "It's just a dream."

"Michael," I sobbed. "I need to get to him."

I felt myself coming to the surface.

"Who's Michael?" the familiar voice asked as I opened my eyes. "There you are."

"What are you doing in my room?" Liam was perched at the foot of my bed, half naked and watching me. I sat up and pulled the covers over my chest.

"Who's Michael?" Liam repeated.

"My brother."

"You have a brother?"

"Had." I wiped at my eyes, trying to hide the tears.

I missed him.

My twin.

Inseparable since conception.

"What do you mean *had*?" he asked, shocked.

It wasn't surprising that he reacted to the news. My mom and I had all but removed any visual memory of Michael from our lives. I still had my box of memories in the top of the closet, but it still hurt to talk about him.

"Michael died last year."

"I'm sorry."

"Why? It's not like you killed him."

"Do you want to talk about it?" he asked as he pulled me into his bare chest. "What happened to him?"

"We were driving home late from Jen's house and a drunk driver ran us off the road. Michael was driving and his side was hit. He died in the ambulance on the way to the hospital. I found out when I woke up five days later."

"Were you close?"

"Michael was more than my brother, he was my best friend," I told Liam. "We were inseparable."

"Yeah?"

"Yeah. He was my twin, my other half."

"I'm sorry you lost him."

"Me too."

No matter how many therapy sessions I went to, I still had nightmares of that night. On nights like this one, I often woke up in a cold sweat, staring off into the dark. When I returned to school after the accident, the sound of a locker slamming would make me jump. It reminded me too much of the sound of the collision.

The stares In the school hallway were the worst.

At first, I had actually considered asking my mom if I could transfer schools. The memories of Michael in that school and at home battered me every day, but since I was already in my last year and didn't have much left until graduation, I tossed the idea out the window.

"Now that we're both awake, I think we should talk."

"You wanna talk right now?" I glanced down at my tank top. "In here?"

"It's not like I haven't seen you naked before."

I blushed.

He placed two fingers under my chin and lifted my gaze to his, then he leaned forward and whispered, "Then again, we don't have to talk at all."

He pressed his lips to mine. As he deepened the kiss, we moved in slow motion until my head settled onto my pillow. Settling half of his body over mine, he slid his left hand up under my tank top. Heat trailed over my stomach, then my ribs and my breathing hitched as he palmed my breast.

The way his body felt molded to mine, brought me back to the night not so long ago when he had held me just like this. Thinking about it still had me clenching any thighs together. I yearned to chase that feeling once again. It took everything in me not to part my legs and let him inside again.

How he made me feel alive.

Worshipped me.

It was everything I wanted my first time to be and more.

And now I was here under the same roof as him.

Pregnant with his child.

And I hadn't told him or another soul about it.

There would be no hiding the changes or the morning sickness.

Eventually no one would buy jet lag as the reason for me being tired all the time.

Because fucking hell, I was tired.

All the damned time.

How the hell did my mom do this?

A sudden pang seared. through my chest as I longed for my twin.

Michael would know what to do.

I laughed at the thought of Michael changing dirty diapers. Cause he would. It was just the type of brother he was. We bickered over the small things like shared bathrooms.

But not the big things, like decking Bobby Ryan for touching my books in the seventh grade. It didn't matter that they were best friends. If anyone mistreated me, my brother was the first one to set it right.

Just about now was when I really needed his unwavering support.

Either that or he could just save me the anxiety and blurt out my condition to mom.

God, I missed him.

An icy wave crashed over me, so I pushed him away.

"Have you been drinking?"

"Only a couple, why?"

"Would you be trying to kiss me if you hadn't been?"

He moved back. "I don't know."

"Then we shouldn't be doing this now."

"Why not?"

"We're family now." As I said it, I couldn't help but add *in more ways than one* in my head.

"No, we aren't. Our parents are married."

"Can you stay here?" I whispered.

"Maybe that's not such a good idea."

Neither did I, but I didn't want to be alone right now.

"Just until I fall to sleep."

"Okay, just until you fall asleep."

The next morning, when I woke up I couldn't help but take in his gorgeous peaceful face.

"Like what you see?" he asked, voice groggy from his deep sleep.

I blushed and looked away. He wrapped his arm around me and

pulled me closer. He kissed my temple, then laid back and closed his eyes. Every time I get close to him I have to remind myself this won't last.

Why was it the one thing that made me think about something other than what I had lost would be the next thing I would lose?

CHAPTER 10

LIAM

The memories of the first night I stayed in her room were still fresh in my mind - it had been a little over a week since then. After we had the long-overdue conversation, the atmosphere between us was so much lighter, and we spent most nights either in her room or mine, laughing and talking until the late hours.

We had yet to take our physical intimacy beyond the point of heavy petting and grinding, with our clothing providing a barrier from going any further. We could both feel the tension in the air, but neither of us knew how to break it. I knew most of what was holding the two of us back had to do with our living situation.

That and our new familial connection.

No matter how much our parents wanted us to be a happy family of four, I couldn't think of Mairi as a sister. Especially when I knew her in the biblical sense. Maybe it would have been simpler had she not been the woman I had a fling with in Paris.

This morning when I woke up in her bed, I could feel her breathing beside me and I knew I couldn't take it anymore. When I woke up with a morning wood as hard as stone, it put all my other hard-ons to shame. I had her exactly where I wanted her, and now it was time to show her how deeply she was affecting me. The sound of us breathing was the only noise in the house as I kissed her and crawled out of the bed.

"Where are you going?" she asked.

"I need to check if anyone is home."

"Why would you do that?"

"Several reasons," I responded.

"What's the first one?"

"That I want you naked and lying in the middle of my bed by the time I come back," I commanded.

I opened the door, glancing out into the hallway before I stepped out, and my footfalls echoed in the silence as I shut her door behind me. In just a few minutes, I had determined that the house was vacated, and the warmth of the coffeepot indicated they had just gone. Thankfully, they stepped out the door without checking in on either Mairi or me. After I made sure the car was out of sight and the door was securely locked, I could hear my footsteps echoing as I climbed back up the stairs.

When I reached the top of the steps, I heard the faint, yet unmistakable sound of Mairi clumsily rummaging around in my bedroom. By the sound of things, she was scrambling to do what I had requested before I left her in her room to check on the parental situation.

I hesitated for a few more moments before I eventually opened the door and stepped through into the room.

And halted on the spot.

There she sat, nestled in the middle of the bed, her hair spread out over the pillows and her body entirely wrapped up from her neck to her toes.

"Are you wearing clothes under there?" I questioned.

She shook her head.

"I don't recall telling you to get under the blankets."

Her cheeks reddened.

"Are you sure you're naked?"

"It was cold."

"I can think of a million different ways to warm you up," I told her as I stalked toward the head of the bed. I leaned forward, as if I was going to kiss her, then I grabbed the blankets and yanked them off.

Letting out a yelp, she frantically waved her arms to prevent the blankets from dropping to the ground.

I was instantly hard at the sight of her.

Naked for the first time in my bed.

As far as I was concerned, she needed to stay like that forever.

Ready and willing for the taking.

I couldn't wait to be balls deep in her wet pussy. She'd even shaved everything except for a little triangle of hair pointed like a beacon.

Straight between her legs.

Which was exactly where I wanted to be. I wanted to feel her heels digging into my ass as I pounded her into oblivion. To hear her scream my name so loud the neighbours know I rocked her world.

"This seems a bit unfair," she told me as she pointed back and forth between us.

"You think so, do you," I teased as my hands went to the button of my jeans. I smirked at the sight of her watching my fingers as I undid the button and pushed my jeans down, kicking them off when they hit the floor.

I reached into the drawer in the bedside table, pulling out a condom and placing it on the top within reach. Then I crawled onto the bed next to Mairi and pressed my lips to hers. I palmed her breast before trailing my fingers down her body until they found their way between her slick folds.

Deepening the kiss, I muffled her moans as I plunged two fingers inside her wet pussy. Her walls clenched around my fingers as I circled her clit with my thumb. Pulling back, I gazed at her face.

Curling my fingers, I thrusted them in and out. Her eyes closed, and she arched her back, pushing her perky nipples closer to my face.

So close I couldn't resist putting my mouth on them.

She mewled as I sucked on one and the other, then kissed my way down her body until I replaced my thumb on her clit with my mouth. Nestled between her thighs, I pulled my fingers from her pussy, chuckling against her when she moaned in protest.

"Don't worry, I'll make it good," I promised. My cock was so hard it could probably drive nails into wood.

"How good?" she breathed.

"So good you might just come with one push inside you."

Kneeling next to her, I squeezed my hard length. Before I had a chance to, she reached for the foil packet on my nightstand. She sat up on the bed and tore into the package. Then she stroked my cock from base to tip. The crinkling of the wrapper was the only sound in the room, other than our heavy breathing. She blushed as she made quick work of rolling the condom down my rock hard length.

Mairi was such a contradiction, so confident in her movements, yet so timid in her actions.

Once I was completely covered, I settled between her thighs. She licked her lips as I pushed them apart. With a roll of my hips, the head of my cock nudged at her entrance.

"Oh God," she groaned.

Her jaw drop open as I pushed forward with a hard thrust. My dick twitched deep within her warm, wet walls. The thought of them clenching me as she came undone almost had me emptying my seed inside her prematurely.

Why did I waste all this time avoiding her?

Her hands gripped the pillow under her head as I pushed deeper and thrust faster. Until the only sound in the room was our breathing and the slapping of flesh. She threw her head back as I thrust one final time.

Plummeting both of us over the edge, together.

CHAPTER 11

MAIRI

For the next week, Liam and I hadn't spent one night alone. Whenever we were in the same room, hiding my feelings and my current condition was more difficult. Our parents were still enjoying their honeymoon phase, so when we were all in the same room it was difficult not to share the same conspiratory looks as we thought of ways to douse their fire.

I tried to phone Jen every day, but every day we seemed to just barely miss each other. Playing phone tag with your best friend from the other side of the world was frustrating, especially when I had such a crazy story to tell her. A story that shouldn't be told via text. I needed to hear her voice when I told her that the man that rocked my socks off and knocked me up, was literally sleeping across the hall from me now.

To be honest, I didn't know how I felt about that.

My mom still didn't know I was pregnant.

I definitely hadn't told Liam I was carrying his unborn child. Until the moment I saw him that first day, I never thought I would have to broach this subject with him. Not to mention that he was in the same house as me and we were sharing the minefield that was our parents as they began their married life.

Trying to ignore those feelings I stuffed down to the bottom of my toes while looking at the father of my child in the eyes was daunting. This move was supposed to open more doors for me and bring me closer to the rest of my family, but now I had to figure out what Liam represented in that future.

If I could ever get a hold of my best friend, she would know what to do. Even if she didn't, I sure as hell needed someone to talk to. After all, she was the only person who knew I was pregnant. At least until I got up the guts to tell my mom. Nothing like having to confess all of your sins in one swoop.

"Hello?" she answered after the first ring, her video popping up.

"Jen, thank fuck! I've been trying to get you for ages."

"Hey chickee," she giggled. "How's Bonnie Old Scotland treating you?"

"Haven't seen much of it yet," I confessed. "Mom's been too focused on her new husband to notice that I don't have a set of wheels."

I wasn't really that upset that my mom was so focused on James. After everything that we had both been through, she deserved to be happy. James seemed to be the only one who could bring her any sort of happiness since Michael died. James always went out of his way to include me, even before they were married, so I was more than a little supportive of their marriage. I didn't have a lot to compare it to since my parents had been divorced for the same amount of time I had been alive.

"Awe," she responded sarcastically.

The only parents who were divorced out of my friends were Jen's parents. They seemed to overcompensate their divorce by allowing her and her siblings an endless spending account. Sure, she had everything that she desired materialistically, but she lacked the relationship that she wanted with her family.

"I'm going exploring tomorrow, even if I have to hop on a bus to nowhere."

"It can't be that hard to get around over there. You should get one of those twenty-four-hour passes on those hop on hop off busses. At least you'd see some sights and get used to the area."

"Yeah, I should try that. Maybe my mom or James would drive me to one of their main pickup points."

"There you go," she agreed. "So, on a more serious note, have you told your mom about the baby yet?"

"Not yet," I sighed. "But the world is definitely trying to make me its bitch."

In more ways than one.

She laughed. "God, you're so dramatic."

"Ironic is what it is," I responded, leading up to the real reason for my call.

"What's ironic?" she asked.

"My stepbrother," I sighed, placing my hand over my eyes.

"Ooh, is he that hot? Don't tell me you want to sleep with your stepbrother? Isn't that kind of forbidden?"

"I've already slept with him."

"What the fuck?" Her eyes lit up. "You've got to be kidding me."

"Nope."

"Well, when you move fast, I guess you move really fast. How did you sneak that by your parents? Don't they sleep just down the hallway?"

I blushed. "No, you're not getting it. I slept with him before we moved here."

"Where else could you have slept with him?" she waggled her eyebrows for effect. "Did you know him over here?"

God, I missed her already.

"I mean I slept with him in Paris. Jen, he's the father."

"You're shitting me right?"

"Nope. Of course my luck would dictate that my new stepbrother is also the father of my unborn child."

"Shit," she started laughing hysterically. "Maybe you're right and the world is really out to get you."

"It's not funny."

"Sure it is."

"Not at all," I groaned. "What am I supposed to tell my mom? 'Hey, mom, so you know how you thought I was studying over Spring? Well, I wasn't. Oh, and guess what... you're gonna be a grandma and your new stepson is the father.' I am sure that will go over just perfect."

I watched through video as she giggled and rolled around on her bed. I stopped talking, crossing my arms over my chest in annoyance, until she calmed down.

"That means your stepbrother is hot," she gasped. "You should sleep with him again. It's not like you can get pregnant twice."

"Shut up," I told her, worried that someone might hear our conversation. "Of course he's hot, but I can't think of him that way. Not anymore."

Part of me thought about telling her I had slept with him again, but I couldn't. If I said it out loud, then it would be real. If it was real, and it went sideways, then I could lose everything.

"What did he say when you told him?"

"I haven't told him about the baby yet."

"You haven't?"

"No, I have absolutely no clue how to tell him. I don't even know where to begin." The truth of the matter was that I shouldn't even be sleeping with him now.

"I'm sorry, Mairi. That sucks," she agreed. "So what are you going to do?"

"I have no clue. Of course he would have to be here at the moment that I decided that I'm keeping the baby," I confessed.

I wanted to tell her I was sleeping with him again, but I didn't know what to think about the situation. For all I knew, the moment I told him about the baby, he'd drop me and then I'd be more heart-broken than I was when he stopped answering my texts.

"You're not just making that decision because he's back in the picture?" she voiced the one question I knew she would. The coincidence of Liam being present in my life would be too great to ignore.

"I can understand why you're saying that, but I decided on the plane over here. The plan just came to me while I was gazing out the window at the clouds. This is a new chapter in my life. Maybe everything worked out for a reason."

"Are you sure you're ready for the responsibility?" she asked, looking concerned.

"I'm positive," I sighed. "In more ways than one now, I guess."

"Yeah," she shook her head. "When are you going to tell everyone?"

"I promise I'm going to tell them soon."

"I can't believe you haven't even told your mom yet?"

"I wouldn't even know where to begin with telling my mom, especially considering Liam is the baby's father."

"How are you hiding all the morning sickness from her?"

"She's too wrapped up in James to notice. For the first week she thought I was getting acclimated to the time change."

"Well, I definitely know you're not going to be able to hide the baby bump for long, chickee," she warned me.

Before I could respond, I heard the floor creek behind me. My stomach dropped. I turned around and Liam was standing in the doorway.

How much did he hear?

"Baby?" he asked, confirming my worst fear. "What baby?"

My mouth dropped open, and my tablet fell out of my hands onto the bed.

"Mairi, are you still there?" Jen asked through the one earphone that I still had in.

"Uh... yeah, but can I call you back?" I asked her when I picked it back up.

"Sure. Love ya, bye."

"Love ya too."

I slid back on the bed and turned to face Liam, holding the tablet to my chest like a shield.

"Boyfriend?" Liam asked.

"Best friend."

He nodded, then repeated his question. "You're pregnant?"

"Uh… Can you close the door?" I squeaked.

"I don't think that's a good idea," he replied.

"Please?" I pleaded.

"Why?"

"Cause I don't want our parents to overhear us talking."

"Why not? Shouldn't your mom already know you're pregnant?"

"Please, just close the door," I repeated.

He shrugged. "Okay."

He closed the door like I asked and stepped up to the foot of the bed. The smell of his cologne made my stomach do flips, not in a morning sickness way.

He looked at the bed next to me. "Do you mind if I sit down?"

"Sure," I replied, placing the tablet on my bedside table. I pulled my knees up to my chest to steady my trembling hands.

"So… you're going to have a baby?" he asked quietly.

"Yes, but my mom doesn't know yet," I whispered. "Please don't say anything."

"When are you going to tell them?"

"Actually, I wanted to find you and tell you first."

"Why?" he asked, with a confused look on his face. "It's your life. It's not like it matters what I think."

"It's your life too," I countered.

"What's that supposed to mean?"

"The baby is yours."

"Yeah, right," he reacted dismissively.

I glanced down at my lap, hoping the silence would make enough of a statement in response. What did he expect me to say? Did he think I was making this up? That would be a pretty shitty thing to do.

He stood up and backed away from me. "You're shitting me."

"You're the only one I've ever been with," I replied, fully expecting him to just waltz out the door. It was only a couple steps away from where he moved to, so what was a couple more steps.

"Please tell me you're over eighteen, cause from everything our parents have been saying you're a lot younger than I thought you were."

"I'm eighteen," I answered with a cringe.

"Fuck," he ran his hands through his hair. "I can't believe you're only eighteen!" He paced the room. "It's bad enough I got you pregnant. But now you're my stepsister and it's going to look like I took advantage of you."

"I've been eighteen since January."

"I thought you were in University."

"I never told you I was."

"No shit."

"I never lied to you. I just didn't tell you the whole truth."

"I thought it was weird that you were in University and still a virgin."

"So you still believe I was?"

"Of course I do," he told me as he sat back down on the bed. "I never had a reason to doubt that you were telling the truth. We only forgot the condom once." He ran his hands through his hair. "Were you even on birth control?"

"I was a virgin."

"You don't have to have sex to be on birth control."

"I hadn't planned on having sex," I responded.

"I can't believe this," he groaned. "I knew I shouldn't have slept with you."

"Are you talking about the first time, or the other night?"

There was a softness in his eyes as he watched me.

"Both," he responded.

It was like he had done a complete one-eighty. I didn't know when I started crying, but suddenly I realized my face was wet. He reached for me, but I flinched.

"I think you should leave," I whispered, pulling further back.

"What exactly am I doing that's so wrong?"

"You shouldn't be in here."

"Why not?"

"Our parents are probably downstairs."

"So what?"

"They might suspect something."

He tilted his head toward my stomach. "I think it's a little too late to worry about that, sweetheart."

I grabbed my pillow and chucked it at him. "Leave."

He furrowed his brows and held the pillow with one hand. "What did I do?"

"Just go," I pleaded.

"You shouldn't be alone."

"I've been alone for four months."

He set the pillow back on the bed and left, shutting the door. I grabbed the pillow, laid down on the bed with it over my face and screamed.

CHAPTER 12

LIAM

I stepped out into the hall.

A baby?

I did the walk across the hall into my bedroom in a fog. I shut the door behind me and flopped down on the bed. I laid there, just staring at the ceiling, as if it held all the answers to the questions of the universe. There were way too many to count, and even less time to figure out the answers. There were four years between the two of us and she was still underage.

Was she going to keep the baby?

Did I want to be a dad?

Did she want me to be their dad?

I hadn't heard enough of her conversation through the door to know any of those answers. All I heard was the word baby and something inside me said I needed to know the answer to at least one question. What I didn't realize was that the response she was about to give me was going to open up a huge list of things I would have to consider.

Would I have still slept with her again if I knew about the baby?

It was one thing to have the girl I couldn't get out of my head move into my house, and another to have her be pregnant with my kid. I still hadn't graduated uni yet. How the hell was I supposed to support a family? Then again, she never said she wanted us to be a family. In fact, she was fairly adamant that she didn't think I should even be in her room, or touch her, even if I was only wiping away a tear.

Before she showed up on our doorstep, I told myself that I wouldn't stop having fun because I had a new stepsister. Now there was the other problem. She was pregnant with my kid. I thought I was just going to deal with a bratty new sister. Instead, fate delivered me the woman of my dreams, who was still too young, and at least eighteen years of future responsibility.

This whole thing would have been easier to navigate if all we had between us was an amazing weekend.

Even when I kept in contact with her I didn't see it going beyond friendship because of the distance between us. In the back of my mind I thought that if she ever walked back into my life, I wouldn't turn down another roll in the hay if she let me. Mairi was just enough wild with her sweet. However, now she was considered completely off limits and a complete and utter disaster waiting to happen.

Which was why now, more than ever, I'd have to be careful.

After laying there for an hour, I called my friend Rick and told him to meet me at the pub. He had just got back into town so he didn't know what was going on in my house yet. My day wouldn't be getting much better, so I might as well have a couple of drinks to numb whatever was going on in my brain.

Our house was in the perfect location.

It was walking distance from the popular local bar. During my first year of uni, I lived in my dorm room, but on the weekends I would stay here purely for the pub. My dad was never at home, so it was the perfect place to take chicks when I brought them home. With the new situation, I wouldn't have the freedom to bring girls home anymore. To be honest, considering the circumstances, I would be a complete asshole if I tried to bring women home.

"Liam," Rick nodded.

"Hey Rick."

"Not that I'm complaining, but what was so urgent you needed a drink?"

"You're never gonna believe who showed up on my doorstep."

"Who?" he asked, taking a drink of his beer.

"The chick I hooked up with in Paris."

"How the hell did she find you?"

"My dad is married to her mom."

He barked out a laugh. "Priceless."

"You can say that again."

"So the hot piece of ass you had in Paris is currently living in your house."

"Yeah, but now she's my stepsister. Feckin' untouchable."

Eric sighed. "Shit, that sucks to be you."

"Yeah, but that's not the end of this train wreck. She's pregnant."

"Yours?"

"Yeah," I sighed.

"You sure?" he asked.

"The timeline is right, and I was the one who took her virginity."

"Shit," he cursed. "What are you going to do?"

"Fucked if I know."

Rick laughed again.

"Fuck you, man! It's not funny." I wanted to punch the smug look off of his face.

"Shit, yeah it is. Your sister's having your baby."

"Stepsister."

"Whatever. Your parents are married."

I groaned. "Don't remind me. She wants to keep it, but doesn't want our parents to know it's mine."

"Well then, you dodged a bullet."

"I guess."

What I don't tell Rick is how I didn't want to be the kid's uncle. Shit,

I wanted kids someday, but just not now. One thing I knew, I didn't want some other jackass to be my baby's father. Mairi didn't seem to want me involved. Maybe I just needed to prove I could be there, and she'd let me.

"Miranda's gonna lose her shit when she finds out."

"Miranda and I haven't dated since February."

"Hasn't stopped her from trying to jump you every chance she gets. How many times have you guys fucked since February?"

"Once," I responded.

"Since before Mairi moved in?"

"Yeah."

"Shit... she's still gonna go psycho on your ass," he laughed.

I ended things with Miranda a couple months before I went to Paris. We'd dated since our first year of college, but had been friends since before that. This past year, I realized we both wanted different things. She wanted to get married, and I wanted to focus on my career. It didn't help that I wasn't in love with her.

Hell, when I thought back, I think I liked the idea of dating her more than the actual dating. She was what I knew, and that was easy. No matter how well we got along, I didn't think she was the one for me. Like an idiot, I had slept with her since I went to Paris. Before anything happened, I made it clear I wanted nothing more. Rick was right about one thing, though.

She was going to lose her mind.

"Enough of this shit, let's get drunk," I lifted my pint and chugged the rest of the beer.

"Hell yeah."

We all stumbled out of the pub at just after midnight, the sound of laughter echoing in the street, and I hailed a cab. I arrived home to a dark house, the only illumination coming from Mairi's room where a warm, yellow light shone through the curtains. I navigated the stairs, carefully placing my feet on each step in order to not make a sound and wake our parents.

I softly rapped my knuckles against the door, the sound echoing in the hallway.

The door opened wide, and Mairi was revealed standing in the doorway. I nearly forgot the purpose of my late night visit as I was distracted by what she was wearing.

My shirt.

All I could focus on was the smell of her hair and the feeling of her lips on mine.

"You're back early."

"I just wasn't feeling it tonight. Besides, I've been thinking about our situation."

"I won't tell our parents that you're the father," she interrupted me.

"Why not?" I asked.

It surprised me she wouldn't tell them the whole truth. I'd told her I would be there for her, but maybe she really didn't want me to be. Women were confusing ninety-nine point five percent of the time.

"Cause it's weird. They'll think we got together here, after we knew we were siblings."

"I'm pretty sure when you have our baby in five months they'll figure it out. My dad knows I was in Paris."

"My mom doesn't know I went."

I raised my eyebrows. Maybe she really wasn't a good girl after all.

"How's that possible?"

"We both know now that our parents were in Vegas getting hitched."

I ran my hand through my hair and exhaled. "Yeah. This is so fucked up."

"You're telling me. I'd already decided I'd raise our child on my own before I got here. Then I walked in the door and here you were and suddenly you're my stepbrother."

"Look. I know this isn't the most ideal situation, but if you truly want to raise our baby, then I want to be involved."

"How?"

"I'll take you to Doctor appointments and whatever else you need. Then we'll figure out the rest when the baby is born."

"How do we explain you taking me to the doctor?"

"Our parents are stuck in their own little dream world. They'll be too busy to drive you and you sure as hell aren't taking transit. Besides, they'll be excited we're getting along. They won't notice a thing."

"Are you sure? You really don't have to."

"Mairi, you're not doing this alone."

She sighed. "Thank you."

CHAPTER 13

MAIRI

I woke up with one thing on my mind.

It was time to tell my mom that I was pregnant, and I needed to do it before she figured it out herself. The only thing I wouldn't do was tell them who the father was. Who knew what they would do if they found out I was having my stepbrother's baby.

I was still trying to wrap my head around it myself.

Before I told our parents, the first thing I had to do was warn Liam, so I went to his bedroom. Liam's door was open, but I still didn't want to just walk in, so I knocked on the door frame. He was bent over his laptop reading emails.

"Come in," he said.

"Do you have time to talk?"

"Sure," he replied.

"I think it's time for me to tell our parents that I'm pregnant."

"I'll go with you," he stood up from his desk.

"You don't have to," I told him, holding my hand up. I wanted to do this on my own. It was my consequence to bear, even if it was his child.

“I promised you wouldn’t be alone. Even if you don’t want to tell them I’m the father.”

“I’m still not telling them.”

“It's up to you.”

I walked down the stairs towards the kitchen. I could feel Liam following close behind. When we rounded the corner into the kitchen, our parents were at the table eating their breakfast. Mom’s laptop was on one side of the table, so Liam and I sat in the chairs across from it. He was next to his dad, and I was closer to my mom. I placed my trembling hands on my lap beneath the table, then I waited for my mom to take a sip of coffee before I began.

“Mom, I have something to tell you.”

“What’s going on?” She set her coffee cup down on the table.

Liam’s warm hand slid on top of mine. Every part of my brain said that I should pull away, but I couldn’t. For reasons unknown, he calmed my nerves and gave me the strength to tell her.

“I’m pregnant.”

My mom stilled, her voice an octave higher than usual. "What do you mean you’re pregnant?"

A storm of nerves twisted in my stomach and I took a deep breath. "I mean... I'm pregnant."

"You're only eighteen dammit!"

I glanced briefly at Liam, and something I couldn’t place flashed in his eyes. Could it have been anger?

“I know, mom. I’m sorry,” I told her as tears streamed down my face.

“How far along are you?”

“Five months.”

“Five months? You’ve been hiding this from me for five months.”

“Yes. I’m sorry I didn’t tell you.”

“Who’s the father?”

“A guy I met at a party,” I responded. It was the truth, but I promised Liam I wouldn’t tell them it was him.

“Does he know?”

I tried my best not to glance at Liam, but he squeezed my hand.

"Yes mom, he knows."

"Well then, where is this boy?"

"I want nothing from him."

"You can't do this alone."

"I won't be alone. I'll be here with you guys."

"Have you though this through? Maybe you should give the baby up for adoption."

"I won't do that mom," I replied.

"Think this through. You're younger than I was when I got pregnant with you and it was tough for me to do it all alone. You're not married and you don't have any means to support yourself."

"I'll figure something out." What she didn't know was that my dad had told me I could work for him part time until I decided whether or not I wanted to go to school. He didn't know about the pregnancy yet.

"Mairi, there is no way you can do this on your own. You're only eighteen, you've got the rest of your life ahead of you."

"Mom, I don't think you understand," I replied.

"I understand enough to know that you're going to ruin your life."

"I'm not ruining anything. If you'd paid attention to anything going on around you besides your new husband, then you would know is the first time I've felt truly happy since Michael's death."

My mom visibly recoiled as if I had slapped her.

"That's not fair," she reprimanded me.

"I wasn't trying to be fair; I was being honest."

"Promise me you will think about it," she repeated like a broken record.

Why couldn't she understand that?

"Mom, I'm never going to change my mind. These babies are a part of me," I walked away, marched up the stairs and slammed my bedroom door.

I could hear muffled voices, but I didn't care. No matter what she said, I had already decided. I would keep my baby and nothing could make me change it. She should have taken a moment to understand how I felt. Tears welled up in my eyes as I laid on my bed and stared at the ceiling.

I must have drifted off because when I heard a knock on my door I looked at the clock and a couple hours had passed.

"Come in," I called and rolled onto my side facing the door.

Liam poked his head through the door. "Hey, sleepyhead. Supper is ready."

"I'm not hungry," I sniffed. I didn't want to face my mom and her constant nagging about me giving up my baby for adoption.

"You should eat," he replied softly.

I sat up, slowly swinging my legs off the side of the bed. "I just don't feel like dealing with them right now."

"So, why don't we go somewhere?" he suggested with a smile.

"Really?" I perked up. It had been a while since I had gone anywhere fun.

"Yeah. I'll take you out to eat and then we'll go to my friend's house."

"Okay," I grinned. "I just need to get into something other than sweats."

"Cool. Come knock on my door and we'll escape together."

He left, shutting the door. What the hell did I need to wear? I was so excited to get out of the house that I didn't even bother to ask him which friends.

What if they were the ones that came to Paris?

If it was them, at least I would know someone. Fifteen minutes and several outfits later I found the most flattering thing. I'd gained ten pounds so far, but what really got me was that my hips were wider, so I knew I already needed new pants. I settled on a wrap-around black skirt that allowed me to adjust the size of the waist. I put on a purple halter top that flared at the bottom to hide my stomach and found some flats.

I walked into the hallway and glanced at myself in the mirror. I'd say one thing for pregnancy, my breasts were bigger. I inhaled deeply and knocked on Liam's door. It swung open, and I resisted jumping him right there. He took a step back and his eyes widened. He scanned my body, paying close attention where my outfit hugged my curves. His eyes sparkled as they met mine. I didn't know how he could be even more attractive than when we first met. He wore dark denim jeans and a black shirt that was tight over his chest and biceps. When I finished perusing his body, I met his eyes.

"You're a knockout," he whispered in my ear.

I blushed. "I've gained weight, nothing fits."

"You're perfect," he replied. "Now let's get out of here."

We arrived at Liam's friend's flat just after eight. My hands were shaking because I'd only met one of his friends before. Liam held out his hand and interlaced our fingers. I immediately felt at ease. I didn't know how he did it, but there was something about him that settled my nerves.

"What can I get you to drink?"

"I'll have some orange juice, please."

"You're not putting vodka in it?" Darren asked from across the table.

I blushed and shook my head.

"She can't drink," Liam explained.

"Why not? Even if she wasn't old enough, we're not in a bar."

"She's pregnant."

"Shit really? Who's the dad?"

Liam was silent and I couldn't see his face because he was looking at Darren.

"Holy shit, no way!" Darren yelled as he looked back and forth between us. "You two don't waste any time. She's only been here for a couple weeks."

Miranda scowled, setting me on edge. I wasn't sure what she was to Liam, but I knew she hadn't been on the vacation in Paris with him. Yet, if I didn't know better, I'd have thought they had something going on by the way she was turning different shades of red.

"This was a bad idea. I shouldn't have come," I whispered in Liam's ear and got up.

He grasped my shoulder. "Don't worry about it."

"This is your life and I am invading it."

"I wouldn't have asked you along if I didn't want you here."

"Are you sure?"

"Yeah, I'm sure."

"Okay."

"So you'll stay?"

"Yes."

"Come sit back down then."

I nodded, but before I sat down, I needed a moment away to calm my nerves. So I went for the most logical explanation and asked, "where is the washroom?"

Surely he wouldn't follow me there.

He pointed. "Down the hall, second door on the right."

"Thanks."

CHAPTER 14

LIAM

As soon as the door to the bathroom closed, Miranda turned to me, "Can we go talk somewhere private?"

"That's not a good idea," I told her. I didn't want to leave Mairi in a strange house with people she had just met so that I could have a private conversation with my ex-girlfriend. The same ex that I had actively been trying to avoid for the past couple weeks.

I shouldn't have slept with her again. I knew she still wanted me, but we didn't work. It was a shitty decision but the last thing I expected was for Mairi to show up a week later.

She just wasn't getting the hint.

"Just for few minutes."

"I'm fine just where I am," I told her. "Whatever you have to say to me you can say in front of them."

"*Liaaam*," she whined. "After everything we've been through, can you just give me this?"

"I don't want to leave Mairi alone," I responded.

"Liam, she's an adult. I'm sure she's capable of being without you for five seconds." She rolled her eyes. "You never would have dated me if I was that helpless."

"She's not helpless," I defended. "She's never met the guys so I don't want her to feel abandoned."

"Please, just give me five minutes," she argued. "Besides, these oafs will make sure she doesn't feel out of place."

I glanced over at the door to the bathroom.

"Five minutes," I warned her.

I followed her down the hallway. When she directed me into the bedroom, I leaned against the door so she couldn't shut it.

She walked partway into the room and when she turned around and noticed I hadn't shut the door behind me; she made a face.

"Aren't you going to shut the door?"

"Why would I?"

She crossed her arms in front of her and replied, "You want them hearing everything I say to you?"

"Depending on what you say, I'll probably tell them everything you say to me," I scoffed.

"Fine."

"What did you *need* to talk to me so urgently about?"

"Why don't you want to be with me?"

"We've been through all of this before. We're better suited as friends."

"You told me you didn't want to date anymore because you wanted to focus more on school."

"That's right."

"Yet when *she* shows up, you change your mind. And now, suddenly she's pregnant and you're all in."

"It wasn't sudden. I've known her for months."

"I find that hard to believe."

I furrowed my brows. "That's the kicker. You don't need to believe that I've known her for months. There is no you and me in that equation."

"I don't understand what you see in her," she replied. "We could have been so good together."

"If you're not going to talk about anything else, I'm going to go back to the table."

"Wait, don't go," she called out just as I reached the door. I stopped and looked back at her. "How do you even know that she's pregnant?"

"Not that I need to appease you with a response, but Mairi doesn't have a reason to lie to me."

"She could be after your money," she argued.

"What money?" I scoffed. "It's not because she needs a place to stay, she already lives with me."

She stepped closer until she was right in front of me again. "Then she's after permanent residence."

"Your grasping at straws, she already has dual citizenship because her parents are from here."

"How do you know it's even yours? It would be just like you to fall for her lies so easily."

I shook my head in disgust. "I won't keep going round and round with you. If you can't accept that I've moved on, then I don't think we should be around each other anymore."

She grabbed my wrist. "No, Liam," she pleaded. "I'm still in love with you."

I sighed. "Miranda, I don't want to hurt you, but I don't feel the same. We want different things. It was the reason I broke up with you. You need to find someone who will love you like you deserve."

"But you're the only one I want," she called down the hall after me.

When I came around the corner, everyone, including Mairi was looking in my direction. Rick and Darren both rolled their eyes at Miranda's antics, while Mairi's eyes were more questioning.

"I think we should get going," I told her.

"You just got here," Rick complained. "We're just getting to know Mairi here."

"You'll have plenty of time to get to know her," I told him. Miranda still hadn't emerged from the bedroom, which was fine by me. With any luck, Mairi and I would be gone before she came out.

Rick got up out of his chair, "I'll show you two out."

"It was nice meeting you," Mairi told Darren.

"Next time I hope you both stay longer. I haven't seen this guy in over a week," he replied.

She nodded her head in agreement.

"Thanks for the invite, guys. See you later."

"Catch you later!" Darren called from the table.

Mairi was a bit withdrawn during our drive back to the house. It made me wonder just how much she might have heard from our conversation down the hall.

"Who is Miranda to you?" she asked when I pulled into the driveway.

"She's a friend of mine from high school," I told her.

"Did you guys date or something?"

"Yeah, but it's over."

"For how long?"

"A couple of years," I replied, not wanting to admit that we hooked up a couple times after we ended things.

We had been friends throughout high school and when she followed me to uni, the familiarity of our shared past made it difficult to see the reason we weren't dating.

So I gave it a try.

"How long has it been over between you?"

"Since February of this year." Truth be told, I didn't really know when it ended between us. We were hot and heavy one moment, and then I was pulling back because our relationship had become more of a friends with benefits arrangement that had run its course.

"I think she still has feelings for you," she responded.

"I only like her as a friend," I assured her. My only regret with Miranda was letting things go on as long as it did. When I explained that although the sex was hot, that I didn't think we would work as a couple, she seemed okay with it.

What twenty-year-old male wouldn't want access to sex without strings and a partner willing to explore whatever fantasies you had?

Then everything changed when I met Mairi.

The connection we formed in that one weekend alone was more than I'd had in two years with Miranda. What I hadn't realized all those years ago was that a deeper connection had the ability to create more chemistry. Which made the sex even hotter than it was with any other woman.

"So there isn't a chance that you'll get back together with her?"

"You have nothing to worry about."

"You don't have to be in a relationship with me because I'm pregnant," she pushed.

"I'm not."

"Are you sure?"

"Yes."

She took off her seatbelt, then responded, "good, because I've seen how much it hurts children when their parents fake it just because they were born."

"That's the last thing that I want," I said as I reached over and grabbed her hand. "I'm not sure what this is between me and you yet, but I want you to know I'm not going anywhere, no matter what."

"Okay."

"Don't just okay me. If we weren't sitting in the driveway, I would kiss the shit out of you."

"Liam." Color rose to her cheeks just before she looked away.

"Go get your cute butt in the house before we get caught."

She scrambled as well as she could out of the car and into the house while I sat there and watched like the sorry sap that I was.

I hadn't been completely honest with her.

I wasn't going anywhere.

Now I just needed to deal with the thorn in my side.

When I was sure that she couldn't hear us, I called Rick.

"Yellow!" he answered.

"Hey, is Miranda still there?"

"No. After the two of you left, Darren went back and coaxed her out of the room. The moment she saw you hadn't stayed, she high-tailed it out of here."

"Do me a favor?"

"Name it."

"Warn me next time if she's gonna be here and we'll make other plans."

"It was that bad?"

"Yeah."

"Sorry man," he replied. "I thought that she just showed up at the door, but after she left, I asked Darren about it and I guess he told her you were coming here. Neither of us knew Mairi was coming with you, so she wouldn't have had the warning."

"I've talked with her numerous times about how we were just friends and that's it would ever be, but she just won't get it through her head."

"She's had it bad for you since we were in our pre-teens."

"And I feel bad about that, but I didn't lead her on. We tried to date because we had so much in common, and we were good friends. It just didn't work."

"Not like you and Mairi?"

"Mairi is different. I don't know what it is, but we clicked."

"I get it, I do," he responded. "I can't believe you're gonna be a dad."

"Me neither. It wasn't in the plans, but I wouldn't change it for the world."

"Let me know the next time you're free and we can go for drinks. I'll make sure Darren knows Miranda isn't welcome."

"I don't want you guys to stop being friends with her because of me."

"She's changed since high school. I don't know what went on, but I don't really hang out with her anymore."

"I hope that's not on my account."

"Not at all."

"Alright, well I should go before Mairi thinks I got lost coming inside."

"Talk later."

I ended the call and went inside.

CHAPTER 15

MAIRI

Liam was good to his word and drove me to my first doctor's appointment. He even took the time to find me a female doctor a short drive from where we lived. The waiting room was filled with other pregnant women, who looked up when we came in. My heart raced as we approached the front desk to check in. The receptionist wrote my name down and had us take a seat. Liam was uncharacteristically quiet, but I completely understood. This appointment was more nerve-wracking because today I'd actually see and hear our baby for the first time.

My hands were trembling, so I grabbed a magazine to distract myself. I tried to focus on the pages as I turned them, but it was hopeless. I couldn't focus on the words, but I continued to turn the pages until I heard my name called.

Standing, I immediately turned to Liam and asked, "Will you go in with me?"

Eyes wide, he responded. "You want me to?"

"I don't want to go alone."

"I didn't think you would want me in there."

"Of course I do, you're the father."

The receptionist placed my medical file in a slot outside the door and ushered us inside.

"You can change into this and then get up on the table," she handed me a hospital gown before she closed the door.

They had covered the white painted walls of the room with posters. The posters depicted several stages of baby development and human anatomy. There was a sheet of paper near the door listing parenting classes. My chest tightened as I thought about the path laid before me. There was so much I needed to do. Then, when I looked around, but didn't see any way for me to hide while I changed into the gown. I froze, panicked both by the seriousness of the situation and my impending state of undress. To my surprise, Liam noticed.

"What's wrong?" He asked.

"Uh... um... can you turn around?"

"Oh... oh... yeah, sorry."

I laughed. "I know I'm acting weird."

"It's okay, I understand," he assured me, as he turned to face the posters wall.

"It's just... I know you've seen me naked before, but that was different."

I changed into the gown and folded my clothes on the chair in the corner. Liam held out his hand to help me up on the examination table. I shivered when my legs touched the table because the room was cold. Liam sat in the corner of the room, with his hands clasped in his lap.

"I'm so nervous," I whispered.

"It will be okay," he stood and leaned next to the table.

A knock on the door made us both jump. I giggled. A younger woman wearing a lab coat and stethoscope walked in the door holding a folder. She closed the door behind her and faced me.

"Mairi Stewart?"

I swallowed. "Yes."

"I'm Dr. McCall," she opened my medical file. "So... it says here that you're eighteen."

"Yes, I'll be nineteen on January second."

Dr. McCall turned to Liam. "And you're the father?"

Liam moved closer and intertwined his fingers with mine. "Yes."

I expected a more judgmental reaction from her. If she disapproved of my condition, she was great at hiding it.

"When was your last period?"

I cringed. "Um... I can't remember, but I know I'm pregnant. I've done the test, and I went to a doctor at home."

"So how far along do you think you are?"

"Around five months," I answered.

"I'll have to lie down on the table and we'll do the ultrasound."

Dr. McCall put on latex gloves and grabbed a bottle of liquid. She rolled the monitor around so Liam and I could see. She rolled up my gown to reveal my midsection, then pushed the elastic of my underwear down. I glanced at Liam's face and his gaze was fixated on the tiny bump, which was becoming larger every week.

"That won't hurt her, will it?" Liam asked.

"No, not at all. It's just going to be cold and she might feel uncomfortable if I need to push harder with the transducer."

Dr. McCall squirted the gel on the wand and rubbed it on my stomach. I gasped at the coldness.

"Interesting," she stated under her breath.

"What's interesting?" I asked, trying to see what she was looking at. "Is there something wrong with the baby?"

She leaned closer to the monitor and turned up the volume.

"As you can hear, there are two heartbeats."

The moment I heard the overlapping beats I lost it. I sobbed.

"What does that mean?" Liam stammered. "Is there something wrong?"

"Both heartbeats are nice and strong," she responded.

"The baby has two hearts?" he asked, dumbfounded.

"No," she chuckled. "That means you're having twins."

Liam exhaled and ran his left hand through his hair, so he didn't let go of my hand with his right. Impending fatherhood had most likely screwed with his brain cells. Liam leaned over and rubbed my shoulder as I continued to cry.

I faintly heard the doctor say, "I'll leave you two for a bit," before the door clicked shut.

Liam pulled me into his arms and quietly held me. When I finally stopped crying, I sat back on the bed and spoke.

"It makes me think about Michael." Finding out we were having twins brought everything rushing back to the surface as if it had happened yesterday.

"I'm so sorry," he replied, gently squeezing my hand.

"No matter what our parents say, I'm keeping them. I know you might not be ready to become a father, and that's okay. I was just supposed to be a one-night stand, even if it was a weekend."

"I'll be here for the three of you," he replied, rocking me to the core.

"Are you sure? This is huge."

I wanted to give him an out, even if our unique step-sibling relationship would inevitably force him to be around for part of the pregnancy and the eventual future. I was prepared to do it alone, and he could just be their uncle instead of a father.

"I've had enough time to think about it. More than anything I want to be their father. If that's not what you want, I want to be in their lives in whatever capacity you'll allow me to be. I still have a year left to finish school, so money will be tight until I graduate and get a full-time job."

"That's what I want too," I replied.

There was a knock on the door, and then the doctor entered.

"How are you both doing?"

"I'm sorry, I kind of lost it for a moment there," I apologized.

"No problem," she smiled, then took a seat. "It looks like you are about five months along. They both have strong heartbeats and you are young and healthy."

"Thank you."

"Is there anything we should be doing?" Liam asked.

"I see that you're already taking prenatal vitamins. I would recommend reading some books, attend some parenting classes and most of all, watch your stress levels," she responded. "You're young and from what I can tell you were in great shape before becoming pregnant, so I don't see anything we need to be concerned about beyond what I've already mentioned."

"Okay," we replied in unison.

"Now, would you like a picture and video?"

I nodded. "That would be awesome. Would you be able to print out two pictures?"

"Definitely."

CHAPTER 16

LIAM

A pair of wandering hands woke me early the next morning.

Opening my eyes just a crack, I peered at the naked beauty who had spent the night in my bed for the third time this week. Her fingers trailed down my abs and disappeared beneath the covers leaving goosebumps in their wake as they made their way to my fast growing erection.

There was something visceral about knowing a woman was pregnant with your child.

It was unlike any other experience I'd had. On top of that, she was changing before my eyes, becoming more and more beautiful.

If that was even possible.

"I wanted to give you a parting gift," she whispered. My cock springing to life just before she wrapped her hand around my shaft.

"What kind of gift were you thinking?" I groaned.

"Why don't I just show you," she replied as she slid down under the covers.

Her breath was warm as ran her tongue up the underside of my dick. She flicked it over the tip, tasting the drop of pre-cum leaking out. It took everything not to thrust into her mouth as her soft lips enveloped the end.

"I think I like it when you show me things," I whispered.

She pulled back, leaving her lips still touching me, allowing me to feel her smile in response. Then she slid her mouth over me and pumped her hand in time with the movement. She hollowed out her cheeks as she continued to suck me off.

She was going to make me come in her mouth if she kept going like this. It felt amazing to have her lips around me, but what I really wanted to do was lose myself inside her. Just as the thought crossed my mind she cupped my balls and I exploded into the back of her mouth like a teenager at prom.

"Holy shit," I moaned as she swallowed my load.

She continued her movements, making me lose my mind, so I slid my hands into her hair and gently pulled her off me.

"Did I do it wrong?" she asked with uncertainty.

"Fuck no," I responded. "I just can't handle anymore."

Pulling her up my body until she was straddling me right above my still hard dick, I smashed my lips against hers. I tasted myself as my tongue slid over hers. Her kiss was hungry and full of desire. She ground down into my erection, moaning into the kiss.

"Shhh," I warned her as I pulled back. "They'll hear you."

My hands went to her hips so I could control her movements. Just one slight movement and I'd penetrate her.

Bare.

Warm, wet walls clenching me as I came deep inside her.

"I still can't believe you'd kiss me after I did that."

"You kiss me after I do the same to you," I told her. "Why is it different just because I'm a guy?"

"I don't know, but it just is."

"Well, it shouldn't be."

She positioned me at her entrance and sunk down, moaning as she sheathed me in her warmth.

We held still for a moment, completely connected.

The sensation was more than I could handle.

Then she started to ride me.

The need to be closer to her had me sitting up. Keeping her seated in my lap, I pressed my lips to hers as she continued rocking back and forth. Mairi moaned into the kiss as I took control of her movements, thrusting upwards.

So much for being quiet.

Fuck it, she felt so good I didn't care what they heard.

Our breathing came in short pants as my cock swelled inside her. She pumped her hips faster up and down, as I arched up to meet her, thrust for thrust. Until we were cascading over the edge, and I was emptying my release into her. Her legs trembled, walls milking me with the last couple of thrusts.

"I should sneak back into my room before they notice," she whispered against my chest.

"Just a couple more minutes like this," I told her.

Our parents had yet to notice our bed hopping.

It had almost become an exciting game of when and not if they would. Over a month had passed since I had completely blown my life to bits. Only to have it reshuffled and structured in a new and exciting way. Mairi was already showing, so I was developing this instinctual need to be more protective of her.

We still hadn't told our parents that I was the father of our babies. The main reason being that her mom was hell bent on her giving them up for adoption. She had yet to wrap her head around the fact that Mairi was an adult and could make her own decisions, even if she deemed them to be a mistake.

Even though we had only just reconnected, there was no way I could imagine leaving them here when I went back to school. So, without Mairi or my father being involved, I had been searching for somewhere for us to live. With both of our parents being so adamant that we were siblings now, I had a feeling that our relationship and pending parenthood wouldn't be accepted.

Deep down, I knew Mairi felt the same way, which is why

neither of us had broached the subject of telling our parents yet. I thought it would be beneficial to ease them into everything. Start with the relationship first, then drop the bomb on them.

Either way, there was going to be a lot of emotions being thrown around. Especially if Alana didn't lay off of the adoption talk. It was getting extremely difficult for me to keep my cool about the situation. After all, I was just supposed to be the brother. I wasn't supposed to have any skin in the game.

I would be damned if she forced Mairi to sign over rights to our children.

I would pack everyone up and leave early for school.

It was one reason I had signed an early lease for the flat I found.

CHAPTER 17

MAIRI

The next morning, a conversation from the kitchen made me pause at the top of the stairs. Orange juice could wait. Like a total creeper, I remained in my perch so I could listen to them. I leaned against the wall at the end of the hallway and got as close as I could without making my presence known.

"Liam, I wanted to wait until the girls were gone, but I think we need to lay some ground rules for both of you."

"What do you mean?"

"You had a girl in your room last night."

"I don't know what you're talking about."

"Don't play dumb with me. I heard her calling out your name. That's what woke me up."

Liam groaned.

"Exactly," James added. "You're lucky it wasn't Alana that heard you. What would she think? You're bringing home women and having sex with them while her daughter is in the room across from yours."

"I doubt Mairi would care."

"It's not whether or not she would care. She's an impressionable young lady. I don't want you to give her the wrong idea."

"And what wrong idea would that be?"

"That it's acceptable to have overnight guests in this house."

"You have overnight guests."

"That's different. I'm married to Alana."

"Don't tell me you waited until you were married to have sex with mom."

"It was a different time back then."

"Exactly. Now is a different time, and it's completely acceptable to have sex before marriage."

"I know it is, son. Just not here. You need to set a better example for her. She's just across the hall from you and doesn't need to be kept awake hearing you with girls."

"It's not like she doesn't know what sex is. She's not that sheltered."

"Can you just do me this one favour and limit it for the summer? You'll be back to Glasgow in no time and back to whatever you like to do in your spare time." James sighed. "Maybe you could stay at their house or get a hotel?"

"We know you're both used to being on your own, but with such tight quarters I think we need to set some new ground rules."

"I'm an adult," Liam argued. "Hell, we're both adults. Are you going to tell Mairi that she's not allowed to have sex?"

"If we have to have the same talk with her we're having with you now, I will leave that to Alana. It would be better coming from her."

"I'd love to be a fly on the wall during that conversation."

"It would be great if you could curb your nocturnal activities until you go back to school."

Nocturnal activities?

"Be thankful Alana didn't hear you. I can't say the same about your sister."

"She's not my sister," Liam argued.

"Mairi is younger than you. She's sheltered and has her head in the clouds. I don't want her to think that this is how I taught you to treat women."

"I don't mistreat women," he retorted. "I have never in my life done anything like that."

"What am I supposed to think? We haven't even met this girlfriend of yours, yet you've snuck her in after dark every night this week. She's gone before we wake up, which means she's chosen to leave or you've told her she isn't welcome to stay. Which couldn't be further from the truth."

"You don't know what you're talking about."

"Whatever the arrangement is, it cheapens your relationship," James replied. "It's no more than a booty call, or whatever you kids are calling it now."

"Dad," Liam groaned.

"Don't Dad me. End the relationship or don't. Introduce us to the girl or don't. The only thing I want from you is for you to take your nighttime activities somewhere else," James huffed. "Now I need to get to the office. Think about what I've said."

Now that they were finished the discussion I could finally get myself a glass of juice. I waited until I heard James leave for work before I went back down. It was bad enough I had to listen to him tell Liam he heard us having sex last night.

I doubted I would be able to ever look him in the face again.

Hands grabbed me as I reached the bottom of the stairs. I yelped as I was hoisted into Liam's arms and deposited on top of the kitchen island counter.

"What are you doing?" I hissed.

"What does it look like I'm doing?" Liam asked as he stepped between my legs.

"I don't think your dad will appreciate my ass print on the island."

"I don't give a fuck," he replied before crushing his lips to mine.

Without pulling away, he grasped my hips, pulling me forward until I teetered on the edge of the counter. Holding me in place with one hand, he used the other to move my shorts and panties to the side.

"Exactly how much did you hear?" he asked as he gazed into my eyes.

I giggled. "All of it."

"I lied when I told him I didn't know what he was talking about." He hummed as he glanced to where I had been bared to him. "I want to leave impressions on you." Then he slid his thumb through my wet folds.

"What if someone comes in?" I breathed as two of his fingers entered me.

"No one will interrupt for hours. Dad's at work and your mom is at a spa."

"Hours?" I asked as his thumb stroked my swollen nub.

He nodded. "Now, lay back," he instructed as replaced his thumb with his mouth, flicking his tongue over my core.

Laying back, my hands went to his head, fingers clasping his hair. Sucking my clit into his mouth, he curled his fingers, hitting all the right spots inside me. He repeated the movements, circling his tongue until I thrashed around on the island.

Squeezing his head between my thighs, I rode his tongue until stars sparked in my eyes. My heart raced. Every part of my skin electrified by his touch. Legs trembling as I soared over the edge.

Before I could come back down, the head of his dick replaced his tongue as he thrust deep inside me. He pumped into me a couple more times, then retreated.

"Don't stop!" I pleaded.

"Don't worry, I'm not finished with you yet," he replied as he grasped the waist of my shorts and pulled them off, taking my underwear with them. Then he lifted the hem of my tank top until it was over my head and still around my shoulders like a vest. He pressed his lips to mine as he thrusted ever so slowly in and out of me.

Then he kissed his way from my neck down to my breast, latching onto my pert nipple.

Sliding his arms under my knees, he spread my legs baring me to the world. Peering between us I watched as the tip of his cook disappeared through my folds. My head fell back as I moaned.

"God, you're beautiful like this," he breathed into my neck, as he moved inside me. Blurting out, "I. Can't. Get. Enough. Of you," with every thrust.

Using his thumb between us, he rubbed my clit in rhythm with his movements as he moved inside me.

"I'm getting close," I told him.

"Fuck yeah," he groaned as he picked up his pace, taking me higher and higher. "Come all over my cock."

His movements became erratic, and then he groaned with his release, stilling after emptying inside of me. He pressed a chaste kiss to my lips and rested his forehead against mine as he regained his breath.

After a moment he pulled back and looked me in the eye. "I can't seem to get enough of you."

Stepping back, he pulled out of me and helped me regain my footing. As soon as my feet hit the ground, I knew I had to clean up.

"I need a shower," I informed him.

"Don't move. I Wanna look at you just like this."

"I can feel your cum coming out of me."

"It gets me all fired up to know it's my seed running down your legs."

I blushed, clenching my thighs together.

"I like that I marked you somehow."

"Liam," I whined. "I should go."

"You're not showering without me."

"Conserving water?"

"Something like that."

Then he swung me into his arms and took me into the shower where he had his way with me again.

CHAPTER 18

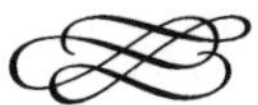

MAIRI

This morning Liam was gone before I woke up. James had secured a tee time for them at the St. Andrews Old Course, so they had to leave bright and early. I was growing increasingly tired as the days went on so I planned on sleeping as late in the morning as I could while he was gone.

I had just rolled over in my bed when my phone buzzed next to me.

Unknown: Hey, this is Miranda.

Unknown: I hope you don't mind, but I stole your number from Liam's phone.

Why would she want to contact me? Before I responded, I added her to my contacts so that I knew who the texts were from.

Me: Hi. No big deal.

Miranda: What're you doing today?

Me: Nothing. Probably just reading my new book.

Miranda: Boring! No Liam today?

Me: He's playing golf with his dad.

Miranda: Then let's have a girls day!

I thought about it for a moment. In the past couple weeks she had been hanging around more and was nice to me when she was there. So I really didn't have a reason to distrust her intentions. It would be nice to have friends here that were girls.

A female other than my mom to talk to.

Me: Okay.

Miranda: You know where the Princes Street Mall is right?

Me: Yep.

Miranda: Meet me in the café just inside the west door.

Me: Sure. I gotta get dressed, then get a ride there.

Miranda: Meet you there at 2.

I glanced at the clock on my bedside table. Phew. I still had a couple hours before we met up.

Me: Sounds good.

Since I had some extra time, I went and had a shower, then got ready to meet her.

I LEFT my mom a note on the fridge so she knew I had gone out, and then called a taxi. When I walked into the mall a couple hours later, Miranda was already there waiting for me. She waved at me from a table next to the pathway by the café.

"Hi," I greeted her.

"Hi. I wasn't sure what to get you, so I just got mine."

"No problem." I didn't expect her to get me anything, but it was probably just as well. She probably didn't know that I was only drinking tea these days. "I'll just go get something and be right back."

"Sure thing," she responded. "I'll be right here waiting."

I went up to the barista and ordered my drink. It wasn't very busy, so it didn't take them very long to call my name, and then I was making my way back to the table where Miranda sat sipping her beverage.

"I hope this is okay?"

"Of course."

She smiled. "I'm so happy you could come meet me on such short notice."

"It's not like I'm up to anything much."

She took a sip of her coffee, then asked, "How have you been feeling?"

"Pretty good. It's an adjustment, but Liam's been a big help."

"That's good."

"Mairi, since you don't know anyone besides Liam I think we need to stick together."

"You want us to be friends?" I felt like the new kid at school asking the other students if they wanted to be friends.

"Of course I do!" she responded.

I hesitated before responding. "Okay."

"Great!" She sat up straight and then continued, "And as your friend I need to be honest with you."

I furrowed my brows.

"Okay."

"I've known him since high school and since you're his new sister, I'm sure he would want us to be close."

"Step-sister."

"I don't know how much Liam told you about me and him."

"He told me everything."

"He did?" She took a sip of her coffee, then placed the cup back on the table, but held it between her hands as if she was trying to keep them warm. Then she tilted her head and continued, "So he told you we've been sleeping together?"

My response felt lodged in my throat.

She nodded. "Well, we are. So, I hope you're not falling for him." She sighed. "Oh honey, you are, aren't you?" she suggested. "I can see it on your face."

I didn't answer.

"Awe... I don't want to see you hurt. He doesn't really love you, you know."

Tears rolled down my cheek. "He told me he did."

Why was I answering her?

"That's cause you're always around and you've trapped him."

"I didn't trap him," I argued.

"Sweety, you and I both know that's not true. In fact, the other night when we were together, he told me he feels sorry for you."

"What night?"

"Tuesday."

The night he told me he was hanging out with Rick and Darren, he was with her?

"I don't need to listen to this anymore," I replied as I got up from the table. "I'm such an idiot. I can't believe I actually thought you wanted to be friends." I pushed the chair back under the table. "Now all I see is a jealous woman trying to convince me to let go of my man."

"That's where you're wrong," she responded. "He was never yours to begin with. Not before Paris, during Paris, or after Paris."

Not wanting to say anymore, I turned and walked out of the café. I walked up the street and turned toward the grassy area on top of the mall.

I needed some air.

There were a couple of empty benches, so I sat on the one with the best view. I sat and people watched for a while. About thirty minutes had passed when I spotted Miranda walking out of the other entrance of the mall.

The only thing I hadn't expected was the person who got out of the vehicle that pulled up to the door.

Liam was here.

He walked up to her, said something, and then suddenly they were kissing.

As my heart lay shattered in the grass beneath my feet, I realized in that moment how foolish I had been to believe he wanted to be with me.

Cause in that exact moment I knew: she hadn't lied.

I was at home and had a bag packed within moments of getting there. It only took me fifteen minutes to get home and with luck I would be gone before he came home. My mom tried to reason with me before I ran upstairs, but I didn't want to listen. So it didn't surprise me when she was waiting at the bottom of the stairs for me.

"Sweetheart, I wish you'd talk to me," she pleaded.

"I don't want to talk about it. I just need to get away for a few days."

After what I saw, I had been up and off of that bench as quickly as my legs could take me.

"I don't understand what the rush is? Are you upset that you're not getting out of the house enough?"

"I get out of the house plenty, Mom," I groaned. "I just want to stay with Dad for a while."

There was no way I could stay here across the hall from him. What had I been thinking? There was no way he was with me other than for the baby. Miranda had said as much. Was he dating her the whole time and just stringing me along because of some stupid sense of responsibility?

I had told him time and time again that I didn't want him to be with me just because I was pregnant. That was the last thing I wanted to happen to our children. Being in a loveless marriage and raising children together just because society deems it necessary was a stupid endeavour.

The child always suffered for it, and I wasn't about to let that happen to our babies.

They would know that they were loved regardless of whether they had one or two parents in their lives. Hell, now I technically had four set of parents. It didn't matter what type of family structure you had as long as there was love.

Because of the literal distance between us, my dad and I hadn't been close over the years. That all changed the moment I called him from the back of the taxi on my way home. He was already parked outside the house and waiting when I got downstairs.

"Hi, Dad," I greeted him. "Thank you for coming so fast."

"Honey, it's so good to see you." He wrapped his arm around me. "I wish it was under better circumstances, but I'll take you any way I can get you."

We loaded my things into his car, and he pulled away from the curb.

The drive over to his house was mostly in silence, which didn't upset me. I had dropped a lot of information into his lap today. Not only was he becoming a grandfather, but I had gotten myself into a situation that I needed him to extract me from. On top of everything, now he would likely have to deal with my mother.

It was about a thirty-minute drive from where I lived to his neighbourhood. He pulled into a gated community, and into a driveway a couple houses in. The building was a two story with red brick siding and a garage. This was the house he now shared with his third wife Camille. Although I had only met her once at their wedding, I had spoken to her several times through video chat, and thought she was a gem.

She was kind and caring, but part of me was worried that my situation could be problematic for her.

We pulled up into the driveway. When we got out of the vehicle, my dad refused to let me take the bags. During our argument over the bags, Camille had emerged from the house and was standing on the steps. Before we got up to the house, Camille walked to the driveway and embraced me. She actually had tears in her eyes, which made me cry too.

"Ladies, why don't we make our way inside. There are too many onlookers out here," my dad suggested.

They showed me to a room, which to my utter surprise they had already decorated it in my favourite colour.

Camille whispered, "when your dad said you were moving back to Scotland, I went shopping and got your room ready. We were excited to have you closer to us and hoped you would want to stay with us on a more frequent basis. I hope you like it."

"I do. Thank you so much."

"This is your home too... for as long as you'd like," she responded, squeezing my hand.

I teared up and hugged her.

"There, there." She patted my back. "Sometimes the men in our lives can be insensitive pricks."

I snorted at her comment.

CHAPTER 19

LIAM

Yesterday had been a shit day.

First, we had to get up at the ass crack of dawn to get to the golf course on time, only to be detoured back to the city because of an accident on the highway. Then, on our way back home, I received a text from Miranda saying that she had seen Mairi at the Princes Street Mall and that she was acting weird.

She said that it sounded like she wanted to move back home and be closer to friends.

I was worried, so I made up an excuse and had my dad drop me off in front of the mall. Then when I showed up to look for Mairi, Miranda latched onto me like some whacked out barnacle. By the time I pushed her away, and did a search through the mall, Mairi was nowhere to be found.

It had been almost two days, and I hadn't seen or heard from Mairi since the morning of our golf trip. She wasn't answering any of my texts. So I called instead, and she sent me straight to voicemail. She hadn't been home in two nights and I was getting worried since she didn't have any friends here.

I searched through my room to see if she had left me a note, but there was nothing.

Then when I heard Alana moving around in the kitchen, I approached her to see if she knew anything. She hadn't been acting frantic over her daughter being gone, but who knew what was happening.

"Where's Mairi?" I asked her.

"She told me she was going to stay with her father for the weekend."

"So she's coming back?"

"As far as I know, but I'm not completely sure," she replied. "After she came home from meeting up with your friend at the mall, she was visibly shaken and I couldn't get a word out of her why she was so upset. She went upstairs and packed a bag and told me she was going to stay with her dad for a couple days."

I schooled my features. "She met up with one of my friends?"

"I think her name was Amanda," she answered.

"Miranda?"

"Yeah, that's her name. I don't know what happened. She really wanted to find friends in the area. She misses her best friend Jen like crazy. I think she needs someone closer to her age to hang around with, especially in her condition."

Now I was even more pissed than I was before I talked to Alana. Miranda made it sound like she had run into Mairi at the mall, not that she had invited her to meet up.

Something had changed in Miranda, and it had to do with more than just our strained relationship.

"Have you talked to her since she left?"

"No, but I'm going to call her tonight to see how everything went. She hasn't told her father about the pregnancy yet."

That was news to me. I thought she had planned to tell him around the same time as she told our parents.

"I hope everything's okay."

"I'm sure it is. When I talk to her, I'll tell her you were asking about her." She smiled. "Liam, I just wanted to tell you how happy I am that you've made Mairi feel at home. She's been through a lot."

"She told me about Michael."

Her hand went to her chest, and her eyes glistened with unshed tears. "She has?"

"A couple of weeks ago."

"That's good. That's good. She doesn't talk about him enough."

"She's still dealing with his loss."

"She misses her brother," she whispered. "We both do." She turned around and focused her attention back on the dishes.

I was the same when my mom died. I didn't want to talk to anyone about it and my dad was a mess so he wasn't able to be there for me like I was sure he wished he could. Things were better now, but we were going through another change in our dynamics because of his new marriage.

I left it at that. Alana and I weren't close enough to have a heart to heart.

MAIRI WOULD EITHER BE COMING HOME with me or I'd be camping out on her doorstep until she took me back. Bag in hand, I was out the door thirty minutes later.

Only to be stopped by the last person I wanted to see.

"Miranda? What the hell are you doing here?"

"I came to see you."

"Why would you do that?"

"Darren told me Mairi left you. Now that she's gone we can finally put this whole thing behind us and be together like we were before she showed up."

"I don't know where you got that idea, but Mairi hasn't left me. Even if she had, I wouldn't be getting back together with you."

"What is so wrong with me that you don't want to be with me?" Miranda whined.

"There's nothing wrong with you Miranda. I just don't feel the same about you as you do me. I've told you time and time again that I only wanted to be friends," I huffed.

"You really love her, don't you?"

"Yes."

"It's my fault," she looked down at the grass.

"What's your fault?"

"I told her you didn't love her."

"Why the fuck would you do that?"

"Because you were moving on without me and I was jealous."

"Miranda, I never lied to you. We've been completely over for almost a year now and you know why."

"I just didn't want to accept it."

When I tried to walk around her, she grabbed my wrist. "Don't go."

I pulled my arm away. "Move on. If I can ever convince Mairi to take me back, we're going to be a family."

"You're seriously just going to leave me here?"

"You just have to keep pushing." I turned and faced her. "So I want you to listen carefully this time. We are done. We were friends at one time, but you've made it completely impossible to be in the same room as you."

"Please don't do this," she cried. "I love you."

It was the last thing I wanted to do to an old friend, but if I truly wanted Mairi back, I'd have to cut all ties with Miranda to make our relationship work.

"It's done. I don't want to see you or hear from you until you get this unhealthy obsession you have with me dealt with. "

I left her standing in my front yard.

~

Twenty minutes later I was pulling up in front of her dad's house. I only knew where it was because Mairi had told me about him buying a new house after his marriage.

"Is Mairi available?" I asked him.

"Let me guess," he greeted me. "You're Liam aren't you?"

"Yes, sir."

"I don't know what happened between you and my daughter to make her finally show up on my doorstep, but I won't stand by and let you hurt her more," he warned me. "She's already been through enough in the past year with the loss of her brother."

"I'm not here to cause any more problems."

He held up his hand, palm facing me. "I don't want to hear any of your excuses. I only want to hear a guarantee that you're not here to cause any problems. I want to know that I can trust you to do what's right."

"That's the plan, sir," I responded. "I don't know what she's told you, but I didn't expect my ex-girlfriend to do what she did. I'm in love with your daughter, and I want a chance to show her exactly how I feel."

"That's what I wanted to hear," he told me. "As her father, I want to tell you to take off and never come back, but she needs you right now more than ever."

"Thank you."

"I'm sure you'll be able to appreciate the importance of protecting your children from what you can, and supporting them when they need a crutch. This is me being her crutch. I'll always be here for her if she falls, but I would like for her to find the man willing to hold her up so that doesn't happen."

"I'll try my best."

"She's in her bedroom down the hall."

"I appreciate it, sir."

He stepped back, allowing me into his house. Once he closed the door behind us, I made my way down the hall in the direction he had pointed me. When I reached her bedroom door, it was closed, so I knocked.

"Give me a minute," Mairi called. I could hear the rustle of sheets and blankets as she moved around in the bed. A moment later, the door swung open and I couldn't help but examine her from head to toe. It had only been a couple days without her and it already felt like forever.

I was being a sappy fuck, but I didn't care.

"What are you doing here?"

"Your mom told me this was where I could find you."

"Why would she tell you that?"

"It's the truth."

"You didn't tell her did you?"

"I didn't tell her I was the father of your babies if that's what you're talking about."

"Good." She crossed her arms over her chest. "Now answer my question. What are you doing here?"

"I came to bring you home."

"I am home."

"No, you aren't."

"This is my home now."

"I thought you said your home is with me."

"Not anymore."

"Why not?"

"Did you even go golfing?" she accused.

"We drove part way there, but had to turn around because of an accident on the highway. They were detouring everyone through neighbouring towns, so by the time we would have made it to the golf course our tee time would be over."

"You made me the other woman."

"No, I didn't."

"I saw you kissing her."

"Who?"

"Miranda."

"For the record, she kissed me."

"Looked pretty mutual to me."

"I've told you before, there's absolutely nothing between Miranda and I."

"I can't believe you expect me to believe that."

"The only place you could have seen us kiss was at the Princes Street Mall. She called me and told me you were there and something was wrong with you, which was the only reason I showed up. She walked up to me when I was looking for you and kissed me. I pushed her away and told her to never do it again and then I spent the afternoon looking for you."

"Really?" she asked as if she didn't want to believe me.

"I have no reason to lie to you."

"She told me I trapped you and that you didn't love me."

"Not true."

"Well, she also said that you slept with her after you had been with me in Paris."

I exhaled. "That's true." She opened her mouth to respond, but I held up my hand. "I slept with her after you blocked me, but not since then."

"Okay."

"So can I take you home?"

"I don't know."

"I know we have a lot to talk about, but I want to make this perfectly clear."

She crossed her arms over her chest. "Go on."

"Before all of this happened, I put some money down on a flat in Glasgow that's big enough for all of us."

"You did?"

"I can't imagine going back and leaving you here."

"You can't?" she breathed.

CHAPTER 20

MAIRI

He took a step forward and placed an errant strand of hair behind my ear. Then he trailed his fingers down my neck, slowly wrapping his warm hand around the back and pulled me into him.

I squeaked, then suddenly he pressed his lips against mine. Wrapping my arms around his back, I pushed further into his embrace.

"So, what's the verdict?" he asked as he pulled back.

"You really want me to move to Glasgow with you?"

"Yes, but only if you want. I can understand needing your mom right now."

"She's still trying to get me to give up our babies. I'm not sure if me staying here will be good for my stress level."

"What about here?"

"I love my dad and Camille has been really great, but this isn't my home. On top of that, they've only been married for a year, I don't think they want two babies in the house."

"I'm sure they would let you stay here if you asked, but that's not what I want."

"Are you sure you can handle us being there with you while you're trying to study?"

"I honestly don't think I'll be able to concentrate without you guys there with me."

"Okay, I'll go home with you."

"Great."

We packed my bag and went back down. Dad and Camille were at the kitchen table when he got to the bottom of the steps.

"He's convinced you to go with him?" Dad asked.

I nodded.

"And this is what you want?" Camille added.

"Yes, this is what we both want," I responded. "Thanks for everything."

"Don't be a stranger," Dad replied. "That includes you, Liam."

"We won't, sir," Liam agreed.

When we arrived back home, I didn't have any idea what we were walking into. If Liam and I were going to do this together, then we needed to tell our parents that we were going to be parents ourselves.

He seemed so confident with the choice we were about to make, and I just didn't understand how he wasn't worried.

Or maybe he was just that good, and he didn't want me to stress out any more than I already was. We discussed at length just how we were going to broach the subject.

He had called ahead and talked to his dad and without divulging the reason, to see if they were both going to be home this afternoon. We had a lot to talk to them about.

Liam set my bags on the floor in the entryway.

"You're back," Mom greeted us, looking surprised, albeit a little confused.

"Yeah," I replied.

"You called Liam to come pick you up. I didn't know the two of you were that close. Why didn't you call me?" she asked. "I would have dropped everything to come and get you."

"I was in the area," Liam cut in.

"Is this about the baby?" she asked.

I shook my head.

"Honey, you're so young. Are you sure you won't consider giving your baby up for adoption?"

"Not going to happen."

"Just think about it. You're so young. You've got your whole life ahead of you, years to have other children when you are ready for them."

"You're never going to change my mind," I responded, crossing my arms over my chest. "These twins are the best thing to happen to me in a long time."

"You cannot be serious!" she gasped. "Twins?" Mom glanced over at James. "One baby is enough, but two is going to be too difficult for you to handle. You can't possibly do this alone."

"She won't be alone," Liam interrupted.

"What are you talking about?" My mom turned to Liam. "I won't be around all the time to help her."

"I am going to help her," he responded.

"Son, I understand you care for your sister, but you're going back to uni in a couple weeks," James interjected.

"For the billionth time, she's not my sister," Liam responded, then dropped the bombshell. "Mairi and the babies will live with me," Liam answered.

"This isn't your responsibility, son," James scoffed.

"Of course it's my responsibility," Liam argued. "It's what any father would do for his children."

"*Your children*?" James looked like his head was about to explode.

"Yes," Liam responded, spine straightening. "My children."

"What the bloody hell were you thinking?" James yelled.

"I was on a trip and I wanted to have a good time."

"Well, it seems you had a really good time that you're going to be paying for the rest of your life."

My mom sat there dumbfounded while Liam and his dad had

their side discussion. Then she interrupted with, "it can't possibly be, Liam. You've only known my daughter since the end of June," my mom piped up.

"That's not true, ma'am. I've known your daughter since March."

"How?" Liam's father asked.

"Remember my trip to Paris, Dad?"

"Yes."

"We met there."

"Impossible. My daughter's never been to Paris."

I cleared my voice and everyone finally acknowledged my presence again. "I've been there mom."

"When?" she yelled.

"Spring break."

"With who? How?"

"I went with Jen. Her dad booked us the tickets and gave us a credit card. You were in Montreal for another conference."

She slumped forward in her chair. "I've been a horrible mother, haven't I?"

"No."

"How could I not be, when my teenage daughter becomes pregnant with her stepbrother's baby?"

"He wasn't my stepbrother."

"How are we going to explain this to people? The scandal."

"Who cares?" Liam answered. "I love your daughter and we are going to have twins."

I looked at Liam. "You do?"

"Of course I do."

"I love you too," I smiled.

He leaned over and gave me a kiss. We must have kissed a second too long because his dad cleared his throat.

"What?" Liam grinned. "I think it's a little too late now, dad."

"Keep the PDA at the breakfast table to a minimum," James responded.

"Look at you with the modern slang," Liam teased.

"This is not the time for smart remarks."

"Of course, we will keep the PDA to a minimum, sir."

ONE MONTH LATER...

We had been staying with my dad and Camille for the past month while Liam and I worked for some extra money. After the conversation we had with our parents, we thought they had accepted we were going to be parents. Neither of us expected them to just be okay with it, since it was a huge ask, but we thought they wouldn't be hostile.

"Are you sure you still want to move all the way to Glasgow?" Camille asked for the billionth time.

Needless to say, our relationship with our parents had become strained since they found out we were going to be parents. Neither of them were happy about me being pregnant, but they were even more volatile about us being step-siblings. I only hoped they would pull their heads out of their asses before the twins were here.

"We've already been through this," I replied.

"I know," she sighed. "I just worry, honey."

Camille had easily slid into my life like she had been there forever. Both her and my dad welcomed us with open arms when Liam brought me back over here only a week after we left. Dad couldn't understand why my mom was willing to lose another child over something so trivial as being in love with Liam.

After all, we didn't know our parents were together before I got pregnant.

"Sweetheart, they'll be fine. Liam will take care of them," my dad assured her.

It all started with telling us we couldn't kiss in front of them, which we agreed to because we hadn't planned on making out in front of our parents. Next, my mom blew a gasket when she saw me in Liam's bedroom, fully clothed, with the door open. After that, they moved their bedroom furniture around so that they could have their door open so they could see down the hall.

They would actually stay awake past their normal time, just to see if we went into each other's bedrooms.

When I threatened moving back into my dad's house or even leaving for Glasgow early, Mom didn't take the hint and kept pushing. When she wasn't trying to convince me to give up the babies for adoption, she was making passive aggressive comments about what people would think when they found out that I was having my brother's babies.

And yes, she said brother!

The final deciding factor was when we went to the doctor for our checkup and she told me I had elevated blood pressure. When she asked what we had changed, we explained our situation further, and she posed the question we had avoided regarding if we had another place to live.

Which we did. I phoned my dad in the car on the way home.

The summer had flown by too quick, but we were both ready for the next chapter in our lives. The flat Liam had arranged for us to live in had two bedrooms and was close to the university.

I couldn't wait to start this new chapter in our life.

It was so close I could even take some evening classes in the second semester.

EPILOGUE

MAIRI

5 Years Later...

Even though we'd had a rocky beginning, everything worked out in the end. The moment the doctor placed our son in my arms, I was overcome with emotion, feeling the warmth of his tiny body against mine. Liam and I had already chosen a few names, but I was still hesitant about honouring my brother by naming our son after him. I didn't know how I felt about it. When he looked up at me with his deep blue eyes, strikingly similar to my twin's, I knew he had to be called Michael James. Then the doctor handed me his sister, and Liam proudly suggested her name should be Paris Elizabeth.

Seeing their faces brought back memories of my brother and I, and it was like I was transported back in time watching an old home movie. The first couple of months after their birth were particularly challenging, due to the postpartum, but also because I could feel the memories of my childhood flooding my mind. Liam was my support throughout the tumultuous moments, and we both made it through with flying colours.

It wasn't long after the twins were born that Liam said to me, "I saw what having my babies did to you, and it makes me want to fill you with more."

Over the last five years, we've experienced so many significant moments. Like when the twins both took their first steps within hours of each other, they couldn't help but giggle with delight, their tiny feet making contact with the ground. Last year, we had a beautiful wedding ceremony with Michael and Paris, our ring bearer and flower girl, standing beside us.

Two months after the wedding, Darren announced that Miranda was pregnant, the result of a rendezvous in the coat check room at our reception. Seven months later, Amelia was born. Less than 24 hours after giving birth, Miranda checked herself out of the hospital, and took off. She vanished without a trace, leaving us in stunned disbelief. Thinking about abandoning my children made me shudder, yet it was clear that some people weren't fit to be parents.

We persuaded Darren to purchase a house close by, so we could be there for him if he needed it. Being a stay at home mom gave me the opportunity to look after his daughter while he continued working, the ideal setup. He was reluctant at first because I had given birth to another daughter shortly before Amelia was born. We quickly convinced him that it would be like having two more tiny bundles of laughter.

A couple months into the arrangement, we found out I was pregnant again. This time was like none of our previous pregnancies, and I ended up on bedrest. My best friend Jen came to the rescue, showing up unannounced on my doorstep, ready and willing to look after both of the munchkins. Amelia and our youngest would undoubtedly be as thick as thieves, little hellions, just like Jen and I were. Paris treated them both like her little dolls, whereas Michael was ever vigilant and had already turned into their little protector.

The best part of moving to Scotland, besides running into Liam, was being closer to my dad and his wife. They really stepped up and helped when our parents retreated into the shadows. Neither my mom nor Liam's dad were happy that we kept the twins. They kept pressuring us, even after I moved to Glasgow to live with Liam.

Our relationship had become so strained that they weren't with us when I gave birth to the twins, but my dad and stepmom were.

My dad didn't just stop with being supportive over our decisions, he also made sure that Liam had a position at his company once he graduated. It might have been nepotism in action, but neither of us cared. We both wanted to move back to Edinburgh to be closer to our families, so my dad gave us the ability to do so. Liam graduated with honors so he was most definitely suited to the position he had been granted.

Besides, what was the use of owning a business if you couldn't help provide for your family.

Dear Reader,

First off, thank you so much for taking a chance on this novella.

I can't believe it's finally finished!

This novella was started in 2017, during my first introduction to the stepbrother trope. No matter how much I tried, I just couldn't get it to work the way I wanted. So, I put it to the side and worked on other stories.

Then I found an anthology for stepbrother books and thought, why don't I sign up and finish this story in time to submit it. Within one week I added 16,000 words to a document that just sat for years.

I'm hoping this will be the first of many novellas I write.

ABOUT KATYA ENSMORE

Katya Ensmore resides in rural Saskatchewan with her #writingbuddy, a Great Dane aptly named Khaos. When she is not spending time with Khaos, she can be found writing or hiding behind her iPad buried in the digital pages of a book.

When it comes to literature and film, she enjoys all things supernatural. She has been writing since she was a child. She currently has several works in progress with hopes to publish more in the near future.

For a complete list of books by Katya Ensmore, check out her website: https://katyaensmore.com or check out her Amazon Author Page where you can also follow for updates on new or upcoming releases.

CLICK HERE TO JOIN THE NEWSLETTER

JOIN KATYA ENSMORE ONLINE

Follow me on Facebook:

https://www.facebook.com/KatyaEnsmore

Join my Reader Group:

https://www.facebook.com/groups/katscreativekhaos

Follow me on Goodreads:

https://www.goodreads.com/author/show/20898957.Katya_Ensmore

Follow me on Amazon:

https://amazon.com/author/katyaensmore

Follow me on TikTok:

https://tiktok.com/@katyaensmoreauthor

Follow me on Twitter:

https://twitter.com/KatyaEnsmore

Follow me on Instagram:

https://instagram.com/KatyaEnsmore

Follow me on Bookbub:

https://www.bookbub.com/authors/katya-ensmore

Follow me on Booksprout:

https://booksprout.co/reviewer/author/view/22531/katya-ensmore

ALSO BY KATYA ENSMORE

LEGACY IN BLUE

Badge Bunny (Viola King)

Back Up (Reed King)

RENEGADE REAPERS MC

Don't Fear the Reapers

Reap What You Sow

Fear the Reapers

STANDALONES

Keeping Our Secrets (novella)

WICKEDLY OBSESSED

A WICKEDLY DEPRAVED PREQUEL

MIRANDA MAY

ABOUT WICKEDLY OBSESSED

Alessandra, mafia princess, heir to the Valentino family. That's been my life from the moment I was born.

It's only been my father and me for as long as I can remember, until Teresa and her twin sons come into the picture. Now I have a new stepmother that I adore, two ridiculously hot older brothers to fawn over much to my boyfriend's chagrin, and a whole lot of training to do before I am ready to take my father's position.

With time, my little crush turns to an obsession, but I know nothing will come of it.

At least, that's what I thought until I turned eighteen and my world became forever wicked.

Wickedly Obsessed is a part of the Sinful Desires anthology, a stepbrother collection, and is a prequel to Wickedly Depraved. This book is intended for readers 18+ due to language and content.

TRIGGER WARNINGS

Torture

Murder

Talk of underage sex

Underage sexting

Gun violence

Use of pressure points to get someone to pass out

Suicidal thoughts and ideation

Cheating off-page (by MMC)

Panic attack

PTSD

Trauma

Possible emotional cheating by FMC

CHAPTER 1

December 2015

Have you ever woken up knowing that today will change the course of your life? Well, today is that day for me.

I stand beside my dad, grinning as he exchanges vows with my soon-to-be stepmother, Teresa. Unlike most teenagers, I'm excited my dad is remarrying. My mom's been dead for ten years. I was only four when she died, and he always said she died in an accident. It wasn't until this year he admitted there had been no accident. No, she was murdered by someone who held a vendetta against Daddy.

Murder? Vendettas? It all sounds like a movie, right? Except this is real life. It's the life you get when your dad is the head of one of the five families. What five families? The Italian mafia's five families, obviously. That's right, I'm a mafia princess and proud of it. I'm fully aware of what that means—at least, I think I do. It's something I'll learn more about this summer since I'll be working with him along with my new stepbrothers.

My eyes dart to them, finding both Luca and Vito looking bored out of their minds. As excited as I am about having a stepmom, I'm not nearly as excited about having new stepbrothers. Not that I have a problem with them—it's actually kind of the opposite.

These two men are hot as sin and only four years older than me. With their thick black hair and piercing green eyes, they're two of the most popular boys in our school. Though they're not boys at all. Even when I met them for the first time a few months ago, I knew they were men, not boys—no matter their age.

They're identical, but I've rarely had a problem telling them apart. They've fooled me a time or two when our parents first started dating, but they're so different that it's easy to tell them apart now. Both stand at six-foot-three, which means they still tower over my five-foot-eight and their love of the gym shows in their wide, muscular builds.

They look so good, I almost feel the need to wipe my mouth to make sure I'm not drooling. Not that I stand a chance with them. I'm too young, and while my body's curves are finally making an appearance, I look nothing like the girls I've seen them with. Which is fine since our parents are getting married, so nothing can happen between us.

Luca catches my eye and grins. I return his smile and turn back to our parents, only to find that they're kissing. I wrinkle my nose because I absolutely don't need to see that.

"Alright, that's enough of that." Vito fakes gagging—at least, I think he's faking. "Please don't traumatize us. You can do whatever you want behind closed doors, but trust me, none of us wants to see that shit."

I giggle, which draws Vito's attention to me, and he smirks. As our parents break apart, he makes his way over to me and throws his arm around my shoulders.

"So what's next on the agenda, Mom? Riccardo?"

Daddy wraps his arm around Teresa with a goofy smile on his

face. "Celebratory dinner at Vincenzo's and then we're off for our honeymoon."

"We definitely don't want to hear about that." Luca throws his arms around his mom and hugs her close. "Congrats, Mom. I'm so happy for you. Well, both of you."

"Yeah, Daddy, congratulations. Welcome to the family, Teresa." I roll my eyes. "And I guess the two of you, too."

Vito gasps, his hand lifting to muss my hair. "Don't pretend you don't like us."

"Not my hair," I whine as I knock away his hand before trying to fix what he messed up.

Teresa tuts at Vito as she comes over to help me fix my hair. "Really, Vito? Alessandra and I spent a lot of time doing her hair. A young lady wants to look good when she's out in public, unlike you two ruffians."

"Does this mean James is joining us?" Luca asks, his disdain clear.

My shoulders stiffen as I glare at him. "I don't know what your problem with James is, but he's a perfect gentleman. Not to mention he's my boyfriend. Of course he's coming. I just have to text him."

"Go ahead and text him then, sweetheart," my dad says with a soft smile. He approves of me and James dating, as he's known him for his entire life.

James is two years older than me and a junior. He's also the quarterback for our varsity football team and my next-door neighbor. We played together as kids, but once I hit high school, things changed between us. We started dating the first week of school. A little fast? Maybe, but also... not really. I've loved James for as long as I can remember.

Now that we're dating, the love I felt for him as a child has morphed into something more, something deeper. Which is why it feels so weird that I'm not only attracted to but feel pulled toward Luca and Vito. Not that it'll ever happen. Number one because I have James, but also how would the two of them ever be interested in me? Super hot and four years older—they're just my forbidden crushes.

"Thanks, Daddy. I'll go do that now and make a quick run to the bathroom before we leave." I shoot him a smile as we step through the doors. I veer toward the left where the bathrooms are while they head to the right toward the exit. I pull out my phone and type out my message.

Me: Wedding's over. We're going to Vincenzo's to celebrate. Daddy specifically asked if you'd be there.

James: That's cause he loves me as much as you do, baby.

Me: I do love you.

James: I love you too.

James: Are the wonder twins going to be there?

Me: Of course they are. We're celebrating as a family. I don't get why the three of you can't get along.

James: It's never gonna happen, baby. No matter how much you want it to.

Me: Yeah, yeah, yeah.

Me: You'll meet us there?

James: Already headed to my car.

Me: Good. I miss you.

James: Miss you more. See you in a few.

With that done, I push into the bathroom and quickly take care of business. Washing my hands, I take a moment to study my reflection. I still feel awkward sometimes, too skinny for my height, but I can see changes in my body already. My hips are widening, and my boobs have gone up a cup size in a week, I swear.

My long black curls fall to my mid-back with the half up-do Teresa wrangled it into. Thick black lashes surround my amber eyes, popping with the black liner and mascara she taught me how to use. I'd been worried about the bold red lipstick that matches my dress, thinking it was too much for someone my age, but Teresa swore up and down that it was perfect for me. She was right. It makes me look older, and I'm beginning to see the woman I'll become one day.

Shaking my head, I grab a paper towel and quickly dry my hands. Everyone's waiting on me, and here I am, staring at myself in the mirror. Talk about self-absorbed. I throw up the door, startling when I find Luca and Vito waiting for me.

"Ummm... what's up?"

Luca pushes off the wall he is leaning against, smiling. "Mom and Riccardo headed to the restaurant. We told them we'd wait for you and give you a ride."

"Okay..." I'm confused about why they'd want to wait around for me, but I won't turn down the chance to hang out with them.

Vito throws his arm around my shoulders, leading me toward the exit. "Look, I know you're only fourteen, but today you look a lot older than that. We didn't want you wandering around by yourself and have some idiot decide he wanted to hit on you."

"Really, we're just trying to make sure we didn't have to kill anyone for hitting on our sister," Luca adds.

"Stepsister," I hiss, not liking it when they call me their sister.

"Right. Stepsister. That's what I said." Luca laughs, grabbing my hand in his.

I bite my lip as butterflies flutter in my stomach at having them both touching me. The worst part is I don't think they realize the effect they have on me.

None of us speak as they lead me to Vito's brand-new Camaro that Daddy got for him. He got Luca a Ducati, but they won't let him take me out on it, no matter how much I pout about it. I love Vito's Camaro though. It's sleek and reminds me of the classic muscle cars that my dad loves so much.

The back seat is pretty small, and when I go to get in, I'm pretty sure Luca gets a flash of my thong and a good portion of my ass. This is the exact reason I hadn't wanted to wear this dress. Well, that and I thought my dad would have a heart attack, but Teresa promised it would be fine. Yet again, she was right. All he'd said was how beautiful I looked and how quickly I'm growing up.

Luca says nothing, so I'm going to assume he wasn't looking.

Thank goodness. The last thing I need is them giving me shit about my dress being too short. Or about the thong I'm wearing.

My face flushes at the thought, and I duck my head as I hurriedly put on my seatbelt. One day, I'm going to stop blushing around them so much. I don't know how, but I'm determined. If there's one thing that can be said about the Valentinos, it's that we're stubborn as hell.

"Got your seatbelt on, Alessa?" Vito meets my eyes in the rearview mirror.

I nod, glancing toward Luca before frowning. "Though Luca doesn't."

"If he wants to be an idiot, then that's on him. But you need to be kept safe."

Vito's words have me ducking my head, trying to hide my blush. My Italian genetics means I have a darker olive skin tone which hides some of the redness but not all of it.

Clearing my throat as Vito starts the car, I ask, "What do you have planned for winter break?"

Today began our winter break, and now we have two glorious weeks off from school. Christmas is less than a week away, and this will be the first one I'm not spending with Daddy. He and Teresa are leaving for their honeymoon tomorrow, and they'll be gone for two weeks—which means they'll be gone the entire time we're on break.

The twins and I told them we were fine with them missing Christmas and New Year's with us. We want them to have this time alone to celebrate their marriage—far from us. There's nothing worse than hearing your parents having sex. Even in our mansion, I've heard them on multiple occasions, and I'd rather be alone for the holidays than hear that again.

Not that I'll be alone since the twins officially moved in. The movers brought over the last of their things last night. Teresa's been living with us since the first of the month, only leaving the big stuff with the boys at their old house. The twins have been staying there by themselves until yesterday. Now they're officially my housemates.

"Not sure yet," Luca says as he turns around to look at me. "We figured we'd see what you want to do and what you have planned."

Oh. Well, that's sweet. I figured they would want to be rid of me as soon as possible. Sure, we're friends, but they have other friends. I thought they'd want to hang out with them.

"I'll be hanging out with James some, but he's going to be working with his dad a lot over break. The Adams invited me over for Christmas Eve. I can see if the two of you can come with me, if you'd like."

Vito snorts. "Not sure James would approve of that."

"I don't care if he approves," I say with a frown. "The two of you shouldn't be alone on the holidays, either. I'll text his mom later. I'm sure she won't mind."

"I won't say no to someone cooking for us." Luca laughs. "You're with us on Christmas day, right? We're going to have to figure out what we're going to do about food."

"I'll cook." I flush again, feeling their attention on me. "Eva will be off Thursday through Sunday, but she's been teaching me to cook. I'm sure I can make us something edible."

Luca shakes his head. "I still can't believe you have a cook."

"*We* have a cook," I interject. "If it weren't for Eva, Daddy and I would've starved. He can't cook for shit."

Vito tuts at me. "Language, Alessa."

I stick my tongue at him even though his eyes are on the road. "I'm not a child. I can say shit. Hell, I can say fuck if I want."

"I don't think your daddy would approve if he heard those words coming out of your pretty mouth, would he?" Luca shakes his head as he turns back around.

Another flush builds at Luca calling my mouth pretty, but I forge ahead. "He doesn't seem to care that every other word out of your mouths is a curse word."

"We're not his little girl, either." Vito's eyes meet mine in the mirror again before flipping back to the road.

"I'm not a little girl." Crossing my arms over my chest, I slump in the seat and pout.

Luca mumbles something that sounds suspiciously like, "We're well aware."

That doesn't seem right though, so I'm sure I misheard him. We all fall quiet for the rest of the short drive, but it's a comfortable silence. I've always felt comfortable around the two of them. Well, since I officially met them.

Before our parents started dating, I only knew the two of them through their reputations. They're the kings of the school and what they say goes. There are even rumors about them killing someone who crossed them. I'm fairly certain those are just rumors, but I wouldn't put it past them. After all, they're about to become part of the family.

Vito parks the car, and Luca climbs out, popping the seat up and offering me his hand. I take it, allowing him to help me out as I tug down my dress so I won't flash anyone else. When I try to pull my hand from his, he just holds on tighter. With a shrug, I let him lead me into the restaurant with Vito trailing us.

"Welcome, Miss Valentino." The pretty blond hostess greets me with a smile before her eyes trail over the twins. Her eyes light up, and her smile turns predatory. "Vito. Luca. It's good to see the two of you again."

Vito glances at her, raising an eyebrow before turning back to scan the restaurant.

Luca sighs, giving the blond a small smile. "Hey, Jenny."

Jenny simpers at his attention. "Are you guys going to the party tonight? Maybe we can hang out?"

"That's not happening," Vito bites out. "I don't know how many times I have to say this before you get the point. You were a one and done. Neither of us wants a second go at your pussy. Stop trying. It's getting a little desperate."

My eyes are wide as I flush again, eyes dropping to my shoes. Rage and lust rush through me, and I can't figure out which one is more dominant. Lust from the way Vito said pussy or rage at the fact that Jenny has apparently slept with not just one but both of my stepbrothers.

I'm well aware they sleep around, but I rarely have to hear about it. And I really don't want to hear about it. It makes me angry, and there's a heavy weight in my stomach I don't want to name.

"Can you just show us the table, please?" I bark, eyes flashing at Jenny. "We're here to celebrate our parents getting married, not for you to try to get in their pants again. Maybe try to be a little more professional next time, yeah?"

Jenny glares at me. "And who the fuck—"

"I'd stop right there," Vito says, his voice scarily quiet. "I wouldn't go trying to insult Alessa. She's about to be the queen of the school, and she can make your life just as miserable as we can. And trust me when I say we will make your life hell if we hear you've said anything unkind about her. Got it?"

Jenny looks like she's about to burst into tears as she frantically nods her head. "This way, please. Your menus are already at your table."

I grin, lifting my head as I follow her to the table with the twins at my side. I probably shouldn't get so much joy out of Vito putting her in her place, but he's right. I am going to be the queen of the school, just like I'll be a mafia queen one day. Ruling the school is a practice run for my future.

Even though my dad keeps saying it's my choice and I don't have to be a part of the mafia, that's exactly what I want. I want to be just like Daddy and in a few months, I'll get my first taste of what that's like.

"There they are." Daddy's voice booms through the restaurant as we reach the table.

"There's my girl," James says as he jumps up from his seat, pulling me from the twins and into his arms. He leans down to brush a gentle kiss on my lips. "You look gorgeous, Lessa."

"Thanks, James."

He pulls out the chair between him and Daddy, who sits at the head of the table with Teresa on his right. I settle into my seat as the twins sink into chairs on their mom's side of the table.

It's quiet as we all flip through the menu. I don't know why I bother since I have the menu memorized. This is Daddy's favorite restaurant, and we usually eat here a few times a month. We've been doing that for as long as I can remember. I don't know if we came with my mom when she was still alive. It's a possibility, but since I have no memories of her, I can't say for sure.

"When do you leave for the honeymoon, Riccardo?" James asks as he closes his menu. I'm surprised he bothered looking at either, since he always gets the same thing.

"First thing in the morning. We fly out at six, and then it's just about a nine-hour flight to Venice. We should land around eight their time."

James grins. "I'm so jealous you're going to Venice. I've always wanted to visit Italy."

Daddy returns his smile. "I'm sure you and Alessandra can go one summer. We'll make it happen."

"Really, Daddy?" I ask, eyes wide.

"Of course, princess. If you want to go, I'll make sure the two of you can go. Probably not this summer, but maybe next summer for your sixteenth birthday?"

I jump out of my seat to throw my arms around my dad. "This is why you're the world's best dad."

"Why?" he asks with a laugh, returning my hug. "Because I spoil you rotten?"

"Well, duh." I press a kiss on his cheek before returning to my seat. I love my dad so much. He definitely spoils me, but I like to think I don't act like a spoiled brat. While he gives me most things I want, he won't hesitate to tell me no.

I also love that he assumes James and I will still be together next summer. I know I'm young, but I think he could be the one. I could see us getting married somewhere down the line—not until after I've graduated college, of course. I don't want to be one of those women who gets married young and starts squeezing out babies.

No, I'm going to run the mafia, which means I need to finish school—Daddy's requirement, not mine—and then work with him until he's ready to retire. I wouldn't mind getting married before he retires, but babies will have to wait until I'm in my thirties. I've got big plans, after all.

"That should be enough time to convince my parents, too." James laughs. His parents are not a part of the mafia, but they know my dad is and they're still friends with him. James's dad owns the biggest construction company in the city, and Daddy always uses him when he's having something built. His mom used to be a model, but now she manages models instead. They make good money, obviously, since they live in the same neighborhood we do.

The conversation derails when the waitress appears to take our orders. Once I've placed my order, my eyes fall on Luca and Vito, who are both glaring at James. I frown, my eyes narrowing as their attention turns to me.

"Stop it," I mouth at the two of them.

Vito rolls his eyes but leans back in his chair and avoids looking at James. Luca grins as he leans forward, putting his weight on his elbows and raises an eyebrow at me.

"Are you sure you don't want to come stay at my place while your dad is on his honeymoon?" James asks. He's been asking me all month, and I've declined him every time. I'm not sure why he's pushing this so hard, but it's pissing me off. The fastest way to guarantee I won't do something is to continuously push me after I've already given an answer. As I said, Valentinos are stubborn.

"No way in hell is she staying at your house," Vito growls. "Alessa is staying at the house with the two of us so we can keep an eye on her."

James makes a face, mumbling under his breath, "That's what I'm afraid of."

I frown, elbowing him in the side. He flushes, and I realize he didn't mean for me to hear his words.

"Sorry, baby. My mom is just worried about you being there with just the twins for adult supervision. I told her I'd ask again."

My face softens at that. I adore his mom. "That's really sweet of her, but I'd be fine on my own. Plus, the twins will be there for me to annoy if I need anything. She acts like I won't call her if I need anything."

James shrugs. "You know how she is."

"And I'm glad she cares so much for my princess," Daddy says with a smile. "But she'll be fine with the twins. Won't she, boys?"

"Of course, she will." Luca nods. "We were actually talking on our way here about plans for the break. We're going to hang out with her as much as she wants us to."

"That's sweet, boys." Teresa's smile is soft as she looks at the twins. "You're such good big brothers."

"Stepbrothers," Luca says, shooting me a wink.

I stick my tongue out at him, knowing he's giving me shit about my comment earlier. James's arm comes around the back of my chair, and I lean back into his embrace as conversation carries on around me.

I'd never allowed myself to think about having a family like this, but now I do, and I couldn't be happier. It helps that I've never seen Daddy look this happy before. Teresa and the twins are good for us.

CHAPTER 2

July 2016

"Alessa, are you paying attention?" My dad's voice snaps me out of my daydreams.

I give a guilty smile. "No, Daddy, I'm sorry."

My dad rolls his eyes as he likes. "Thinking about that boyfriend of yours? Or maybe it's your birthday party that's got you distracted?"

I shrug, flushing because neither of those is what I'd been daydreaming about. No, these daydreams featured my stepbrothers. Something I will never admit out loud—not even to my best friend, Lyla. I'm sure she has her suspicions about how I feel about Vito and Luca. Luckily, she's never called me out on it, so I haven't had to decide if I would need to lie to her or admit the truth.

"I was asking if you were sure you wanted to do this job with the twins. This one is going to be bloody. I don't want to send you on a job and traumatize you. You can still decide you want no part in the business." He raises his hand to silence me when I open my mouth to argue with him. "I know what you're going to say, but we won't make that decision until after you graduate from college. You might discover a new passion between now and then.

"You know, if you decide not to follow in my footsteps, I have the twins now. If you choose another path, the two of them will run the business when I retire. If you decide you still want to be in charge, they'll act as your right-hand men—even act as your underbosses, if that's what you want. They've already decided this is the life they want. They've made it abundantly clear they'll stand by your side or run the business, depending on your decision."

Warmth rushes through me at their confidence in me. Vito and Luca have already expressed their support for me throughout the summer, which is sadly almost over. We've been working for my dad for almost two months, but school starts in less than two weeks. The upside to that is my fifteenth birthday is just around the corner on the twenty-first of July. Daddy has a gigantic party planned for me, and I can't wait.

I've done none of the "bloody" work with the twins yet, as they and Daddy don't seem to think I'm ready—until today, that is. I don't know what has changed their minds, but I'm actually excited about it. A little weird? Maybe. But in this family? Not at all.

"Yes, Daddy, I'm sure. I can do this. I need to see all aspects of the business—not just the parts you deem safe. I'll never be able to make an informed decision if I don't see what all it entails."

Daddy smiles softly, nodding. "And this is why I think you're ready. The twins are still a little resistant to the idea, but I think they just don't want to ruin your innocence."

Oh, I'd like them to ruin my innocence all right.

No. Bad Alessandra. That is so not what he's talking about. Plus, that's something James will get to experience. In fact, I'm thinking about asking him to take my virginity on my birthday. I have my own room at the hotel where we're having the party, so it would be easy enough for us to spend the night together.

Teresa had the talk with me at the beginning of the summer and got me started on birth control, just in case. She said teenage hormones can get out of control and that ending up pregnant would destroy not only my plans for the future but James's as well. Which I get. Honestly, I probably would've gone to her about birth control at some point, so it was nice that she came to me.

"Silly boys," is all I say to my dad. "I'm ready for this. I promise."

"Good. The boys will be by to pick you up soon. They'll take you back to the house. Listen to them on what to wear—they won't steer you wrong. In fact, listen to everything they tell you. They're in charge tonight."

I nod, trying to keep my excitement at bay. "I understand, Daddy. I will listen to everything they say and follow directions. I know I'm not the boss yet."

"That's a good girl, princess." He glances at his phone when it goes off. "Looks like they're here. Be good tonight."

"I'm always good, Daddy," I sass as I hop up from my chair and head for the door. I'm almost as excited to see the twins as I am for my first torture session tonight. I wonder if we'll end up having to kill the person and who they are. What did they do that Daddy has to have them questioned? Maybe the twins will know.

I take the elevator downstairs and hurry to the door, finding Luca and Vito leaning against Vito's Camaro. They both grin at me as I run down the stairs and throw myself at them as if I hadn't seen them this morning.

They catch me between the two of them, laughing.

"I think she's happy to see us," Vito says.

Luca snorts. "Or maybe she was just tired of doing paperwork, and she's just glad we're here to rescue her."

"Shut up." I smack Luca's stomach, barely able to stop myself from stroking the rock-hard abs he's hiding under his tee. Why do they have to be so hot? "I'm excited about tonight."

"I still think you should wait until next summer," Vito grumps as he walks around the driver's side.

"I'm ready for this, Vito, and I will not let you bring me down. And what about you?" I turn to face Luca as he swings open the passenger side door. "Are you going to be a Mr. Grumpy Pants about this, too?"

"Did you just call Vito Mr. Grumpy Pants?" Luca laughs so hard I'm surprised he doesn't fall to the ground as he grasps his side. "Oh, tonight is going to be so much fun with you there, Alessa."

I lean up to kiss Luca's cheek. "And this is why you're my favorite."

"What the fuck?" Vito practically shouts as he turns to the back seat while I climb in. "You're not allowed to have favorites."

"The fuck I'm not."

"Language, Alessa. One of these days, I'm going to take you over my knee and spank the brat out of you."

I fight not to rub my thighs together at that, my pussy suddenly soaked. Not really sure why that turns me on. Spankings aren't something I've had since I was a child and that only happened once or twice. It must be all the porn I've been watching, so I'll be prepared to lose my virginity. The spanking in those looked fun.

I know what you're thinking. Porn is nothing like sex in real life, and I'm sure that's true. But it's the only reference I can get my hands on, and it's hot as hell. I've spent many nights with my hands down my pants as I watch. I've been watching all kinds too. I've watched gay and lesbian porn, plus the regular kind. My favorites are when there are two or more guys with one girl. Especially when the guys are together.

My phone alerts me to a text, pulling me away from those dangerous thoughts as Vito pulls away from the curb.

James: Wanna come over and watch a movie tonight? My parents are out.

Me: I wish I could. Daddy has me doing a job with the twins tonight.

James: What kind of job does he have you doing at night?

Me: You know I can't tell you that.

James: This is dumb. I don't know why you want to work for your dad.

James: Or why he thinks you should work for him? You're only fourteen.

Me: Almost fifteen!

Me: And I want to. I like working for Daddy. This is my future. You know that. If you can't deal with it...

James: Yeah, that year makes all the difference.

James: Of course I can deal with it, I promise. I just really wanted to see you tonight.

James: Especially since I have the house to myself.

Me: I know. I would've liked to hang out with you, too. How about I make it up to you?

James: Hmmm... how do you plan to do that?

Me: I have a room by myself at the hotel on the night of my party. Nowhere near my dad's. You should stay the night.

James: Yeah?

Me: I'd really like it if you did. And I can think of some fun ways we can celebrate my birthday.

James: I like the sound of this.

Me: Good. Do you forgive me?

James: Always. Text me when you're done with the job. You know I can't sleep without talking to you first.

Me: You're making me blush.

James: I can think of some better ways to make you blush.

"Will you stop sexting with your boyfriend and get the fuck out of my car?" Vito's tone has me frowning as I glance up at him. He looks pissed, and I don't understand what the hell's going on.

"Excuse me?" I undo my seatbelt, reaching forward to stab my finger in his chest. "I don't know who the fuck you think you're talking to, but you will not speak to me like that. Asshole."

Without another word, I climb out of the car to find Luca waiting for me. I'm so angry at Vito right now that I'm close to tears.

"Who does he think he is?" I spit out as Luca's arm goes around my shoulders and pulls me to his side.

"He's just being an asshole. Ignore him."

I roll my eyes and try to bite back my anger. I hate when I fight with either of them—it's usually Vito. Luca prefers to go with the flow, while Vito seems to enjoy making me angry. They'll be leaving for college soon, and then they won't be around as much. I'm going to miss them, and I want to spend as much time with them as possible before they leave.

But when he pisses me off like this, I want nothing to do with him.

"Alessa," Vito calls after me, but I ignore him, choosing to finish my conversation with James.

Me: Sorry, baby. I've got to get ready for this job. Keep those ideas in mind for tonight's phone call.

Me: You know, an orgasm always makes me sleep better.

James: Jesus fuck.

James: You can't say shit like that.

Me: Sure I can. I just did.

Me: Go fuck your hand while you think of me.

Me: Love you.

James: Saints above. You're going to be the death of me.

James: Love you too. Be careful tonight.

"So how are things going with James?" Luca asks as I slide my phone into my pocket.

My eyes narrow as I turn to look at him. I know the three of them don't get along, and the twins have no problem talking shit about James. Not that I let it stand. I always give them a piece of my mind when they start in.

"Down, kitten," Luca says with a grin. "I'm genuinely asking. He's still treating you right?"

"Of course he is." I scoff. "Like I'd let anyone mistreat me."

"I know you wouldn't, but I thought I'd ask." We pause at the bottom of the stairs. "Wear something comfortable in black. You have black tennis shoes, yeah?"

I nod. "Black and comfortable. Got it."

"We've got thirty minutes until we leave." Luca glances over his shoulder. "If you don't want to get into a screaming match with Vito, you should probably head upstairs now."

I look over my shoulder to see Vito making his way up the stairs to the front door, anger radiating from him. "Good call. I'll be back down in thirty."

I give him a quick wave and scurry up the stairs. I'm not actually afraid that Vito and I will get into a screaming match. I have no problems screaming at him—it's how we Italians show our love, after all. It's more that I'm afraid I'll forgive him too quickly. Because I hate being angry with them, I usually end up folding first. I'm not in the mood for that right now.

CHAPTER 3

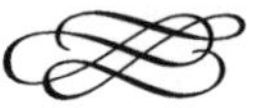

True to my word, I'm downstairs in less than thirty minutes in all black. I'm wearing my most comfy black jeans and a plain black tee that bares just a hint of my stomach—it's the boobs. I'm already up to a C cup, so a lot of my shirts now bare my midriff. Not that I mind.

Instead of black tennis shoes, I'm wearing a pair of black ankle boots with a small heel. My boots are so much more comfortable than my tennis shoes. Plus, they'll help my ass look amazing.

Luca comes running down the stairs seconds after me. "Look at Baby Valentino, all dressed up and ready to torture."

I shake my head, glancing down at my outfit before focusing my attention on him. "This is definitely not me dressed up."

"Nah, I know. But you look good, and you still followed directions—except the shoes." He puts a finger to my lips when I go to argue with him. "I think they're a good choice. Just as good as tennis shoes, but they're what you're used to wearing, so you'll be more comfortable."

"You're aware that we're going to torture someone and not seduce them, right?" Vito's voice is still grumpy.

I turn to him with a glare. "Luca said to wear all black and make sure it was comfortable. I'm comfy, and it's all black. You don't need to look if it offends you. Prick."

I spin on my heels, once again pissed at Vito. I'd reined in my anger while in my room, but he just had to piss me off again, didn't he? What the hell is his problem? He never used to be like this with me, but this has been happening more and more the later in summer it gets.

I don't know what crawled up his ass and died, but I will not put up with it. If he wants to ruin the last of our time together before they go off to college, then I'll let him. But I will not play along. I might not be the queen bitch of the mafia yet, but I'm still a queen bitch.

"Jesus, Alessa. That's not what I meant." Vito growls his annoyance. "I'm sorry, okay? I don't mean to be such an ass. I just... I don't want this for you."

"Don't want what for me?" I ask, throwing my hands in the air as I face him.

"This." He waves around the house. "The mafia. The killing. The torture. Any of it. You deserve better."

I scoff. "This is my birthright, and I embrace it fully. This is what I want. I don't want some boring life living in the suburbs, popping out kids while I work a job I hate."

"Hate to break it to you, baby girl, but you live in the suburbs now," Luca says with a grin.

"You know what I'm saying." Rolling my eyes, I focus on Vito again. "Honestly? I don't care what you want for me. I care what I want for me, and this is what I want. I'm sick of you treating me like a child and trying to keep me away from the dirty parts of this life. This is the life I choose, Vito, so get your shit together."

Vito takes a deep breath before giving me a sharp nod. "You're right, and I'm sorry."

I stare at him in shock, waiting for the other shoe to drop. He just wraps his arm around my shoulders and drags me to the car. "Stop looking at me like that, Alessa. You act like you've never heard me admit I'm wrong before."

"I haven't. You never admit you're wrong, even when it's very obvious that you are."

He shrugs. "Well, it's something I'm working on. At least with you. Now shut up and get your game face on. Today's the day you learn how to torture someone."

He leaves me at the passenger door, and I quickly crawl into the backseat, waiting for both of them to climb inside before I inundate them with questions.

"Who are we torturing? What did they do? Will I actually get to torture him, or are the two of you going to make me sit on the sidelines?"

Luca laughs. "I'm going to need you to take it down a notch there, Alessa. No one should be this excited going into a torture session."

"Eh. Let her be excited. It is her first time, after all." Vito shoots me a grin in the mirror before starting the car. "Did your dad really not tell you anything about tonight?"

I shake my head. "He didn't bother to tell me about it until right before the two of you showed up. Pretty sure he wanted the two of you to get me up to speed."

"Sounds like him." Vito groans. "Luca, you fill her in while I drive."

"Sure." Luca spins in his seat so he can see me. "The torturee is George Mann."

My eyebrows shoot up. "I know George. His daughter Amanda was besties with me and Lyla until we hit middle school. George always went on all of our field trips, and he was the one who watched us on play dates because his wife was a hotshot surgeon. They live just up the road from us, and Daddy always invites the Manns to parties. I don't know why I didn't put two and two together to realize he worked for Daddy."

"Technically, he's not a part of the family," Luca says. "He's the accountant for the family, which means he's only an associate. He's been stealing from your dad for years without him realizing. Now, he knows."

I shrug, pushing away the emotions threatening me. "If he stole from the family, he has to pay for that. I assume we're looking to get some kind of information out of him, and that's why he's not dead right now."

"You're one smart cookie. We have the amount he's stolen, but it looks like he didn't just steal it for himself. He wasn't good at covering his tracks, depositing it into an offshore account in his name. But half of the money went into another account in a name we don't recognize before being sent to other accounts all over the globe, and we can't trace it. If he tells us who else was stealing, he might live through the night." Luca shrugs.

"Or not," Vito adds.

"Riccardo gave us instructions to get the information from him, however we have to. He didn't say we had to kill him, but he also didn't say we can't." Luca shrugs. "Now that you're aware it's someone you know, are you sure you want to do this?"

Do I want to torture the guy who was practically a second father to me while growing up? Not especially, but that's the way of the business. Anyone can betray you, even those that you trust implicitly. It's something Daddy has been trying to ingrain in me since I was young, but he's especially been harping on it this summer. I wonder if it's George's betrayal that caused that.

"I have to do this. If I can't do this, then I can't run the business. This won't be the last time someone close to us betrays us. I'm not naive. I know how the world works. Is it going to be easy? Probably not, but I won't know until I try, will I?"

"Brave princess." Vito smirks, and I feel myself preening under his attention.

Turning my head, I glance at the streets around and realize I don't know where we are. It seems we're in the industrial part of town —someplace I've had no reason to go to before tonight. "Where are we going?"

Luca winks. "Riccardo gave us a building on this side of town that we had redone for our sessions. It's not much further."

I settle in for the ride, watching the buildings as they pass by before remembering James had sent me a message while I was getting ready. I pull out my phone and see he sent me a video. I snag my earbuds from my pocket, not knowing what he might have sent me. Better not to let the twins hear it, just in case it is something spicy.

Pressing play, I'm happy I put in the earbuds. I lick my lips as I watch James stroke his cock before coming all over his stomach. My thighs clench as he lets out a guttural, "Fuccccck."

He continues lazily stroking himself as he lifts the phone up so I can see his face. "Love you, Lessa." He smirks, licking his lips before the video ends.

Since I'm still a virgin, we obviously haven't slept together, but this is far from the first time I've seen him come. Lately, a lot of our goodnight phone calls end up turning into video calls as we get ourselves off. My birthday can't come soon enough.

I quickly put away my earbuds and phone as the car comes to a stop outside a nondescript building. It looks like every other building on the block. Kind of boring if you ask me. If I ever build a torture room, it's going to be something fancier, I decide. No industrial buildings for this queen.

We climb out of the car, and the twins lead me to a door with a code panel outside of it.

"Come here, Alessa," Vito says, stepping to the side. "The code is 072101. You need it to get into and out of the building, not to mention getting in and out of the rooms inside."

"072101," I repeat, and it takes me a moment to realize it's my birthday. My brow furrows as I turn to him, but he's already punched in the code and heads inside. Luca quickly follows him, and I have no choice but to do the same. I'll just need to ask them about it later.

We walk down a long hallway before it opens up into a large room. I'm surprised by how quiet it is. It seems none of the outside noise is making it in here. When I voice this thought aloud, Luca grins.

"It's soundproofed. We don't want anyone walking by to hear us."

"That makes sense," I say, as I take a few moments to study the room. There's a drain in the center of the room, a chain hanging from the ceiling above it. That also makes sense. Better the blood goes down the drain rather than getting everywhere. Less cleaning—something I can get behind.

There's an entire wall of cabinets on the far side of the room along with various pieces of furniture—chairs, tables, and some things I don't even know what they are. Something else to ask about, eventually.

"What's in the cabinets?" I ask as I wander toward them.

"Torture tools."

I spin around to face Vito. "All of them?"

He laughs at the look on my face. "They're not all full. In fact, we saved one for you. Figured if you were going to get into this, then you should have a place to put the tools you prefer."

"I get my own torture tools? And a cabinet to put them in?" I grin, clapping my hands. The twins laugh at my glee but nod.

"Since we don't know what you'll like, we'll put out a little of everything tonight," Vito says, his hand landing on my lower back and leading me toward the cabinets.

I gape as he swings open the door and I take in the massive amount of knives, daggers, and baseball bats, of all things. I reach out to touch the knives but hesitate with my fingers mere inches away.

"You can touch any of them you'd like. Just be careful, they're sharp." Vito reaches in to grab the knife I'd been about to touch. "This one is a butterfly knife. I'm not surprised it was the first one to call to you. We'll have to teach you how to use it—I have some practice ones at the house—but this is something you can carry on you at all times."

Vito takes the time to explain each of the different knives to me and the different ways they can be used. He pulls a couple of butterfly knives, machetes, throwing knives, ka-bar knives, daggers, and scalpels out and places them onto a rolling table Luca pushes over.

"Baseball bats are more about brute force. Probably not going to be a favorite of yours, but we'll try it at least." Luca grabs a few from the cabinet and sets them on the table.

They show me the other two cabinets holding so many things I never would have considered using to torture someone. Plus, some things that could be interesting to see how they worked. Anything I show an interest in, they place on the table, adding a few other items as well.

"So now what?" I ask as we close the last cabinet.

"I assume you wore these clothes because you don't mind them getting bloody?" Vito asks, eyes raking up and down my body.

I shrug. "I figured they would. I'm not concerned about it."

Luca laughs. "He's trying to tell you we'll be burning our clothes when we're done. If you don't want to do that, we have some jumpsuits you can wear over them."

Glancing down, I shrug again. "I'm outgrowing them, anyway. They're fine to be burned."

"Well, in case you ever have to come here in a hurry and don't want to burn your clothes, the last cabinet has jumpsuits." Vito gestures toward the cabinets. "Always shower before you leave. We'll show you where we do that when it's time."

I'm guessing that one of the doors off this room must lead to the showers, but I'm curious what the other rooms are. "What do all the doors lead to?"

"Most of them are holding rooms for whoever we're going to torture." Luca doesn't meet my eyes, making me suspicious.

"Most of them?" I cock an eyebrow as I glance between the two of them.

Vito laughs, wrapping his arm around my waist as he leads me to the door closest to where we entered. "Luca is embarrassed."

"Embarrassed of what?"

Vito says nothing, typing in the code on the pad and throws the door open. It takes me a minute to realize what I'm seeing, and as soon as I do, my body heats. I'm sure I'm blushing to the tips of my hair at this point. Now I know why Luca is embarrassed.

"You have a sex dungeon," I blurt as I spin around to face them.

Vito waggles his eyebrows at me, a smirk firmly in place. "See, I knew you'd know what it was. We sure do."

"It's not like we use it." Luca's eyes are on the ground, and I see a faint blush on his cheeks.

"Speak for yourself, brother." Vito laughs again as he pulls the door shut and leads me to another room a few doors down. He sobers quickly. "This is where we've been keeping George. He's been here since late last night, so I'm sure he's eager for this conversation. You want to do the honors?"

I punch the code into the pad and push open the door, wincing as screamo metal blares from the room. I lift my hands to my ears and yell to Vito, "How didn't I hear that before now?"

I can't hear his response, but I'm able to figure out what he's saying by reading his lips. "Soundproofing."

So they'd not only soundproofed the warehouse as a whole but also the individual rooms. While that makes sense, the screamo metal does not.

I drop my hands with a sigh of relief when the music cuts off. "What is up with the music?"

"It causes sleep deprivation—another form of torture. Very few people can sleep with the lights on and that music playing." He gestures into the room where George is chained to the wall, slumping so the metal cuffs dig into his skin and he looks absolutely exhausted.

"Alessandra?" George sounds so relieved to see me. "Thank goodness you're here. Can you explain to these two they've made a mistake? I'll forget all about it if you let me go now."

I raise an eyebrow as I turn back to Vito and Luca. They just smile, shrugging. It's interesting to me that George thinks I'm here to save him. Though, I guess most people wouldn't think that an almost fifteen-year-old mafia princess was coming to torture them. A thought hits me, and I smile.

"Keys, please." I hold my hand out until Luca drops them in my hand. "Poor, George. I can't believe they did this to you."

I move over to unlock the cuffs but don't catch him as he falls to the floor. His shoulders slump forward as I move to unlock the cuffs around his ankles. Once he's free, I wrap an arm around his waist and help him stand.

I find the twins standing in the doorway, but they say nothing as I lead George from the room and toward the exit. I don't know what they're thinking, but they're obviously trusting me. A thrill runs through me at the trust they're putting in me. Honestly, I feel like if I walked out of here with George right now, they'd let me.

Too bad for George, that's not at all what I have planned.

I pause at the end of the hallway that leads to the exit. "Oh, dear. I don't have the code to get out. Hmmmm, guess that means we'll have to torture you after all."

"What?" George stutters, pulling away from me until his back hits the wall. "Aren't you here to take me home?"

"No, Mr. Mann, I'm not. You stole from my family and have information that's important to us. I'm here to get that information from you."

He just stares at me for a moment, obviously shocked, before he decides to take his chances and throws himself at me. He's exhausted and not overly in shape, so it's easy for me to dodge him, even in these close quarters. It's also easy for me to kick the back of his knees while he tries to push himself off the wall he'd fallen into when I'd dodged his blow.

When I kick the right one, George lets out a scream, telling me I've torn something, and he's not happy about it.

"Did I forget to tell you Daddy has had me in self-defense classes since I was six? I'm actually surprised you didn't know that." I snicker as I stand over his collapsed body. He's clutching his knee, tears falling down his face as he screams. "How pathetic."

I kick his ribs and turn back to the twins. "I can't carry him."

"We've got it, princess," Vito says with a laugh.

He and Luca easily lift him to stand between the two of them and lead him over to some kind of rack they must've pulled out while I was busy playing with George. I watch, fascinated, as they strap his arms and legs down to the rack with metal cuffs that leave him spread eagle and arms stretched out. Then they lean the rack backward so it looks like a table.

"I like that," I say as I make my way over, circling the rack and George as I run my fingers along the rack. "Would I be able to do that?"

Vito nods. "Go ahead and try."

I grab the top of the rack and push it, finding it easier than I expected to move him to a standing position. I lay it back down, and once it's back in place, George turns to me with pleading eyes.

"Please, Alessandra. It wasn't my idea. You don't have to do this."

"Okay," I say easily. "All you have to do is tell us whose idea it was. If you tell us that right now, you can leave."

George's lips slam shut as he shakes his head. I just shrug, turning back to the twins. "I guess it's the hard way. I'm excited. What's first?"

Luca slides a scalpel into my hand. "First thing is to get his shirt and pants off. You can always get him completely naked, but then you'll have to see his old, shriveled up dick."

I wrinkle my nose at that. "Yeah, no. He can keep his underwear on. I definitely don't need to see that."

Vito snorts. "The scalpel is sharp enough to cut through his clothes and if you happen to cut him while doing it? Well, he won't like it much, but we will."

I focus my attention on George. "This is your last chance. Just give us a name, and this doesn't have to go any further."

George shakes his head, and I sigh, sounding put out, but really I'm glad he's not making this easy. As long as I don't focus on his face, then I think I can do this. I place the scalpel at the neckline of his shirt, sliding it down and easily slicing through the material. Blood pools on his skin as the material falls away and I find myself fascinated by it.

"Oops. Guess I pushed a little too hard."

I continue to his pants, realizing the waistband might be a bit of a problem. It's harder to cut through the material there, but I manage it, running the scalpel down his left leg and moving onto the right side. I push the blade further into his skin on this leg, watching as blood spills down to the floor. A quick horizontal cut across the front of his pants and they fall away. Luca pulls the remnants of his clothes away as Vito moves to stand beside me.

"You might've cut just a little too deep on that one," he says, gesturing to his right leg that's bleeding heavily.

"Oops?"

Vito laughs, grabbing a ka-bar. "That's okay. We'll just cauterize the wound."

"How?" I ask as I trail him to the side of the room until we come to a stop beside a burning furnace. "Oh, I didn't even see this."

The sound of creaking wheels has me spinning around, only to see Luca pushing the rack toward us. I must look confused because Vito laughs at me.

"The furnace is too far away from where he was. The knife would've cooled too much by the time we made it back over. You want it as hot as possible." Vito opens the small opening on the front, and I bend over to see hot coals burning inside. He pulls on a glove before sliding the metal of the knife into the coals. He leaves it there for a few moments, and when he pulls it out, the metal is glowing red.

He leans over, pressing the hot metal to the cut I'd left on George's leg, and he lets out an ear-splitting screech that has me smiling. The smell, on the other hand? I'd rather never smell that again.

"That must hurt."

Vito snorts, nodding to Luca, who pushes the rack back to the center of the room. Vito shuts the door to the furnace, and we follow Luca.

Luca leans over the rack, slapping George across the face. "Oy, stop screaming. We just saved your life. Are you ready to give us a name?"

"Fuck you, you piece of shit. I'm not telling you a damn thing."

"Oh, good," Vito says with a laugh. "That's what I was hoping you'd say. After all, we still have so much to show Alessa about the fine art of torturing someone."

And show me they do.

I get to take a cattle prod to him, and I learn how to use a baseball bat to hit him over and over, breaking bones but avoiding internal injuries. I'm not a huge fan of the baseball bat, as it requires more upper body strength than I have to use it repeatedly. But it is quite effective.

I learn about waterboarding and dry-boarding. I even get to cut off one of his fingers, but once again find it's not the easiest thing to do for someone of my stature. But as soon as I hold up his finger, grinning down at George, he bawls.

"Fine. I'll tell you. Just make it stop."

I lay his finger on the table holding our tools and lean down so I can coo in his ear as I push his wet hair from his face. "That's a good boy, George. Tell us whose idea this was and it'll all stop."

"Vincent Andretti! He's the one that came to me and convinced me it would be so easy—that we'd never get caught."

I pat his cheek condescendingly. "Thank you, George. Don't you feel better now?"

"Feel better? No, I don't feel better, you psychotic bitch! No wonder Amanda stopped hanging out with you. She must've felt the darkness—the craziness—you were hiding from the world."

Anger rages through me. This asshole just called me a psychotic bitch. Any chance he had of walking out this door just went out the window. Swinging my attention back to the twins, I shake my head.

"Vincent is my dad's—"

"Consigliere. We know." Luca's already pulling out his phone. "I'm going to call Riccardo and let him know so he can get someone on the problem as soon as possible. The two of you can figure out what to do with him."

"We need to kill him," I cut off whatever Vito was about to say. "I want to kill him."

Vito says nothing for a moment, just watches me. "Are you sure? Taking a life can change you."

I nod, already having made my decision. "Yes, but you're going to need to talk me through it. I don't actually know how to kill someone."

"There are lots of ways to kill someone. You can make it long and drawn out or make it quick." Vito glances down at George as he continues to spew vitriol. I've already blocked out his words, but it's clear Vito doesn't like what he's saying. "Will you shut up?"

Vito grabs a piece of the shirt I'd cut off of him earlier and shoves it into his mouth. He's still making noise, but it's muffled enough we can't make out the words. "So much better. What was I saying? Oh, right. Ways to kill him." Vito taps his fingers on his lips as he looks over the table of trays.

"You enjoyed cutting, right?" At my nod, he grabs the butterfly knife and hands it to me. "I know this one was your favorite. As long as you keep it sharp enough, it'll do. Come here."

We walk to the top of the rack, and Vito wraps his hand in George's hair, yanking it back and bearing his throat to me. "I think slicing his throat is the most effective. He won't die right away, but it's bloody and easy enough to do. But you have to cut deeply enough that they can't be saved. Not that we'll have that problem with George, but in general. It's also not a good way to kill someone silently. Go ahead and try it."

When Vito releases George's hair, I step up behind him and replace his hand with mine. I pull back hard enough that George's neck goes completely rigid. I can hear him pleading through his gag, but it's easy enough to push that away. I watch his pulse beat rapidly against his skin as I lift the knife to his throat.

Vito adjusts my hand until I'm holding the knife further down and back. I glance at George once more and realize I feel nothing at the thought of taking his life. No guilt. No joy. It just is what it is.

I push the knife into his skin, and it cuts like a hot knife through butter, a trail of blood spilling from the cut. With no further hesitation, I pull it across his neck. Blood sprays out, soaking the floor and George's upper body, and I can hear him gurgling beneath the gag.

Note to self—make sure you're behind someone when slitting their throat unless you want to take a bath in blood.

"The gag will make him drown in his blood faster, won't it?"

Vito nods. "More than likely."

"Okay." I hand the knife back to him before glancing down at my clothes. Now I see why they burn their clothes after torture sessions. I'm covered in blood. Obviously, not as much as George, but even though they're black, I can see every spot of blood on my clothes. "Shit, I didn't bring a change of clothes."

"Yeah, I should've thought of that," Luca says as he walks back over, glancing at George before focusing his attention on me and his brother. "We have a pretty decent stash of clothes here so you can wear something of ours. We should probably show you to the showers."

The twins lead me past the rooms and down a hallway I hadn't noticed earlier. At the end of the hall is a door without a keypad, which turns out to be a locker room.

Luca throws open a locker, revealing towels and washcloths. "There's shampoo and body wash in the showers. If you're going to make a habit of coming here, you'll want to get your own stuff. You'll just have to smell like us until you can get home and clean up again. Clothes are in the locker next to this one. Everything will be too big for you, but there's sweatpants and shorts in there with drawstrings, so you should be fine."

Vito nods his head to the end of the rows of lockers to reveal a wide open area with shower heads attached to the wall. In one corner, a curtain hangs over an enclosed area. "Guess it's a good thing we didn't take out the stall, huh? I'll put the shampoo in there, and we'll start with the body wash. Then we'll switch."

"Uh, okay..." Apparently, we're all going to shower at the same time. Sure, I'll be behind a curtain, but seriously? What have I gotten myself into?

Luca ducks into the stall, hanging a towel from a hook that will keep it outside of the water flow, and hands me the washcloth. Vito sets the shampoo on the floor before turning back to me, arms crossed over his chest. "Throw your clothes out here. Everything has to go—bra and panties, too."

Well, fuck. Why didn't I think about that? Ugh, I'll need to get some cheap bras for torture time, I guess.

"Got it. Now move." I shove past them, and once the curtain is closed behind me, I quickly undress and toss my clothes over the curtain. The water is so freaking cold when I turn it on, but it quickly warms.

"Ready to trade?" I jump at the sound of Luca's voice.

"Ummm, yeah. One sec." I quickly finish washing out the shampoo—my third round of shampooing. Grabbing the bottle, I cling to the shower curtain as I pull it aside so I can hand him the bottle.

My eyes immediately drop to his cock as soon as I realize he's naked—which, of course, he is. He's showering. How else would he shower? Get it together, Alessa. But I can't look away as I lick my lips. I've only seen James's cock this close up before, but I've seen a lot while watching porn.

James's dick is long and girthy enough that I worry about whether he'll fit but Luca? He's not as long as James, but he's thick—so fucking thick. I don't even know if I'd be able to fit my hand around it. And then it grows under my gaze, and my eyes dart up to his face. His eyes are hungry as he grabs the shampoo from me and replaces it with the body wash.

"We'll be done in just a minute so we should be dressed and out of here by the time you're done," is all he says before spinning and heading back toward the showers he and Vito are using.

I can't help but watch his ass as he walks away. Damn. I really didn't need to see him naked. When Luca steps beneath the shower head again, my eyes find Vito. He's stroking his hard cock when his eyes lock on me. He just grins as he works himself, and all I can do is stare at him as he does so.

"Stop jacking off and finish showering, asshole. The cleanup crew will be here soon." Luca punches Vito in the shoulder, and it breaks our staring contest.

I duck behind the curtain, making sure it's closed as I lean against the wall. What the fuck was that? My pussy is pulsing and all I want to do is get myself off.

Fuck. Fuck. Fuck.

This is wrong, so wrong. Even with that thought rushing through my head, my hands slide up my body so I can cup my tits. I twist my nipples, fighting back the moan that threatens to spill from my lips.

I can't let them hear me. They can't know I'm getting off after just seeing their dicks. Then they'll know how I feel and I can't let that happen.

One of my hands snake down my body until I'm circling my clit as I continue to abuse my pebbled nipple with my other hand. I'm dripping wet, and I know it won't take long to come.

My eyes fall shut as I imagine Vito with his cock in hand, Luca next to him as they both stroke their lengths. Why is that so fucking hot?

I have to shove my fist into my mouth to muffle my cries as I fall apart to the image of my stepbrothers jacking off.

As I come down from my high, tears fill my eyes, and guilt rushes through me. It's bad enough that I have a crush on them, but now I've masturbated to images of them? That's so far beyond okay—especially because I have a boyfriend. I highly doubt James would be okay with this if he found out.

I have to get over this. I have to shut down this crush. They can never be mine. I have James and I love him. I don't care what I have to do, I'm going to get over this. I will not jeopardize my relationship over this.

Having made that decision, I step beneath the water once more and begin scrubbing off the blood covering my skin. I focus my attention on James and the phone call we'll have before bed. I think tonight is a good night for a video call. That'll wipe away the memory of the twins jerking off with no problem.

I choose to ignore the little voice inside calling me a liar.

CHAPTER 4

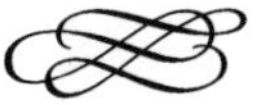

It's finally my birthday.

Fifteen doesn't feel too much different from fourteen, but that'll change tonight. By the morning, I'll no longer be a virgin.

There's a knock on the door to my hotel suite that startles both me and Teresa, who's currently checking my hair and makeup. We laugh together as I call out, "Just a moment."

"Why don't you put on your dress, figlia?"

I beam at her as I jump up. I love that she calls me daughter. As someone who can barely remember her mother, it's nice to have a mother figure. Besides Susanna, James's mom, who is the only other woman in my life who has filled that hole inside me. I have zero plans to call her mom—it would make things even weirder for me and this forbidden crush I have on Vito and Luca.

I dart into the dressing area, pulling my dress off the hanger. I really need to get over this stupid crush. I have the world's best boyfriend in James, and here I am thinking about my stepbrothers. There is definitely something wrong with me.

At fifteen, there's really no reason for me to have this fancy of a birthday party, but Daddy insisted, and who am I to turn that down? The invitations were all hand delivered by one of Daddy's associates dressed in a tux—definitely over the top—and they were fancy as hell. Formal attire is required, and while I don't mind putting on a pretty dress, I can't help but wonder how many people will actually show up with that kind of requirement. I guess I'll find out soon.

It had taken forever for me to find a dress that me, Teresa, and my dad all approved of. He wanted me dressed demurely, and neither Teresa nor I were having any of it. I'd wanted a more risque dress, and it had been Teresa who found the perfect dress. Daddy seems to think it covers enough skin but shows off the body I'm so proud of.

It's a deep emerald color that looks amazing against my skin tone. The material is silky against my skin. It fits like a glove from its strapless, sweetheart top to where it tapers into my waist before clinging to my hips and thick thighs. From just above my knees, it flares out until it drags on the floor with a small train on the back. Teresa called it a mermaid dress, and I can see why it has that name.

"Come on, Alessandra," my dad calls. "You don't want to be late for your entrance."

Checking my reflection in the full-length mirror once more, I pull my heels on and step back into the room. As soon as Daddy's eyes land on me, they fill with tears.

"Oh, Alessa. You've grown into such a beautiful woman. You look just like your mother." He smiles softly, and I can feel his love, his pride, for me. When he holds his arms out to me, I go into them willingly.

"I love you, Daddy."

"I love you too, princess." He pulls back and lifts his hands to hold my face in his hands. "Don't you go growing up on me too fast. You're still my little girl, even as you're blossoming into a woman."

I grin up at him. He might be a hardened mafia boss, but he has no problems showing his love for those he deems important to him. "I'll always be your little girl, Daddy. No matter how old I get."

He kisses my forehead before pulling away and nodding. "As it should be. Well, ladies, shall we get this show on the road?"

My dad leads us from my suite and to the elevator. I watch as the floors descend to the first floor, butterflies a flight in my stomach. Tonight is a big night for me. My dad might not know just how big, but I'd told Teresa, and she'd made sure I was ready. As excited as I am for the party, I can't wait until it's done and over so I can take James back to my suite.

As the doors open before us, Daddy offers one arm to me and one to Teresa before leading us over to the ballroom where the party is being held. The doors are closed, and I can hear the emcee calling for everyone's attention before announcing my arrival.

Over the top? Absolutely, but sometimes you just have to go with the flow. And let's be real, there's a lot about Daddy that's over the top.

I don't know how they knew I was standing outside the doors, but who am I to question it? The doors open onto a landing with stairs leading to the ballroom. We stand at the top for a moment, and my eyes scan the room, looking for James. Before I find him, Daddy is leading us down the stairs while all eyes are on us.

My eyes lock with Luca's when I find him and Vito standing at the bottom of the stairs. As soon as my feet are firmly on the ground, he reaches out to take my hand in his.

"Happy birthday, Alessa." He presses a kiss to my hand that sends a shiver down my spine. I hope no one else saw that. Why haven't I been able to shake this crush yet? I really need to get over it.

"Thanks, Luca. I appreciate you coming to celebrate with me."

Luca nods, and when I try to pull my hand free, he continues to hold on to it for a moment longer before passing it to Vito. Vito also presses a kiss to my hand, looking up at me from beneath his eyelashes.

"You look beautiful, Alessa. Happy birthday."

"Th-Thank you," I stutter, not liking their attention on me while their mom and my dad stand at our sides.

"Lessa!" James appears at my elbow, drawing me into his arms as he pulls me away from the twins. He kisses me deeply there in front of everyone—my parents, the twins, my friends, and my dad's business associates. My body heats as his tongue brushes mine, even as I'm thinking about how inappropriate this kiss is. Not that I care enough to pull away.

When James breaks the kiss, he's smirking down at me. "How is it that my girl gets more and more beautiful every day? You look exquisite."

"You're lucky I like you, Adams," my dad calls with a laugh. "Do me a favor? Maybe don't kiss my daughter like that in front of me again? It makes me feel a little stabby."

James flushes as he pushes his blond hair from his eyes. "Of course, Riccardo. I'm so sorry. I don't know what came over me. Well, that's not true. Lessa had me under her spell, and I forgot for a moment where I was."

"Bullshit," I hear Vito mutter under his breath, and when I glance back at him, he forces a smile. I don't like it.

"Why don't we let Alessandra and James go greet their friends? After all, this party is all about her, hmmm?" Teresa says as she places her hand on my dad's chest.

Daddy nods. "Enjoy yourself, princess. But you and I are having a dance later, okay? I made sure they had the song I wanted—you'll know it when you hear it, and I expect you to meet me on the dance floor."

"Of course, Daddy. Thank you." I hurry back over to press a kiss to his cheek, though he has to duck down so I can reach. That's what happens when your dad is over six feet tall.

James wraps an arm around my waist and leads me away. I'm surprised as it seems everyone I invited has shown up. I guess the formalwear wasn't as much of a turnoff as I thought it would be.

"Have you seen Lyla?" I ask James, glancing up at him.

He nods. "She's hiding in the corner."

I laugh, unsurprised by this information. "Let's go see if we can drag her out, then."

Lyla isn't a big fan of people, and she hates being the center of attention. I'm sure it's hard being my friend sometimes because I'm a social butterfly. I know almost everyone we go to school with. I don't know how much of that is the mafia princess thing, but I get along well with everyone. Except maybe Amanda. She's been a little cold toward me since her dad went missing. I don't know if she knows her dad was involved with my dad or what, but she's definitely been avoiding me.

I almost wish I could tell her he's dead so she can have some peace of mind, but I know I can't. And they're never going to find his body. I can't even be mad at her for avoiding me. After all, I'm the one that killed her dad—not that there's any way for her to know that. I'm not sorry for killing him because it's what he deserved. But I am sorry that she's having to deal with him being missing. She did nothing wrong, but he stole from my family—from the mafia—and thought he could get away with it.

No one in Daddy's world is questioning where Mr. Mann is. They all know how my dad takes care of business—how we take care of business. Maybe some of those rumors have hit Amanda's ears, and that's why she's being cold toward me, but I honestly couldn't care less. After all, she's the one who abandoned mine and Lyla's friendships when we hit middle school.

"Lyla," I call out when I finally spot my best friend. It had taken us longer to reach her than I would've liked, but we kept being stopped by well-wishers and people who wanted a few moments of my time.

"Alessa, you look amazing, girl." Lyla grins, eyes roaming over me.

"So do you." And she really does. Her bright pink dress against her umber skin. Her braids piled on her head in an intricate updo that I have no idea how she could've done on her own. But I know my girl, and she wouldn't have let anyone else touch her hair. "That's a brilliant color on you."

"I know, right?" The two of us laugh together as James rolls his eyes.

I blow him a kiss as I wrap my arm through Lyla's. "I hope you didn't think you were going to get away with hiding in the corner. I need my bestie by my side for my party."

"I thought I'd at least try." Lyla shrugs. "But no, I didn't actually think I'd get away with it. Come on then, birthday girl, let's get our party on."

Lyla and I head for the dance floor with James trailing us. He's used to the pair of us by now, and I don't even feel bad about it. Once we hit the dance floor, my attention will be on James while Lyla seeks out another female to dance with. She might not overly care for crowds, but she's always on the prowl for hot girls.

We lose ourselves to the music, dancing until my legs can barely hold me up any longer. Lyla has her arms wrapped around a hot blond on the dance floor and waves us off when I check in on her.

James leads me to an empty table on the edge of the dance floor where I drop into a seat, glad to be off my feet. "I'm going to get us some drinks. Water?"

"God, yes, please."

He leans down and kisses me deeply before heading toward the bar. I settle back in my seat, eyes scanning the room. It seems everyone is having fun—both my friends and Daddy's associates, though they're definitely segregating into two very different groups.

"What are you doing sitting over here all by yourself, birthday girl?"

I turn to find Luca sitting beside me, and I shrug, waving toward the bar. "James went to get us some water. I needed a break from dancing."

"Grinding on the dance floor will do that to you." Vito drops into the seat on my other side, his words sharp.

Rolling my eyes, I ignore his comment. "What are you doing? I expected you to have already found a hookup for the night by now. Figured you'd be up in your room fucking already."

"Worried about our sex life, are you?" Vito smirks.

Yes.

"Of course not. It's just your usual MO." I force myself to keep my eyes on the dance floor.

Vito leans in, his chest bumping against my arm as he whispers, "Liar."

"Fuck off, Vito." I narrow my eyes, turning to him with a glare. Which turns out to be a mistake, seeing as his face is inches from mine. I can't help the way my eyes fall to his lips as his tongue darts out to wet it.

"Nah, baby girl, I don't think I will. I think you want us right where we are."

Luca sighs heavily. "Knock it off, Vito. It's Alessa's birthday, and she doesn't need you being an ass."

Glancing over my shoulder at him, I give him a grateful smile. "Once again, proving why you're my favorite."

Vito just laughs as he leans back in his chair. "Say what you want, baby girl, but we all know I'm your favorite."

"Not likely."

Before Vito can respond, James hands me a bottle of water, and I smile up at him as he greets the twins. "Vito. Luca."

"James." Luca nods in acknowledgment while Vito ignores my boyfriend.

"Vito, you're in my seat."

Our conversation cuts off when loud pops fill the air. My eyes widen, realizing they're gunshots. Someone is firing a gun at my birthday party.

"Get down, James!" I scream, but it's muffled as a hard body hits mine, taking me to the ground. I try to wiggle out of Vito's hold, but I'm not going anywhere as I continue to scream James's name.

Tears stream down my face as the gunshots continue to sound throughout the ballroom, my voice straining as I yell for my boyfriend. When Luca crawls up beside us, I see a gun in his hand.

"I have to find mom and Riccardo. Keep her safe."

"No, Luca! Don't leave. You can't."

Vito shushes, trying to calm me down. People are running for the exits, and I still don't know if James is safe. With the way Vito is holding me, I can barely turn my head, so I can't see what's going on.

"James is okay, baby girl. He's under the table." He lifts enough so I can crane my neck and see he's telling the truth. "Luca knows what he's doing, but we have to make sure our parents are okay. We don't know if this is an assassination attempt or if someone is just trying to cause problems. Either way, we need to make sure they're both okay."

His words finally sink in, and I understand. I try to scan the room —or at least the small part of the room I can see from my place beneath Vito. My eyes land on the dance floor, and I see multiple people lying there, unmoving as blood pools beneath them. When my eyes lock on a dark-skinned body clad in hot pink, I scream again as more gunshots sound out around us.

No. Not Lyla. Not my best friend.

Please let her be okay. I don't know what I'll do if something happens to her. Maybe she's not hurt. Maybe she's just playing possum. Please let her only be playing possum.

But I already know she's not. I can see the pool of blood beneath her, and all I can really hope for is that she's not dead. Please let us be able to get her help in time. She can't die. She just can't.

"Alessa, please listen to me. I need you to calm down. I need you to be quiet until we know it's safe. They could target you. I'll do my best to keep you safe, baby, but I'm only one man."

I understand what he's saying, but it's like I'm no longer in control of my body. I can't seem to stop my screams or make myself look away from Lyla.

"I'm so sorry, Alessa. I didn't want to do this."

I have a moment to wonder what he's talking about before his handle circles my neck, pressing down on two spots. It doesn't take long for black dots to appear in my vision as I struggle against his hold, but it's no use.

As I drift into the darkness, I send up a prayer that my friends and family are safe.

CHAPTER 5

"Alessandra? It's time."

I turn my head to stare at Teresa, who's currently standing in my doorway. I just stare at her blankly, trying to understand what she's trying to tell me.

"Oh, Alessandra, I'm so sorry." Tears slip down her face as she hurries across the room to cup my cheeks in her hands. "I know this is hard for you, but we need to get you dressed."

"For what?" I croak, my voice rusty from lack of use. I've barely spoken to anyone in the eight days since my birthday.

Teresa tries to smile but fails as she wipes away her tears. "It's Saturday, figlia. We need to get you ready for Lyla's funeral."

Oh. Right. I vaguely recall her telling me about that the other day. Not that I paid much attention, too lost in my grief and guilt.

If only I hadn't let Daddy insist on throwing me a party. If only I'd made sure Lyla stayed by my side the entire night. There's so many things I would change if I could. So many things that could've prevented my best friend from dying. Only, I can't turn back time, and I can't change events that have already happened.

I remember very little from that night after Vito knocked me out

—something that both Luca and James punched him for. Daddy also yelled at him for close to an hour after everything was done and said. I remember waking up still in the ballroom as EMTs rushed around, one of them trying to speak to me.

I remember waiting at the hospital while Lyla went into surgery. I remember her mom falling apart when the doctor came to inform her Lyla had died on the operating table. I remember James holding me close through it all. But that's it.

Over the following days, I learned it was some startup that thought they could take out both my dad and his heirs—me and the twins—in one swoop. They hadn't, and now they're the ones dead.

But so is Lyla. Lyla had done nothing wrong. She was just there to help me celebrate my birthday. I was her only link to the mafia. She never should've been in that position. There was no reason for her to be shot.

Not that she was the only one who was shot that night—though she's just the only one who died. Some of Daddy's men were shot, and so was the girl Lyla had been dancing with. They also shot Luca —something that freaked me the hell out, but it had just been a graze. He'd let them stitch him up before he'd joined us to wait for news on Lyla.

Daddy, Vito, and Luca are all avoiding me. I've barely seen them since that night. I know it isn't just work keeping them away from me. I've seen the guilt in all three of their eyes whenever they look at me. Teresa has tried her best to help me, but I know I've been pushing her away.

James has really stepped up, though. He's been by my side every day from the moment he's awake until his mom calls him to come home for dinner each night. Then he comes back until he gets another phone call, telling him he has to come home and sleep in his own bed.

James's dad, Ted, and mine had a huge blowup the other day. Ted said he didn't want James around me or my family ever again. He said I was poison that was slowly killing his son—that their deal was off.

Daddy hadn't taken that well. Neither had James, who'd gone to break up the fight while I laid in my bed sobbing. Neither of us could figure out what deal Daddy and Ted apparently have.

James said he didn't care what his dad said. He loved me, and he would never leave me. I think he'd be better off out of my life, and I think his dad had a point.

I am poison.

Lyla's dead because of me. James could've been hurt because of me. One day, he will be hurt because of me. I don't want that for him, and when I'd tried to convince him it might be for the best that we break up, he'd lost it. He's never raised his voice to me before, but he sure did that day. Then he'd stalked out of the room and I haven't seen or heard from him since then.

That was two days ago.

Even though I know it's for the best, it hurts so much that he just walked away after telling me how much he loved me. That he'd never leave me. But he did leave me. Part of me feels like I deserve it, but that doesn't make it hurt any less.

I squeeze my eyes shut as it all becomes too much, tears cascading down my cheeks.

I can't do this. I can't say goodbye to Lyla—especially not without James by my side.

But what choice do I have? I have to go to the funeral. Not just because it's expected but because I owe it to Lyla. I owe her so much, and I'll never be able to repay her for the years of her friendship. The very least I can do is say goodbye and be there for her family.

"I wish there was something I could do to take this pain from you." Teresa pulls me into a hug that I gratefully fall into. That she's still trying after I pushed her away means the world to me.

I cling to her for a few minutes before pulling away, wiping at my face. "I haven't picked anything out to wear."

"That's okay, Alessandra. I'll pick something out for you. Why don't you go take a shower? We'll forgo makeup today."

I snort. "That's probably a good idea."

While Teresa heads into my closet, I make my way into the bathroom. I shower quickly, and I stare off into space as I dry off. It's really hard for me to focus on anything right now. I think part of that is me not wanting to think about anything.

I don't want to think about the fact that I'll be starting school in a few days without my best friend. I don't want to think about the fact that James and I might have broken up. I don't want to think about how this is exactly what being a mafia princess means. I just don't want to think. I don't want to feel.

I don't want to live.

That thought is the hardest one for me to deal with. A lot of it is because I feel unworthy of living, but I also know that's the guilt talking. There's a hole inside of me, and I don't know how to fill it.

I've told no one about the thoughts I've had about ending my own life, afraid of what they might say or do. I know it won't make anything better—it won't fix anything. In fact, it's likely to make things worse for everyone. That's probably the only reason I haven't tried to kill myself. I don't want to think about the mess I'd leave behind.

A soft knock on my bathroom door pulls me from my thoughts. "I've got a dress laid out on your bed. Why don't you get dressed and I'll meet you downstairs in ten minutes? You really should try to get some food in your system before we leave."

"Thanks, Teresa." I ignore her comments about eating something, knowing there's no way I can force down any food.

I don't remember the last time I ate. Maybe I'm trying to kill myself slowly without realizing it.

No.

I shake my head, clearing away my thoughts as I step into my room. I get dressed quickly, paying no attention to what Teresa has picked out for me and definitely not glancing in the mirror. I don't care what I look like.

I find Teresa, Daddy, and the twins in the kitchen.

Daddy takes one look at me and sighs. "Oh, princess."

He pulls me into a hug that I don't return. I'm not mad at him exactly, but I'm not happy with him. He should've been there for me for the last week, not avoiding me. Now he thinks he can just hug everything better?

I don't think so.

"I'm sorry you're having to go through this. I never wanted the business to touch your life like this." He brushes a kiss against my head. "But the twins and I spent the last week torturing every one of those assholes to make sure we got them all."

I pull away with a frown. "So you weren't avoiding me?"

"What?" My dad looks confused as he shakes his head. "Absolutely not, but I'm sorry I made you feel like I was. I just wanted to make sure that we took care of those responsible for Lyla's death, and we got them all. I promise you, princess."

"That's good." I ignore the fact that there are tears in his eyes, not being able to deal with them. I know he has to be hurting too. Lyla and I have been inseparable since preschool. Her parents were my parents, and he was Lyla's dad just as much as he's mine. "Thank you for making them pay, Daddy."

My voice sounds wooden even to me, and I can see the concern on his and Teresa's faces. I turn my head to look at the twins, pleading with them to save me. I can't deal with this right now. I'm still a little hurt and unsure if they've been avoiding me.

Sure, Daddy said they've been torturing people, but that wasn't a twenty-four-hour job. Where have they been between that? Because they certainly haven't been here.

"Riccardo, I think Alessa should ride with Vito and me. If we head out now, we can swing through a drive-thru. I'm sure she'll eat if there are french fries involved." Luca gives me a soft smile.

"I don't know..." Teresa starts.

"No, that's what I want," I cut her off. "French fries sound amazing."

They really don't, but I need to get away from my dad and Teresa —preferably without hurting either of their feelings.

"Fine," my dad says with a sigh. "But don't be late."

Luca nods as he jumps to his feet, Vito following at a slower pace. "Of course, Riccardo. C'mon, Alessa."

Luca throws an arm around my shoulders, and as much as I want to duck away, I don't. I let him lead me from the kitchen and out the door before I step away from him.

"Thanks for the save."

Luca grabs my hand, pulling me to a stop. "Will you look at me, Alessa?"

I close my eyes, taking a deep breath before turning to do just that. I find Vito standing just behind him, both of their faces worried. "What?"

"Why are you acting like this?"

"Like what? Like my best friend is dead and we're on the way to her funeral? Like my boyfriend and I got into a fight two days ago and I haven't seen him since he walked out the door? Since I realized I'm toxic to everyone around me? Or that I've finally realized just how little I mean to the two of you? You'll have to be a little more specific."

Instead of waiting for an answer I don't want to hear, I yank my hand from his and head for the car. I climb inside, deciding I'll just have the driver take me to the church. I can sit with Lyla's family and support them. When I go to slam the door, it's yanked out of my hands and swings open to reveal two very pissed off twins.

Rolling my eyes, I scoot over on the seat so they can climb inside. They both climb inside, but Luca picks me up and sets me between the two of them.

"We're heading to the church now, but stop at McDonald's on the way," Vito barks at the driver before raising the partition.

"I don't actually want french fries. I was just agreeing to that so Teresa would let me leave. She has an obsession with feeding me, and I have no desire to eat."

"Too fucking bad," Vito spits as he turns on the seat to face me. "Now, what the fuck is this about the two of us not caring about you?"

I cross my arms over my chest as the car pulls away from our house, refusing to answer him. I don't want to get into this right now. I never should've said it in the first place, but there's just so much anger inside of me, and I can't always keep it inside. Sometimes I just snap—like I did with James.

"Damn it, Alessa. Talk to us." Luca's hand lands on my thigh, and he squeezes. "I'm sorry we haven't been around. Like your dad said, we've been a little busy with the assholes who shot up your party."

I scoff. "You've been torturing people twenty-four hours a day? That seems highly unlikely."

Luca's face softens. "We should've checked on you. I'm sorry. We just didn't know what to do to help you besides making those men pay."

"You should've been there for me. That's what you should've done. Luckily, I had James with me except for the last two days. I've been alone with my thoughts since he walked out and trust me when I say that isn't somewhere anyone wants to be right now."

"What's that supposed to mean?" Vito growls, forcing me to look at him.

"Nothing. It means nothing. Just leave me alone."

Luca sighs, shaking his head. "I'm sorry, but we can't do that. We did that for the last eight days, and it apparently pissed you off. Tell us what's going on. Let us be there for you. Please."

I shake my head as my heart splits open again. He sounds like he cares. So does Vito, in his own psychotic way. I want to hold on to the anger, though. It's better than feeling like I'm being split apart by the pain and guilt. There's no fucking way I'm telling them how I've thought about ending it all.

"It doesn't matter."

Vito growls, his hand clamping down on my other thigh. Now so isn't the time to be turned on, but my body doesn't seem to care. Having them both touching me like this is too much. They're too much.

Everything's just too much.

"It does matter," Vito says. I turn toward him, even though I know my best course of action is to continue to ignore them. "You matter."

I scoff but say nothing, forcing myself to look away from him. I want to believe their words, but their actions have told me something different. I need to learn to deal with things on my own. This week has taught me I can't rely on anyone but myself. Not my dad. Not the twins. Not even James.

Teresa has attempted to be there for me, so maybe I can count on her. But if I count on one person, I'll want to count on others. No, it's obvious to me now that being a part of Daddy's world means you can't rely on others. They'll only let you down or betray you.

Both men withdraw their hands from my legs and lean back into the seat. They're both practically vibrating with annoyance—which probably gives me more satisfaction than it should. When we stop at McDonald's, they order a shit ton of food that they better not expect me to eat.

And yet, I'm still surprised that as soon as we're pulling away with food in hand, they both try to shove food at me. "I'm not fucking hungry. I don't want to eat. I told you this. Why won't you listen to what I tell you?"

"Because you're not telling us anything. You're hurting and won't talk to us. If you won't let us help you, then the least we can do is make sure you get some food in you so you don't pass out at the funeral." Luca's voice is soft, but I can hear the anger and hurt in his words.

I don't want to hurt them—truly, I don't—but I don't know what else to do. I'd needed them and they hadn't been there. All I do is hurt everyone around me.

"Everyone would be better off if I'd been the one to die," I mutter. I hadn't meant to put voice to those thoughts, but I guess the cat is out of the bag now.

"What the fuck are you talking about!" Vito screams, and I duck my head, squeezing my eyes shut against the tears already threatening to spill.

Luca's hands are gentle as he pulls me into his lap. "Shut up,

Vito. She doesn't need you screaming at her. That will not help the situation in the least."

I lay my head on Luca's chest, clinging to him as I fight back my tears. It's a losing battle when he presses a gentle kiss to my forehead. Tears stream down my face as I bury my head, trying to hide from them.

"None of that, Alessa." Luca is gentle as he forces me to look up at him. "I know you're hurting and there's probably a lot going on inside your head right now, but I need you to tell me what you meant."

Looking up into those piercing green eyes, I know he will not let it go—neither of them will. "I'm poison, Luca. I ruin everything I touch. My best friend is dead because of me. James is fighting with his dad because of me. I'm fairly sure we're broken up when all I was trying to do was keep him safe and happy. I don't want them to fight because of me. Then there's the two of you and Daddy. You disappeared like I was too much to deal with. Like I was nothing."

Done with my word vomit, I duck my head again. I don't want to see the moment they both realize I'm right. When they realize I'm not worth it—that it would have been better if I'd died.

"Nothing would be better if you were dead."

I'm surprised by the emotion in Vito's voice, daring to glance at him from beneath my eyelashes. I'm even more surprised to see tears dancing in his eyes as he reaches for my hand.

"This family would be nothing without you in it. We'd be devastated if anything happened. Your dad, our mom—they wouldn't be able to survive it. As for the two of us? We'd live the rest of our lives with a hole in our hearts, never able to be truly happy because you wouldn't be there."

This time, I lift my head to stare at him in shock. I don't even know what to say to him. Luckily, Luca speaks, so I don't have to.

"This world would be bleak without your light, Alessa. I'm sorry we made you ever feel you meant nothing to us. The truth is, you mean more to us than you should." Luca won't meet my eyes when I turn to gawk at him. "Promise me you won't do anything to hurt yourself. Please don't take away the light. It's the only thing that keeps us sane in this crazy world we live in."

I feel like they're admitting to something that I'm just not understanding. Surely, they can't be saying what I think they're saying. I glance between the two of them, though they're both avoiding eye contact with me.

Vito clears his throat. "As for James, I'm sure he was just hurt by you trying to push him away. We'll help you fix things with him. Hell, we'll even try to get along with him for your sake."

"Really?"

Luca laughs. "Yeah, we can do that for you. It's obvious how much the two of you love each other, and it isn't fair the way we've treated him."

"I think you'll find we'll do just about anything for you, Alessa," Vito says quietly. "Even put up with your golden boy next door."

"I... uhhh..." Not knowing what to say, I try to pull away from Luca to return to my seat between them, but he just tightens his hold.

"Please don't. I'm not ready to let go just yet."

I duck my head as I flush, burying my head in his chest once more. If I'm honest with myself, I'm perfectly content to remain here for as long as he wants. Vito moves to sit beside his brother and holds my hand in his. We remain quiet the rest of the way to the church as I let them hold and comfort me.

When the car comes to a stop, we all sit there for a moment. None of us are willing to break the bubble we're cocooned in.

A knock on the window has us pulling away from one another, and Luca opens his door to find the driver standing there.

"Yes?" Luca asks with raised eyebrows.

"Ummm... we're here. I didn't want to just open the door..." he trails off. "I should have just waited until you were ready. I'm very sorry, Mr. Colleti. This is my first day driving."

Before either of the twins can bite his head off, I lay a hand on each of their arms. "It's okay. They were just giving me a moment to myself before we headed inside, but we're ready now."

I nudge Luca until he sighs and climbs out of the car, with me still in his arms. When he sets me down, he pulls me against him in a hug. Seconds later, I feel Vito at my back.

"You've got this, Alessa. We're here for anything you need. Just tell us what you need, and we'll do it." Vito presses a kiss to the top of my head, and I allow myself a moment to soak in their warmth.

"Thank you both, but I think I need to do this on my own." I step out of their arms and give them a sad smile. "But maybe you don't go too far?"

Luca nods. "We'll be just a few steps behind you all day. I promise."

I nod and straighten my shoulders before heading inside. I find Lyla's parents standing at the top of the stairs leading into the church. Making my way over, I stop in front of them.

"Mr. and Mrs. Brown, I just wanted to say again how sorry I am about Lyla. She didn't deserve this. I'll understand if you'd rather I didn't attend her funeral, but I'm hoping that you'll allow me to."

"Oh, Alessandra. First of all, I don't know how many times I have to tell you to call us by our first names." Jordan Brown is a force of nature, and she's been insisting I call her by her first name since I was ten years old. It felt just as weird then as it does now, but I'll do anything she asks of me right now.

"Of course, Jordan. Aaron. I'll work on it, I promise."

Jordan pulls me into her arms, and I can hear the tears in her voice as she speaks to me. "This isn't your fault, Alessandra. We don't blame you for this. Hell, we don't blame your dad for this. The only people to blame for this are the men who shot up a fifteen-year-old's birthday party. Please don't pull away from us because you think we blame you or hate you or whatever you've convinced yourself of. Look at me."

I pull back enough to look at her, finding her face as wet with tears as mine.

"You're family. Lyla might be gone, but you're still ours. Mason and Everett have already lost one big sister. Please don't take the other one from them. I don't think any of us could survive it if you stopped coming around." She brushes the tears from my face. "We love you and, of course, we want you here. Lyla would've wanted you here. Do you know how pissed off she'd be to find out anyone—including yourself—was blaming you for this tragedy?"

I laugh—though it comes out as more of a sob—because I know she's right. "I know you're right, but that doesn't make it any easier to not blame myself."

"That's okay. Anytime you need to be reminded that this isn't your fault, you just come to me. I'll set you straight." Jordan smiles through her tears as Aaron lays a hand on each of our shoulders.

"*We'll* remind you." Aaron looks exhausted, but here he is supporting both his wife and me as we fall apart in front of the church.

I nod, hugging them both—which does nothing to stem the flow of tears—before stepping back and glancing around. "Where are Mason and Everett? Are they not coming?"

Jordan shook her head. "They're with their grandmother. Everett is too young to understand what's going on and Mason didn't want to leave his side. I think he's afraid his little brother might be taken away from him, too."

"Let me know when it's a good time to come by and see them," I tell her, knowing I need to be there for those two little boys.

Aaron ruffles my curly hair. "You can come by anytime, and you know that. Obviously, they won't be home today, but maybe come by tomorrow. Mason's been asking for you. I think he's afraid something happened to you as well."

"I'll be there as soon as I'm awake. It'll be good to see them."

Jordan brushes her hand across my cheek. "You're such a good girl. They'll be thrilled to see you. As will we. We should probably head inside. That's where we're greeting everyone as they arrive. You'll sit with us. We have room for you and James," she glances over my shoulder, "and the twins, too. Whoever you need, but it would mean the world to us if you sat beside us."

"Of course I'll sit beside you." I take a shaky breath. "I think I'll stay out here for a bit, but I'll see you inside?"

"Yes, you will." With one last squeeze of my hand, Jordan and Aaron head inside the church.

I can feel the twins' gaze upon me from where they wait at the bottom of the stairs. I'm not ready to go inside the church, but I'm not sure what to do while I wait for the funeral to start. Figuring we can head back to the car and maybe I can eat some of those french fries after all, I spin around.

James is standing at the bottom of the stairs between the twins. His blond hair is a mess, like he's been running his hands through it over and over. His face is one of absolute despair. "Lessa..."

Not letting myself second guess my instincts, I run down the stairs and throw myself into his arms. He lifts me off the ground and clings to me.

"Why don't we head to our car? The two of you can talk, and we'll make sure you aren't bothered?" I pull back enough to stare at Vito.

"Did you..."

James laughs. "Did they call me? Yeah, they did. They said you needed me. That we needed to talk, and I came as fast as I could."

I mouth a quick thank you to the twins over James's shoulder as he starts toward the town car we'd come in. "How did you get here?"

"I took my dirt bike." He nods his head to the bike parked haphazardly near the stairs we'd just left.

"Your mom is going to be pissed."

He shakes his head. "She already knows. I told her you needed me and she told me to take the bike. Her and Dad are also not seeing eye to eye when it comes to you. In fact, Dad is in the doghouse right now."

"I don't want that. I don't want to cause problems in your family."

James sets me down, swinging the car door open and gesturing for me to go ahead. He glances over his shoulder at the twins. "Thank you."

"We did it for her," Vito grumbles. "Don't fuck this up. If you hurt her again, we'll be hurting you."

"Yeah, yeah, yeah," James grumbles as he climbs in behind me. As soon as the door shuts behind him, he's leaning in and kissing me. It's a fairly chaste kiss for us and over much quicker than I would have liked. "Let's get one thing straight, Lessa. You're not the one causing issues in my family. That is all on my dad. He's being an asshole, and neither Mom nor I are going to put up with it."

"That doesn't make me feel any better," I mumble. "It's still me you're fighting over."

James shakes his head. "No. We're fighting over the fact that my dad is being a stubborn asshole. The reason Mom told me to take the bike and not her car? It's because she's refusing to ride to the funeral with him. She told him he had until the end of the weekend to get over his nonsense or he could find somewhere else to stay."

I gasp. "No, she can't do that. They can't break up over me."

"They won't." James's face softens. "Even if they did split up, it would be because of Dad's stubbornness. He won't let it get to that. He's going to hold on to it as long as he can, and when Mom tells him to get out, he'll let it go. Don't worry about him. How are you? Why did Luca call me?"

I bite my lip, eyes falling to my hands in my lap. "After you left the other day, I was alone, and I started to think maybe it would be better if I was gone—that it would've been better if I'd died instead of Lyla."

"No. Never. Look at me, Lessa, please," he begs until I lift my head to meet his eyes. "I'm sorry I left you alone. I was just so angry that you were trying to end things 'for my own good' that I couldn't stay. Sometimes I can be just as stubborn as my dad. I didn't want to let go of my anger. But if you'd just called, I would've come. I never want you to think we'd be better off without you.

"If you weren't here, I don't know how I would find the will to live. You're my everything, Lessa. I don't care how many people say we're too young to feel that deeply. It's true. You're my past, my present, and my future. Without you, my life has no meaning. I love you so much, Alessandra Valentino."

Once again, my eyes fill with tears, but this time they're happy tears. "I love you too, James Adams."

He pulls me in for another kiss, this one slow and sensual. I love him so much it hurts. Yes, I'm young, but I know he's my future, too.

A knock on the window breaks us apart, and I hear Luca's voice. "It's almost time for the funeral to start."

James leans over to brush his lips against mine once more before opening the door. Once we're standing outside again, I lean up to kiss each of the twins' cheeks. "Thank you."

"You're welcome," they both murmur as I move back to James's side. They trail behind the two of us as we make our way into the church and for the first time since my birthday, I feel happy to be alive.

This is what Lyla would've wanted for me—to be alive and happy while celebrating her much too brief life.

CHAPTER 6

August 2017

Leaning against James's house, I'm fighting tears as he and the twins put the last of his stuff in his car. I'm so not ready for this. This past year has been hard enough with James by my side, but now he's off to college, just like the twins. While the twins' school is about five hours away, James will be a little closer to home. His school is about two hours away.

Sure, it'll be easier for him to come home, but he's going to be so busy with school, I know the visits won't be as frequent as he thinks. I'm trying to be okay with it—with being on my own. No Lyla, no James, no twins. Even though I'm technically still the queen of the school, I don't have any real friends. Only people who pretend to be my friend for the status.

If I'm honest, I don't even really care. It's been hard for me to want to get close to anyone after Lyla's death. I'm fairly certain most people don't want to get close to me for the same reason. Not that there have been any issues since that day. Daddy shut down those men and scared anyone else from trying to take over our city. It probably helps that the heads of the other four families came in and showed their support, bringing their heirs along with them.

It had been pretty cool to meet the heirs as they're close to my age. I think some heads of the families thought they might match one of their sons with me, but that shit wasn't going to fly with me. I made a few friends among the heirs and their families, but they're not exactly in the same city.

The five families each run their own city, and together they run the Northeast. Our family runs Corcoran. The Alessi family, headed by Elio, runs New Vienna. His heir's name is Dario, and he's three years older than me. His sister, Aria, is only a year older than me and I kind of love her.

Then there's the Rossi family, headed by Sergio, who runs Cerulean. Valeria is their heir, and she's my idol. Five years older than me, and she's such a badass. Something me and her youngest sister, Natalia, both agree on. Natalia is my age, and I'd like to say we're tentative friends.

The fourth family is the De Lucas. They run Achille, and they're headed by Gabriella. Yes, a woman, because in our world it doesn't matter your gender, just your determination. Her heir is Matteo, who's only a year older than me. He's pretty cool, and his mom was definitely trying to hook us up.

The last family is the Messinas, headed by Giovanni and oversees Greycliff Bay. Their heir is Enzo, who's ten years my senior. I wouldn't say Giovanni was trying to set me up with his heir, but I'm not a hundred percent sure about that. I don't think he cared which of his sons I ended up with, as long as it was one of them. He brought the four boys. Paolo, who's six years older, Francesco, who's two years older, and Dante, who's two years younger. I made it clear to all four of them I wasn't looking to make a match, as I'm not single.

It was nice getting to meet so many of the players I might work with in the future. Though I know there are tons of other players throughout the rest of the country. I know next to nothing about them. I'm guessing that's something Daddy will get to eventually.

James shuts the trunk and brushes his hands over his jeans. "I guess that's it. Thanks for helping, guys."

Vito just grunts, but Luca laughs, slapping his hand on James's back. "It's not a problem. We were glad to help. Plus, it'll be easier for Alessa if we're here after the two of you say goodbye."

James's eyes find mine, and he grins. "Thank goodness for that. We don't want any repeats of last year."

"There will be no repeats of last year," I say as I make my way down the stairs to stand in front of him. "I'm still working with the therapist, and I'm okay. I'm sad to see you go, but I'm also so excited for you. I wish I could go with you. This will be good for us."

James laughs as he wraps his arms around me. "I don't think it'll be good at all, but I get what you're saying. Distance means nothing to love like ours."

"Exactly." I lean into him as I go up on my tiptoes to kiss him. He still has to duck down a bit because I swear he's gotten even taller. The kiss is short and sweet—we already said our goodbyes last night when he snuck into my room and made love to me all night long. "I love you, James. I'll miss you and still expect my nightly phone calls, but I want you to enjoy your college experience, yeah?"

"I promise I'll try not to sulk about being so far from you, and nothing can keep me from our nightly calls." He kisses the tip of my nose. "Enjoy the week with the twins. I wish I didn't have to leave early, but they have that stupid orientation this week."

I run my hands over his chest. "I know, baby. We already talked about this. You're going to your week of orientation. School's already started for me, anyway. It's not like I have a ton of free time right now and the twins will make sure I don't get into any trouble this week. After that, it's just me, so we'll see what kind of trouble I can get into."

James narrows his eyes. "You better not get into any trouble."

"Like I would. I'm the perfect, well-behaved mafia princess, didn't you know?"

All four of us laugh, but I know James needs to leave. He'll stand here all day to keep talking to me. I give him a huge smile, barely able to keep back my tears. "Go. Call me later, and you can tell me all about campus, but you have to leave in order to see it."

"I love you so much, Lessa." His lips brush over mine once more before he steps away.

"Love you too."

The twins move to stand on each side of me as James climbs into his car with a sad smile. He waves at us before he backs out of the driveway. I keep waving until his car disappears around the corner and only then do I let the tears fall.

"It's okay, Alessa," Vito says as he scoops me into his arms. I lay my head against his chest and just let the tears fall.

Luca's hand runs up and down my back before Vito starts across the lawn to our house. "We've got you. Let it all out."

I take them at their word and sob as Vito carries me home. We end up in my room, settling on my bed with one of them on each side of me. I don't know how long I cry for, but finally, I settle down.

"Feel better?" Luca asks.

I snort. "Not especially, but I'll be fine. It's just going to suck with all three of you away at school and me here all on my own."

"The year's still early. There's still time to make friends." Vito plays with my hair as he stares down at me.

Over the last year, the three of us have grown so much closer. Hell, they're actually friends with James now. So, I guess the four of us have grown closer. I still harbor that stupid crush of mine, but I've learned to ignore it. After all, I'm only human, and my stepbrothers are hot as hell. Of course, I have a crush on them. That doesn't mean I'll ever act on it.

"I don't know if I want to," I say, voice quiet as I stare off into space. "I don't really want to drag anyone into this world. I think I'm content to have acquaintances for the next two years. I'm still in contact with the other heirs and some of their siblings. They're already in this world and understand what I'm going through, so I think they'll be the friends I need, ya know?"

Luca sighs. "Won't that be awfully lonely for you? None of them are close to here, and some of them are off to college, too."

I shrug. "I don't know yet. I'm not afraid to be alone. Everyone I love is just a phone call away. And who knows? Maybe Vito is right. Maybe I'll make friends with someone. I'm just not in a hurry. Some time alone might be good for me. Help me figure out who I am, beyond being a mafia princess or James's girlfriend."

"I won't lie, Alessa. We're worried about you. We don't like leaving you here with no one to turn to." Luca has joined his twin in playing with my hair, and I let my eyes fall shut. It's so relaxing to feel their hands brushing through my strands.

"I promise I'm okay. I won't hurt myself, and if I ever feel the need, I'll tell someone. Trust me."

Vito grunts but doesn't argue with me. Luca, on the other hand, I can practically feel his worry.

I crack an eye open to look at him. "Since when did you become such a mother hen?"

"He's always been a mother hen." Vito snickers. "You just draw it out of him more."

"Well, you're just going to have to get over it. It's time for me to stand on my own. I need to prove that I can do it—to myself, to Daddy, to the two of you. Hell, even to James."

I roll onto my side, dislodging their hands from my hair as I pull Luca closer until his arm is under me and I'm tucked into his chest. Vito presses against my back, his arm tossed over me and Luca. It doesn't take long for me to drift off to sleep in their warm embrace.

I WAKE SLOWLY, blinking to clear the sleep from my eyes. My room is almost completely dark, the only light coming from the moon through the window and a small crack in my door.

Hearing hushed voices outside my door, I wonder if that's what woke me. I climb from my bed and creep over to the door.

"It's not appropriate," Teresa hisses.

"Mom, we're not doing anything wrong." Luca's exasperation is leaking into his words. "James left today, and she didn't need to be alone."

"That might be true, but the way the three of you were clinging to one another? That isn't how siblings act. It's not right. What if it was Riccardo who walked in on you and not me?"

Vito scoffs. "He would've thought we were offering comfort to his daughter—which is exactly what we were doing. That's all it was and all it'll ever be."

"You better damn well make sure that's all it is. Don't you think for a second that I don't see how the two of you look at her when you think no one is watching. She's your sister, for God's sake. It's disgusting."

"No," Luca barks, surprising me. I've never heard him speak to his mom that way before. "She's our stepsister. We are not related by blood. We know Alessandra is off-limits, but you will not make us feel bad for what we feel. There is nothing wrong or dirty about it—even if we never plan on acting on it. Now, lay off."

It's Teresa's turn to scoff. "I will not lay off. You might be grown, but I'm still your mother. I only want what's best for you. Can you imagine what people would say if they knew? What Riccardo would say?"

"If they knew what, Mom?" Vito's gruff voice betrays his anger. "That we're attracted to a woman four years our junior? That's in high school? Or is it that you're married to her dad? It doesn't fucking matter because it's never going to happen. We're her friends, and it'll remain that way. We'll be there for her whenever she needs us, regardless of your opinion on the matter."

"We would never take advantage of her—something you should know, seeing as you raised us. Even if we were to act on our feelings, it wouldn't be now. She's too young and has her entire life ahead of her. We wouldn't hold her back from that. Something, once again, you should know." Luca lets out an exasperated sigh. "I'm done having this conversation with you, Mom. I love you, but nothing you say is going to change how we feel or us being there for her. So just drop it."

"We need to get back in there before she wakes up," Vito adds. "I don't want her waking up alone. She needs us right now."

Shit. I dart back to the bed, diving under the covers as the door swings open to reveal the twins. I sit up slowly, blinking at the pair of them as if I'd just woken up. "What's going on?"

"Nothing, Alessa," Luca says as he climbs back onto the bed. "Let's just go back to sleep."

"And what if I don't want to go back to sleep?" I don't think I can go back to sleep—not after hearing all of that. My mind is absolutely blown and running in a million different directions right now.

Vito grins at me. "What do you have in mind, then? It's after midnight. There's not much to do right now."

I frown, reaching for my phone. "Shit. I missed James's call."

"It's okay, Alessa. I answered when he called. I explained that you were a little upset about him leaving and that you were passed out. He said he'll call you tomorrow." Luca rubs my back, trying to call me down.

I'm annoyed that I missed talking to him because I'm already going crazy with him gone. Not to mention the bombshell I'd just overheard. Shit, I really am a mess.

Turning back to Vito, I shake my head. "Bullshit. There's a ton to do. It's Saturday night. I can name off at least ten parties happening right now."

"You want us to go to a high school party?" Vito asks, obviously not enthused by the idea.

I wrinkle my nose. "Well, no. The only reason I mentioned parties is because I know they're going on right now. I think there's plenty of trouble we can find outside of going to a party."

Vito grins. "Trouble, you say?"

"No." Luca shakes his head. "We're supposed to be keeping you out of trouble, not helping you find it."

"Where's the fun in that, Luca?" I pout, crossing my arms over my chest. "I bet if we went trawling the streets, we'd be able to find some asshole who thinks he's big and bad, trying to take advantage of some woman."

Luca's eyes narrow. "And what does that have to do with us?"

"I was just thinking a torture session is just what I need to feel better. You want me to feel better, don't you?"

Vito laughs, throwing his arm around my shoulder. "I'm loving this new side of you, Alessa."

"What? The side that enjoys torturing assholes?" I grin. "You should. The two of you introduced me to this side of myself. Bet you didn't think I'd like it as much as I do, did you?"

"Nope," Luca says with a laugh. "But you know we'll never say no to helping you torture someone."

"Do you want me to ask your dad if he has anyone he needs us to torture instead of picking up some rando from off the side of the road?" Vito tilts his head, watching me as I consider it.

Sighing, I agree. "Fine. See if Daddy has anyone, but if he doesn't, we're going to find someone."

"Torture isn't usually in a sixteen-year-old's repertoire, you know that, right?" Luca laughs as he shakes his head. "You don't have to torture people. Your dad doesn't. Well, I guess he does sometimes, but it's not really a job for the head of the family."

"Don't care," I sing-song. "I'm not the head of the family yet, and I enjoy it. Daddy says he doesn't care if I torture people as long as they deserve it. He says he was the same way when he was my age. He said it's a good way to let out the darkness that runs through our veins."

"That's dark as fuck," Vito says as he pulls his phone out of his pocket. "I like it."

"You would." Luca rolls his eyes, pulling me against him as Vito calls my dad. "I don't care that you need to torture people. You know that, right? Vito is the same way, and I'm not judging either of you."

I turn my head to look up at him, noticing for the first time how his eyes drift to my lips. Damn, overhearing that conversation has me seeing things from a new perspective. "Not you, though?"

"I don't need to torture people. I need to kill people."

My eyes widen in surprise. "I never would've guessed that."

"Vito and I try to lock down our darkness when we're around you. We don't want to scare you."

"You don't."

We're both silent as we stare at one another, the air around us tense. Is he thinking about kissing me like I'm thinking about kissing him? I almost wish I hadn't heard his and Vito's confessions to Teresa.

Not only do I have a boyfriend that I love, but I know how much trouble we'd cause if anything happened between the three of us. It would hurt so many people. James, Teresa, and Daddy are only the tip of the iceberg of who we'd hurt by giving in to this.

I understand why they'd told Teresa this couldn't happen—that we couldn't happen. We'd burn our whole damn world to the ground if we gave into this tension between them. If they can remain strong, then so can I.

"You're in luck, princess. Your daddy has two men for us to torture tonight. We just have to pick them up and bring them to the warehouse."

Vito's voice breaks me and Luca from our little stare down, and I clap excitedly. Is it weird that I get excited about torturing people? I'm sure it is for some people, but this is the world I live in. I might as well enjoy it, right?

"Let's go do this then." I grin as I climb off the bed and head to the bathroom to freshen up. When I step back into the bedroom, the twins' heads are bent as they whisper between the two of them. "Everything okay?"

Luca grins as he lifts his head. "Yup, everything's great. You've still got clothes at the warehouse, right?"

"Yup," I say, popping my p to be annoying. "I just stocked up my locker."

It's Vito who nods. "Good. We're just going to duck into our rooms real quick, and we'll meet you downstairs."

"Okie dokie."

I watch them duck into the hallway before pulling my shoes on. Overhearing their conversation changes some things, but also, not really. The overall situation is still the same. I have a crush on two men I can't have. So what if they're also attracted to me? It can never happen.

I want them in my life, so I'll keep dealing with it just like I have been—by ignoring it. It'll get easier one day, right? It has to, but even if it doesn't, this is the way it has to be.

CHAPTER 7

May 2019

I'm grinning from ear to ear when Stacy throws her arms around my neck. "We did it! We're done. We're officially no longer high schoolers!"

I return my best friend's hug, just as excited as she is to be done.

I met Stacy in the second half of our junior year. She moved to the city when her dad took over as my dad's underboss. The previous underboss, my uncle, died of a sudden heart attack. We'd been devastated, and there was no one in the family who Daddy felt was ready for the role. I know he'd originally wanted the twins to move into the role, but they weren't done with school yet.

The twins had tried to say they'd quit school and Daddy had said no. He's very determined that the three of us finish college before we become fully entwined in the family. As much as I would've loved having the twins home full time, I'm glad Daddy said no. If he hadn't, I never would've met Stacy.

Her dad, Lorenzo, had grown up in Corcoran alongside my dad. When he was twelve, his parents died in a car crash, so he had to move to New Vienna to live with his aunt and uncle. Turns out his aunt and uncle worked with the Alessi family. It had been natural for him to become part of the family when he was old enough and had worked up to being a capo.

When Daddy called the head of the family, he asked if he could ask Lorenzo to be his underboss. Elio Alessi knew he wouldn't be able to offer the same role to Lorenzo, and it would be good for the relationship of the two families, so he agreed. Lorenzo had been ecstatic and moved his family here—which included Stacy and his wife, Alondra.

She'd been exactly what I needed—someone already involved in the mafia and someone who needed a friend just as badly as I did. It took my goth bestie a bit of time to accept being friends with the head cheerleader, but I eventually wore her down. Now, we're practically inseparable. I even introduced her to Lyla's family, and they welcomed her with open arms, glad that I'd finally let myself befriend someone else.

"C'mon, Stace, let's go find our families," I say with a laugh, breaking away from her.

I'm so thankful that I told my family and James to meet me outside of the stadium where our ceremony was held. Watching families file down and try to locate their graduates is crazy. I'm so glad I thought ahead. It's probably because we'd had the same problem four years ago when the twins graduated and then two years ago when James graduated.

Stacy and I push through the crowds of people and exit the front entrance. I see a few others seem to have had the same idea, but my family is easy to spot. There's Lorenzo and his wife standing beside Daddy and Teresa. On their other side are James's parents. The biggest surprise, though, is finding Lyla's parents there as well.

Tears fill my eyes when I see them, even as a smile lights up my face. Lyla should've been graduating today as well, and I hate she isn't, but I'm proud of the memorial I'd put together with Stacy's help. I'm grateful they were here to see it. I'd told no one I was doing it except Stacy because I'd been afraid someone would try to stop me.

When my eyes lock with Jordan's, she mouths a thank you even as her own eyes fill with tears. I guess I was worried for no reason. Deep down, I should've known no one would try to stop me from honoring my late friend.

"Lessa!" James's whoop is the only warning I get before I'm picked up and spun in circles. I cling to his neck as I throw my head back, laughing loudly. As soon as he sets me back on my feet, his lips are on mine.

"Oh my god, James. Will you knock it off? You're acting like you didn't see her this morning." I can practically hear Stacy rolling her eyes.

I hear the twins snickering, and I can't help but smile into the kiss. James reluctantly pulls away, shooting a mock glare at Stacy. "I'm just proud of my girl. Don't be jealous."

"Jealous of who? Alessandra?" She snorts. "Unlikely."

James laughs as he releases me, pulling Stacy in for a hug as the twins rush me. They try to hug me at the same time, and we end up in some kind of weird group hug.

"I'm glad to see you two, but I can't breathe." I laugh as Luca and Vito step back, sheepish looks on their faces. "I'm glad you made it back in time."

"We wouldn't have missed it for the world. We jumped in the car as soon as we finished our finals." Luca grins.

I loop an arm through each of theirs, leaving Stacy and James to trail behind us as we head toward our parents. "How long are you here for?"

Vito's nose wrinkles. "We have to head back on Monday so we can start getting our stuff packed." He boops me on the nose when I pout.

"You'll see us on Wednesday. The parentals said you guys were going to head up a day early and spend the night at a hotel." Luca leans over so he can rest his head on mine as we walk—something I'm sure can't be comfortable for him.

"We are. It was my idea. I figured I could check out the campus before I head there in the fall."

James makes a noise behind me. "I still can't believe you're not going to school with me. We've spent the last two years apart, and you choose your dad's alma mater over going to school with your boyfriend? Who does that?"

"Wahhh," Stacy teases as James lets out an oof, telling me my bestie hit my boyfriend. "Stop being a baby. It's also where her mom went."

James's arms wrap around my waist from behind. "I know. I'm just kidding, baby. You know I don't care what school you go to. And it's not much further away from my school than it is to here. We'll make it work just like we always do."

I turn my head to kiss him quickly before pushing my ass back into him. "We will. Now, back off before you make me trip."

"Like the twins would ever let you fall," he says with a scoff.

He's not wrong. My stepbrothers would do anything to make sure I don't get hurt—even keep me on my feet if I trip. I don't get to respond as we've reached the parents. There are rounds of hugs for Stacy and me from each of the parents, and I'm not sure I've ever felt so loved—even from James's dad. Things have been awkward between us for the last two years, but I think that's because he feels guilty about the way he acted.

"What's the plan for tonight?" Vito asks. "Are we having a party or what?"

I shake my head. "No, James planned a surprise for tonight, so we're going to be heading out soon. But I'm all yours after we all go out to lunch tomorrow. No party, though. You know how I feel about parties."

I haven't had a party since my fifteenth birthday party. I know I'll have to one day, but that day definitely left me a bit traumatized. I'd rather not revisit it anytime soon. Maybe one day.

"Well, that sucks." Luca pouts. "Can't believe we came all the way up here for your graduation, only for you to run off with your boyfriend."

I roll my eyes at him, not bothering to respond. James just laughs, throwing his arm around me. "You snooze, you lose, buddy. You should've thought of it first."

There's another round of hugs from everyone, and then James and I are on our way. "Are you finally going to tell me what we're doing?"

"No," he drawls. "That would ruin the surprise."

"You're an idiot."

James grins. "But you love me, anyway."

"You're right, I do."

"Then that's all that matters."

I shake my head as I settle back into my seat. I don't mind that he's surprising me—in fact, I kind of love it—but would it be so horrible to at least give me a hint? He's been keeping this surprise super close to the vest. Even his mom said she didn't know what he had planned.

I wonder what he has planned. Is it something exciting? Romantic? Both, maybe? I bite my lips as I run through what he could have planned. I'm going to blame my preoccupation for not noticing where we're heading sooner.

"Are we heading home?" I ask, confused.

James laughs, glancing over at me as he nods. "We are. That's where the surprise is."

Hmmm… this is getting more and more interesting. What could it possibly be? By the time he pulls up to my house, I'm practically bouncing in my seat.

"C'mon, James," I beg. "Tell me, please."

He just shakes his head, climbing out of the car, and hurrying over to my door. He opens it, offering me his hand so I can climb out. I'm pouting but realize there's no point in asking him to tell me what he has planned since I'll find out soon. When James offers me his arm, I accept.

Instead of heading into the house, we circle behind it. Walking past the pool area, he leads me into the gardens. The gardens were apparently Mom's pride and joy—besides me. Or, at least, that's how Daddy tells the story.

Growing up, I spent a lot of time in the gardens to feel closer to a woman I missed without ever really knowing. Once I started high school, things changed, and I didn't have the time to come out here regularly. Or maybe it's because I didn't need to feel as close to my mom once I had Teresa. Who knows why, but it's nice to be walking here now.

I gasp when we approach the gazebo buried deep within the gardens. Daddy always likes to tell the story of how he proposed to my mom here. The house has been in our family for generations, and when he came of age, his parents gifted the home to him as they were ready for a smaller place. The gardens hadn't been what they are now, but Daddy always said how much he loved spending time with my mom out here.

Fairy lights twinkle all around the gazebo and candlelight flickers, adding to the glow as the sun sets behind us. James leads me up the stairs, and I find a blanket with tons of pillows laid out before us. He helps me sit before pulling a picnic basket from seemingly out of nowhere.

"Well, this is certainly a surprise," I say with a grin. James isn't known for being super romantic, and I'm okay with that. He's very good at sweet gestures, but this surpasses anything he's done in the past. It's the best kind of surprise.

James laughs as he pulls some of my favorite foods from the basket—lasagna, stuffed mushrooms, garlic bread, to name a few—before he pulls out a bottle of champagne and two glasses.

I raise an eyebrow, pulling a laugh from James. He's not twenty-one yet, so he can't buy alcohol. "Who did you con into getting you champagne?"

"There was no conning. I asked the twins to get it for me. They only agreed because I told them it was for a surprise for you after graduation." James rolls his eyes as if annoyed by the twins, but I know better. Things have been so much better between the three of them these past few years. Something I'm ever so grateful for. Because I'd never be able to choose between my boyfriend and the twins.

"That was sweet of them." I glance around the gazebo, a soft smile on my lips. "This is sweet of you. I haven't been out here in ages."

James piles food on a plate before handing it to me, humming his agreement. "I know, and I wanted to do something special for you. I know it's been hard with me being away at college and now we'll be even further apart. I want to relish the time we have together, celebrate it. Celebrate us."

"Damn, when did you get so romantic?" I giggle.

"I've always been a romantic," James starts to say, but my giggles cut him off. He shoots me a mock glare before grinning. "Okay, so I'm not the most romantic guy out there. I want to be better about that. You deserve the world, Lessa, and I want to give it to you."

I lean over to kiss him, though I can't stop smiling, which makes it a little more difficult. Then I dive into the food, moaning at the taste. "Mmmm, you had your mom cook for us, didn't you?"

"I sure wasn't going to do the cooking. I wanted the food to be edible, and she was more than happy to help. She knows your favorites as well as I do."

I can't help but grin at him for another moment, allowing myself to really study him. He's always been an attractive guy, but he's all man now, and I love it. He's always spent time in the gym since he's an athlete, but everything is more pronounced now. He's put on more muscle since I last saw him. His hair is longer than I've seen it in a while and he's rocking at least two days' worth of scruff on his face. I kind of love it.

Shaking my head, I turn my attention back to my food and devour it quickly. James's mom is an amazing cook. She might not be Italian, but she learned a few Italian recipes from our cook so she could make me my favorites. She's just all around amazing and while it would have been nice to have my mom around, I never really knew her. Susanna Adams is the first mother figure I remember having and then Teresa as a teenager. They're the women who shaped me into who I am today. Well, the two of them and my dad.

Once we're done eating, James pours us a glass of champagne. I'm cuddled against his side as we just enjoy each other's company. Until James clears his throat and I turn my head to look up at him. I frown when I realize he looks nervous. What could he possibly have to be nervous about?

"What's up, James? You seem tense."

James chuckles, taking a deep breath as I turn to face him. "I love you, Alessandra. I have since we were kids. Being your first and only in everything has been the best experience in my life. I've been thinking, and there's another first and last I'd like to be in your life."

My eyes widen as he pulls a box from beneath the blankets. It's suddenly hard to breathe as he pops it open, revealing a beautiful ring. I'm shaking as he takes it from the box and grins at me.

"I want to be your husband more than anything in the world. Please tell me you'll do me the honor of being my wife?"

Dread fills my stomach as tears well in my eyes. He can't be doing this right now. It's too soon. We've talked about getting married, and I absolutely want to marry him—after college. Why is he asking me this right now?

"James... why?" I croak, my eyes shifting up to meet his.

James's head jerks back, and his face falls. "Because I love you and want to spend the rest of my life with you. We've talked about getting married. I thought this was what you wanted."

"Yeah, after I graduate college. I'm not even eighteen yet. I want to be your wife, one day in the future. I thought you understood that."

James grins at my words, shrugging. "So, we'll have a long engagement. I'm okay with that. I just want everyone to know you're mine and since we'll be at different schools, I thought this would be a good way to show that."

All I can do is blink at him as I process his words. He wants to show everyone that I'm his? With a fucking engagement ring? Not only does that not make sense, but it's also insulting as hell.

"No. That's not a reason to get engaged." I run my tongue across my teeth as I try to rein in my anger and annoyance. "Have I done something to make you not trust me? To make you think you need to collar me to make sure that other men know I'm taken? You've been away at college for two years, and I've trusted you implicitly, but now that I'm going myself, you want to own me? I'm not a possession you can own."

"That's not what I meant..." James shakes his head, and I can see the panic building in his eyes. "I love you, Lessa. I want us to get married. I want you to wear my ring. I want you to be mine."

I carefully set down the glass of champagne before standing. James hurriedly does the same, reaching out to me, but I step out of his reach.

"I don't know what the hell you've been learning at that college of yours, but what you're suggesting is possession, not love. I don't like it, and I won't put up with it. So, no, James. I won't be marrying you or accepting your ring. Not until you prove that you're worthy of me. Because all of this? This isn't you, and the person you're acting like isn't someone I want to be with."

James's jaw clenches but says nothing. I don't mean to laugh, but what the hell does he have to be pissed off about? He's the one who is acting like he wants to own me. No one will ever own me—no boyfriend, fiancé, or husband.

"So I'm not worthy of you?" James scoffs. "Of course, I'm not. I should've known you'd look for any opportunity to break up with me so you can jump into the twins' beds. How fucking stupid do you think I am?"

Oh, boy. This is going to get ugly, isn't it?

"First of all, I said nothing about breaking up with you. I wasn't even remotely thinking about that, but it's obvious you have been. Second, the twins? They're my stepbrothers, my friends. I thought you moved past your jealousy."

"I'm not jealous of those douchebags," he practically screams in my face, and it takes everything in me to not punch him dead in the face. I think he's forgotten who he's dealing with.

"You are so jealous of my friendship with them. It's why I wanted the three of you to be friends so you could put that behind you. I don't know what happened between spring break and now to make you act like this? But you're sadly mistaken if you think I'm going to allow you to speak to me like this. I've never heard such disrespectful things come out of your mouth before—and never aimed at me. What changed, James? Why are you acting like this?"

James shoves the ring in his pocket, pacing along the gazebo as he refuses to meet my gaze. "You really don't see the way they look at you, Lessa? They want you. They want to bend you over and fuck you until you forget your own name. And I'm not an idiot—I've always seen the way you stare at them with desire in your eyes. For the longest time, I thought it was just a small crush that you'd get over eventually—but you haven't, and I don't think you're going to."

"So what if I'm attracted to them? It's not like I'd act on it. I'm allowed to be attracted to other people even when we're together. Being in love doesn't make you blind, but it also doesn't mean you'll act on those impulses. Why do you keep ignoring my question?" I ask, tilting my head at him. "What brought this on? What made you act this way?"

"Damn it, Lessa! I slept with someone else! It's hard with you so far away, and I got drunk, and it just happened. I didn't mean for it to happen. I'm so fucking sorry. I didn't want to tell you because I knew you'd be pissed and I didn't want to hurt you, but that's what changed." James drops to his knees in front of me, laying his head on my stomach as his arms circle around me. "I thought if we got engaged, I wouldn't be tempted again. I need you to forgive me."

I stare down at him in shock. He'd slept with someone else and had thought getting engaged was the answer? What an idiot. Why are men so dumb? I squeeze my eyes shut, fighting back my tears as betrayal sits heavy in my stomach. He cheated on me. What's to say he won't do it again? Can I trust him after this? Can I forgive him?

"Was it just once?" I ask, voice shaking as I lose my battle with my tears.

James tenses for a moment before leaning his head back to look at me. Tears fall down his cheeks as he slowly shakes his head. "No. It happened a few times."

I bite my lip to keep myself from sobbing. Once I've got myself under control again, I nod. "Do you want a relationship with her?"

James makes a face. "It's... not a woman, Lessa."

I jerk back from him, nearly falling down the stairs in my surprise. "Are you gay? It's okay if you are. That's not something you can control. I just... need to know?"

"No," James says as he shakes his head. "I'm bisexual. I've always been bisexual. I just didn't know how to tell you."

"Did you think I would judge you for that?" I swipe at my cheeks, trying to wipe away the tears, but they keep coming. A part of me feels bad that he didn't feel comfortable enough in our relationship to tell me, but the other part? That part is pissed as hell. He'd been keeping that from me, and he cheated on me more than once.

"Of course not, Lessa. I just didn't know how to bring it up." James runs a hand over his face. "This is so not how I thought this night was going to go. I love you so much, Lessa."

I lift a hand to my lips, trying to hide the way they quiver. "I love you too, James, but I think this makes it very clear that what we need is a break—not an engagement. I need time to figure out if I can forgive you for cheating. I also think you need time to explore your sexuality without having to worry about a girlfriend. I hope I can get over it eventually, but I also know I would always wonder if you were cheating on me if you don't take time to figure out what you want."

"I want you, Lessa. I've always wanted you and I always will. Please, don't do this," James pleads.

"I think we need this. I need this. Why don't we take the summer and next year to figure out what we really want? What we need. I'll always love you, James, no matter what happens." I'm barely able to hold back my sobs at this point. "But I can't be around you right now, and I don't know when I'll be able to."

I spin on my heel and run for the house. I need to get away from him, away from this feeling of betrayal.

Fuck. I definitely didn't expect to end my night this way—betrayed and broken. What a way to begin the rest of my life.

CHAPTER 8

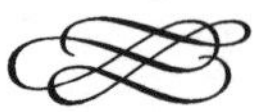

I jerk awake when my bed dips. I have no idea what time it is or when I fell asleep. My eyes feel puffy, and I can barely peel them apart to see who's in my bed. I'm only slightly surprised to see the twins crawling in on either side of me. I say nothing as Vito settles against my back, his arm thrown over my waist as Luca lies facing me.

"Hi," I croak, clearing my throat before continuing. "What are the two of you doing here?"

Luca's face fills with sympathy as he reaches up to stroke his hand down my cheek. "James called and told us what happened, so we hurried home to check on you."

"How are you doing, baby girl?" Vito asks as he nuzzles my neck.

I squeeze my eyes shut, my chest tight as I fight against the tears wanting to spill forth again. "How do you think I'm doing?"

Vito growls, leaning up on his elbow so he can look down at me. "Want us to go kick his ass?"

I'm shaking my head before he even finishes asking. "No. Absolutely not."

"We totally will if you want us to," Luca says, sighing when I shake my head again. "That's unfortunate. I was looking forward to kicking his ass."

"The two of you are his friends, and he's going to need you right now. You can't be mad at him." I pause. "What exactly did he tell you?"

"We absolutely can be mad at him." Vito's voice is doing the growling thing again. "He cheated on you. He hurt you. He might be our friend, but so are you."

Luca squeezes my hand. "He said he proposed—like an idiot—because he felt guilty for cheating on you. Apparently, he's bisexual and just told you. You said you needed a break—for the summer and the next school year."

I nod. "That about covers it. I know the two of you are protective of me, but you can't turn your back on James. I think the three of us are the first people he's told outside of maybe some people at his school. I can't be there for him right now—I'm too hurt—which is why I need the two of you to be there for him.

"Don't even try to argue with me," I say when I hear Vito taking a breath behind me. I roll onto my back so I can see both of them. "What he did doesn't mean I don't still love him. He's been my best friend for years longer than he was my boyfriend. He's going to be confused and hurting right now. He's going to need you, since I can't be there for him. But you can't give him shit about being bisexual."

Vito scoffs. "Like we give a shit about his sexual preferences. What we care about is that he hurt you."

Luca sighs. "Of course, you have to bring that up—making sure I feel guilty enough to not be angry. I would never turn my back on someone because of their sexual orientation—especially not when it's the same as mine."

"You're bi?" I screech, sitting up in the bed to stare down at him in shock. "Why didn't I know that?"

"There was no reason for you to know. There's been no one I've been interested in enough to bring home to meet the family—man or woman—so there was no reason to tell you." Luca shrugs and I try not to be hurt by his words. But I am.

"Do I give off vibes that I'm anti-LGBTQ or something? Why didn't I know that two of the most important people in my life were bi?" I bury my face in my hands. This shouldn't be hurting me so much, but on top of everything with James, I'm basically an open wound.

"Of course, you don't, Alessa." Luca pulls me into his arms. "It's just a part of me, and I'm so open with it, I didn't think about needing to tell you. That has nothing to do with you, but I'm sorry I hurt you by not telling you."

I shrug but lay my head on his chest. "It's fine. I get what you're saying, I'm just a little..."

"Prickly?" Vito offers.

"Sensitive," I say, glaring at Vito, who just smirks and shrugs at me. "You're an asshole."

"See. I told you that you were prickly."

"I'll fucking show you prickly." I struggle in Luca's arms, ready to grab the knife in my bedside table and leave a new hole or two in Vito.

Luca chuckles, tightening his arms around me. "Let's just stay here, hmmmm? There's no need to stab Vito. If we stabbed him every time he pissed us off, he'd be dead."

"How did you..."

"Know that you were thinking about stabbing Vito?" Luca laughs, his body shaking against mine. "Because you usually want to stab Vito, and I know your knife is nearby."

"Whatever." I pout as I settle against Luca, getting myself comfortable.

"Come on, princess, I'm sorry. I just wanted to make you laugh." Vito's face pops up in front of me.

I laugh, a bitter sound that holds no humor. "And what do I have to laugh about right now? I found out my boyfriend cheated on me and kept the fact that he's bisexual from me. Oh, but he's not my boyfriend anymore because I don't know if I'll be able to forgive him. Plus, I think he needs to be single so he can explore that side of himself. He can't do that while he's tied to me."

"Always thinking about everyone else." Luca presses a kiss to the top of my head. "Most people would focus on the betrayal they feel at their partner's betrayal. But, here you are, worried about making sure he has the freedom to explore his sexuality. How are you only seventeen?"

I shrug. "I've always been mature for my age. No matter how hurt I am right now, I will always worry about James's well-being. He's my best friend, and I want him to be happy—even if that's not with me. I just want all the people I love to be happy."

"And that's what makes you a much better person than me." Vito reaches out to brush at the tears I hadn't realized were falling. "If I were you, I'd want me and Luca to kick his ass. You've got to be careful with that empathy. When you become head of the family, others will try to use that against you."

I cock an eyebrow at him. "Caring about others doesn't make you weak, Vito. It makes you human, and I plan to keep my humanity intact even when I become head of the family. But it also doesn't mean I'll let people walk all over me."

"Plus, we'll be there to watch her back for any snakes trying to slither up behind her." Luca grins at me before sobering. "Do you want to talk about James?"

"No."

Luca laughs. "Let me rephrase that. Do you need to talk about James?"

I shake my head. "Not right now. I'm sure I'll need to eventually, but right now I just want to forget about the horrible night I've had."

"What do you need from us, Alessa?" Vito leans forward to rest his forehead on mine. "Whatever you need, it's yours."

If I was in a better mood, I would absolutely use that to get them to do something embarrassing, but I can't even find joy in that. "Right now, I need to sleep. I think it would be easier if the two of you stayed. And when the two of you head back to school, I want to come with you."

"You'll only be two days behind us," Luca starts, but I cut him off.

"No. Vito asked what I needed, and this is what I need. As soon as we have lunch with our parents, I want to leave Corcoran and come with you back to Wildwood. It'll get me away from here, and I can wander around campus, get to know it before I start in the fall."

Vito turns to Luca with a shrug. "I did tell her anything she needed, and it's not like she's putting us out or anything."

"I'm just not sure our mom or your dad are going to agree to it." Luca makes a face. "And you're still underage. I'm not getting arrested for kidnapping."

I snort. "They wouldn't call the cops if you took me to campus with you. Leave Daddy to me. Teresa will go along with whatever Daddy says and how can he say no to his princess, who just got her heart broken?"

"With that innocent look on your face and some fluttering of your eyelashes—maybe a tear or two—and I think you'll convince him easily," Vito says with a grin. "You are Daddy's princess, after all."

I grin because I know I have my dad wrapped around my finger. I'm not ashamed of it, and I rarely try to use it to my advantage, but if either he or Teresa tries to tell me no, I'll pull out the big guns.

A yawn racks my body, and I blink against my sudden tiredness. "I think I'm ready to sleep now. You'll stay, right?"

My eyes are already falling shut as Luca lowers me to the bed. Both of the twins kiss my forehead as sleep pulls me under.

"Of course, Alessa. Whatever you need—we're yours." I smile at Luca's words.

"We're not going anywhere, baby girl. We couldn't even if we wanted to." Vito's words are the last I hear as sleep overtakes me fully.

~

It's easier to convince my dad and Teresa than I thought it would be. As soon as they hear about what happened with James, they're practically shoving me out the door with the twins. They send us home from the restaurant as soon as we're done eating, so I can pack a bag and we can get on the road.

"I thought they'd put up a bit more fight than that." Luca scoffs, glancing at his brother before turning in his seat to look at me. "Especially Mom. You don't think Riccardo is planning to kill James, do you?"

"Daddy would never."

Vito raises his eyebrows, meeting my eyes in the mirror. "Your dad would never, what? Order someone to be murdered? Kill someone for hurting his princess? Because I can tell you that both of those are something he absolutely would do."

"Daddy wouldn't dare do anything to James." I hesitate, pulling out my phone and sending a quick message to my dad. Just to be on the safe side, of course. I know he wouldn't hurt James. Okay, I'm like ninety percent sure he wouldn't.

"If you're so sure, then why are you texting him?" Luca laughs.

I wait until I get confirmation from my dad that he won't hurt James before I put away my phone and focus on Luca once more. "I could've been texting anyone."

"You could have been, but you weren't. You were texting your dad. What did he say?"

Crossing my arms, I roll my eyes. "He would neither confirm nor deny any plans he had for James. But he promised not to hurt him since it meant so much to me."

"He totally had something planned." I can see Vito's shoulders shaking as he attempts to hold back his laughter.

I won't admit it out loud, but I think they're right. It's suspicious that my dad wouldn't just come out and say he had nothing planned for James. But since he promised me he wouldn't do anything, I know whatever he had planned won't happen now.

Yes, I'm still hurt by what happened with James, but I also get it.

Honestly, if he would've come to me before anything happened, I would've been fine with talking about opening our relationship. I know people are more than capable of loving more than one person at a time. It would've been an uncomfortable conversation, but so what?

It's the betrayal of him cheating on me that hurts the most. I don't care that it was a man he's been sleeping with. It's that he's been hiding it from me and then he tried to propose to me. I know men mature slower than women, but I'm seventeen years old—almost eighteen now—and I'm already handling this better than James did.

I believe he regrets his decisions, but he kept doing it, even knowing it was wrong. It's these kinds of things that are making it hard for me to move past all of it. And, yes, it's only been a day, but I don't enjoy holding onto things like this. The twins might give me shit about me being too soft, but I hate being mad at the people I love. I'm terrible at holding a grudge.

Who needs the added headache of being mad all the time? Certainly not me. I'd rather just let it all go. But in this case? I'm not sure I'll be able to let it go anytime soon. I'm hurt, betrayed, and so angry. All of that anger isn't just directed at James, though. I should've noticed that something was going on. I shouldn't have gotten so complacent in our relationship. Don't get me wrong, this is mostly on James, but I hold a small amount of blame that I won't push off on him.

"You're awfully quiet back there," Luca says as he grabs my hand. "Should we be concerned? Is this going to be like when you lost Lyla?"

I force a smile as I look up at him, shaking my head. "No, nothing like that. I promise I won't get lost in my head. I'll let the two of you know if I feel myself slipping. I have no intention of hurting myself, Luca."

"Okay, Alessa. I just wanted to check. I know this is hard, but we'll be here for you every step of the way."

Vito clears his throat. "Okay, enough of the serious stuff. We have almost three days before our parents show up. What are we going to do to corrupt our sweet stepsister until then?"

I snort. "That you think I'm not already corrupted is hilarious. And don't act like being sweet is a negative personality trait. I can be a lot less sweet if that's what you're into, V."

Vito smirks, and I know he's accomplished what he set out to do—to distract me from all the shit. It's exactly what I need. I have no intentions of thinking about any of it this week. I can worry about it when I get home. This week, I'm going to enjoy some time with the twins on campus, and then I'm going to watch them graduate.

Once we get back home, I know Daddy will put the twins through their paces as they're officially accepted into the family. He just better not think I won't be right there beside them. I'm going to need the two of them if I plan to make it through the summer. Plus, I can show them how good I've gotten at torture. I know they'll be proud of me. Daddy sure was.

"I've never been to a college party before. We should definitely go to at least one of those." I grin when Vito makes a face.

"I hate parties," he says.

I stick my tongue out at him. "That's because you suck."

"Nope, that's Luca." Vito laughs when Luca punches him in the arm. "Hey, now. I'm driving. You're not allowed to hit the driver. Especially not when Alessa is in the car."

I giggle. I've always loved how the two of them are together. They have a sibling bond that I know our parents wished the twins and I shared. Sure, I love them both, but I never have and never will think of them as brothers. We're friends, and that's the relationship we'll keep.

"Okay, so we'll take you to a college party. I'm sure someone is throwing one tonight since the semester is over. I'll text a few people and find a good place for us to drop in." Luca glances up from his phone. "What else do you want to do while we're on campus?"

I shrug. "I really just kind of want to wander around. I've been on campus a few times, but never with free rein. And it's not like Daddy is going to let me stay on campus. I'll be staying in the same apartment as the two of you."

"Of course you are. It's the most secure building in the area, so he won't have to worry about you. He didn't actually buy the place with us in mind. He was always hoping you'd go to Wildwood." Luca shakes his head. "I know he didn't want to pressure you about which school you chose, but he was so fucking excited when you told him you'd be attending his alma mater."

"Yeah, I noticed that," I say with a laugh. "I guess it's a good thing I decided not to go to school with James. That would've sucked."

Vito reaches back to grab my hand, squeezing it lightly before returning it to the wheel. "It would have, but you would've handled it like the badass you are. But we're also grateful you chose Wildwood. We already have some people who have agreed to keep an eye on you."

"Excuse me?"

Luca's head drops forward when he sighs. "That's not at all what happened. We have some friends who aren't graduating this year, and we asked if they'd watch out for you. Not that we think you can't take care of yourself, but it's nice to have someone to watch your back—especially your first time away from home."

I consider him for a moment before nodding. "You're right. It would be helpful to know some people on campus already, so thank you for that. Will I meet any of them before your graduation?"

"I'm sure we can make that happen." Luca glances back at his phone when it goes off. "We're in luck. One of the guys is having a party tonight. You'll be able to meet him and maybe a few others."

"Sounds great." I yawn, wrinkling my nose. "I'm gonna take a nap, I think."

"Okay, baby girl. Get some rest. You'll need it for the party tonight."

I laugh at that. Like I've never been to a party before. How different can a college party be from a high school party?

Closing my eyes, I lay my head against the window and let sleep pull me under.

~

LATER THAT NIGHT, I'm eating crow because it turns out a college party differs greatly from a high school party—or at least this one does. I've never been huge into parties in the first place, but I feel so out of place here.

"Are all parties like this?" I whisper to Luca, eyes wide as I take in the living room.

Luca snorts. "Probably not all of them, but this is a school filled with rich assholes who like to throw their money around. Stephen is the guy throwing this party—he's family—and he doesn't live here. He just bought the place so he could throw parties here."

"Are you kidding me?" This place is freaking huge. Three stories of modern lines and wall-to-wall windows. It's only a ten-minute walk from campus, meaning it was a two-minute walk from the apartment the twins have been staying in—the apartment that will be mine in three months. I'd thought the apartment was over the top, but this place? And it's just for parties? That's insane.

Don't get me wrong. I know my family is well off, and I could totally afford to do the same, but why? We're only here for four years and to buy an entire house just for parties seems wasteful.

"Yeah, he actually lives in the apartment across the hall from us. You'll find that most of the family's kids live in that building while attending Wildwood."

Of course, all the mafia kids are staying in the same building. It explains the extravagance and security. Gotta keep the heirs and spares safe while they're away from the nest, after all. I wonder if that means Matteo, Natalia, and Aria have apartments there too, since they all go here. Well, Natalia will begin in the fall with me.

Something to wonder about later because right now, I'm here to have a good time with the twins and meet some people who I'll be attending with in the fall.

Glancing down at the simple black dress I'm wearing, I glance between the twins. "You're sure I'm dressed okay?"

Vito rolls his eyes. "I wish there was more material to your dress, but yes, you're dressed fine. With that being said, you need to stick to either mine or Luca's side at all times. We don't need anyone to take advantage of you."

"Okay, Dad," I say with a roll of my eyes. "Hope you're cool with dancing then because I will be dancing—and maybe not by myself."

Vito makes a face. "Fine."

I reach up to pat Vito on the cheek. "That's a good boy."

"Somebody's asking for a spanking," he growls.

I fight the shiver that wants to run through me and just grin. "I'm not one of your playthings, V. Now, what kind of drinks do they serve at rich college kids' parties?"

It turns out that it's not keg beer like all the college parties you see on TV. Nope, these fancy fucks have full bars manned by bartenders. And I mean multiple bars. There's one on each level and one by the pool in the backyard. The bartenders also have most recreational drugs that we can order, just like it was a drink.

Each floor has a dance floor with various types of music playing. On the first floor, in the kitchen, there's a catering staff ready to serve us with all kinds of hors d'oeuvres—something they happily point out when we duck inside. There are also bedrooms on every floor, many of them being used by couples and groups—some with the doors wide open. I hadn't been prepared for the live porn and the twins had laughed as my blush spread.

The pool is in use, as is the massive hot tub beside it. And it seems like everyone is naked, even some people lying beside the pool. This party is beyond insane. I don't even know what to do with myself, though I'm trying really hard to play it cool with the twins. After all, I don't want them to be embarrassed by their younger stepsister.

"Vito! Luca!" a masculine voice yells out across the din in the backyard. All three of us turn to find a tall Viking of a man climbing from the pool completely naked.

I'm sure it's rude to stare at someone's cock at these kinds of parties, but hot damn. This man has a fucking tree trunk between his legs. Thick and long, with a slight curve. I can't decide if I want to run away or climb him like a tree.

"You've got a little something here," Luca says, wiping at the side of my mouth.

I bat away his hand. "Shut it, Luc. How am I just supposed to ignore his cock? It's fucking massive."

"That's alright, sweet thing," an unfamiliar voice says, causing my eyes to widen. "I don't mind you staring. I wouldn't even mind if you want to touch or lick it."

I turn to find the man standing in front of us, grinning at me. He raises his eyebrows as his eyes travel up and down my body. "Oh, you are a pretty little thing, aren't you? I'm Stephen. Who might you be?"

"This is Alessandra Valentino, and she's only seventeen, fuck-face." Vito shoves at Stephen's head. "Put your goddamn dick away. I don't want to see that damn thing."

"Ahhhh." Stephen's smile falls as he sighs, leaning over to grab a pair of pants and yanking them. "Of course, she's off limits."

"I'm off limits?" I ask, confused.

Luca snorts. "Of course you are. You're still underage, and you're the Valentino heir. Your name alone will keep the worst of the worst away. Stephen's going to make sure the rest of the assholes stay away as well."

Stephen picks up my hand, pressing a kiss to it. "As sad as it makes me, I will be nothing but a gentleman with you, pretty Alessandra. And if I get to beat the hell out of some idiots along the way, it'll make my day."

"That's... sweet? I guess?" I laugh. "I guess it's good that I have no plans on dating anytime soon, huh?"

Vito's finger hooks under my chin, lifting it until I meet his eyes.

"We're not worried about you dating, Alessa. We're worried about the assholes who only want to get in your pants."

"You're worried about hookups? And what if that's what I want?"

Stephen sighs again. "Are you sure she's off limits?"

"Yes," both of the twins bite out, their attention never leaving me.

"Alessa, you're hurting right now. We won't let you do something you'll regret tonight." Luca rubs his hand along my lower back. "When you come back in the fall, if you want to hook up with every guy on campus, we won't try to stop you. Stephen and the others are only here to watch your back. They won't stop you from doing something you want—though they'll make sure you're of sound mind to make those decisions."

I pout, glancing at Stephen. "And what if I want to sleep with Stephen?"

"Look, baby, you're hot as hell, but that isn't a complication I need in my life." Stephen laughs. "How about we just be friends?"

"Fine." I grin at him before grabbing Luca's and Vito's hands. "Now, I want a drink, and then we're dancing."

"Vito dancing? That's something I'd like to see," Stephen says, but it's quickly followed by a groan. Turning my head, I find him bent over while Vito glares at him.

"Really, V? Can we go a few hours without you punching someone?"

Vito shrugs. "Probably not."

"We'll see you later, Stephen," I call and drag the guys inside.

We end up having more than one drink before finally making it out to the dance floor. I have a pleasant buzz going as I move to the beat, hips swinging and arms in the air. It's not long until I feel bodies push against both my back and front. I don't have to open my eyes to know it's the twins.

The songs are getting slower and dirtier and our dancing reflects that. I have one arm looped around Luca's neck where he dances behind me, his hands low on my hips as he rolls against me, his dick hard. I have my other arm wrapped around Vito's neck, our foreheads pressed together and his leg between mine.

Luca's hands tighten on my hips slightly before he presses me harder on Vito's thigh. My clit rubbing across it with each roll of my hips. My mouth drops open, my breathing picking up as the three of us continue our sinuous movements. When Luca's hands travel up and down my torso, just brushing against the bottom of my tits, my eyes fall open in shock and heat rushes through me. Vito's hand comes up to rest against my cheek, and I can't help melting into his touch as Luca's lips trail along my neck.

Is this really happening right now? How did this become my life?

The corner of Vito's mouth lifts into a semblance of a smile when his eyes follow the movement of my tongue as it darts out to wet my suddenly dry lips. Then he's leaning down toward me. My eyes fall shut, and I know this moment is going to change our relationship completely, but I can't find it in myself to care. I've wanted this for so long.

Vito's lips brush against mine, and I'm in heaven—until someone bumps into him and then we're a tangle of limbs as the three of us hit the floor.

"Fuck." Vito quickly rolls off me, turning to look at the asshole who'd bumped him. "Watch where the fuck you're going."

The guy turns around, mouth open to spew bullshit, I'm sure. As soon as his eyes land on Vito, his anger disappears, and he pales significantly. "I'm sorry, Vito."

"Whatever. Just get the fuck out of my sight."

I scramble to get out of Luca's arms, my body throbbing and needy, but the moment is over. I'm partially grateful for that, but mostly I'm disappointed. This really isn't the time for this to happen. Not with the James situation so fresh. I won't use the twins as some kind of rebound. What I feel for them is so much deeper than that—but I know if something happened between us tonight, that's exactly what I'd be doing.

I smile as the twins climb to their feet. "Do you mind if we head home? I think I'm all partied out for the night."

Luca's face falls, and Vito is back to scowling.

"Are you sure, Alessa?" Luca asks, and I hear the hope in his voice.

I don't want to hurt him, but this isn't the right time, and we'd all end up hurt if we continued this tonight. I nod slowly. "Yeah, I'm exhausted. I think I just need to go to sleep."

Luca forces a smile as he nods, throwing his arm around my shoulders. "You didn't sleep well last night, so that's understandable."

I know calling it a night is the right decision, but why does it hurt so damn much?

CHAPTER 9

Things between me and the twins are awkward for the next few days, but as soon as our parents arrive, it's like nothing happened. We watch the twins graduate, and I'm just as proud of them as our parents are. Especially Vito, who has always hated school. But Daddy told them they had to graduate college before he'd bring them into the family full time, and they did it.

When we're back home, Daddy pulls them into his office to talk about their future in the business. I'm not invited, but that's just because Daddy is sadly mistaken about how I plan to spend my summer.

I push open the door like I own the place. Daddy, Luca, and Vito all turn to face me as the door shuts behind me, and I smile as I skip further into the room.

"It seems my invitation to this meeting got lost in the mail," I joke as I plop into the chair beside Luca.

"You didn't get an invitation because you're not supposed to be here, princess." Daddy gives me a smile that's somehow both patient and a little condescending.

I cock an eyebrow, focusing on my dad. "Are you discussing what you plan on having the twins do this summer?"

Daddy's eyes narrow slightly. "Yes, which doesn't involve you."

"That's where you're wrong, Daddy. Whatever you have the twins doing, I'll be right there with them. Silly of you to think otherwise. It would be much easier if I was here for the conversation than have Luca or Vito explain it to me later, don't you think?"

Daddy's eyes shut as he lifts a hand to rub between his eyes. "Even if I forbid you from joining them this summer, you're still going to do it, aren't you?"

"Yup." I pop the p, still grinning at my dad. "I'm glad you realized that so quickly."

I hear Vito snicker on the other side of Luca but don't turn away from my dad. I really want him to say I can stay for the meeting, but if he makes me leave, the twins will fill me in. The three of us are a team and it's time Daddy fully realizes that.

"Princess, I love you," my dad begins, his exasperation clear, "but you're going to be the death of me. You realize this is going to entwine you in the business more, don't you?"

I nod. "Of course, Daddy. I know you said I don't have to decide until after I finish with college, but this is what I want. I want to be in the business. I want to take over for you when you retire. I've known that for a long time. You're the only one who hasn't realized just how serious I am about it."

Daddy turns his attention back to the twins. "Are the two of you okay with this?"

Luca grins at me before nodding. "Of course. It's better to have Alessa involved than her trying to follow us. Plus, she's part of the team and has been for years."

Vito just shrugs. I wrinkle my nose at him before sticking out my tongue. What a douche. He'd miss me if I wasn't there with them—even if he won't admit it. I make things more fun, and he knows it.

"Fine. You can stay and work with the boys this summer. At least I know they'll keep you safe."

I explode from my chair, running around the desk to throw my arms around my dad. "Thanks, Daddy. You're the best!"

My dad laughs as he returns my hug. "Okay, go sit down. I'll go over what I already told the boys, and then we'll move on from there."

I'm still grinning as I drop into my seat, eyes on the twins. Luca shoots me a wink, reaching out to grab my hand in his and giving it a squeeze. Vito rolls his eyes, but his mouth lifts at the corner, telling me he's happy that Daddy agreed. Looks like I'll have a busy summer, which means less time to think about James and his betrayal.

TWO WEEKS LATER, I find myself in the torture warehouse with the twins. Sadly, Daddy hasn't had anyone for us to torture until now. I can't wait to show the twins what I learned this year. I guess being friendly with the other heirs is good for something. When Sergio Rossi and Gabriella De Luca, as heads of their families came to meet with my dad, their heirs, Valeria and Matteo, came with them. It turns out I'm not the only female who likes a good torture session.

The three of us had a lot of fun in the torture warehouse over that weekend. We all learned from one another, and it was a blast.

Luca laughs when we walk inside. "I see you've been redecorating."

I shrug as I come to a stop behind him. "It's just so boring in here. It needed a splash of color. Plus, it throws people off when you bring them out here."

"I would imagine so." Vito groans. "Did you have to make it so bright?"

Running my eyes over the space, I take in the changes I've made. I had three walls added to block off most of the warehouse from view and painted the walls a happy yellow. Luckily they're far enough away from where we actually do the torturing that not too much splashes on them.

"If you don't like it, you can move stuff around, but I like the yellow walls. No one is expecting to get tortured in a room painted so cheerfully. Let's do this. I can't wait to show you what I learned this year."

"Who taught you something about torturing that we didn't?" Vito tilts his head, eyes narrowing on me. "And why were you torturing with someone that wasn't one of us?"

I laugh. "Someone sounds jealous."

"I'm not fucking jealous. I just want to know who the hell you let into our fucking warehouse." Vito absolutely sounds jealous and I kind of love it.

"Daddy had someone for me to torture while he was meeting with Sergio and Gabriella. Valeria and Matteo came down with them, so I brought them along."

Vito grumbles under his breath while Luca just shakes his head. "Are they where you got the idea for the cheerful walls?"

I nod. "Valeria says she has rooms set up for torturing instead of a warehouse. One is a white room—which I know we already use the individual rooms for—but she showed me pictures of her torture space and her walls are a pastel pink. That wasn't a happy enough color for me, so I went with yellow."

"Well, if it makes you happy, then I'm happy to work in the yellow room," Luca says as Vito heads towards one of the holding rooms to grab our victim. "Vito won't admit he's jealous, but he is, and so am I. I like to think of torture as something that's ours since we taught you—even though I know you've had to do it a lot on your own while we were away at school. But maybe you'll have some new tricks to teach us."

"Don't worry," I say as I lean into him. "Torture is our thing, but it got a little lonely with you away. I promise from now on, I won't play with anyone else except the two of you."

Luca's eyes dilate, and I bite down on my lip as I stare up at him. Things haven't quite gone back to normal between the three of us. Any time it's just the three of us, there's a tension in the room that isn't easy to ignore. I wonder if they think of that night as much as I do.

Luca leans toward me, eyes on my lips, and I wonder what it'll be like to kiss him. I've imagined it a million times, but I know my imagination won't live up to the real thing.

A grunt and the slam of a body hitting the table have us jumping apart. Turning around, I find Vito has dragged out our torture victim. He's already strapping him down, the unconscious man's limbs moving easily.

"It really is much easier when the two of you are here," I say, clearing my throat when I realize it's come out a bit hoarsely. "I always have to bring along a bodyguard because Daddy worries, but I always have them do the heavy lifting. The last one that came ended up puking everywhere. He's not allowed on Alessandra duty any longer."

Vito laughs. "Not everyone has the stomach for torture—even when they're not the ones doing it. And there are even fewer people who can deal with the way you torture, baby girl."

I preen under his proud words. I'm aware I'm a little fucked in the head, seeing as I love to torture people and that I love hearing the twins say how proud they are of my torturing skills.

But, hey. YOLO, am I right?

"Just you wait, V. I'm gonna blow your mind with what I can do."

"I'll just fucking bet." I barely catch Vito's muttered words, but it's enough to make me blush because I don't think he was talking about my torture skills.

"Well," I say brightly, trying to ignore the desire building inside of me. "If you boys will step out of sight. I enjoy letting them think it's just little me, who couldn't know a thing about torture, here. It makes it so much more fun when they realize just how scared they should be."

"I'm a little scared," Luca admits with a laugh as he drags Vito to a spot where they can watch, but the man won't be able to see them.

I shoot them a grin before grabbing some smelling salts and

running them under the man's nose. He jerks awake, trying to pull at his restraints before his eyes land on me.

I blink up at him, an innocent smile in place. "Hey, mister, are you alright?"

The man turns his head from side to side, trying to sit up and see if there's anyone else in the room. When he sees nothing, he turns back to me. "Where am I? What am I doing here?"

I shrug. "I don't know. Daddy had me in his office, but I got bored and wandered around. I found you like this."

"And who's your dad?"

"Riccardo Valentino."

The man's eyes go wide, and I can hardly hold back my glee at the instant fear I see there. But I have to because I really love this game.

"Please. You have to get me out of here. I did nothing wrong. I don't know why your dad has me here, but I'm just a dock worker."

I tap my finger on my chin as if I'm considering his words. "Hmmm... Daddy doesn't bring people here if they did nothing. Usually, he only brings wicked men here. How do I know you aren't a wicked man?"

"I promise, I'm not. It was just a case of being in the wrong place at the wrong time, I swear."

"For the women killed? It was definitely a case of them being in the wrong place at the wrong time. But for you, Davis? No." I let my crazy shine into my smile, and I swear the man visibly gulps. "It's not my Daddy you should fear, by the way."

I gesture for the twins to join me. "After all, it's the three of us that take care of the torturing. All those stories you've heard about the people my dad has tortured in the last four years? Yeah, that wasn't him. That was us."

Davis babbles, offering excuses and begging for mercy, but I just ignore him as I pull over my tray of goodies. I don't even bother putting them away anymore since it's usually just me here, but I guess I'll have to learn how to share the space again.

"Vito, would you mind getting him naked for me?" I ask over my shoulder as I set up my new favorite toy.

"Absolutely, princess." There's a swish in the air, telling me he pulled out a butterfly knife. When the man screams, I smile. Vito must have given him a few cuts while removing his clothes.

I drape the clamps over my arm as I turn back to watch Vito remove the last of Davis's clothes. Luca comes over and picks up a clamp with a frown. "Are these nipple clamps?"

Instead of answering him, I just grin and move to stand beside Davis once more. "Oops, looks like Vito got a little knife happy. I'd say I'm sorry about that, but I'm really not. You deserve everything we're going to do to you today. Daddy says I'm supposed to find out how you were getting information on the women you killed, but that it's not absolutely necessary. I think he knows that I just want to make you hurt. Because, yes, no matter what you do or don't tell me, you're dying today. It's the least I can do for those women."

"You crazy bitch," Davis screams in my face, which just makes my smile grow.

"I really am, and I enjoy it a lot. Though I don't think you're going to enjoy this nearly as much as I am." I grab one set of clamps, putting them on his nipples. He winces at the pain, and I roll my eyes. If he thinks that hurts, he's screwed for what's coming next.

I take the other set of clamps, which are bigger and quickly secure them on his balls. He screams like a damn baby. Why is it that the men who target women are always the biggest babies? Too bad for him, it's just going to get worse.

"Luca, would you be a doll and hand me that butt plug?"

Luca is laughing as he grabs the buttplug and hands it to me. "This is definitely creative, Alessa. I'm still not one hundred percent sold on it yet, but I'm definitely intrigued."

Ducking down, I shove the butt plug up Davis's ass—without lube, of course—grinning when Davis lets out a horrified scream. Then I turn around to face the twins. "Oh, this is just the beginning."

Not wanting to ruin the surprise, I grab the long length of chain and clip it to both sets of clamps and the buttplug. I hold up the end of the chain, ignoring Davis's pitiful whimpers and whines. "Got any guesses what I'm going to do with this?"

The twins glance at each other and then at my tray before shaking their heads. "I've got no fucking clue, Alessa, but I'm definitely looking forward to finding out," Vito says with a smirk.

I didn't actually expect that they'd know what I was going to do. I slide my tray over and lift the sheet that covers the cabinets beneath my tray. I hook it to the battery—this bitch is stronger than a car battery when turned all the way up—and grab the remote.

"I don't recommend touching Davis or the chains," I tell them with a smile before I hit the button that starts the electricity running through the chain at a relatively low rate. Davis's body jerks on the table, and I glance down to find I hadn't started at the lower voltage I thought I had. I turn it off, giving him a break since I really had meant to start lower. Davis lets out a groan as the electricity stops flowing. "Oops. Guess we're starting out strong."

"Jesus Christ, Alessa." Luca's eyes are wide as he turns to face me. "Did you just shock his nipple, balls, and up his ass all at once?"

I nod proudly. "I told you I learned some new tricks. Though, I usually start with a lower voltage. My bad."

Vito steps up behind me, pulling me firmly against him so I can feel how hard he is. "Baby girl, that was fucking hot and you're definitely going to share your new toy."

"I'll be happy to share it any time, V." I press the button again, my smile growing as I watch Davis's body twitch again and this time he even lets out a scream.

"How about you turn that off for now and let us play for a bit? Then you can use it some more." Vito grabs the remote, quickly cutting it off.

I pout as I look up at him. "Fiiiine."

"Brat," he mutters as he goes to pull away from me, but I grab ahold of him and roll my hips, so I move along his hard shaft trapped inside his pants.

"But you love it."

"Fuuuucccck." Vito's head comes to rest on the top of my head. "You're right. I like it a lot."

And once again I find myself in dangerous territory, so I duck out of his hold. My face is hot, and I know I'm blushing—not to mention my drenched panties—but luckily neither of the twins comment on it as I ask, "What should we do next?"

We're a month into summer before I run into James for the first time. It was bound to happen, and I'm surprised it took this long. That doesn't mean I don't completely freeze the moment my eyes land on him in the middle of the grocery store.

He's pushing a cart, following his mom, who is rambling about who knows what. He looks tired and a little beat down. His blond hair is dirty and his clothes wrinkled. The scruff he'd been sporting is now a full-blown beard, and I don't know how I feel about it.

I bite my lip, wondering if I can get away before they notice me.

"Alessandra!" Susanna calls out. "Oh, darling, I haven't seen you since your graduation."

She sweeps me into her arms, and it's obviously too late to get away, so I force a smile on my face. "Hi, Susanna. Yeah, I've been busy this summer. The twins are working for Daddy full time now, and I've been tagging along with them so I can learn the ropes a little better."

She frowns at that. "I hate the idea of you being involved in his business, but you're an adult who can make her own decisions." She glances over her shoulder at James, who is frozen in place as he stares at the two of us. Glad it isn't just me.

"James, get over here and say hello to Alessandra." Susanna sighs, rolling her eyes as she turns back to me. "I hope this isn't too uncomfortable. I know what happened and I know you broke up. But you've been friends for so long, it breaks my heart to see him like this. He's falling apart without you—and I'm not trying to guilt you into anything. He messed up, and I'm aware. But if you could at least say hi to him, it would make me feel better."

"Of course, Susanna," I say, fighting back tears. There's not much I wouldn't do for this woman and saying hello to James is something I can give her.

"Uh, hi, Alessa." James stutters through his words as he runs a hand through his dirty hair before he tries to straighten his clothes. I almost smile at the sight, but it doesn't quite make it to the surface.

"Hi, James." I nod, not knowing what else to say and not fully comfortable.

No one speaks for a few moments before Susanna lets out a sigh. "It was good seeing you, Alessa. Stop by the house any time you want. If you tell me when, I'll bake you some treats."

"And I can stay in my room or not be there," James offers.

I glance up at him to find him fighting tears. My own eyes fill again as I duck my head and nod. "I promise I'll do that, Susanna. I need to go now."

"Of course, Alessa." There's sadness in Susanna's voice that I choose to ignore. I can't deal with that right now. All I can do is focus on not sobbing in the middle of the grocery store as I rush outside.

Somehow, I make it to my car before I fall apart. Leaning forward against the steering wheel, I sob. I haven't really dealt with how I'm feeling after finding out about James's betrayal. I've been burying myself in the work we've been doing for my dad and ignoring it.

Not the healthiest of ways to handle it, and I should've known this moment would come. Hurt, betrayal, anger, love—they all race through me all at once, along with other emotions I can't even name. It's overwhelming and, of course, it's happening in the middle of the parking lot at the grocery store. Why would it happen somewhere more convenient?

Though, is there really anywhere convenient to have a break-down? I'm not sure there is.

A knock on the window has me gasping and jumping in my seat.

I swipe at my tears as I turn my head, not wanting anyone to see me like this.

"It's just me, Alessa. Open the door, yeah?"

"Luca," I sob as I throw open the door and jump into his arms.

"Shhh, it's going to be okay. Why don't we grab your stuff, lock up the car, and Vito will drive us home?"

"But..." I choke on my words. "How did you know?"

Luca glances to the side, and I follow the motion to find James standing there, tears streaming down his face before he hurriedly turns away. "James called me. He didn't think you'd want him to see you like this, but he was worried."

I can't even answer him as another rush of sobs takes over me. I don't like to see James crying and breaking apart. I don't want him to be broken. But I'm also not ready to forgive him.

Luca says nothing as he lifts me into his arms, calling out, "Grab her purse and stuff? I'm going to get her in the car."

I settle my head against his chest, eyes falling shut as I listen to his heart beating while I continue sobbing in his arms. The car must not have been far because within moments Luca is bending over, but instead of laying me into the backseat, he climbs in with me still in his arms.

My eyes open in time to see Vito pushing the front seat back and laying my stuff in the front seat. He gives me a soft smile that I'm more used to seeing on Luca's face than his before swinging the door shut.

After he climbs into the driver's seat, he turns around to face me. "I know it's hard to believe, but this will pass. Things will get better."

"But not if you keep holding it all inside." Luca presses a kiss to my forehead. "We haven't pushed you to talk about it, but that ends now. You need to deal with it. I can't stand seeing you like this—neither of us can."

"Okay," I choke out, squeezing my eyes shut again. "But later, please?"

"Later is fine, baby girl," Vito says, his hand coming to brush over my hair. "For now, let it all out. I'm going to drive us home, and then we'll both hold you until you're done falling apart. After that, we'll talk about it."

"Okay," I sniffle, burying my head further into Luca's chest. I don't want to talk about it, but seeing James has proven one thing to me—I *need* to talk about it.

CHAPTER 10

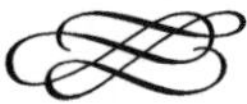

I close my eyes behind my sunglasses, enjoying the heat from the sun as I lounge on a float in the pool.

"Are you just going to sunbathe in the pool all day? Because that's going to be quite dull for Vito and me."

I turn my head to look at Luca and Vito standing beside my float. It's my eighteenth birthday, and Daddy gave us the day off. Since I'm still not big on birthday parties, we decided to have a low-key day at home. We watched a couple of my favorite movies this morning before heading out to the pool. We haven't been out here long, but I should've known they wouldn't be content to just lounge.

"You're both big boys. I'm sure you can find some way to entertain yourselves."

Vito smirks. "Oh, I can think of plenty of ways to entertain myself."

My eyes narrow, not liking the sound of that. Before I can respond, my float is tipping over, and into the water I go. I choke on the pool water, obviously not having been prepared for it, as I push myself to the surface.

I cough a few times as I tread water, annoyed that both twins are tall enough to touch the bottom of the pool and I'm not. "You're both dicks."

I swim to the edge of the pool, pushing my wet hair out of my face. Now I'm going to have to take a shower before we go to dinner tonight. Fuckers.

"Oh, come on, Alessa. We were just fucking around." Vito appears beside me, arm wrapping around my waist so I don't have to keep myself afloat.

"Well, douche canoe, I hadn't planned on getting my hair wet and now I'm going to have to shower before dinner. Which also means I'm going to have to blow dry my hair. All of that means less time in the pool for me."

Luca presses against my back, setting his chin on my shoulder. "We're sorry, Alessa. We thought it would be funny—"

"Which it was," Vito tacks on.

"Shut up, Vito, you're not helping." Luca sighs. "Forgive us, please. I don't want you to be mad at me on your birthday."

I sigh, leaning my head back to lie against him. "There is one way to make it up to me."

"Oh, yeah? What's that, brat?" Vito asks.

I grin at him. "Presents!"

"And who said we got you anything? Brats don't deserve presents."

"Yes, they do. And of course you got me something because you love me."

Vito makes a face but nods. "Fine. If we give you your presents now, will you stop being mad at us?"

I consider it for a moment before nodding. "Absolutely. Bring me presents."

They both laugh before Luca pushes me out of the water and helps me until I'm kneeling on the deck. I turn around just in time to see them both launch themselves from the pool, arm muscles bunching in a way that makes me want to lick them.

The pool probably wasn't the smartest idea. Oh, well. *C'est la vie* and all that. I climb to my feet, eyes never leaving them as I chew on my bottom lip. Why do they have to be so hot?

"See something you like?" Vito's voice breaks me from my thoughts. I flush as my eyes dart up to meet his eyes and then Luca's.

"Shut up. The two of you know you're hot. I'm going to shower and blow dry my hair. I expect presents to be waiting for me when I'm done."

I spin on my heel, heading for the house without waiting for a response. Vito mutters something, but I don't quite catch it. I'd stop to ask what he said if I didn't need so desperately to get away from them.

I take a quick shower, but blow drying my hair takes forever with how thick it is. It's almost an hour later when I make my way downstairs to find the twins in the living room. I'd thrown on a pair of shorts that are so short, my ass is almost hanging out and a t-shirt that belonged to one of the twins at some point before I stole it. I didn't bother to put on a bra because why wear one if you don't have to?

"Presents," I say, holding out my hands and wiggling my fingers.

Luca makes a face. "Presents will have to wait a bit. Your dad called, and he has a job for us."

"On my birthday?" I whine, pouting. "Isn't there someone else who can do it?"

"Unfortunately not." Luca stands up and I realize for the first time that they're both dressed in dark jeans and button-down shirts.

"I'm guessing it's not a torture session?"

Vito shakes his head. "No, this is more of an undercover thing to find out some information."

"What should I wear then?"

"As much as I hate to say it, something sexy. It might be easier for you to use your feminine wiles to get the information." Vito doesn't look happy about it at all, something that sends my stomach fluttering.

"Okay, I can do that. Be back in a flash."

I run back upstairs and into my closet, trying to figure out what to wear. I have plenty of sexy clothes, but I need to keep the heat in mind. I really don't feel like wearing a dress. The last thing I need is some douche trying to slip his hand under my dress while I'm trying to get information from him.

My go-to would be my black leather pants, but it's way too hot for that. An idea forms in my head, and I pull open some drawers until I find what I'm looking for. I got them last summer but haven't worn them yet. The black leather shorts are high waisted with ties criss-crossing up and down the sides, meaning I can't wear panties with them.

I grab a black band tee I altered into a crop top with the sleeves torn off that will show a hint of my bra—maybe I'll wear a red one. That'll be eye-catching. My high heeled over the knee boots pair nicely with the outfit. I throw on some makeup, including a smokey eye and bright red lipstick, and then I'm ready to go.

I hurry down the stairs to find the twins waiting for me. Vito's the first one to see me, and he shakes his head. "Nope. Go back upstairs and put something else on."

I just laugh, brushing past him. "I'm a grown-ass adult, V. I'll wear whatever the hell I want, and there's not a damn thing you can do about it."

"I could just throw you over my shoulder and bring you back upstairs."

"You could," I say as I glance over my shoulder. "But then I'd just come back down wearing the same outfit."

"Not if I stripped it off you and burned it." Vito cocks an eyebrow as if daring me to try him.

Not that I would mind if he stripped my clothes off, but there's no way I'm letting him burn them. I look good in this outfit, and he's not my boyfriend—even if he was, he wouldn't have a say in what I wear—so he can get the fuck over it.

"You look good, Alessa." Luca wraps an arm around my waist and starts leading me toward the door. "Vito is just going all alphahole on you. He can't help himself sometimes."

I snort when Vito growls behind us but says nothing. It's not until we climb into the car that I realize I don't know where we're going. "Where are we going and what information does Daddy need us to get?"

"He sent us an address and told us to text him after we're inside. Then he'll tell us what he needs us to find out." Luca rolls his neck before turning back to look at me. "Honestly, it's weird as fuck, but I looked up the address, and it's for some club, so who knows what he needs us to find out?"

"I guess going to a club on my birthday isn't so bad, but isn't it really early for heading to a club? Don't they usually open later?"

Vito laughs. "Yeah, usually, but maybe it's someone who works there. Or maybe there's a private party. Who knows? We tried to get more information, but he wasn't very forthcoming."

"That's a little strange."

"Yeah, no kidding." Vito shrugs. "We should be there in thirty, and then I guess we'll find out what the hell is going on."

I settle back into my seat. There's no point in worrying about it until we get there. Daddy usually has a reason for what he has us do. I'll just have to trust him, like always.

When Vito pulls up in front of the club, a valet appears out of nowhere and opens his door. Luca's door swings open a second later, leaving the three of us wondering what the hell is going on.

"Mr. Valentino is waiting inside for the three of you," the valet says when we don't get out of the car.

Luca and Vito hesitate for a moment before climbing out of the car. After Luca steps out, the guy who opened his door leans in to pop the passenger seat forward, but Luca lets out a growl and does it himself. He offers me his hand, and I allow him to haul me out of the car and into his side.

"I don't know what the hell is going on, but you stay by my side, okay?" Luca mumbles as Vito comes to stand on my other side.

I just nod, stomach turning as I wonder what the hell we're walking into. What is Daddy up to?

Two men man the double doors leading into the club and swing them open as we approach. We step into a dark hallway with an unmanned booth to one side. At the end of the hallway is another set of double doors, and it's well soundproofed because no sounds make its way to us.

The three of us march to the double doors before pushing them open.

"Surprise! Happy birthday!"

I jerk in Luca's arms as the chorus of yelling voices sound out. We're at the top of a short set of stairs, while Daddy and Teresa stand at the bottom, beaming up at us. My fingers seek Vito's, and he quickly intertwines them as I forget how to breathe.

I told Daddy I didn't want a birthday party, and he'd agreed, but I should've realized he gave in much too easily. Italians celebrate eighteenth birthdays like others celebrate fifteen or sixteen. Of course, he threw me a surprise party—which would be great if I wasn't terrified of having a birthday party after my fifteenth birthday, where I lost Lyla.

My breath is coming in pants now, my body shaking, and I'm frozen in place as images flash inside my head. Gunshots sounding and Vito's body covering mine. The fear that rushed through me as Luca took off with a gun in hand. My worry over James. Lyla's unmoving body lying on the floor, blood pooling beneath her.

"Fuck. She's having a panic attack," Luca murmurs as he lifts me in his arms and I bury my face in his chest. I can feel us moving down the stairs, but I can't catch my breath enough to tell them I need to leave, not go further into the club.

"Alessandra?" Daddy's voice is close, worry coloring his tone. "What's going on?"

I hear Vito snarl. "She told you she didn't want a party. Then you threw her a surprise party and didn't tell me or Luca. We could've at least prepared her if we'd known. If I had to guess? She's flashing back to the last birthday party she had where her best friend fucking died."

Tears stream down my cheeks as Vito and Daddy's voices drift away. Luca opens a door and steps inside. The noise muffles as soon as the door shuts behind us.

"Fuck. Alessa? Are you okay?" Luca scoffs as he tries to pull away from me, but I cling to his shirt. "Of course you're not okay. Come on, baby girl, I'm just going to set you on the counter."

I reluctantly release my hold on his shirt and allow him to do just that. As soon as my ass is on the counter, I pull him into me with my legs wrapping around his hips and my arms around his neck. I'm clinging to him like a koala as I try to extract myself from memories of my fifteenth birthday party.

Luca holds me close for a moment before tilting my head back so I'm staring up at him. "I need you to breathe with me."

I blink up at him, confused by what he's trying to tell me. I feel like I'm hearing his words through a fishbowl and I can't comprehend them. He gives me a soft smile and grabs one of my hands, lowering it to his chest. I feel his chest rise, hold for a few seconds and then lower.

Oh, breathing. Mine is still coming in pants, whimpers falling from my lips along with it. There are black spots floating around the edge of my vision, and I know I need to get it under control or I will pass out. I mimic his breathing until I no longer feel like passing out. It takes another few moments for my hearing to come back properly.

"That's a good girl. Just keep breathing. You're so strong, Alessa." Luca's words make me smile as I look up to meet his eyes again. "There's my girl."

I hear a snort behind Luca and glance around him to find Vito standing there. "Are you okay now?"

I nod at him before leaning back to lay my head against the mirror at my back. "What the hell was Daddy thinking?"

"That's what I want to know," Vito says with a growl.

I giggle. "Did he not tell you after you finished snarling at him?"

Vito shrugs. "I didn't exactly wait around to hear his answer. I wanted to make sure you were okay."

"As okay as I can be." I shake my head, sighing. "This is not what I wanted."

"Just say the word, and we're out of here," Luca tells me, hand stroking over my cheek.

I consider it for all of ten seconds before I shake my head. "No. Daddy went to all the trouble of planning this party. The least I can do is go out there and try to enjoy myself. Plus, Valentinos don't give up."

"No, they sure don't." Luca's hands move to my waist so he can lower me to the floor.

As soon as my feet hit the floor, I wrap my arms around his torso, laying my head on his chest. "Thank you for helping me, Luca."

"Always, baby girl, always." He presses a kiss to the top of my head, and I pull away.

I turn to the mirror and groan. I'd wrecked my makeup. Thank goodness, I always think ahead. Happy to see Luca held onto my bag, I grab it from him and pull out what I need to fix my face. Within five minutes, I'm back to normal, and besides the small tint of red to my eyes, no one can tell I'd fallen apart.

Spinning on my heel, I smile at the twins. "Welp, let's get out there. We have a party to enjoy."

"Yeah, right." Vito rolls his eyes but pulls me to his side. "If you need to leave at any point, just tell me or Luca and we're out of here."

"I will. I promise."

The three of us leave the bathroom to find my dad and Teresa waiting for us. Daddy rushes over to me, taking my face in his hands. "I'm so sorry, *bambolina*. I thought you were just being stubborn about not wanting a party. I didn't mean to hurt you."

"You haven't called me *bambolina* in years, Daddy." I give him a soft smile. "You don't need to worry about me. I'm not a little doll anymore. Definitely no more surprise parties. I really didn't want a party, but that's just my fear talking. I'm stronger than that so now that I've made a smashingly dramatic entrance, why don't we head out there so I can enjoy the party you planned for me?"

"You are so strong, Alessandra. I'm proud to call you my daughter." My dad kisses the top of my head before stepping back to offer me his arm. "Nothing would make me happier than escorting you to your party."

"*Amore mio*," he says as he turns to Teresa, "the twins will escort you in."

"Of course they can." Teresa shoots a smile in my dad's direction before sobering as she focuses on me. "I'm glad you're okay, Alessandra, and I'm sorry for the part I played in the surprise. I should have realized the trauma you would hold from what happened with Lyla."

"It's okay, Teresa. I know the two of you were coming from a place of love and it's not like I explained why I didn't want a party." I reach out to squeeze her hand as my dad leads us back into the club. I glance at Daddy's suit before glancing down at my clothes. "I think I'm underdressed."

Daddy laughs. "Not exactly what I would've suggested you wear, but considering the story I told the twins, I'm unsurprised. It doesn't matter what you wear, Alessandra, you're always beautiful. Just like your mama. She was like a chameleon, always able to adapt to new situations easily—just like you."

I hum, unsure of how to respond to that. It has been a while since my dad spoke of my mom. When I was younger, he would tell me stories of her often since I had no memories of her. As I grew older, the stories slowed before stopping completely when he met Teresa. I didn't realize how much I'd missed those stories.

"You stopped talking about her. Why?"

Daddy glances at me, letting out a sigh. "I didn't want to be disrespectful of Teresa, but that wasn't fair to you. We'll take a day off next week, and I'll tell you all the stories you want to hear."

"I'd like that, Daddy. Thank you."

Then we reach the club floor again, and people are surrounding us—some wishing me a happy birthday and others checking that I'm okay after my entrance. It's overwhelming, and I don't know where the twins are. Finally, the music starts playing and someone drags me away from the crowd of people.

Once we're free, I realize it's Stacy. I throw myself at her, hugging her tightly. "Thank you for saving me."

"You're welcome. I saw that look on your face and knew if I didn't do something quickly, you were going to give everyone another show." Stacy pauses, looking over me. "You look okay, but are you?"

"Okay enough," is my response. "Daddy and Teresa worked hard to put this together, I'm sure, so the least I can do is pretend to have a good time."

Stacy shrugs. "Or you could actually have a good time."

"That would be ideal, but I'm not sure if it's going to happen. I will try to have a good time, I promise," I reassure her when her mouth pops open.

She crosses her arms over her chest and nods. "I guess that's fine."

Rolling my eyes, I throw an arm around her shoulders. "Please tell me Daddy set up an open bar. That will help immensely."

"Then we're in luck because he sure did and they're not carding."

"Hell, yes! Let's go do some shots and then hit the dance floor." Grinning at my bestie, I realize I really want to enjoy my party. Just because I didn't want one doesn't mean I can't have fun, right? And what are the chances of someone shooting up my birthday party again?

With that cheerful thought, I drag Stacy to the bar for tequila shots.

I've got a good buzz going as Stacy and I tear up the dance floor. The alcohol has definitely kept me from remembering why I didn't want a party. It's still there, always in the background, but it's easier to ignore.

What's not so easy to ignore—my ex-boyfriend sitting at a table beside the dance floor, his eyes never leaving me. The pain doesn't hit me as hard this time. I've seen him a handful of times since that dreadful day in the grocery store, and each time has been easier. I no longer feel the need to cry just from seeing him and the hurt doesn't burn as deeply. I can tell he wants to talk, but I'm not sure if I'm ready for that. Though, can anyone really be ready for that kind of conversation?

"You should go talk to him," Stacy yells beside my ear.

I wince away from her loud voice, knowing that I wouldn't have heard her if she hadn't yelled, but damn. "I don't know if I'm ready."

I don't shout like she did, but she still seems to understand. "You are. Honestly? It'll probably make you feel better."

Stacy gives me a little push toward James's table, and there's no way to miss the hope in his eyes. I feel a little sick to my stomach about having this conversation with him, but we'll both be heading off to school soon. If not now, when?

He jumps up from his seat as I near him, a small smile on his lips. "Hey."

I don't hear his greeting, but since I can't seem to tear my eyes away from him, I'm able to figure it out easily enough. Stopping in front of him, I offer him my hand. He doesn't hesitate to take it, not even questioning what I'm doing.

There's no way I'm having this conversation here in the open, especially not since we'd have to scream at one another to be heard. Daddy told me they roped off the VIP area so no one could go up there, but that I could bring whoever I wanted up there. I assume it'll at least be quieter, so I head straight for the stairs leading up to it, pulling James along with me.

There's a man standing at the bottom of the stairs. He says nothing, just lifts the velvet rope blocking the entrance and steps aside. I drop James's hand because it's beginning to feel a little too familiar. Just because I know we need to have this conversation doesn't mean I'm planning to get back together with him. I still think this break is what we need. James needs this time to explore, and maybe one day we'll find our way back to each other.

I sigh in relief when I reach the top of the stairs, finding that the VIP area is actually a closed off room. Pushing the door open, I find it blissfully quiet. The same music from downstairs is piping through the room but at a much lower volume. There's a wall of windows along one side of the room that looks down at the club. I pick out Stacy's blond head from the dancers and smile.

James clears his throat, and I turn around to find him standing awkwardly just inside the door. "I like the new look."

I laugh. "Sometimes you just need to let go of the old and embrace the new, right?"

I hiss when James winces. "That's totally not what I meant. Fuck. Look, this conversation is going to be awkward as hell no matter what, so let's try to not take each other's words the wrong way, yeah?"

"I can try." James chuckles, but there's no amusement in the sound. "Why don't we sit down?"

I walk over to a booth and gesture for him to join me. We both settle on opposite sides of the table, just staring at one another.

"How have you—"

"What have you—"

We laugh together, and I feel more at ease. Sure, this is the man who broke my heart, but he's also been my best friend since we were children. There's a lot more between us now, but I know he'll always be a part of my life. I need him to always be a part of my life.

"Let me start, please?" James waits for my nod before continuing. "I know I fucked this up so bad. I've been tearing myself up for months. I don't know what the hell I was thinking by proposing to you. I knew what your answer would be, but I was just so desperate to keep you. But that never would've been fair to you. I regret so much about how I handled everything."

"I wish you would've told me about being bisexual." I hold up a hand when he tries to speak. "Let me finish. I could've been there for you while you were struggling, but I get it is something really personal and hard to share. I'd like to think if you'd come to me, we could've talked it through and maybe even tried an open relationship, but who knows how I would've reacted. I hate that you betrayed my trust and then tried to hide it, but I get it.

"I understand why everything happened, and I even understand where you were coming from. I'm working on forgiving you. I really am, but I'm not there yet. With that being said, I hate not having you in my life. This isn't me saying we should get back together. I still stand by what I said that day. I think you need time to explore that side of you and you can't do that when you're in a relationship. I don't know what this year will bring the two of us, but I'd like us to be friends. Friends who talk and text—who keep up with each other's lives. It's going to be hard for both of us, I know. I still love you and I always will—no matter what happens. I also believe that you can love more than one person at a time. This guy you met? Do you love him?"

There are tears in James's eyes as he stares at me. "Do you really want to have this conversation?"

"Want?" I snort. "Not especially, but if we're going to be in each other's lives, we need to have it."

"I don't love him—yet... but I think I could." James shakes his head. "Too bad I probably fucked that up, too."

I reach out to take his hand in mine. "Then fix it, or at least try to. I don't know what you've done to make you think you fucked it up, but a little groveling never hurts."

James snorts. "Yeah... I don't know if that'll be enough."

"All you can do is try. I want you to be happy, even if that's not with me. Will it be hard to see you happy with someone else?" I shrug as tears fill my eyes. "Probably, but that's something I can deal with. You need to be true to yourself, just like I do. We can't help who we love, but what we can do is not lie to the people we love. You can't ever lie to me again, James, or I'll punt you out of my life so fast your head will spin."

"Honestly, I'd do just about anything to stay in your life, Lessa. This summer has been miserable without you. I promise to never lie to you again. Even if the truth hurts one or both of us."

When I smile this time, it's genuine. "I promise to never lie to you, either. I think being honest with one another is the only way we'll ever find a way past this."

James sucks on his teeth, and it's obvious he wants to say something, but he remains quiet. I snort. "You're not being very subtle about wanting to say something. Just say it."

James winces. "I feel like by asking this, it's going to upset both of us."

"Do you want to know the answer?"

He nods slowly. "I think I need to know the answer."

"Then ask."

"Are you in love with the twins?"

That definitely wasn't what I thought he was going to ask. Fuck. I guess we're doing this too. I play with the ends of my hair as I nod. "Yes."

He takes a deep breath as he nods. "I thought so. Have you..."

"What? Slept with them?" I scoff. "I only kissed Vito once for like a second. But since we're being honest, it's coming. We've been fighting it for so long, and we're all single. I'd love for it to happen."

James winces, and I wrinkle my nose. "Too much?"

"No. I mean, yes, but I need to hear it. This won't be easy for either of us, but just like you want me to be happy, that's all I want for you. If the twins make you happy, then I hope the three of you can figure it out." James sighs, running a hand over his face. "Would it be okay if I hugged you?"

This question has me grinning and sliding from the booth. "Yes. I'd really like that."

James stands, pulling me into his arms. I wrap my arms around him, laying my head on his chest as I close my eyes. I've missed this so much. James gives the best hugs, and I could've used a few of those this summer. Too bad I was hurting too badly and so angry with him.

No, I won't focus on that right now. I'm going to focus on the present and future. If I want to have him in my life in some capacity, I need to let go of the past. Maybe not today or tomorrow, but sometime soon I'm going to have to let it go.

"What the fuck is going on here?" Vito's voice cuts through the room, and I wonder how I missed him entering.

James and I break apart, turning to see both twins standing there. Vito looks even more pissed than usual with a scowl on his face, but it's Luca's face that breaks me. Hurt paints his features as he refuses to meet my gaze.

They must think we've gotten back together.

James glances from the twins to me and then back again before holding up his hands. "I think it would be best if I left. In fact, I think I'm just going to head home. Thanks for talking to me, Lessa. It means the world to me. I'll text you tomorrow, yeah?"

"Sounds good. Thanks for coming, James." The entire time I speak to him, I keep my eyes locked on the twins. These assholes better not try storming out of here before letting me explain what they interrupted.

I mean, it was just a fucking hug. Why are their panties so twisted?

From the corner of my eye, I see James slide by the twins and duck out of the door, but still keep my attention locked on the twins. As soon as the door shuts behind him, I cock an eyebrow. "Why are you so pissed off, V?"

"That asshole broke your heart, and you're up here letting him paw at you? Of course, I'm pissed! We've been holding you together all summer, and you're just going to get back with him?"

I shake my head. "Who said I got back together with James, asshole? Maybe if you'd asked questions instead of making assumptions, you wouldn't be so angry right now."

"You were hugging him, Alessandra." Luca still won't meet my eyes as he speaks.

"And?" I lay my hand on my cocked hip. "I'm my own person. I can hug whoever the fuck I want."

"But that asshole?" Luca's eyes finally meet mine as he clenches his jaw.

I just raise my brows. "You mean, your friend?"

"Doesn't mean he isn't an asshole," Luca mutters, looking abashed as he drops his head.

Vito's face is red when he steps up to me, practically growling. "Are you really stupid enough to just forgive him? He fucking broke you. He doesn't deserve you."

"Oh? And who does?"

"We do!" He yells, throwing his hands in the air. "I know you're not stupid, Alessandra. Luca and I have been in love with you for years. We never made a move on you because it was inappropriate—you were underage and dating James. But we're the ones who held you when you cried your heart out over him breaking your heart. We're the ones who made sure you stayed busy. We're the ones you leaned on."

I bite my lip, blinking up at him. I really don't like that they keep calling me Alessandra, but I can't help smiling when I realize what he just admitted. "You love me?"

Vito's eyes get comically wide, telling me he hadn't meant to spill that secret. He just shrugs as his eyes fall away from me, obviously embarrassed.

"Hmmm... that's convenient, seeing as I'm in love with the two of you as well."

Vito's head jerks up, and I can see the hope in his eyes. With a grin, I throw myself at him, knowing he'll catch me. Hooking my legs around his hips, I press my lips to his. He opens his mouth under my assault until our tongues are dancing together and I feel Luca press against my back.

I break the kiss, turning my head to take Luca's lips. I love how they both kiss so differently. I lose myself in the kiss, rolling my hips against Vito as I seek friction to help the ache between my legs. Luca breaks the kiss, and I lean forward to kiss Vito again but freeze at Luca's words.

"We can't do this."

I struggle in Vito's arms when what Luca has said really sinks in. I need to get the hell out of here. There's no way I can deal with their rejection right now. Damn it, I came with them. How am I supposed to get home? James already left, and Stacy's been drinking. Tears fill my eyes as Vito finally sets me on the floor.

Shit. Shit. Shit.

I'm already darting for the door when a hand wraps around my arm. "No. Shit. That's not what I meant, Alessa."

Luca pulls me off balance, so I tumble into his arms. My chin quivers as I keep my head ducked low. He lifts my chin with his finger as he crowds me against the wall. "We can't do this *here*. I don't want to do this here. I want to take you home and spread you out on my bed while we pleasure you all night."

He brushes a kiss against my lips before leaning his forehead against mine. "We know what you taste like now, baby girl. There's no way we're letting you go now."

"Then what are we waiting for?" I ask, glancing at Vito over Luca's shoulder. "Take me home."

CHAPTER 11

After that, the twins whisk me out of the club as quickly as they can. We don't bother waiting for the valet, Vito just grabs the keys and tosses the valet a tip. The car is easy enough to find, and I'm climbing into the backseat within minutes.

"Scoot over, Alessa," Luca says, bending over to look at me.

"What? Why?"

"So he can see how many times he can get you to come before we get home," Vito offers from the front seat as he turns around to give me that signature smirk of his.

"Oh," I squeak but scoot over. Who the hell would say no to that?

Luca climbs into the backseat with me, pulling the door shut, but leaves the seat folded up. He's on me before Vito can even put the car into gear. This kiss is just as heated as our first.

His lips never leave mine as he pushes me back until I'm lying with my back on the seat. His fingers graze the hem of my shirt before pushing it up and only then does he break our kiss. He leans back as his big hands squeeze my tits through my bra.

"Fuck, I can't wait to see your naked tits. You've got amazing tits, you know that, right? I want to fuck them."

I giggle at the look on his face, and he pouts. "I don't think you're taking this seriously enough."

"And I don't think *you're* taking this seriously enough, brother. Get our girl off or we'll switch and you can fucking drive." I can't see Vito since I'm lying down behind him, but I'm sure he's shaking his head.

"Whatever." Luca ducks down, pulling my bra to the side and flicking his tongue over my already hard nipple. I was already wet, but now? I'm absolutely dripping. Not the best feeling when you aren't wearing panties and have leather pressing against your pussy.

I wiggle beneath him, trying to make myself more comfortable.

Luca pulls back to look at me with a frown. "Are you okay?"

"Ummm... I can't exactly wear underwear with these shorts and leather against a wet pussy isn't the best feeling."

I hear a grunt from the front seat. "Mmmm, say pussy again, baby girl."

"Uh... pussy?" I say hesitantly.

"It's not nearly as sexy when you say it like that," Vito complains.

"Just shut up and get us home. Let me worry about Alessa." Luca shakes his head. "I think I can help with that, baby girl."

Luca's hands slide down my sides until he reaches the ties on each side of my shorts. I open my mouth to explain how the ties work, but he already has them undone and sliding down my legs. Well, okay, then.

I expect Luca to climb back up after he pulls off my shorts, instead he ducks down between my thighs and runs his nose up my slit. He lets out a groan. "You smell delicious."

My cheeks heat at his words. I've never been with anyone besides James, and while he'd been okay at eating me out, he'd never been overly excited about it—not like Luca, who sounds like he's going to die if he doesn't get a taste of me. I wonder what other differences I'll discover between sex with James and the twins.

Luca sucks my clit into his mouth, and I gasp, back arching off the seat. He pulls back, flicking his tongue over and over. My fingers lock into his hair, trying to pull him closer when he pulls away. He's barely touched me and I'm already close to coming. I guess that's what happens with years of buildup.

Luca chuckles when I try to redirect him to my clit. "Don't worry. I'll take care of you. I know what I'm doing down here, I promise."

I huff but loosen my grip. He dips down further, his tongue sliding between my folds and holy shit that feels good. James never fucked me with his tongue, and it's an entirely new experience.

Fuck, I need to stop thinking about James.

Luca continues to fuck me with his tongue, and it feels amazing. I roll my hips to meet the thrust of his tongue. I'm practically riding his face—not that he seems to mind if his groans are anything to go off of. When his thumb finds my clit, it sends me right over the edge.

"Fuck!" I scream, my fingers tightening in his hair as I squeeze his head between my thighs. My body shakes, and I grind against his face until I come down.

Realizing he might need to breathe, I jerk my legs apart and pull his face away from me. "I'm sorry, Luca. I wasn't trying to suffocate you."

"I wasn't done," is all he says before diving back between my legs. Vito's chuckle sounds through the car as Luca continues to lap at my juices before turning his attention to my clit. He slides two fingers into my pussy while he sucks on my clit and I don't know how he expects me to come again already.

I try to explain that to him between pants and gasps, but he just ignores me. And makes me come two more times on his fingers and tongue. He's gasping as he pulls away. I can't even get my body to move, so I just watch as he swings his head around to look at Vito. "How much longer until we make it home?"

"About ten minutes."

"Good." Luca bends down, scooping me into his arms before he settles back on the seat. He sits me on his lap, facing the front of the car and pulls my shirt back up, yanking the cups of my bra away from my tits. "We're going to give Vito a show, baby girl. I can't wait until we're home to be inside of you, so you're going to ride my cock. Vito can watch your tits bouncing as you take what you need."

I mewl at the picture he's painting. I lift on my knees, glancing between my legs. "Undo your fucking pants."

Luca doesn't hesitate to undo his pants. He shifts to slide both his jeans and boxer briefs down his hips enough to free his cock. It slaps against his stomach, and I lick my lips.

Of course he's got a big dick—not that I'm complaining.

I reach back and take his cock in my hand, stroking it a few times before lining it up with my pussy. I sink down slowly, head falling back as I let out a moan at the stretch. It takes a bit of work to take him all in, but when I do, I'm rewarded with a kiss.

"You take my cock so good, baby girl. Now, let's give Vito a good show, yeah?"

"Yes," I cry out, already moving up and down his cock. I catch Vito's eyes in the rearview mirror and reach up to tweak my nipples.

Luca lets me ride him at my own speed for a few minutes before his hands tighten on my hips. "Okay, baby, I'm going to help you out now, okay? We only have a few minutes until we get home and I want to make sure we both come before then. I want you to work your clit for me."

"Okay."

Luca lifts my hips before slamming me down on him as he thrusts up. He hits a spot that has me seeing stars and keeps hitting it as I bring my hand down to work my clit like he told me to.

"Fuck, Luca. You should see the way her tits are bouncing with how hard you're fucking her. It's so fucking hot. Baby girl, I'm so hard for you right now. I want to fuck my hand while I watch you, but I'm afraid I'll crash the car."

I moan at Vito's words, feeling my orgasm building up fast as Luca fucks me hard and fast. The car comes to a stop, and my eyes pop open, finding that we're sitting outside the house. Luca adjusts my hips, and his next thrust sends me spiraling.

Luca groans as my pussy squeezes him, his name falling from my lips like a prayer.

"I'm going to come, Alessa. God, I love you." Three thrusts later and he's coming inside of me.

Vito has turned in his seat as he strokes his cock, eyes on me. Pulling off Luca, I lean forward so I can suck Vito's length into my mouth.

"Oh, fuck. You don't have to—" Vito moans, hips stuttering as he pushes his cock further down my throat. "Your mouth feels like heaven. I'm not going to last."

I pull off his cock and shoot him a smile. "Come for me, V. I want your cum filling my mouth."

"Oh, Jesus," he murmurs as I return to sucking his dick, going as deep as I can and swallowing.

"Jesus can't save you now, brother," Luca says with a laugh.

But Vito doesn't answer, since he's too busy coming down my throat. I swallow down everything he offers before pulling off his cock and licking my lips. "Yum."

"Alright, we need to get inside immediately," Luca says, pushing me forward into Vito so he can reach the door handle.

I grab the back of Vito's head and pull him in for a kiss. I know he has to be tasting himself on my lips, but he doesn't seem to care. I'm ripped away from the kiss by Luca, who's dragging me from the car.

"Wait! My shorts!"

"I've got them." Vito holds them up so I'll stop struggling in Luca's arms.

"But I'm still naked."

Luca laughs as he jogs toward the house. "Actually, you're only half naked, but don't worry, there's no one around to see you."

I squeal when he tosses me over his shoulder. I try to brace myself on his thighs but give up and decide to bite his ass instead.

Luca stumbles for a second before bringing his hand down on my ass. "Bad girl. You're going to make me drop you doing things like that."

I just giggle as he pushes open the front door and I lift my head to find Vito has already caught up to us. Luca doesn't put me down, thundering up the stairs with Vito hot on his tail.

"Ummm... should we really have come home for this? What if our parents come home?"

"Well, sweet girl," Vito says, and I lift my head so I can look at him while he talks. "When we moved in, we had your dad soundproof our rooms. Even if they come home, they won't know what we're up to. Well, they might have an idea that we're with someone, but they won't know it's you."

Soundproofed rooms? What the hell? I wish Daddy would have soundproofed my room. It definitely would have made things a lot less awkward for me and James, because I'm pretty sure everyone in this house has heard us having sex at one point or another.

Fuck, I'm doing it again. I can't keep thinking about James while I'm with Luca and Vito. That's not fair to any of them. It's just hard for me to not compare my time with James to now, since he's the only person I've ever had sex with.

"You okay down there?" Vito asks with a frown. "You look like you're thinking awfully hard."

I shake my head. "No. Just getting lost in my head. We all know how much I love doing that."

"That we do," Luca says with a laugh, his hand coming down on my bare ass again.

"Stop it, Luc," I squeal. It's not that I mind him spanking my ass —in fact, I like it very much—but we've barely made it up the stairs. One of the staff could come across us at any moment. I don't even know how we'd explain this away since I have nothing on my bottom half.

I sigh in relief when Luca pushes open the door to his room and steps inside without us having run into anyone else. Suddenly, I'm airborne. I bounce on the bed before sitting up and glaring at Luca.

"I'd appreciate a warning next time, asshole."

Luca just laughs as he pulls off his shirt. His hands drop to his pants, and my eyes search out Vito. I find him already naked and moving toward the bed. I rip my shirt over my head, reaching behind me to unclasp my bra before throwing it who knows where.

"I was planning on doing that," Vito says as he crawls up on the bed.

"You were too slow." I shrug, knowing I'm being a brat.

"Such a brat." Vito pushes me back onto the bed, laying his body atop mine as he kisses me. It's easy to lose myself in his kiss. His cock is already hardening again when he pulls back to look down at me. "You're fucking gorgeous."

"So are you." I turn my head to find Luca lying beside us. "Both of you are."

"Of course we both are—we're identical." Luca winks at me as Vito pumps his hips, gliding his cock between my wet folds and bumping my clit with each pass.

I moan, my head rolling back to rest on the pillow. It doesn't take long for my hips to begin moving, meeting each of Vito's thrusts. "Fuck me, V. Please."

"I will. Just as soon as you come again." Vito licks his lips. "Luc, why don't you help our girl come? Lick those pretty nipples of hers?"

"Hell, yes!" Luca moves closer and takes one of my nipples into his mouth. His hand moves to the other, twisting and pinching it between his fingers. Having both of them touching me like this is too much, and I come hard.

"That's our girl," Vito purrs. He rolls over onto his back, taking me with him so I'm straddling him as Luca moves to press against my back. "Have you done anal before?"

I frown, wondering why he's asking. "A few times. Why?"

Luca trails his lips along my neck. "Well, there's two of us and we each have a cock. We enjoy fucking girls together, which means one of us in the ass and one in your cunt."

"Will both of you fit?" Because I certainly don't see how they could.

Luca chuckles. "Oh, yeah, baby. We can both fit. That's if you want us to."

Do I want them both to fuck me at the same time? Hell yeah, I do. If they say it's possible, I believe them.

I nod slowly. "Yeah, I want that."

"Good girl," Vito says, sending a shiver up my spine. "Luc, grab the lube."

"On it."

Vito's hands tighten on my hips before he lifts me up and settles me over his cock. "You're going to ride me while Luca gets your ass ready. Then when he's ready, we'll hold still until he's inside you and then we're both going to fuck you."

My pussy clenches down on nothing. Feeling desperate, I reach down and take Vito in hand before lowering myself onto his length. We both hiss as I take him completely inside of me. I hesitate when I feel Luca climb back on the bed, but Vito helps guide my hips.

"Don't worry about him. You just worry about riding my cock."

I nod, letting my eyes fall shut as I move up and down his dick. I love the way he fills me up just right. When I feel Luca's hand on my ass, his finger rubbing against my puckered hole, I keep moving.

"That's it, baby girl. Just keep riding Vito's cock. We're going to make you feel so good." Luca's words make me flutter around Vito's dick, pulling a groan from him. Luca laughs before pushing a finger inside of me.

I let out a dirty moan as he pushes it even further inside of me. I might not have done anal all that often, but I kind of love it. Luca fucks me with his finger, quickly adding a second.

"Oh," I cry out. "I feel so full."

"Wait until you have both of our cocks inside of you." Vito smirks, waggling his eyebrows at me. I slow my movement as Luca works his fingers inside of me. I keep the slower pace as he stretches me out until I just can't take it anymore.

"Give me your cock, Luc. Please."

Luca's fingers pause their movement while Vito just laughs. "You heard her, Luc. She's tired of your fingers."

"It'll be my pleasure," Luca whispers against my neck before pushing me forward to lie on Vito. I hum, enjoying Vito's arms around me—even though it means we've had to pause our activities.

I can't wait to find out what it feels like to have two cocks inside of me. Obviously, I've imagined it before, but there's no way I could know what it really feels like. I've watched porn and read some smutty fiction that included it, but this isn't really something you can understand without doing it.

Then Luca's back, his cock pressing into me. I relax until he slips inside of me. Oh, fuck. He's barely inside of me, and I can tell this is going to be overwhelming. Luca works himself further into me, and I feel so stretched, so full, and he's still not finished.

"Fuck," I hiss.

Luca freezes. "Do you need me to stop?"

"If you stop, I'm going to stab you."

Vito laughs, causing me to clamp down on both of them. They both groan before Luca continues pushing inside of me until his hips are flush against my ass.

"Fucking finally," Vito murmurs before lifting his head to kiss me. "Do you need a minute or—"

"Fuck me. Both of you. Now."

"Yes, ma'am," Luca murmurs before doing just as I asked. The two of them alternate, one pulling out while the other thrusts back into me and it's all too much. Within a handful of thrusts, I'm falling apart on both of their cocks. As soon as I've come back down, they move together so that I'm either really full or way too empty.

I can't focus on anything but the sensations racking my body. The way my nipples drag across Vito's chest, the way he rolls his hips to make sure my clit rubs against him with each thrust. I feel like I'm floating in sensations, another orgasm building and building.

When Luca's arm snakes between me and Vito, pinching my clit, there's nothing I can do but fall apart. I scream both of their names as the best orgasm I've had in my life rushes through me. They both come together, or at least close enough together that I can't tell who came first. Their cum is hot as it paints my walls—in both the front and back. That's going to be messy.

Both twins call out my name, and it's the last thing I hear before I black out. I don't know how long I'm out for, but when I come to, I'm on my back, and one of the twins is between my legs, wiping up the mess they made.

"There she is."

I turn my head to find Luca lying beside me, his elbow bent so his head lies on his hand. "Yup, here I am."

My voice is a little hoarse, telling me I had probably overdone it on the screaming. "You're sure no one could have heard us, right?"

"Even with as loud as you were screaming, no one would've heard you," Vito says with a laugh as he looks up from between my legs. "I promise. Hell, our parents probably aren't even home yet."

I nod, eyes feeling heavy. "You wore me out."

"Well, seven orgasms is a lot." Vito sounds smug as he throws the washcloth into the laundry basket before settling on my other side.

I hum my agreement. It really is a lot. "I should probably go back to my room before the parentals show up."

"Nope." Luca pulls me to him until he's spooning from behind. "We're not even remotely close to being done with you."

Vito scoots closer, hitching my leg up and over his with a laugh. "But we should probably sleep now. You'll need the rest for when we wake you up and do it all over again."

Heat rushes through me even as my pussy yells at me. "A nap sounds good," I say, eyes already falling shut. "I love you both."

Vito's lips brush against mine. "I love you too, Alessa."

"I love you, too, baby girl," Luca murmurs against my ear.

And that's how I fall asleep with a smile on my lips, snug between the two men I thought I could never have.

~

I WAKE UP SLOWLY, blinking against the light filtering in through the window. Wow, I haven't slept that well in a while. I smile as I realize I'm still sandwiched between the twins. Vito's wrapped around my back, his cock hard against my ass. My head is pillowed on Luca's arm, and his head rests atop mine. His legs tangle with mine, and when I try to move, I feel his hard cock as well.

I guess guys aren't lying when they talk about morning wood. Which gives me some ideas about how I can wake them up. After all, they'd both woken me up many times throughout the night with their cocks inside of me.

Wait. Fuck.

Glancing at the alarm clock beside the bed, I see it's after ten. I shouldn't have fallen asleep in Luca's room—no matter how soundproofed it is. There's no way Teresa and Daddy aren't up yet. Sure, their bedroom is on the other side of the floor, but if either of them came looking for me and I wasn't in my room? What am I supposed to tell them? There's no way I can tell them I was fucking the twins all night. That won't go over well—of that, I'm absolutely certain.

I extract myself from their arms as I try to form a plan. I'm going to have to leave the room. If Daddy or Teresa come knocking on the door, they'll easily be able to tell what happened. We'll have to break the news to them eventually, but I'm not ready for that. How can I be? We'd admitted we loved one another, but we hadn't talked about what this meant. I'd definitely prefer to do that before our parents find out.

Climbing from the bed, I hunt for my clothes. My shirt is destroyed, and my bra is missing. There's no way I'm going to put those shorts back on. They'll be sticky as hell from when I had them on in the car. And since I hadn't been wearing panties, I don't even have those to slip on.

Spotting the button down one of the twins wore last night, I grab it and pull it on. Glancing in the mirror after I finish buttoning it up, I realize it hits me mid-thigh. As long as I don't bend over, I'll be fine.

All I have to do is sneak across the hall to my room. That shouldn't be too hard.

Turning to look at the twins once more, I smile. Maybe I should wake them up? I chew on my lip before deciding against it. I'll come wake them up once I've gotten cleaned up in my room. Then we can talk about what exactly this means and how we're going to handle it all.

With a final nod to myself, I open the door and slip into the hallway.

"What the fuck is going on here?"

I freeze at the sound of Teresa's voice. Turning slowly, I find her standing outside my bedroom door.

"Why are you coming out of Luca's room dressed like that?" There's anger in her eyes as she shuffles across the hallway until she's standing in front of me. "Please tell me you didn't sleep with your brother?"

"Stepbrother," I hiss. "We're not blood related."

"And you think that makes it okay? It doesn't. I told those fucking boys to stay away from you. This can't happen. I won't allow it."

I scoff. "You won't allow it? The three of us are adults, and we can make our own decisions. You don't get a say in it."

"The three of you..." Teresa trails off, pushing open Luca's bedroom door. Her hand covers her mouth as she sees both of the twins lying naked in the bed. Shaking her head, she pulls the door shut before grabbing my wrist and dragging me across the room to my bedroom.

"Let me go!" I try to shake off her hold, but she digs her nails into my skin, not letting go until we're both in my room with the door shut behind us. "I don't know who the fuck you think you are, dragging me around—"

"Shut your mouth, Alessandra, and listen to me. There's a reason I told those boys to stay away from you. I should've realized they wouldn't listen, but I'm trying to save their damn lives."

That brings me up short. "What are you talking about?"

"I'm talking about the fact that when your dad married me, we made an agreement. He'd bring the boys into the business and treat them like they were his own, so long as they stayed away from his precious princess."

I shake my head, not believing her. "That doesn't sound like Daddy. Not to mention, he's been the one pushing us to work together ever since the summer I turned fifteen."

"Yes, because he wants them to work for you. He wants them to support you if you decide to become head of the family. You're female, so he's allowing you the choice of whether you do so. If you were a male? You'd have no choice. That was the other part of the agreement. If you chose to not be involved, the twins would run the family." Teresa shakes her head, tears falling down her cheeks. "But if he finds out that they both slept with you? He'll have them killed."

I consider her for a moment before shaking my head. "No, he won't. First of all, it's not just sex. I love them, and they love me. We're going to be in a relationship. Daddy never interferes with my love life, and this will be no different."

"Oh, you sweet, naive girl. Even with as much as you know about the business, you still think your dad is soft." She snorts. "I wish this world worked the way you think it does. You don't have to believe my words. I can prove it to you."

I scoff. "And how are you going to do that?"

"You don't think I could marry your dad without signing a contract, do you? I'll show it to you. It's all there in black and white. Come with me."

"Where are we going?" I ask, not immediately following her.

"To my room. I have a copy of the contract in a safe."

"Don't you mean yours and Daddy's room?"

Teresa laughs before sighing. "You really do have blinders on, don't you? Riccardo and I don't share a room. We never have. This was a marriage of convenience. Your dad needed a wife and backup heirs, and you needed a mother. My previous husband was a part of the family too, just not high up. He owed some people a lot of money when he died, and since the boys were old enough, they were planning to make them work off the debt. Your dad offered to pay it off, and he'd make sure we lived in the luxury we had before my husband started gambling it all away."

I shake my head because it makes no sense. She's talking about the man who'd told me just last night that he hadn't wanted to talk about my mom since marrying Teresa because he thought it was disrespectful of his wife. I can't coincide the picture of a cruel man Teresa is trying to paint for me with the man who raised me.

"Show me."

Without another word, Teresa leads me towards the wing that houses their room—or rooms, I guess, if what Teresa is telling me is true. She leads me past Daddy's bedroom to the room next door. I follow her inside, admitting to myself it looks lived in.

Teresa swings a picture away from the wall, revealing the safe—something that doesn't even make me blink. We have safes like this hidden all over the house. Daddy runs one of the five mafia families in the area, so of course we do. She pulls a folder and what looks like a recorder from the safe, nodding for me to join her at the table on one side of the room.

"I have more than the contract as proof," she says, holding up the recorder. I nod for her to play it, and she does.

"Would you state your name and that you agree to the recording?" A male voice I don't recognize filters from the speaker.

"I, Riccardo Valentino, agree to have this meeting recorded."

"I, Teresa Colletti, agree to having this meeting recorded."

"Excellent. For the record, I am Nico Romano and I am a lawyer, working with both parties for an agreement on a marriage contract." The lawyer clears his throat. *"You've both had time to review the contract?"*

Both Daddy and Teresa give affirmative responses.

"And are there any questions or concerns from either party?"

"I did have a question," Teresa's voice is hesitant.

"Of course, that's why we're having this meeting."

"In the section about my boys, I understand most of it. They're to start training with you immediately so that you can train them to either take your place when you retire or work directly under Alessandra. That I get." There's a pause. *"The part I don't get is this clause here. It says Vito and Luca are only allowed a pre-approved relationship with Alessandra?"*

Daddy clears his throat. *"Alessandra is still very young, but she will marry James Adams when she's of age. It is something that I arranged with his father when they were young. The two of them are practically inseparable, so I don't expect any resistance from either of them. Your boys are older and attractive. I would be surprised if my princess didn't develop a crush on them. But even if it is mutual, they must not act on it. It would be inappropriate, and I will not allow my daughter to deal with the things that would be said about her having relations with her stepbrothers. Not to mention what it would do to her and James's relationship."*

"And what would happen if something did happen? I don't expect it to. I just prefer to know all outcomes."

It's the lawyer who speaks next. *"If any of the terms in the contract are broken, it will be immediately nullified, and the twins will be removed from the family."*

"Removed from the family? But that means—"

"Yes, we're all aware of what it means, Teresa. If you don't think you can keep your boys away from my daughter, then we shouldn't bother moving forward."

"No, I can make sure that won't happen. Will they be allowed around her at all?"

"Of course. They'll be her brothers. I will begin their training at the same time I begin hers."

"Okay, then I'll sign. Thank you for answering my questions."

Teresa turns off the recorder, lifting her eyebrows. "Do you believe me now?"

I bite my lip, wondering how I've missed this side of my dad. What did he mean when he said that he arranged it with Ted? Holy shit, is this the arrangement they argued over? They never would explain it to me or James.

"I do, and I see what you're saying, but me marrying James is no longer a given. I think Daddy would understand."

"I don't think he would. Your dad has a plan for you—even if he hasn't filled you in on it. And my boys? They're just spares. I know he cares for them, but it won't matter." Teresa drops her head in her hands for a moment and when she lifts it again, her eyes are pleading.

"Please, Alessandra, they're all I have left. You're leaving in just a few weeks for school, and you've already seen what long distance can do to a relationship. I'm begging you to let them go. Don't put their lives in danger. I couldn't stand it if something happened to them."

Squeezing my eyes shut, tears stream down my cheeks. I can't deny the words I heard my dad say. While he hadn't come right out and said it—obviously, since he was being recorded—he implied he would kill them if we became romantically involved. I'd love to say he would change his mind after four years, but I can't. I can't because I don't know this side of my dad. It's a side I've never seen, and I'm terrified.

"I don't want them to get hurt because of me," I murmur. "But what am I supposed to do? What's done is done."

"You could leave. Right now. I'll call and get the jet ready for you. You can take Stacy wherever you want. Just stay away until you head to school. Then, when you're home for Christmas break, it will all have blown over."

I snort. "Yeah, I don't think five months is going to make much of a difference. What the hell am I supposed to say to them?"

"Nothing. You can't say a word to them. I know my boys, and they'll say fuck it and take their chances with your dad. We can't let them do that. Go. Pack a bag. Leave immediately and don't answer when they call."

For the second time this summer, my heart is splintering. I don't want to walk away from them. I love them, but I don't know how Daddy will react because I don't think I really know him at all.

I can't take that chance—not when it's their lives we're talking about.

"Okay." I stand up, nearly knocking over my chair in my rush. "I'll throw some clothes into a suitcase and call Stacy on the way to pick her up. I don't know how much longer they'll sleep, so I need to leave now. You'll have to pack up my room and have everything shipped to the apartment. I'll send you a list or something."

"Thank you, Alessandra. I know this hurts right now, but it's for the best."

I shake my head at her. "I really don't think it is, but I won't gamble with their lives."

Without another word, I rush from the room and back to mine as quickly as I can. I can barely see what I'm throwing in the suitcase through my tears, but within ten minutes, I've packed as much as I can. I'm sure I've forgotten some things, but it's not like I don't have a credit card to buy anything I've forgotten.

I hesitate before leaving my room. I know Teresa said I couldn't have any contact with them, but I'll be damned if I leave without a word. Setting my bags down, I scribble out a quick note. With it in hand, I grab my bags and set them outside my door.

I hope they're not awake because if they try to stop me; I don't think I'll be able to walk away. I'm just not that strong. I can't even seem to get myself to stop crying. I'll have to have a driver take me to Stacy's because there's no way I can drive in this condition. Looking at the note once more, I bend over and slide it under the door.

Pressing a kiss to my fingers, I touch the door before hurrying over to grab my bags and get the hell out of here. As I clamor down the steps, all I can think about is the note—wondering if it's enough and knowing it's not.

I'm sorry. I wish things could be different.

EPILOGUE

May 2023

Leaning back in my chair, I run my hands over my face with a sigh. I'm about to give up on studying. Tomorrow is my last final, and I'm reaching the point where I don't think I can stuff anything else into my brain. Senior year is no joke, but after tomorrow it's all over. The only thing I'll have after that is graduation. And then I'll need to figure out what I'm going to do with the rest of my life.

My phone rings, and I answer it without glancing at the screen. "Hello?"

There's a moment of silence, and I'm just about to pull the phone away from my face to see who called me when I hear his voice.

"I honestly didn't think you'd answer."

My stomach falls, and my hand tightens on the phone. Why is Vito calling me? Why didn't I check to see who was calling?

"V? Why are you calling me?"

"You need to come home. Now." Vito sounds just as brutish as ever.

I snort, biting the inside of my cheek to keep from snapping back at him. "Why? You know what? It doesn't matter. I'm studying for my last final that's in the morning. I can't do this with you right now."

It's been four years since I've seen the twins. And almost as long since I've seen my dad or Teresa. Why is he calling me now?

Fuck. It doesn't matter. I don't have the time or patience to deal with him right now. I'm already pulling the phone away to hang up when his words catch my attention again.

"Damn it, Alessandra. Do you think I'd be calling you if I didn't have to? You made yourself very clear four years ago that you wanted nothing to do with us." He swears. "Look, I wouldn't be bothering you if I didn't have to be. We need you home as soon as possible."

"Vito, there's nothing for me there. My dad already knows I plan to take the summer for myself. I'll be back in the fall."

"Fuck. Why are you so fucking stubborn? I didn't want to do this over the phone. You have to come home because my mom and your dad are dead."

The phone falls from my grasp, hitting the floor. I can hear Vito's voice filtering from it, but my mind is fuzzy. My dad is dead? He can't be. I just talked to him this morning.

"Alessandra!! Alessa!! Fuck. Baby girl, please answer me!!"

I shake my head as Vito's words finally penetrate the fog and I grab my phone once more. My voice shakes as I ask, "Did I hear you, right? Teresa and my dad are dead?"

"Yes. Fuck, I'm sorry. I didn't want to tell you over the phone, but you weren't listening to me. Are you okay?" Vito curses. "Of course you're not okay."

"I need you to tell me what happened. I just talked to my dad this morning. What happened? How..."

"How did he die?" Vito sighs. "Someone put a hit out on him. We knew that someone was targeting him and we tightened security, but somehow we missed this and didn't get there in time. I'm sorry."

I shake my head before realizing he can't see it. "Don't put that on yourself, V. If there was a hit out on him, then these were professionals. There wasn't much you could have done."

"It's time for you to come home, Alessandra. It's time for you to take your spot as head of the family."

I almost drop my phone again. I still don't know if I want to be head of the family. Being away from it all these last four years—being away from them—made me realize there could be more to my life than the mafia. Finding out that my dad wasn't the man I thought he was, changed everything. Things haven't been good between the two of us since I went home that first Christmas.

I'd confronted him about what Teresa had told me. He didn't deny any of it, just sat there staring at me blankly before asking me what I expected. Apparently, arranged marriages are still a thing, and he expected me to marry James. Even after he broke my heart, my dad expected me to forgive and forget. Regardless of what I wanted.

My dad's the one who broke my heart that day. It's the day I stopped calling him Daddy because I wasn't a little girl anymore. I'd stalked out of the house and headed back to campus, refusing to speak with my dad for months. I haven't been back to the house since that day. I even stopped speaking to James because there was no way I was being forced into a marriage if it wasn't what I wanted.

Occasionally, I still feel bad for never explaining things to the twins and James. I know my silence has hurt them. God, this is all such a fucking mess that I'm not prepared to deal with.

"Alessa?"

"Sorry, V. As you can imagine, this is a lot to take in at once. I have to take my final in the morning. I'll pack up what I need and throw it in the car so I can head straight there when I finish." I hesitate. "I'm sorry about your mom, V. Are you okay? And Luca?"

He snorts. "We're about as okay as you are. We'll see you tomorrow."

Without another word, he disconnects the call, and that's when the tears start falling. With my dad dead—I still can't believe he's dead—there's no choice for me any longer. I'll have to take my place as the head of the family and with only half the training I should have gotten.

On top of that, I have to face the twins again. Fuck, I'm probably going to see James again, too. I don't know what he ended up doing after he finished college. I hurt all of them when I left and stopped answering their calls and texts, but it's what had to happen. Teresa had been right about the twins and me. The three of us couldn't happen. My dad would've had them killed, and sadly, James was an unwitting player in it all, and I just couldn't deal with it.

But he's dead. So what's going to hold you back now?

I push that thought away because it doesn't fucking matter. What matters now is finding out who the hell put a hit out on my dad and make them pay. I won't even have time to grieve my dad and stepmother properly. Let alone, get a grasp on emotions with everything left so unresolved with my dad.

One thing at a time.

Right now, it's time to pack up the essentials and then go to bed. I'll take my final in the morning before making the five-hour drive home. The twins will have already started looking into it, and we'll make a plan from there.

Fuck, I can't believe my dad is dead.

The End

~

ENJOYED THIS STORY? Want to read more about these characters? Pre-order Wickedly Depraved, releasing on September 10, 2023.

ABOUT MIRANDA MAY

Miranda is a new author who has been writing since high school, but never considered being published until now. When she discovered reverse harem books, she knew it was time to share her stories. She has plans to write paranormal romance, urban fantasy, omegaverse, and contemporary—all reverse harem/why choose/polyam stories.

Growing up a Navy brat, Miranda has lived in many places. She currently makes her home in Piney Flats, TN with her husband and adorable corgis, Luna and Trixie. Don't worry if you've never heard of it, it's a teeny tiny town less than an hour from the Tennessee/Virginia border. When not writing, Miranda spends most of her time reading or playing Dungeons and Dragons like a true geek. She also has an almost unhealthy obsession with corgis—so don't be surprised if she brings them up.

JOIN MIRANDA MAY ONLINE

Check out my website.

Join my Facebook group, Miranda May's Masquerade.

Subscribe to my bi-monthly newsletter.

Follow me on Amazon.

Like my Facebook page.

Follow me on Goodreads.

Follow me on Bookbub.

Follow me on Instagram.

Follow me on TikTok.

Follow me on Twitter.

READ MORE BY MIRANDA MAY

SECRETS OF SORLPHI

A Fae Realms Series.

Paranormal RH Romance.

Silent Secrets | Book One

Sinful Secret | Book Two

Sinister Secrets | Book Three

HEATED

Series of RH Omegaverse Intertwined Standalones.

Knot My Reality | Book One

Knot Their Reality | Book Two (July 21, 2023)

STANDALONES

The Music That We Make (June 9, 2023)

A PNR Rockstar second chance story.

Wickedly Depraved (September 10, 2023)

A Dark RH Mafia Romance.

ANTHOLOGIES

A Whale of a Time

Eleven spicy RH whale shifter short stories.

featuring The Music That We Make

Sinful Desires

Stepbrother Forbidden Romance anthology.

featuring Wickedly Obsessed

Personal Demons

Releasing June 30, 2023

Dark PNR/Paranormal stories dealing with mental health issues.

featuring Caged

A STEPBROTHER ROMANCE

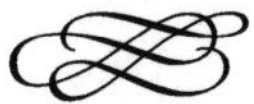

BRE ROSE

CONTENT WARNINGS

An Unexpected Encounter is a Why Choose romance where our FMC will now have to choose between her love interests. It will end in a cliffhanger for the Sinful Desires Anthology but will have a HEA when released in the full novel at the conclusion of the anthology.

Please be advised that the story will contain the following content/trigger warnings. If any of these are triggering for you please do not read. If any other warnings not listed are noted please contact author at breroseauthor@gmail.com.

- Body Shaming
- Fast Burn
- Exhibitionism/Public Sex
- Mistaken Identities
- Bullying from a parent

If these do not bother you then happy reading.

CHAPTER 1

SELENA

My plane is set to take off in two fucking hours and I still need to get to the airport and check in. Racing around the room, I hurriedly pack my bag.

I promised my mom that I'd be there with a smile on my face. Deep down, I was happy for her. She found love again. Losing Dad was hard on her, especially the way he suffered in those last few years as cancer slowly deteriorated his body, taking him from the healthy, muscular athletic trainer, to looking like the king from that dragon show everyone raves about.

It just seems like we're saying goodbye to the chapter of our life that housed him and ushering in a new one with, what was his name again - ahh, shit, I know it started with an 'A'. It's one of the reasons I went out drinking last night with my friends, got stone-cold drunk, and woke up in a panic next to a naked, chiseled body this morning. His name is a black hole in my memory and I don't have time to dwell on it. I quickly dressed and got out of there as fast as I could. Which leads me to the predicament I'm in now, trying to get everything done to get to the airport before my flight takes off and I have to explain the shitshow of events to my mother.

I'm walking out the door to wait downstairs for the Uber I ordered, trying to juggle my coffee, purse, phone, and keys in my hand as I lock the door. The shrill ringing of my phone almost causes me to drop the aforementioned coffee. Seeing my mother's picture flash across the screen, I quickly answer.

"Mom," I huff out, short of breath as I try to lock the door, only to fumble and drop the keys to the ground.

"Selena Reign Middleton, please do not tell me you're still at home!" she practically screams in panic through the line, and I wince.

"No, Mom. I'm at the airport. Just heading to the gate." God forgive me for lying, I just hope she buys it.

"Selena, I may be old, but I'm not dumb. If you miss your flight, I'm going to kill you. Abel's sons are already going to be late, just barely making it for the ceremony. I need you here," she chastises me.

"Mom, I know how important this is to you and I won't be late. Well, the only way I would be is if the flight is delayed, so don't worry. I'll see you this evening. I'll call you before I board my connecting flight, so you know when to expect me. Now I have to go. I love you. See you soon." I disconnect the call, awkwardly slide the phone into my bag, and lock the door. Hurrying to the elevator, I step inside while juggling all the items I have. It's only after I hit the button for the first floor do I let my back rest against the wall and blow out a deep breath.

I miss you, Dad! If you were here, I wouldn't be going through this. Dealing with Mom's criticism all on my own. Seeing her marry another man who isn't you.

The Uber arrives just as I step out of my apartment building and onto the sidewalk. A middle-aged gentleman with graying hair, receding hairline and a potbelly exits the driver's side as the trunk of his car pops up and helps me store my luggage away.

"Selena?" he asks.

"Yes," I smile, handing him my last bag.

"Heading on a trip? I saw I was taking you to the airport," he asks, no doubt trying to make idle chit-chat.

"Yeah, my mother is getting married. I'm actually going to meet her husband and his children for the first time," I tell him as I move toward the rear passenger door and climb inside his royal blue Toyota Camry. He closes the trunk, then seconds later he opens the driver's door and slides in behind the wheel. I scrunch my nose when the smell of smoke and body odor hits me.

It's then I realize I never showered and reek of sex. God help me now. Hopefully, the stench in the car will overpower the smell coming off me.

"Second marriage?" He glances at me in the rearview mirror.

I just sit there, staring at him, as he looks back at me. My lips are pursed, not wanting to talk about my life with some random stranger. Guess my silence wasn't an obvious enough clue that I didn't really want to talk, so I finally speak up.

"Yes, Sir, my dad passed away a few years ago. She met Abel on a single's second chance cruise and, well, two months later, they're getting married," I tell him, reaching in my bag and pulling out my phone to send my mom a text. *Selena, why in the hell do you keep telling this guy all this information? He could be a killer.*

Me: Mom, when I get in, I'm just going straight to the resort and checking in. If everything goes well, I should be there by three and we can have an early dinner.

Mom: That sounds perfect. Abel wanted to take me for a moonlight cruise on his boat. His sons will be here tomorrow afternoon, just in time for the wedding. They had to rearrange their shifts at their new job.

The driver, bless his heart, must finally get the picture that I don't want to talk. I immerse myself in my phone, scrolling through all my emails, answering the ones I need to, and deleting the spam. A little while later, as we pull up in front of the airport, I finally cleared out the nearly three hundred emails that sat in my inbox.

I never thought being an accountant would require answering this many emails, especially when it's not even tax season. I've been lucky in my career, starting off as a freelance accountant. Word of mouth spread quickly, and I gained a steady clientele, affording me the ability to work from home, as well as set my own schedule.

"Have a wonderful trip and congratulations to your mother," he tells me sweetly. I'll need to remember to give him a good driver review on the app.

Gathering my suitcase, garment, and toiletry bag, I rush inside the airport, straight to the check-in counter, all the while praying I have everything I need and I can get through the check in line quickly.

"Okay, ma'am. Here's your boarding pass, but you need to hurry. Your plane is set to take off in fifteen minutes and they've already begun boarding," the pimply face boy tells me. I mean, when did they start hiring teenagers? Because that's what this boy looks like.

"Shit!" I panic, gathering my purse and racing toward the checkpoint. The whole process is eating away at my time. Put all your items in the bin, including your shoes, walk through the metal detector, and pray it doesn't go off because it'll only delay you more. Once you make it through there, you still have to wait for the bin to make its way down the conveyor belt to you.

Once it does, I slide my shoes back on and race through the airport to my gate like I'm heading toward the finish line on the track field, with my eyes on the gold medal.

"Wait, wait!" I scream out as I see the attendant getting ready to close the gate.

She hears my screams and looks like she thinks about it for a moment before stopping.

"You're lucky," she tells me.

"Thank you, thank you," I rush out, breathless.

She quickly checks my boarding pass and directs me toward the plane. All eyes are on me when I step inside, especially the little old lady at the front who's glaring at me like I held the plane up for hours.

Ignoring everyone, I head down the aisle to the seat assigned to me. Relief washes over me when I sit down, having made my first flight on time, and I blow out a breath. If I had missed my connecting flight, I didn't know what I would have done. The stewardess goes through her pre-flight spiel and the next thing I know, we're in the air.

It only takes about an hour to get to the next airport and once again I'm off and running to the next terminal. Thankfully, they weren't closing the gate in my face, but I was one of the last ones to make it there. By the time I make it, I'm worn out. I feel like I haven't been able to catch my breath since this morning. It doesn't help that I woke up with a hangover.

Making my way down the aisle, I look for my assigned seat. When I finally spot it, I stop dead in my tracks, staring at the guy occupying the window seat next to mine who's hot as sin. He's got dark brown hair, so dark it's almost black, and a chiseled jaw. Tattoos wrap around his exposed forearm, disappearing underneath the sleeve of his shirt.

He looks up, eye fucking me, as I sit down beside him. Did it just get really hot in here?

"Fuck, you are fucking gorgeous. Looks like I get the amazing company of the most beautiful woman on the plane," he tells me, causing the blood to rush to my cheeks, as I let out a little schoolgirl giggle. *Ahh shit!* Where in the hell did that come from?

"Cocky, aren't we? But I'm sure there are far prettier women than me on the plane that would cream their panties for lines like that. Ones that can actually make it to the airport on time. That's just not me." I joke with an awkward laugh as I buckle my seatbelt when the airline attendant begins her safety speech, pulling my attention back to her.

I can't help but keep casting sideways glances at the deliciously handsome man next to me. The scent of his cedarwood cologne makes me rub my thighs together and all I want to do is climb into his lap and ride him until we both see stars, my cum covering his cock. *What the fuck is wrong with me? Settle down Selena and get your hormones in check.*

I've never been a prude when it comes to sex, but I am known to be more on the reserved side. But from the quick fuck last night, to the racing dirty thoughts of the man sitting next to me, you'd think I was a common street corner prostitute.

I feel the stroke of a hand across my arm and jump as my hairs stand on end from the electrifying touch. Shooting daggers at the culprit sitting next to me, he smirks.

"Seeing how we're buddies until the plane gets to the next stop, I thought I'd introduce myself. I'm Elias, twenty-nine, single, no kids, good job. And what about you, Princess?" He grins and shifts slightly in his seat, so he's facing me.

Wanting to have a bit of fun, I decide to fuck with him a little and knock his cocky ass down a notch or two. "I'm Veronica, thirty-one. I look good for my age. I have six kids with six different fathers. I live off men because I hate to work and I'm currently looking for husband number four. Do you want to apply?" I lean closer to him and bat my eyes.

He looks shocked for a moment, before howling with laughter, scaring the people sitting around us. I can feel everyone's eyes on us for a second before the plane begins to move, taxiing down the runway, getting ready to take off.

"You almost had me. I love a girl with a sense of humor. The marriage part I'm not sure about, we've only just met. But I'd certainly fill out the boyfriend application. You seem like a girl that'll really keep me on my toes. Want to give me the real details now?" He gives me a flirty, confident wink. You know, the one all the cocky bastards use that has girls dropping their panties in seconds.

"Wow, you're deranged, aren't ya? All that and you still want to apply, or are you just looking to get your dick wet? A little hit it and quit it?" I can't help the evil smirk taking over my face.

"Oh, you wound me!" He places his hand over his chest and mocks a pained look on his face.

"Do all the ladies fall for these lines of yours? Because for you to be using them, either they must, or you're a glutton for punishment."

I chuckle, but damn if I don't secretly want to fall for every single line he's given me.

I'm feeling like a floozy, as my mother would call it, having slept with a man last night whose name I can't recall. And now this guy, who I'd take into the bathroom on this plane right now, just to join the mile high club. Just the thought of that has me squeezing my legs together to ease the ache that's taking over my core. A move that doesn't go unnoticed by my handsome neighbor.

"Are you okay, Princess? Something you need help with?" He leans closer with a cocky smirk on his face.

He thinks he's embarrassing me, but he's not, so I decide to play along. "So, are you going to follow me to the bathroom, slam my face up against the wall, and fuck me from behind?" I let out a low moan and bite my bottom lip as I give him a wink.

He grins, looking up toward the seatbelt sign that is now showing we can move around the cabin, and stands, taking my hand in his. He leans down and whispers into my ear, which sends shivers down my spine. "Your wish is my command. Meet me there in a minute." Releasing my hand, he turns and heads toward the bathroom, leaving me breathless, needy, and extremely wet. What the fuck do I do now?

CHAPTER 2

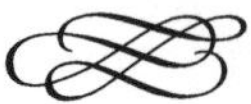

SELENA

I sit there for a moment, biting my lip as I try to decide what the fuck to do. Was he serious? I don't even know this man. Am I really ready to have round two of fucking a goddamn stranger?

Fuck it! You only live once. I'm horny as hell and damn if I don't deserve to join the club. Standing slowly, I nonchalantly make my way to the bathroom, where I know Mr. Hotty is waiting for me. Passing the rows of seats, I keep my eyes locked on my destination.

Walking to the back, I see two bathrooms and no fucking clue which one he went in. I don't have to wonder for long though as the door to my left opens, and a tattooed muscular arm reaches out, snaking around my waist, and pulls me inside.

He shuts the door behind me, then pushes me back against it, flipping the switch to occupied. Leaning his head down, he places it by my ear and whispers, "I was afraid you changed your mind, and I was going to have to come in here and fuck my own hand. You're the hottest fucking woman I've ever seen." He growls as he shifts his head to the left, devouring my lips in a kiss that has my toes curling and stars dancing in my eyes. Fuck! If it's this good already, I can't imagine what it'll be like when he fucks me.

His hands slide down my body as he kneads my breasts, before moving down to my skirt, lifting it up, and ripping my panties off. "That's better." His fingers glide through my hot core and rub small circles over my clit, applying just enough pressure to have me moaning in ecstasy. "Shhh, Princess, don't want anyone to know what we're doing in here." He chuckles quietly, the rumble of it sending shock waves straight to my core.

His fingers continue to slide through my wet folds and I instinctively rock against them, as shocks of electricity hum through my body. A second later, they disappear and I let out a disapproving groan.

"Shh, Princess, we need to hurry. We don't have much time." He reaches down with his hand before I hear the rattling of the metal on his belt as he undoes his pants. Pulling out his dick, one so massive both in girth and length, I ponder on how it will even fit inside of me. What is up with these men? Both men in the last two days have had monster cocks.

He takes the head of his beast and strokes it back and forth between my lips, teasing me. "Please, fuck me," I beg, not wanting to wait any longer.

"As you wish." He lifts my leg up over his arm, and grabs his cock in his other hand, lining the head of it at my center. Sliding it in slowly, my body screams as it adjusts to his size. I moan at the fullness I feel while he stops to give me time to adjust before he begins pumping in and out of me at an increased speed.

"Oh, God!" I cry out into his shoulder, trying to keep my voice low but failing miserably.

"If you can't be quiet, Princess, I will gag you with your shredded panties." He places the pad of his thumb over my clit and begins to rub it vigorously as he pumps into me faster. The scream builds in my throat and right when I think I can't hold it back any longer, he captures my mouth with his, swallowing all my sounds.

A rap on the door has me freezing, but only spurs him on. "Be out in a minute," he calls out.

"A minute?" I whisper as I feel a fluttering in my stomach, signaling I'm close.

"Oh baby, I'm close. Once you come, I'm exploding inside of you." He's true to his word. Not even a minute later, I orgasm hard. When my pussy clamps down around his cock, I feel ropes of his hot cum filling me up.

I collapse into his arms as we both ride out our release, breathing hard as we try to catch our breath. When we're both done, he lowers my leg and pulls his cock out, leaving me feeling empty. Using my ripped panties, he cleans me a little before balling them up and placing them in his pocket. "I think I'll keep these to remember you by. Now, head back to your seat. I'll meet you there in a minute."

Before opening the door, I roll off some toilet paper and wipe my legs, making sure to remove all traces of our encounter. Looking in the mirror, I see a thoroughly fucked woman staring back at me. I run my fingers through my hair, straightening it up the best I can. He lets out a laugh, but I don't care. Turning the knob, I walk out and keep my eyes on the ground, not wanting to look at the stewardess who is standing there with her arms crossed across her chest, tapping her foot on the ground, like a teacher scolding their pupil.

"Sorry," I tell her sheepishly, as my face heats in embarrassment before I scurry off down the aisle back to my seat.

Paranoid, I feel everyone's eyes on me, all of them knowing what I've just done in the bathroom. Shaking those thoughts away, I keep going. It's only when I go to sit that I remember I have no underwear on. Damn him.

A couple of minutes later, Elias comes strutting down the aisle like a prized horse at a fair, sliding past me and sitting down. Leaning into me, he places his mouth right by my ear and whispers, "Thanks for the mile high fun, Veronica, and the panties. They'll be used as part of my spank bank."

Fuck me! The only saving grace is that when this man brags to his friends about the girl he banged on the plane, it will always be Veronica. No one will ever think we are one and the same. We sit there in silence, him with a cocky ass grin on his face and me burning with embarrassment. I can't believe I just did that.

Needing to take my mind off of it, I bend over and search through my bag, pulling out my book. I've recently been reading smutty romance, and it's become an addiction. Right now, I'm caught up in this shared world series of fairy tale retellings, and I'm dying to see how this retelling of Robin Hood ends.

I can feel him, every time he leans in over my shoulder to take a peek at what I'm reading, and each time I shift my book so he can't. "Come on, Veronica, I want to read and get cultured too," he whines, causing me to just shake my head in disbelief. Really? He wants to keep talking? I really thought he was the hit it and quit it type of guy.

He finally gives up, shifting his gaze to the window, staring out of it aimlessly. How do I know? Because I'm sneaking glances at him out of the corner of my eye.

He really is gorgeous. One of the hottest men I've ever seen in my life, but there's something that I'm just noticing now that seems oddly familiar. Is it the profile of his face, the dimple on his cheek when he smiles? Shaking it off, I go back to reading.

The plane has finally begun its descent, and the stewardess starts her spiel. I can finally be on my way to my mom, see her wedding, and get back home. I love her, but she can be so overbearing sometimes. '*Selena, it's time you settled down, got married, and had me some grandbabies. You know you're not getting any younger, and soon all the good men will be snatched up.*' She just doesn't know when to give it a rest. I already live with the guilt and loss of my father, knowing he will never walk me down the aisle, or be there to bounce his grandkids on his knee as he regales them with stories of me as a child.

A tear slides down my cheek and I hastily reach up to wipe it away, but not before he notices. "Veronica, are you okay?" His concern causes my heart to melt a little.

"Yeah, just thinking of my dad. He passed away a couple of years ago," I tell him softly, my voice cracking as I try to not break down. Every time I talk about him, it ends with tears.

"I understand. My mom passed away about six years ago from cancer. We thought she could beat anything. She beat it twice, but it kept coming back with a vengeance, finally winning. We were there with her until the moment she took her last breath. There's not a day I don't think about her or want to pick up the phone and call her. So I won't tell you that you'll finally get over it because you won't. You just learn to deal with it a little better. The breakdown and tears become less, but never go away." He smiles gently, his eyes holding so much compassion.

God, could this man be more perfect? He knows exactly what to say to console you, and can fuck like a god. Too bad I won't see him again after today. It's for the best, though. I have no clue where he's from and I always self-sabotage relationships, anyway. Especially the good ones. I've never been able to accept that good shit can happen, always waiting for the next shoe to drop that'll throw me for a loop. So I learned to be the one to drop it first. That way, I never get hurt. I'm just alone a lot. Maybe that's why I did the random hookup last night and today.

The plane lands and begins to taxi to the terminal. Almost there. I can see his hands sliding up and down the length of his jean-clad legs nervously. "So, Veronica, is there any way I can get your number? Call you sometime, maybe meet up and go on an actual date?"

God, I want to say yes, so fucking bad, but I can't. Why? Because I'm really attracted to this guy and I know if it went well, I'd do something to push him away. Until I can learn to deal with that, I can't hurt other people. Maybe hit-and-run sex is the way to go. No ties, no feelings for the most part, and no information. That way we can't contact each other.

"I'm sorry, you're hot as fuck, and I really, really like you, but I don't see it going anywhere. We most likely live nowhere near each other, and a date just seems a step backward after what we just did." I glance at him just as the stewardess calls for us to disembark and he's staring at me. Without saying another word, I stand up quickly, snatching my bag up from the floor, and race down the aisle, pushing my way in front of the other passengers.

I need to get off this plane before he tries to convince me to change my mind.

"Veronica, Veronica." I hear called out from behind me and start walking faster. I know the airport will be crowded and it'll give me the chance I need to disappear into the masses.

I burst into the terminal of the airport and hit the ground running. The bathroom up ahead gives me the opportunity to do just what I wanted, to disappear. Making a quick shuffle to the right, I head in the door and straight to a stall, shutting the door behind me as I let out a sigh of relief.

Did I really just run like a madwoman from the hot guy who wanted to take me on a date? That would be yes because I'm a fucking idiot! Selena, you need to get your shit together. At that moment, I make a vow to myself that the next time I'm asked out or someone wants my number; I give it to them. Also, my real name would be good as well.

I hang out in the bathroom, relieving myself, and freshening up until I'm pretty confident the coast is clear and I head out to the baggage claim to collect my luggage.

Luck is on my side. I catch a glimpse of him, bag in hand, heading toward the exit door for the airport. Crisis averted. But my heart plunges a little, knowing I screwed up a chance for what I bet would've been an amazing date.

CHAPTER 3

SELENA

The cab ride from the airport was uneventful. I get checked in and head to my room. Walking in, I look around and check out my new home for the weekend. The room is large with a king size bed, table, and dresser with a large flat screen television sitting on it. In the corner is the wet bar, which I will definitely be hitting up, especially if I have to deal with my mother. The curtains are pulled back, showing me the balcony. Mom and the new stepdaddy definitely picked a nice place.

I drop my bags and flop down on the soft bed in exhaustion. All I want is a nap, but I know I need to give my mom an update, so I pull out my phone and send her a message letting her know I'm here and checked in. Do you think she would let me rest? No, she wants me to meet her and my future stepdaddy, Abel, for a late lunch in the lobby restaurant.

Reluctantly, I agree, smooth out my dress, and head for the door, but stop dead in my tracks when I remember that fuck head took my underwear. Rushing back over to my suitcase, I open it and reach into the mesh pocket, pulling out a pair. There is no way in hell I'm sitting down at dinner with my mom and Abel pantyless. Nope, no fucking way that is happening. I quickly step into them and shimmy them up my legs, smoothing my skirt out once I'm done. Snatching up the room key, I walk out the door.

Once I've made it downstairs, I head straight for the restaurant and spot Mom immediately. She's seated at a table, snuggled up against an older man with salt and pepper hair, muscled arms, and a pair of dark-rimmed glasses. He's gazing at her, a huge smile lighting up his face and I just watch them for a moment. My mom is so happy. The happiest I'd seen her since my father passed away. As much as we can bicker at times, seeing her happy makes me happy. She deserves it. It gives me hope; that maybe there is someone out there for me when I eventually get my shit together. I mean, hell, she found love twice.

Stepping up to the table, I clear my throat to pull them out of the tunnel vision they have on one another. "Mom, you look beautiful," I tell her, as she stands, moving around the table to pull me into her arms, squeezing me tightly.

"Selena, I'm so glad you are finally here. Abel's son arrived here as well but went to see the tailor. He needed to get his tuxedo fitted to make sure it didn't need any alterations before the wedding. We had hoped they would've gotten here earlier, but their work schedule didn't allow it. Luckily, they all wear the same size, so he is trying them on for all three, especially since Ezekiel may not get here until the morning of the wedding." My mother pouts and Abel jumps up to comfort her, making me want to hurl. I can already tell she has him wrapped around her fingers, falling for her charade of woe is me.

"Oh, pumpkin, it'll be okay. My sons wouldn't miss this for the world and the wedding is going to be amazing." He turns her around to face him and kisses her on the forehead. Damn if it doesn't instantly soothe her. He extends his hand out to me, and I reach out to shake it, but instead, he pulls me into a hug. "I finally have two beautiful women on my arm, my future bride and her daughter. I'm the luckiest man alive." He squeezes me, acting like we've known each other for ages, and as nice as he seems, being held in his arms is fucking creeping me out.

Pulling out of his hold, I step back and take a seat at the table. "Are you excited, Mom?" I ask, trying to get the lunch back on track. The need for a nap is strong, as well as a shower.

"Absolutely. Abel is such a good man. Now, tomorrow night, we have the rehearsal dinner. In the morning, the seamstress here just wants to meet with you quickly to check that your dress fits. I know the last time you came and saw me it did, but it looks like you might have put on a few pounds." Of course, she would sneak a snarky comment in. My mother weighs a buck twenty-five, and because I have a butt that would make J Lo jealous and thighs any man would want wrapped around his waist, she assumes I'm fat. 'Get with the ages, Mom,' I want to scream at her. Men want a thicker woman now, not a beanpole.

"Ahh, Pumpkin, I think she looks fine," Abel says at the same moment our server steps up to the table. She's a fuller size woman, with her auburn hair pulled back into a fierce bun, wearing a white shirt and some black slacks.

"Good afternoon, my name is Buelah and I'll be your server today. Can I get the three of you started with some drinks and appetizers?" She looks around the table, holding her order pad poised in her hand.

"I'll have some water and a house salad, please," I announce, wanting to be done with this meal as fast as possible. My mom has always been a little much, but since my dad passed away, her patronizing comments have gotten worse.

"Salad is a great option for you," my mother cuts in snidely and I see red.

"And I'd like to order my food as well. I had a late night and then had to rush to the airport and burned off a lot of energy on the flight. Can I get your thickest, greasiest burger and some fries smothered in bacon and cheese, please?"

My mother sits there, her mouth dropped open in shock, disgust, and whatever other word you can think of to describe it. Abel just has a smile on his face. "I love to see a woman with a hearty appetite and not afraid to order what she wants."

My mother turns slightly in her seat and slaps him across his chest playfully. "That is until she's as big as a house, then they move on to the skinny girl. Don't fill her head with delusions."

Tired of it already and wanting to get on with this so I can get back to my room, I ask Mom the question that'll get her off the subject of my weight. "Why don't you order so you can tell me all about the wedding plans and what we need to do tomorrow?"

She quickly orders her bird food and Abel orders the same as me, minus the cheese on the fries. Then she does exactly what I expect. She talks about herself for the rest of the lunch. I have to admit it's her favorite topic, but it sounds like the wedding will be absolutely beautiful, and apparently, I'm gaining three stepbrothers out of the deal. Ones I'll probably only see on holidays when all the family gets together and never see again until the next family event.

I don't know how many times I yawned during the meal, but we are taking our last bite when I know I can't sit there any longer. My mom hasn't stopped talking, so I have to butt in. "Mom, I'm exhausted. I'm going to head to my room and take a nap. I'll meet you in the lobby at nine tomorrow morning. We can go get breakfast, go to the dress shop, and then get our nails done. Have a mother-daughter day."

"That sounds wonderful. Just make sure to wear something a little less wrinkled tomorrow." Her eyes cross and her lips purse.

Seriously! I was on a plane for God knows how long. And well, I did have some amazing sex on the plane, but she doesn't need to know that.

"Well, if you'll excuse me then, and yes, Mother, I will ensure I look appropriate. Abel, it was lovely finally meeting you. And I look forward to meeting my future brothers." With that, I stand and leave the restaurant, heading toward the elevator. Ready to take off these clothes and take a nice, long, hot bath.

As I step inside it and turn around, I swear I see a familiar face. The one I left in bed when I snuck out of his room this morning. It's not possible. What would he be doing here? I must be seeing things, or did my one night stand come back to haunt me? We are stuck staring at each other until the doors slide shut, cutting off our view of each other.

Great, if he's here, then I either have to work to avoid him or have another round of amazing fucking sex.

Pressing the button for the sixth floor, the elevator jerks, moving upward as I step back, resting against the wall. It halts to a stop on my floor, dinging as the doors fly open.

Dragging my ass out of it, I head straight to my room, locking the door behind me once I'm inside. The luxurious king-size bed is calling to me, but I need a shower first. I haven't had one since yesterday evening before going out, and in that time I've had sex twice.

I head straight for the bathroom, finding the largest tub I've ever seen in my life. It's big enough for two people and my mind immediately shifts to having sex in it.

Putting the plug in place and turning the water on, I adjust the knobs, making sure it's hot before pouring in some of the bubble bath I spotted on the sink. There's no way in hell I'm letting this tub go to waste.

Undressing and dropping my clothes to the floor, I climb in, letting my body sink into the warmth of the bubbly liquid, and lay my head back. It feels so good to wash away the stress of the day, more specifically, my mother.

Now if I could just get out of tomorrow.

CHAPTER 4

ELIJAH

I can't believe Dad is getting married to a fucking woman we've never even met. Hell, he's barely even mentioned her. If she's trying to get to him for his money, the cunt is in for a rude awakening. My brothers and I will shut that shit down fast.

Stepping into the resort, I look around and let out a sigh. Eli was supposed to meet me in the lobby, but he isn't here yet. I wasn't supposed to be in until later tonight, but was able to get everything handled in Chicago and left early. I head to the receptionist to check in, but as I look out across the lobby, my jaw drops.

I see the most beautiful woman in the world, just as she turns around, her eyes locking on mine. She's gorgeous, with curves in all the right places and long wavy hair. I'm stunned by her beauty, but she's looking back at me like she's seen a ghost. The elevator doors close, breaking the spell I was under, taking her away from me. I wonder what that look was about?

Shaking it off and hoping like hell I get to run into her before I leave, I step up to the counter to check in. Eager to get up to my room and rest. The flight here was long and I still have to fly back and finish packing the last of our shit for the movers. We had a last-minute change in our duty station and got lucky. We were reassigned to station 29 in Jefferson, Georgia.

Zeke went a week before us and found us a house since he was just coming off leave from an accident. So he's there. His plan is to fly to our home in Georgia from the wedding with us, pack, and then we'll ship our cars except for one and head to our new home.

I've just barely stepped away from the desk, key card in one hand and my luggage rolling behind me in the other, when I see my dad exit from the restaurant. He has a stick thin brunette with him. Guess this is the new bitch of a stepmother.

"Son," he calls out from across the room, not calling me by name. I bet it's because, at this distance, he doesn't know which one I am. It's mine and Zeke's running joke to see how long it takes him to figure it out.

We had fun growing up as identical twins. The only difference is a slight scar above my right eyebrow from a drunken fight one night during our senior year of high school. We both liked the same girl and were dating her when some douche she dumped the prior year tried to slut-shame her. Yeah, that didn't fly with either of us. He got one good swing in before I fucked him up.

"Hey, Dad, is this the new wife?" I ask, trying to keep it civil until I have a chance to fully vet her, and believe me, I will.

"Yes, this is Julia Middleton, soon to be Carter," he says playfully as he pulls her in closer to him and she places her hand on his chest, flashing a rock that could pay the yearly mortgage on our new house.

Yep, gold digger!

"Nice to meet you, Julia," I say sweetly, even though I have to bite down on the side of my jaw to keep from screaming at my dad to get a clue.

"You as well. And which one are you?" she asks, in a nasally voice.

"I don't know, Dad, why don't you tell her," I say, eager to see his answer, so I can tell my brothers the new tally on right versus wrong answers.

I see him, staring intently at my face, knowing it's the one surefire way he can get it right. "Of course, this is Elijah. Elias headed straight to the tailor when he got here. We weren't expecting you and Ezekiel until tomorrow at the earliest."

"Yeah, I got done early. And Julia, where is your daughter? What is her name again?" I ask, eager to see if the gold digging apple falls far from the tree.

"Selena, she was exhausted from her travels and went to her room to rest. I'm sure if not before, you'll meet her tomorrow at the rehearsal dinner. Now if you'll excuse me, your father is taking me out sightseeing so I'm going to go change," the bitch says before kissing my father, putting on a show about it, then saunters off, making sure to sway her hips. My father's eyes follow her the entire way as his head moves left to right, in sync with her hips.

"So, Dad, are you sure this is what you want?" I ask, cutting to the chase.

"Of course it is. Why would you ask a question like that?" His voice is harsh, as he looks at me sternly.

I know I pissed him off with the question, but I'd rather he be pissed at me than the bitch taking him to the cleaners. "Because one, that flashy ass diamond on her finger, or two, the fact you only knew her for what, three months tops."

"First off, it's none of your business. When you find the love of your life, you know it and you don't need to wait because time won't change anything. I was lucky enough to have found two loves and I'm not wasting time being unhappy," he barks at me before storming off in the same direction she left.

Fuck, maybe I should've handled that more tactfully. Shrugging it off, I head for the elevators. The doors start to shut, but a duo of bleach blonde, overly tanned women hold them open for me as they run their tongues across their lips.

"Hey there, all alone?" the one on the right asks, as they both erupt in giggles.

"Umm, for now, yes. But I'm here with my brothers for my father's wedding," I tell them, trying to be nice.

They step closer, their giggling becoming louder and more annoying. I push the button for the sixth floor but instantly regret it because now they know which floor I'm on.

"Brothers, huh? How many? I mean, there are two of us. We don't mind sharing. I'm Barbie and this is Bebe."

All I can think is, of course, it is. "Elijah," I tell them bluntly. God, can this elevator move faster?

He must hear my prayers as the elevator jumps to a halt and the doors open. "It was a pleasure, ladies. Enjoy your stay." I quickly step off and head down the hall to room 606, walking faster than normal to get away from them.

Looking back over my shoulder as I hold the key up to the scanner, I see both girls with their heads sticking out of the elevator door, watching exactly where I went. Opening the door, I step into the room, giving them a forced smile and wave before shutting it behind me.

Maybe I should check with the desk about changing rooms. I have a sinking feeling that them knowing where I'm sleeping, will come back and bite me in the ass.

Dropping my bag onto the bed, thrilled that Dad booked us a suite of some sort. Two beds in one room and one with its own bed and a small sitting area. At least Dad thought ahead and made sure we'd all be comfortable.

Sitting down, I pull out my phone and open the group chat with my brothers

Me: When are you two asshats getting here? I just met the new step bitch...

Zeke: That bad?

Zeke: Was her kid with her?

Me: No, but I'm sure we will get the pleasure of meeting her tomorrow. Are you even going to be here?

Zeke: I should be there tomorrow night if I can

catch the flight. If not, I'll take the red eye out and be there first thing on the day of the wedding.

Eli: Both of you fuckers suck. How did I get stuck with trying on not one but three tuxes, especially since your ass is here, Jay?

Me: Oh, is the big macho man gonna cry cause he had to try on some tuxedos for his brothers?

Eli: Haha joke all ya want, but this guy got himself inducted into the mile high club on his flight here. I just hope I can run into her before we leave and get her number.

Zeke: Dude, you're doing about as good as me. Last night I met this fine ass chick at the bar, ended up having the best sex of my life, and woke up to an empty bed this morning. She snuck out, no note, nothing. I plan to hit that bar every night until I find her again. I don't even know her name.

Me: Well, I just saw the hottest girl getting on the elevator and I plan to find her, so hands off. Look at us all getting some kind of lady luck at the same time.

Me: Watch out though because I ran into a couple of blonde barbies that, and I quote, like to share.

Zeke: That's okay, I want to find the girl from last night.

Eli: Same, I'm going to be searching for the girl from the plane, anyway. I have one last suit to try on and then I'm headed to the resort.

Me: See you when you get here.

Zeke: Off to the gym.

God, I can't wait until we are all back in the same place again. For brothers, we're really close. We all went into the same profession, firefighting. We tried to live separately but hated it, hence living and working together. If we hadn't all got stationed at the same firehouse,

I would've found something else to do until I could. But it would be in Jefferson without a doubt.

Standing up, I decide to hit the shower. Maybe I can get a nap in when I'm done. I can feel the exhaustion creeping in. There's also a mysterious beauty I want to meet, but I need to find her first. It's going to be like finding a needle in a haystack, especially since I have nothing to go on but what she looks like.

But it's a treasure hunt I'm ready to take on.

Opening my bag, I pull out my toiletries and a change of clothes, then head to the bathroom. My two plans for the weekend racing through my mind. Find the mystery girl and get rid of the future step bitch.

CHAPTER 5

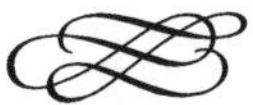

SELENA

My wake-up call comes in from the front desk promptly at eight-thirty am. Yeah, I know I'm cutting it close, but I don't fucking care. Going through my suitcase, I grab the lavender linen sundress that I wadded up like yesterday's newspaper last night, just to make a point. Mommy dearest didn't want wrinkles, so guess what she's getting. Serves her right for trying to fat shame me.

Dressing quickly, I snake my hands through my hair, getting out all the tangles and pulling it up into a messy bun before applying a little mascara to my lashes and calling it a morning. We're just going for a dress fitting and a mani/pedi, so there's no need to be dressed to the nines.

Picking up my room key and my purse from the nightstand, I head out the door. I have exactly four minutes until I'm late, and I can guarantee you she's already tapping her foot on the floor with a look of disdain on her face. *How dare I keep Julia waiting!* Stepping up to the elevator, I press the down button, and when the doors open, two blondes with fake boobs and tiny waists are giggling inside.

"Are you sure this was the floor?" bleach blonde one says to the second as they step off, blocking me from entering.

"Excuse you," bleach blonde two belts out as she turns her nose up at me. They move past me, the door shutting before I can get in it.

Reaching out, I push the button again, catching the elevator before it leaves the floor, and the doors spring open for the second time. I step inside but not before glancing to the left to hear the blondes giggling as bleach blonde one looks over at me. "Did you see how fat she is? Glad she wasn't on the elevator with us. We could have plummeted to our death."

"Can you believe people let themselves go like that? Please kill me if I do." Bleach blonde two acts like she's gagging.

Unfortunately, they accomplished just what they wanted. They hit me with the one insecurity I try so hard to overcome; my weight. Now I get to listen to my mother criticize me about it. They've sucked all the joy from wearing the wrinkled dress out of me, and I just hope the poor unfortunate soul who they are looking for has better sense than to fall for those heinous vultures.

The elevator goes straight down to the first floor, not stopping at any other floor. Stepping out into the lobby, true to form, Mom stands there, arms crossed over her chest, with a scowl on her face, tapping her toes on the floor. Kill me now. What I wouldn't give for this to be a roadrunner cartoon, and me as Wile E. Coyote, where the dynamite is ready to blow me up, or the rock fall on my head.

"Really, Selena, you weren't raised in a barn. Did you not listen to anything I said last night? If it wouldn't make us late, I'd send you back to your room to change. Are you trying to embarrass me?" She turns quickly and rushes toward the hotel doors, still mumbling under her breath. I just drop in behind her and follow her out to the waiting cab, sliding into the back seat behind her.

"I didn't have time to iron it, Mom. But it's not that bad. It's the material and after the first time I sat down, it would wrinkle anyway." I try to placate her, but she brushes me off without acknowledging what I said.

"Now, I'm getting the last fitting on my dress. I just pray the sizes the sister shop sent over are correct. The last thing we need is to have to change the dress altogether." She stares at me harshly, allowing her eyes to take a moment to peruse my body. "I swear you've gained at least twenty more pounds since I saw you last."

I close my eyes, take a deep breath, then open them to look out the window. It's not even worth the waste of breath to argue with her. She'll always be right and well, it is her day. Dad wouldn't want me to upset her. He was the buffer between the two of us, never allowing her to nitpick at me, and his death left a huge gaping hole for her to step through and berate me.

I zone out the rest of the way, only mumbling, "Oh really," "Yes ma'am," and "You're the most beautiful bride," at random parts of the conversation when I was paying attention. Finally, we're pulling up in front of a fancy dress shop, one of those high couture ones you see movie stars at. The front of the building is an enormous window, allowing you to see inside. Stepping through the door, you're immediately greeted by a hostess, of all things, handing you a flute of champagne. Guess nine-thirty in the morning isn't too early to start drinking.

"Mrs. Middleton, so lovely to see you again," a tall, slender, middle-aged woman with dark hair pulled back into a tight bun says as she makes her way over to Mom, giving her a kiss on each cheek.

"Yes, it is, Darla. Lovely to see you again. I was hoping you would be here for my last fitting, and please call me Julia."

"I wouldn't miss it for anything. Tomorrow is the big day and I can't wait to see you walk down the aisle. And who is...this?" She lets her eyes trail up and down the length of my body, a look of disdain on her face.

"Oh yes, this is my daughter Selena. Please allow me to apologize in advance. I was not aware she had gained weight, and I just hope her dress fits." Go ahead Mom, you are really taking advantage of every chance you have to ridicule me. Wonder what she would think if I told her about the guy from the club and the plane. Apparently, I wasn't too big to get thoroughly fucked in the airplane bathroom.

"I'm sure we can handle it." The snobby bitch even has the audacity to roll her eyes at me. "Now let's get you fitted and Delores can handle Samantha." She gestures toward a woman just stepping out of the back, who's wearing glasses and a measuring tape draped over her shoulders.

"It's Selena, and that sounds perfect. I don't want to delay the rest of our day, and I would love the surprise of not seeing you in your dress until tomorrow." I know it may have come off catty, especially with the glare my mother shoots my way, but she pissed me off.

"Wonderful, Julia, come along with me. Delores, can you help Selena?" And with that, she links her arm with my mother, and they head off toward what I assume to be a private dressing area.

"Hi, Selena. Are you ready?" Now that she's up closer, I can see how timid she is. Darla must nag on her as much as my mother does me.

"Yes. My dress should already be here. I had my measurements sent over and I'm hoping to only need a few alterations." I smile, trying to assure her I am most definitely not like my mother.

"Okay, I can take you back to the dressing room and go get it. Then we can see where we stand with alterations." She gestures in the same direction as my mother, and my stomach cringes in pain.

"Are there any other changing areas, preferably as far away from my mother as we can get?" I ask, praying to whatever god is listening...

Delores' face changes drastically, her meek, scared face now replaced with one of relief. "Yes, we do." And just like that, we are heading in the completely opposite direction of my mother and the other bitch.

Chapter break

"Oh my gosh, it fits you like a glove!" Delores cries out as she steps away and looks at me in my bridesmaid dress. "Okay, now, you can look, close your eyes and turn around, so I can make sure it's perfect."

Doing as she says, I close them and turn. I can feel her moving around me as the breeze from her quick movements hits me. "You can open them now."

Taking a deep breath, I open my eyes, gasping when I see myself in the mirror. I look amazing. The dress hugs my curves perfectly, the side slit displaying my tan thighs. The teal dress has a sweetheart neckline with small shimmering jewels lining it. A thin strap over each shoulder holds the dress in place. "It's beautiful. You made me look amazing."

"Oh no, Selena. You made the dress look beautiful. It's almost as if they made it for you. The measurements were dead on. We don't need to make any alterations. We'll have it steamed, then delivered to your hotel by the end of the day."

My mother picks that moment to step inside. "Oh my god, Selena. Look how tight that is on you. I knew you gained weight. Delores, we will need to have it taken out. There's no way I can have her looking like a pig stuffed in a blanket."

All the joy I felt when I looked at myself in the mirror was now gone. My face no longer holds the smile it once had. Turning away from my mother, I look back to the mirror where Delores stands, as she mouths, "I'm sorry."

"Selena, get out of that dress so they can get to work on it. We need to hurry if we want to make our nail appointment." She turns and marches out of the room, the bitch hot on her heels.

"I'm not taking anything out. They're crazy. This dress fits you perfectly," Delores announces with a huff that has my smile returning. I like this woman, she has moxy.

She helps me out of the dress, letting me know she intends to let them think she's doing adjustments, but really isn't, and that the dress will be delivered by the end of the day. Thanking her, I hurriedly change and leave to meet my *wonderful* mother in the lobby.

"Selena, come along now," my mother calls out just as I step into the lobby. Not wanting to hear her bitch anymore, more than she already has, I follow. "Did they note the alterations that need to be made?"

"Yes, Mother, even said they would have it done by the end of the day and the dress delivered to the hotel."

"Very well then. Let's go get our manicures and pedicures done, then grab some lunch. Please eat a salad today, Selena. We wouldn't want all the work the seamstress is doing today to be in vain." I wait for her to walk away before I roll my eyes. Lord, just give me the patience to get through this.

The nail salon was conveniently just two shops down from the dress store, and we made it there well before our appointment time. Something I didn't point out to my mother. It wouldn't have done any good if I did, she would have disagreed with whatever I said, anyway.

Mom goes to check us in and I use the moment of freedom to walk over to the case holding all the different colors of polishes, letting the tips of my fingers trail along the line of bottles until I land on the perfect shade of metallic gray that would go amazing with the deep burgundy dress.

"Selena, couldn't you go with a more classy shade, like a nude, pink, or even a French manicure?" I yelp at my mother's words. Damn, I didn't even hear her come up behind me. "Selena, was that necessary? You are causing a scene."

"Forgive me, Mother, how juvenile of me to scream in fright. As far as the color, I love it and it's what I'm getting. Are they ready for us? Suddenly, I'm feeling tired and not hungry at all." I've had my quota for the day of my mother, and there's no way I can make it through this and lunch.

She huffs, but before she can say anything, we're called over to the chairs for our pedicure. I keep waiting for my mother to say something, but she doesn't. Instead, she pulls out her phone and begins busily typing away on it.

"Mom..." She throws her hand up, halting me from saying anything else. *Yep, I've pissed her off.*

The rest of the appointment goes by in silence. Well, for me anyway. My mother, on the other hand, talks to everyone else whether they want to or not. When we're done, she heads straight for the counter to pay.

Taking a deep breath, I step up to her, knowing I need to fix this. As much as I hate how she speaks to me, especially about my weight, I never want her mad at me. "Your nails look beautiful. There's not going to be a bride who looks as beautiful as you."

"Thank you. Abel is meeting me here for lunch and should be here any minute. Then we're going for a carriage ride. You are free to do whatever it is you want to do today. Just remember, the dress rehearsal is at seven tonight. If everything goes well, it will only take about thirty minutes." She doesn't wait for me to respond. She signs the credit card receipt and turns to head for the door, where Abel appears out of nowhere.

Hailing a cab, I head back to the hotel. Angry at myself for letting my mother get to me. At no other time am I self-conscious about my weight, unless I'm around her. She has me so out of sorts that I don't even realize that I've gotten on the elevator and off on my floor until I notice I'm headed in the wrong direction. 617 is the other way. Turning, I walk back, passing by the ice machine, when a deep husky voice speaks as he snakes his arm around my waist.

"There you are. Seems like this is my lucky day."

Looking over my shoulder, I recognize the unexpected face, just as he turns my body to face him, slamming his lips against mine in a toe curling kiss.

CHAPTER 6

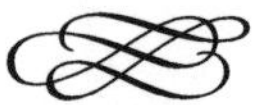

ELIJAH

I'd just come from 'the brunch from hell' with Dad, only to get to my room and have no ice. I needed a stiff drink, and it was barely one in the afternoon. Eli and Zeke owe me for this shit. Eli for sleeping in, rambling on and on about how he did his part by trying on the tuxes, and Z for still not having his ass here.

Picking up the ice bucket and the room key, I open the door and head down the hallway to where I saw the vending machines. Imagine that, even ritzy resorts have them. Guess rich people like snacks too.

I hear the sexiest voice mumbling something about wrinkles, weight, and heading the wrong way, and lift my head to catch a glimpse as she passes by. The bucket and all its icy contents drop to the floor, not phasing her, as I catch sight of the beauty from the elevator.

"There you are? Seems like this is my lucky day," slips from my tongue as I take hold of her shapely waist and pull her toward me. She glances at me over her shoulder before I turn her around and claim her lips.

She gives in to me so willingly, with no fight like I would expect from a woman when a strange man kisses and gropes her. "You found me, but how?" she asks through a moan.

Fuck, did she see me yesterday?

Deepening the kiss, my tongue slides along the seam of her lips and she opens for me, allowing it to slip inside to massage hers. Gripping her hip tighter, I move us back into the tiny area housing the ice machine and one lone snack vending machine. There's just enough room on the other side of them for us to duck in, so we are out of sight.

I release one side of her hip, bringing my hand up to run my fingers through her hair, and pull back to look at her. "God, you're fucking gorgeous."

"Fuck me," she moans out breathlessly. "Here and now. I need it."

Shit! Is this goddess for real? She reaches down and undoes my jeans, then reaches in and pulls out my already hard cock, grasping it in her hand, and begins stroking up and down my shaft.

"Are you sure? I don't have a condom, and what if someone sees?" Am I really afraid to be seen fucking in public?

"I'm on the pill and it didn't matter last time. Fuck me or I'm gone," she moans as she drops to her knees, opening her mouth and taking in the length of my cock, sucking me like there's no tomorrow.

My brain is beyond functioning at this point, but damn if I can fight against what my body wants. I arch my back, trying to keep from coming. Fuck if this woman isn't a master at sucking dick. Reaching down, I grasp her hair in my hand, holding her head in place as I start fucking her face. Her gag reflex is on point.

"Damn baby, if your pussy is as amazing as your mouth, I'm never letting you go," I growl out, fighting the urge to come.

She huffs out a laugh with her mouth full that sends ripples of vibrations along my shaft before she pulls off with a pop, standing back up. The absence of her wet lips wrapped around my dick makes me crave her even more.

"I said fuck me," comes boldly from her, causing my cock to twitch with excitement at her dominance.

"Don't you want to go to your room? Hell, we can go to my room. My brother's there, though."

"Seriously, less talking and more fucking. I need your cock in me now. I've missed it," she says breathlessly, already shimmying her panties down her legs and stepping out of them, leaving them abandoned on the floor.

Wait! What did she say? We haven't... but before I can think anymore; she reaches down, cupping my cock in her hand, and begins stroking it.

Fuck me!

Reaching down, I lift her leg, then remove her hand as I grasp my cock, angling it at her entrance before slamming it inside of her. She's so fucking wet and ready for me. Normally I'd want more. I'd take the time to explore every inch of her body, eating her pussy until I had my fill. But this little minx is primed and ready and there's no way I'm going to let her find someone else to satisfy her craving.

"Faster," she calls out, before wrapping her hands around my neck.

"Damn, you feel so tight, baby girl." Adjusting my grip on her leg so I can cup her ass with my hands, I lift her from the floor, pressing her back firmly against the wall, and continue to thrust my cock up inside of her tight, dripping wet cunt.

At the rate I'm going, and the way her sweet cunt is gripping my dick, I'm not going to last much longer. Her moans become more erratic before she cries out, "Fuck, I'm coming!"

I pump into her faster, feeling my balls tighten, signaling I'm close to my release as well. "Me too, baby, me too. Do you want me to pull out?"

She doesn't even answer, just takes my mouth, slides her tongue inside, and rides out her orgasm. Increasing my speed, it's only a couple of pumps later before I'm shooting my hot load inside of her tight little hole. Once I'm done, I just hold her there, allowing my body some time to come down from its high.

"You can let me down now," she says, and I slowly lower her back to the ground, making sure she's steady on her feet. Bending down, she picks up her underwear, balling them up in her hand, before smoothing down her dress.

"Fuck, babe, I wasn't expecting this. Can I get your number? See you again?" There's no way in hell I want her to escape. I think I just found my wife. A woman who knows what she wants and takes it, a wild side to her, and is hot as hell. She's the fucking unicorn of women.

"I got to go. Sorry, I don't remember your name, but honestly, I didn't expect to see you here." She pushes past me, rushing down the hallway, leaving me dumbfounded.

Hold up... I never gave her my name. What is she talking about? I wonder why she mentioned we fucked before? Was I drunk and don't remember?

Once I have my bearings back, I step into the hallway, but she's already gone and I don't have a clue where. Putting my dick back in my pants and zipping them back up, I pick up the bucket from the floor, refill it with ice, and head back to the room.

Opening the door, Eli has finally woken up and is sitting on the edge of his bed, scrolling through his phone. Hearing me open the door, he starts speaking. "Looks like the rehearsal dinner is canceled tonight. Apparently, the new step-monster is so distraught by the way her daughter treated her today that she just can't go through it. Dad's taking her to some overnight spa retreat and will see us in the morning. Guess the daughter is just as much a bitch as the mother."

When I don't say anything, he looks up at me. I've shut the door, but I'm still standing there, the ice bucket cradled close to my chest, as I gaze dopily into space. "Okay," is all I can manage to get out.

"Earth to Jay. What the hell, man? Did you even hear a word I said?" He laughs.

"No rehearsal tonight. Stepmommy's upset because of her bitch daughter. Who the fuck cares? It'll give me time to go find my future wife," I tell him, moving over and setting the ice bucket down on the table.

"Your future wife? You've lost me, man. What in the world is happening today?"

I walk over and sit down on my bed, facing him. "Eli, man, I saw her again."

"The girl from the elevator?"

"Yeah. There I was at the ice machine, and she walked by. I called out to her, kissed her, then she told me to fuck her. We did it in the hallway right beside the ice machine. She's everything I want in a woman."

"So where is she?" he asks.

"She left, told me sorry she forgot my name. Granted, she may be a little crazy, because a couple of the things she said made absolutely no sense. But Eli, she's perfect. Come out with me tonight and help me find her. We can look for your girl from the plane too. I have a feeling they'd get along great."

"Sure, why not. Maybe Zeke will be here in time to go with us. I'm going to take a shower. Want to get some lunch when I'm done?" Eli asks, standing and moving over to his suitcase, taking out his toiletry bag.

"I mean, I worked up an appetite, burning off a lot of calories by having the best sex of my life." I burst out in laughter as Eli just shakes his head at me.

One thing is for sure, I'm going to find my mystery woman. Hell, I didn't even get her name.

CHAPTER 7

SELENA

Oh my god! What just happened? I ask myself as I rush down the hallway back to my room. I can't believe I just did that. Not to mention the fact that he found me here. How did he know where to find me? Has he been stalking me? Shit, he could be here to kill me, and what do I do? Have sex with his fucking ass beside the ice machine.

It didn't stop me from taking what I wanted, some fucking good ass dick. I don't know how I came across two men in the last few days that have made me orgasm like no other, but damn if I don't love it. If he wants to pleasure me like that, then I'll gladly let him tie me up and lock me in a basement, making me his own personal sex slave.

Pulling my keycard out of my purse, I scan it and push the door open, stepping inside my room. It's still a mess from this morning, with clothes tossed about, so I quickly hang them up, then sit down on the edge of my bed, falling backward.

All the euphoria from my wild sexcapade drifts away, knowing that I have to go yet another round with my mother tonight. I love her dearly, but I can't stand being around her.

"AHHHHHHH," I scream out in aggravation. At the same time,

I hear my phone ping, letting me know I have an incoming message. Dread fills me with who it could be from. My top guess, mother dearest.

Mom: The rehearsal tonight has been canceled. The wedding planner will meet with Abel and the boys tomorrow, and then us.

Wow! Okay, not that I'm complaining, but why? Is she really not even going to say?

I'm about to reply when another message pops up.

Sam: Bitch, it's been almost over 24 hours since you left with no contact. Are you dead? 😵

I can't help but cackle at my best friend. He's the best, and I have no clue what I'd do without him. He's comforted me through every visit with my mother. But before I can chat with Sam, I need to find out what the hell's going on with this damn rehearsal.

Me: Why was it canceled?

No need to pussyfoot around, blunt and to the point is how I like it.

Mom: Really, Selena? You have the gall to ask me that after today? My nerves are shot after the way you behaved. How you talked to me. I could barely contain my emotions and Abel felt it was best to take a night for me. He's booked us an overnight couple's retreat to pamper me. I expect to see you in my suite tomorrow at 10 am sharp.

Me: Mom, don't you think you're overreacting just a little bit?

Mom: No, I don't! Just look at you now. I'm turning my phone off. See you tomorrow, Selena. Hopefully, this bitchy attitude of yours will not make a presence.

Could she be any more dramatic? Standing up, I head over to the minibar, pulling out a bottle of whiskey. Why, thank you, Mom.

Opening the bottle, I lift it to my lips and take a long swallow of the bitter brown liquid.

Good, now I can get drunk tonight, have a hangover tomorrow, so I won't care what she says, then come back to my room and crash for the rest of the day. Opening the minibar, I pull out two more bottles, and make my way back over to the bed, kicking off my shoes and sitting down, resting my back against the headrest and picking my phone up.

Sam: Are you in jail? Did she finally make you crack? Do I need to sell my body to raise money for bail and an attorney?

Sam has me laughing so hard that I choke on the liquid in my mouth. It flies out in a fit of laughter.

Me: I'm alive, not in jail, but very much headed toward being drunk.

Me: Apparently I was rude and embarrassing today, even though she took every opportunity to fat shame me. So no rehearsal tonight and me and the minibar are getting to know each other on a very intimate level.

Sam: Seriously, you fat? Not to be rude, Lenny, but is your mom on some kind of drug? You have a body other women would kill for. Men would die to be with, well, all men but me. Sorry baby, it's all about the sausage for me, tacos make me want to hurl.

Me: And that's why I love you. Want to come out here and save me?

Sam: NO!

Me: Fine, be that way! Here I was going to tell you about the hot guy from the club who hunted me down here and we just fucked in the hallway of the resort, not to mention the guy I met on the plane who inducted me into the mile high club.

Sam: Yes. You slut. I love you, baby... Shit. Jose is here, I have to go. I'm about to get my own world rocked. Promise me when you get home, we have a bestie night complete with pizza and alcohol.

Me: Promise.

One thing is for sure, I lucked out in the best friend department. And at the moment I'm lucking out in the alcohol department too.

Chapter break

ELIAS

"Zeke just messaged, said he's on his way here from the airport," I call out to Jay, who's in the bathroom, primping, hell-bent on finding his girl from earlier. Shit, I can't even make fun of him. I want to find Veronica. I know it isn't her real name, but with nothing else to call her, it's all I have.

Jay pokes his head out of the bathroom, removing the toothbrush from his mouth. "Fuck yeah, he gonna go out with us? "

"I imagine so. Fuck man, just got a message from Dad. Let me see what he says."

Could the rehearsal be back on now? That will really throw a wrench in Jay's plans for the night.

Dad: I want you and your brothers to message your new sister and take her to dinner. Get to know her and perhaps persuade her to be nicer to her mother tomorrow. It would make your old man happy.

Ughh! I groan out in disgust.

"What is it, Eli?" Jay calls from the bathroom.

"Seems Dad wants us to play nice with the new sister and take her out to eat."

He comes out of the bathroom, a scowl on his face as he buttons up his shirt. "No way, man. I want to find my girl, not babysit."

Me: Dad. Come on, don't make us. We haven't even met her, know what her name is, or even have her number.

Dad: You will do this because I asked you. Selena is going to be your sister, and you need to get to know her. Here is her number 555-647-9555. Now I expect you and your brothers to do it.

Me: Fine.

Dad: Also meet me in the wedding hall at 9:30 am. The wedding planner will be going over how the ceremony will go before she goes and meets with Julia and Selena.

"Jay, apparently we have to do it. Make Dad happy. I'm going to message her. Let's get it over with, then we can dump her and head out and find our ladies, and then find one for Zeke."

Needing to get this done, I open a new message and type her number in it.

Me: Hey this is Eli, your soon-to-be stepbrother. Dad messaged and wants me and my brothers to take you out to eat. Get ready and we can meet you in the lobby.

I figured if we eat in the resort restaurant, then we don't have to worry about bringing her back here. I wait a few minutes but when I don't get a reply I feel relieved. If she doesn't want to answer, at least I can tell Dad I tried.

But it seems luck isn't on my side. A few seconds later, my phone pings with an incoming message.

Stepbitch: Thanks but I'll pass. Jose, Jim, Jack and the Captain, and I are all having a good time right now.

Me: Wow. You are a slut, aren't you?

Stepbitch: And you're a fucking dick, so I guess we're both good. So fuck off.

"She's definitely a bitch who apparently is screwing four guys up in her room." Jay just turns his nose up at that.

"What a slut. Think she learned it from her mother? Eli, are we really going to let him go through with this tomorrow?"

"We don't really have a choice." I sit down on the bed, stretching my legs out as I lean back on the headboard, picking up the remote and scrolling through channels until I finally stop on ESPN.

Jay continues to bitch, but I barely pay attention to a word he says. Too busy fuming at the way the little whore messaged me.

A knock on the door pulls both our attention and Jay jumps up to answer, his carbon copy standing on the other side.

"Who's ready to drink?" Zeke says loudly, stepping past Jay to enter the room, and dropping his bag on the floor. "Did you get to meet the new steps?"

"Nah man, apparently the new sister pissed the step monster off and all plans tonight were canceled. Then Dad wanted us to take the sister out, but according to Eli, she's holed up in her room with four guys and gave us their names." Jay gives him the play-by-play as he flops down on the bed.

"What were their names?" Zeke asks as he sits down on the edge of Jay's bed, facing me.

"Jack, Jose, and two others I just can't remember," I tell him, as he gives me a furrowed look before doubling over in laughter.

"Dude. That's alcohol. The stepsister is getting drunk in her room, not having a train run on her," he says when he finally catches his breath.

"Whatever, she's still a fucking bitch. Let's go. I want to find the woman from the plane and Jay wants to find his girl from the hallway."

"Sounds good. Would be even better if my woman was here, but when I get back home, I'm going to find her."

We all stand up and head out the door, with me in the rear, making sure to snatch up the key card from the desk.

Fuck the step monster and the step bitch. It's going to take everything in me not to object to this damn wedding tomorrow.

CHAPTER 8

SELENA

The incessant ringing of the phone wakes me from my drunken stupor. I barely remembered to call downstairs last night and schedule a wake-up call before I attacked the mini bar like a wino who hit the motherload. How dare that asshole message me and demand that I meet them in the lobby, and to top it off, call me a fucking slut. He doesn't know me from Sam, yet he has the nerve to call me such a derogatory name, so fuck him and the high horse he rode in on.

Picking up the phone, I tell them thank you, knowing it won't stop until I do. As much as I want to curl back up into the warm comfort of my blankets, I fling them off and sit up, giving myself a little internal pep talk. '*Come on, Selena, you can do it. A ceremony lasts what, ten minutes max, show your face at the reception, do your toast, then you can get the hell out of there.*'

I head to the bathroom to take a quick shower, brush my teeth, and throw on some clothes. Mom has a hair and make-up stylist coming to her room to take care of us, so I don't have to worry about doing any of that. Per her words exactly, "She didn't want me looking whorish on her day and embarrass her." Is there some game where whoever calls me a slut the most wins some jackpot?

I don't need my purse today, but I pick up the room key card from the table, before grabbing the dress I draped over the chair when room service delivered it last night. Taking a deep breath, I mentally prepare myself for my mother and step out the door.

The hallway is quiet. The only other soul in sight is an older woman, probably about seventy, heading in the same direction as me toward the elevator. She ends up going down while I go up to the ninth floor.

It feels like my soul is being sucked from my body the longer the elevator ascends to the floor until finally it comes to a screeching halt and the doors slide open. Stepping off, I begin the walk of dread until I end in front of their room at precisely ten am sharp. Lifting my hand, I knock on the door.

I could just walk in, but I don't. Who knows what kind of lecture could stem from that, and on the off chance my new stepdaddy is still in there, I don't want to walk in on my new stepfather's bare ass as he's railing my mom. Now I need to bleach my eyes because that's all I can see.

The door flies open, but it's not my mother. It's a brunette who's about my age, with a white blouse and black pencil skirt, standing in front of me. "You must be Selena. Your mother was beginning to worry we'd have to hunt you down since you were late." There's a sternness to her voice, but her eyes hold a whole different story; I see compassion. She must see the woman my mother truly is.

"Mom said ten, and it's ten. So I think I'm right on time and not late," I joke, as the woman steps to the side, allowing me space to enter the room.

"Selena, you know that is still late. You should have been here thirty minutes ago. And the way you're looking right now, it's going to take a miracle to make you look presentable," she says with a sneer, as the woman standing in front of her doing her makeup gives me an awkward smile.

"Well, good morning to you, Mother, and what an honor it is to be a part of your special day, even with how horrendous I look." Looking over, I see a table already covered with breakfast foods, coffee, and orange juice, and I make a beeline right to it.

I make a cup of coffee first, needing it to deal with my mom, before picking up a croissant and covering it in a maple spread. Mom's nasally voice pipes up behind me. "Selena, don't you think you should go for something with fewer calories? The bread will make you bloat even more and we already had to let out the dress yesterday."

Groaning, I turn to her, before plastering an evil smile on my face and take a huge bite out of it as I glare at her. "I think I'll be okay. Plus, no one will be looking at me with how gorgeous you're going to be." That puts an instant smile on her face because she loves to hear how great she looks.

"Yes darling, that's true. How was your night with your new step-brothers?"

"Don't know. I didn't go because I was having too much fun with Jose, Jim, Jack, and the Captain." The woman who answered the door, who my mother still hasn't taken the time to introduce, covers her mouth with her hand, as she attempts to stifle a laugh.

"Really, Selena? Here only one day and already fooling around with four men? You should be ashamed. God help me. If Abel finds out about it, I'm going to kill you. Do you make it your life's mission to embarrass me?"

"Calm down, Mom. It's alcohol. I was raiding the minibar and didn't want to go out."

"Even worse, now he'll think my own flesh and blood is an alcoholic, which he'll attribute to one of the reasons you're so damn fat."

And that's when I felt my blood boil. It took every ounce of my being not to storm out of the room and jump on the first flight back home. One would expect their mother to love them unconditionally. Guess she didn't get the memo. I make a vow to myself at that moment that if I ever get pregnant, and have a child, especially a girl,

I'd never expose her to my mother's venom. I'd love her no matter what.

"Selena. Hi, I'm Cassandra. Why don't I go ahead and take care of your hair while Layla is finishing your mother's hair? Then once Mayrene is ready, she can go over how the wedding entrance and so forth will go. I know the guys all showed up early, and she was able to take care of their part pretty quickly." She comes over to me, gesturing toward a chair set up on the other side of the room away from my mother.

"That sounds great." Taking another huge bite of my croissant, I head over to her.

"If you could just change into this button-up shirt, that way your makeup and hair won't be messed up by pulling your shirt over your head when it's time to get dressed," she whispers but not low enough that Mother's eagle ears didn't hear.

"Why didn't you listen to me when I told you what to wear, Selena? Honestly, it's like everything I say goes in one ear and out the other," my mother gripes.

"You're right, Mother, I'm such an ungrateful child. It's a shame you got burdened with a child like me." Turning away from her, I pull off my shirt, put the other one on, and drop into the chair.

I sit in silence the rest of the time, not saying a word unless I have to while my mother bitches about me. Once Cassandra has my hair up in one of the most beautiful braids I've ever seen, she moves over to my mother, before giving my shoulder a reassuring squeeze and whispering in my ear, "Don't listen to her, you look beautiful."

Layla changes places, now done with my mother, and comes over to me, turning my face into a work of art that even has my jaw dropping when I look at myself in the mirror.

"Okay ladies, before we get dressed," Mayrene says loudly, "let's go over the wedding march. Selena, obviously, you will go first down the aisle. You're going to stay behind the door until the music starts, then step out. Wait for a count of five and then begin your walk. Abel and his sons will be waiting at the altar with the pastor. Once you are in your spot, then the wedding march will play and that's when Julia will step out. Everyone will take in her beauty before she makes her way down the aisle." She continues on, and I listen, making sure I know what to do and when to do it. I'm just ready for this day to be over.

"Did you hear all that, Selena? You looked like you were falling asleep. Is being a part of my day too much for you?" my mother bickers at me.

"Yes, Mom, I heard it all." That's all I have the effort to say because honestly, I would rather have a root canal than be here right now.

"Okay, Cassandra, if you could help Selena into her dress, then Layla and I will help Julia."

I pick up my dress and wave Cassandra toward the bathroom, not wanting to undress in front of my mother and listen to the comments I know would come once she saw my nearly naked body.

Once I'm in nothing but my thong, Cassandra holds open the dress for me to step into, then pulls it up the length of my body. The satin material feels wonderful against my body and compliments my skin color.

"You look stunning, and this dress fits you like a glove. I'd kill for your body," she says, as her eyes rake down my body, and I get a feeling she may just be into me.

"Don't let my mother hear you say that. She'll think you've gone mad."

"I'd be mad any day to have a woman looking like you on my arm." Yep, she's definitely interested in me. Too bad I'm into men and not women.

Stepping back out into the room, my mother turns to face me, dressed in a classic white mermaid dress, and she looks beautiful. Like an older version of the woman in her and Dad's wedding picture.

"You look beautiful, Mom. Abel's a lucky man," I tell her because I can't lie about that. To everyone but me, Mom is so sweet, caring, and loving. Hopefully, once they're married, he keeps her so busy that she has less time to see or call to harp on me.

"Okay ladies, time to head down. The men are already there and ready to be in place. No way of them accidentally seeing the bride before the big reveal," Mayrene announces as she moves over to my mother, placing the final touch on her look, her veil, the very one she wore in her wedding with Dad.

Picking up my room key, I slip it into the bodice of my dress for safekeeping. The clothes, well, they could stay here. I'd get them later or Mom could toss them for all I care.

We make our way down the hall to the elevator, stepping inside once the doors open. Mayrene pushes the button for the twentieth floor, which I learned this morning is where the ballroom is located. The ride is quiet except for the banter back and forth between Mayrene and Mom, who never once speaks directly to me. A blessing if you ask me. Once we reach the floor, the doors open and I quickly exit, with everyone else following suit.

"If you'll just follow me, I'll get us to where we need to be without anyone seeing. All of the guests should be in the hall waiting, as well as the groom." Once she's done, she heads down a hallway tucked off to the side, Mom following behind her as I take up the rear.

Soft music emanates out of the hall, filling the room foyer where we're waiting. "Okay, Selena it's time," Mayrene announces.

Stepping up to my spot to head down the aisle, I wait for the music to kick on, making sure to paint a happy smile on my face. I'm going to get through this. Then Mom will be so occupied with her new husband that she can ignore me and I can enjoy the rest of the time I have here.

The music starts playing, which is my cue to turn the corner and head down the aisle. Stepping out from behind the door and looking up, I'm frozen in place. My eyes go wide at the sight before me and my heart begins to race. Standing directly beside Abel are three faces, two of them identical that I know very well. Three who have made my body feel so amazing and now I know who they are and they are off limits. *Shit!* I slept with my stepbrothers. I don't have any time to process, to think, as I begin my march down the aisle toward three faces holding the same look of shock as me.

Fuck me!

To Be Continued...

(I know just when it was getting good! lol)

~

PreOrder Now

https://books2read.com/u/bpNOdE

ABOUT BRE ROSE

Bre Rose writes under a pen name in both the contemporary and paranormal, why choose genre primarily, but does have works that are MF. Bre is a native of North Carolina and mother to three amazing sons and two feline fur babies more affectionately known as her hellhounds.

She's always been an avid reader then progressed to becoming an ARC, BETA and ALPHA reader for some of her favorite authors. After some encouragement she decided to tackle writing the stories in her head and is loving every single minute of it. When she isn't reading or writing she enjoys traveling the world and still has some places to mark off her bucket list. She also enjoys spending time with her family and advocating for the differently abled population.

To keep up to date with all upcoming releases and all things Bre then simply join her facebook reader group Bre's Rose Petal Readers.

ACKNOWLEDGMENTS

First as always, I want to thank my family, my sons Dustin, Brandon and Nathaniel. Y'all mean the world to me and I couldn't imagine this life without you. To my extended family, my bestie Melissa, I love you more than you could ever know. Thank you for being my support when I need it the most. I can't wait to give you your story.

To my teams, Alpha, Beta, Arc, Street and Tik Tok you ladies and guy (Love ya Michael) mean the world to me. Thank you for always being there, encouraging me and sharing my books to the world. Where would I be without you?

Shayna, my PA, my right hand, what can I say? You keep me on track with everything I need to do feeling defeated. You are always there to tell me how amazing I am, one day I will believe you. I know I am not the easiest person, sometimes being way too needy, but you never once complain. Thank you for your invaluable proofreading and editing skills as well as the ability to make some kick ass paperback wraps. I am so happy that I get to be a part of your success as you skyrocket with your talent. I wouldn't be here today without you

Lastly, to my readers, I appreciate all of you. It is your support and enjoyment in reading my work that keeps me wanting to write more. I hope to be able to bring you stories for years to come. I know that ending left us heartbroken but I promise Sierra will have a happy ending with her men.

ALSO BY BRE ROSE

https://books.bookfunnel.com/breroseauthor

Memphis Duet

Finding Memphis (Book 1)

Saving Memphis (Book 2)

Memphis Duet Omnibus

Memphis Spinoffs

Unbreakable

Memphis Beginnings:Novella

Prophecy Series

Shay's Awakening (Book 1)

Shay's Acceptance (Book 2)

Shay's Ascension (Book 3)

Beyond the Pack Series w/ Cassie Lein

Rise of the Alpha

Destroying the Alpha

Claiming My Alpha

(Coming June 2023)

Brighton High School Reunion Shared World

Reuniting With Desire

(coming July 2023)

Fairytales with a Twist Shared World

Charleston Curse

(coming June 2023)

Merciless Few MC Shared World

Kentucky Chapter

Sinner Choice

(Coming August 2023)

Standalones Stories

Love On the Ice

(coming October 2023)

Morelli Family Series

Assassin's Seduction (Book 1)

(Coming Jan 2024)

Sports Romance w/ Cassie Lein

All on the Field Kindlevella

(on going)

All on the Field Ebook

(Coming 2023)

Breaking Hearts Duet

Against All Odds

CLAIMING SUTTON

IRIS JAMES

ABOUT CLAIMING SUTTON

See, little sister, I knew you wanted it.

Once Landon has me in his grasp, there is nowhere to go but down. I try to resist, to push aside my body's reaction to him, but with the house to ourselves and his devilish tongue, my resolve weakens.

So here we are, only months after our parents' union, committing one of the highest sins, but Landon's touch creates a fire within me, stoking the need I didn't know was there.

I fall deeper into his forbidden arms until it's too late, but finder's keepers. He's mine, and I'm his.

His little *step*sister.

Claiming Sutton is a stepbrother-themed short story in the Sinful Desires anthology, following Sutton and Landon's beginning. The couple will have cameos in future stepbrother works.

CW: dubcon

CHAPTER 1

SUTTON

My last night of freedom tastes like vodka and bad decisions. I'm supposed to be at my brand new house with my mother and brand new stepfather, but at the last minute, I got cold feet. I called my mom and told her I was late packing up, so I wouldn't be able to make it until tomorrow morning. In reality, I booked a hotel room and decided to get drunk at this bar. I started slow with beer, but that wasn't dissolving the anxiety fast enough, so some shots got me to this level. I expect the next few will bring me well past it into sweet oblivion.

My artsy and independent mother left for a wellness retreat three weeks ago and came home with a rich husband. She claimed he was her "twin flame," and with that, we uprooted our lives. Mom put our small two bedroom house on the market, packed up, and left with strict instructions that I was to follow. My time is up, and here I am.

At nineteen, I'm a little aimless, and I can admit that. Mom was content to let me take a year off after high school before going to college, but I've been playing with the idea of continuing to work and taking another year off. I'm not sure what I want to do, and the idea of taking out loans so I can drift aimlessly at an expensive school sounded like torture. How fortunate for me that my new stepfather was able to swoop in and fix all my problems.

This move to Woodbury comes complete with a fully staffed mansion, my mother turning into a pod person, an acceptance to Brighton University where my new daddy is an alum and generous donor, and a new stepbrother I assume will want nothing to do with me. That feeling will be mutual.

It was hard to say goodbye to the house I grew up in, and the few friends that I have, but I'm trying to embrace my mom's excitement over this fresh start. Maybe this is everything I've needed. Or it'll be absolute hell, and I'll be moving into a small studio apartment soon.

I knock back another shot and barely wince as the cheap liquor slides down my throat, warming my insides as it goes. My hotel is across the street, so I'm not worried about stumbling back there later. The chilly night breeze hits my back when someone opens the door, and I

debate putting my leather jacket back on, but this top makes my tits look good, and vodka makes me horny. His scent assaults me before I see him. It's an intoxicating mix of cedar and vanilla, which has me licking my lips. The man this scent belongs to sits a few stools down from me and orders whiskey.

I shift my focus back to the two shots still in front of me and play with one of the empty shot glasses that hasn't been cleared yet. I can't seem to control my eyes from wandering back to the sexy guy that walked in. He has dark brown hair that's shorter on the sides and longer on top, which would give me something to really hold onto if... no, that's not happening. His blue eyes look dark and annoyed when they flash at me, but something changes in them before he looks away quickly.

Well, okay then. A moment later, there's another burst of cold air, and this time the person responsible sits next to me. He has dark hair too, still cute but not as sexy as the guy to my right. The new guy offers me a friendly smile and motions for the bartender. I politely smile back and tip another shot back while he orders a beer.

"Are you celebrating or wallowing?" He takes a drink of his beer, and I decide to see if he'll do for the night.

"I guess that depends."

"On?"

"How my night ends."

He laughs and gets comfortable on his chair, angling to face me. "I would love to help make this a celebration. I'm Derek." He extends his hand in my direction, and my manners kick in.

"I'm Sutton. It's nice to meet you." I shake his hand, and I swear I see the other guy whip his head in my direction.

"Can I buy you another drink?" Derek watches me with interest as I take the last one in front of me.

"You sure can. I'll take a beer. Thank you." He orders my drink and leans into me.

"I come in here a couple of times a week, and I've never seen you before. Are you new in town or new to this establishment?"

I smile as his hand settles on my leg. "Both, actually. I just moved here today. I'm staying across the street tonight because I can't get into my place until tomorrow." I bite my lip and hope it's giving sexy and not cannibal vibes.

Derek takes another drink from his beer before squeezing my leg. I watch his eyes drift over me, taking in my leopard print booties, black leggings, my lace trim top, and eventually, my actual face. I can see the lust in his eyes, and I know I've got this in the bag.

"I live here, so I've never had a reason to stay there. I've heard it's a nice place though."

"It's incredibly nice. Want to come see for yourself?" I was planning to have a few more drinks, but I want to have enough of my wits about me to tell Derek to leave when we're done.

"I'd love to. I'm ready when you are." He basically starts chugging his beer, so I stand up and grab my leather jacket off the back of my chair while he finishes. He throws some money down on the bar for the drinks. "I'm just going to run to the bathroom quickly, and we can get out of here."

I nod at him. "I'll be waiting." I watch him as he walks to the men's room and pull out my phone.

I'm just about to text a friend what I'm doing in case I get murdered tonight when the air shifts my hair, and I turn around. Standing over me is the sexy guy that had been sitting a few chairs away. His blue eyes, which seemed so dark, are much lighter when they're glaring down at me.

"What are you doing?" I don't know who this sexy asshole thinks he is, but he's breaking a very basic rule of humans and invading my personal space.

"You're not leaving with him." He steps closer to me, and my back hits the bar behind me.

"Actually, I am, and I'll tell you one very important reason why. Because I feel like it, and it's none of your fucking business." I reach up and pat him on the head, which is a considerable reach from my five-foot-four height to his obviously over six feet self.

"You can either tell him you changed your mind and leave with me, or I'll rip his head off his fucking shoulders, and then you can leave with me. Either way, baby, you're mine." He smirks, and I almost want to yell at my vagina for getting all tingly and wet at his words.

I kind of want to see if he'll do what he says, but I also can tell by his size that he could probably kill Derek, and that seems like an extreme thing to allow to happen this evening. I shrug at him instead.

"Fine, bossy. Let's go." I gesture toward the door, and he grabs my hand to lead me out.

Right as we get to the door, Derek calls out, "Hey, Sutton! What are you doing?"

I stop to turn around and address Derek, but Mr. Bossy answers instead and reminds me that I didn't even ask what his fucking name is. I'm so going to end up on a *Dateline* special. "Sorry, Derek, she's with me. Feel free to fuck all the way off." Derek looks between me and my potential serial killer and raises his hands up, clearly making a decision. "That a boy, Derek."

Within a moment, I'm being pulled across the street and into the luxurious and well-lit lobby at The Franklin Hotel. I decide that, at the bare minimum, I should know this guy's name before he knocks my head against the headboard.

"While I'm totally into this whole mystery thing you've got going, what's your name?" We come to a stop at the elevators, and he peers down at me with those gorgeous blue eyes.

"Landon." It seems like he's searching my face for some kind of reaction, but I've got nothing for him.

The elevator door dings, and we step inside. I hit the button for floor twelve and let the nervous excitement take over. I hope this guy knows what he's doing because I'm so ready.

CHAPTER 2

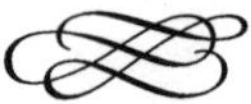

LANDON

From the moment I saw her, I wanted her. When I first walked into that bar, I was in a bad mood and didn't feel like talking to her yet, but when that guy waltzed in and thought he could have her? Fuck no. I thought for a moment it would all be over when I told her my name, but she didn't have anywhere near the same reaction to mine that I did to hers.

She smiles at me as she produces her room key and flashes it in front of the lock. The door opens, and she stops before letting me enter.

"I'm Sutton, not that you asked."

"I heard you tell that loser at the bar." She huffs and steps into the room, so I can walk past her.

"Would you like a drink? I have a couple of beers in the mini-fridge." I watch her as she holds onto the wall and slides her booties off, so I grab the beers and hand one to her when she's done. "Thanks."

She tosses her jacket onto the chair in the corner of the room and takes a long drink of her beer. I watch her throat move as she swallows, and I'm out of patience. I march over to her, grab the beer from her, and set it down before I pull her into my chest. Her breaths come faster, and I close the distance between us, capturing her mouth with mine. Our tongues tangle and battle for dominance, but my girl here is going to learn her place.

I grip the back of Sutton's neck and grind myself into her. My whole body shivers when she lets out an obscene moan at the contact. She takes a step back from me and starts sliding her skintight leggings down. I follow her lead and unbutton my shirt, followed by my belt and jeans. We're each standing there in our underwear, and she's even sexier than I imagined. She licks her lips as she takes in the sight in front of her, and almost like she's reading my fucking mind, she drops to her knees and pulls me out of my boxers.

Her mouth wraps around my dick, and I know I'll be a goner in no time if I let her finish me off this way. "Oh fuck, your mouth is perfect, baby." I keep one hand behind her head and stare down with fascination as my dick disappears into her mouth over and over.

Finally, when I know I'm getting close, I pull her away, pick her up off the floor, and toss her onto the large white bed behind her. She lets out an adorable yelp, and I pounce on her. I bite her lower lip and tug on it before I consume her again, slowly working my way down her body. Her breasts are perfect and practically begging me to put them in my mouth once I get her bra off. I lick and suck one nipple before showing the same attention to the other. I keep moving down her body until all that's keeping me out is a pair of lacy, black panties.

"Hey, those are my favorite!" Sutton whines when I tear them to shreds and throw the scraps behind me.

"You don't need to wear underwear anymore." I dive into her pussy before she can answer.

"Fuck, holy shit." Sutton's legs fall to the side as I suck on her clit and slowly push a finger inside her.

She's soaked and so ready for me. I want to make her come like this, so I pick up the pace. I press down on her clit and rub circles that have her grinding into my hand. I can tell how close she is, so I keep the pressure and rhythm exactly the same. Minutes later, when she explodes all over my face, it's absolutely perfect. She's tangy and sweet like strawberries, and I don't think I'll ever get enough. I need to be inside her.

Sutton is still breathing heavily and trying to come down from that high as I move and line myself up with her entrance. I should be asking about birth control or putting a condom on, but I can't even imagine putting a barrier between myself and this girl. I know basically nothing about her, but this overwhelming urge to fill her up and mark her as mine has taken over, and that's exactly what I'm going to do.

"Wait, I'm on birth control, but do you have a condom?" Well, that settles that.

"I do, but I'm not wearing it." I thrust into her, and she cries out.

I have to take a deep breath before I start moving because she feels even better than I imagined. She's so fucking tight; I could die a happy man like this. Sutton wraps herself around me like she's afraid I'll stop what I'm doing. Zero chance of that happening. She's kissing me anywhere she can reach, my mouth, my neck, and it's driving my need higher and higher as I continuously pound into her tight pussy. I pull back enough, so I can reach my hand between us and circle her clit.

"Oh god, Landon, please, please." Fuck, I didn't think this could get any better, but the sound of my name on her lips as she begs shoves me even closer to the edge.

I pinch her clit, and it immediately sets off her second orgasm. I keep fucking her through it, but watching her fall apart underneath me is so fucking sexy that I spill into her a few moments later. I already want her again, but I roll off her and lie beside her while we both try to catch our breath. She starts to laugh, but I'm confident enough to know it has to be about something other than what we just did.

"Would you like to share with the class?"

She holds up a finger while she composes herself. "Sorry, I'm just shaking my head because I had this brief thought as we were leaving the bar that you better know what you're doing." She starts laughing again.

"I trust that I've alleviated that fear." I grin at her and let out a chuckle of my own.

"Fuck yeah, and then some. I'm actually going to need you to alleviate me of a few other things." She rolls over on top of me and starts grinding against me.

"Oh, baby, I'm happy to be of service." I lift her up and drop her down onto my already hard dick.

She gasps as she takes my entire length in one go, but she's more than wet enough for it. Sutton is a fucking siren as I let her take control. I watch her tits bounce and pull her closer so I can suck on her pretty pink nipples. I thrust into her and revel in the way her body holds onto me so tightly. She can feel it too, even though she won't be ready to admit it yet. That's okay, I've got time.

"Shit, Landon. Don't stop, don't stop, I'm going to come." Her breathy voice and the way she's writhing on my dick have me coming a second after her.

Her breathing starts to even out as she lies on top of my chest, and I want nothing more than to fall asleep and maybe fuck her a couple more times, but I should go. It'll make tomorrow that much better. She clears her throat and slowly slides down to the bed.

"Listen, this was... well, fucking awesome. I need to be up and out of here really early tomorrow though, so would you mind taking off?" She grabs the blanket and covers herself with it.

I hold back the chuckle that wants to get out and smile. "No, I've got a big day tomorrow too. This was fun." I don't know if she's expecting more, but she watches me quietly as I get dressed.

I don't think she notices when I grab her shredded panties and slip them into my pocket, but I wouldn't care if she did. I make sure I have everything on me, then walk over to her and grab her chin. She lets out a little sigh as I slam my mouth onto hers and kiss her goodbye.

Without another word, I leave her room and head outside to my car.

Sleep well, little sister.

CHAPTER 3

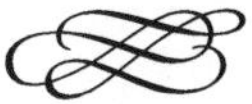

SUTTON

Light pours in through the curtains that I forgot to close, but I let out a sigh of relief when I remember I made Landon leave last night. Nothing is worse than the awkward lingering goodbye of someone you had sex with and never want to see again. Although, if I'm being completely honest, I'd totally fuck Landon again. He's hot and has this weird intensity about him that draws me in and wants to let him do whatever he wants with me. I shake my head. We didn't even exchange last names or phone numbers, so that ship has sailed.

I'm only fifteen minutes from my new home, so I take my time showering and getting ready. I'm going to attempt to make a positive first impression on my new stepfather and stepbrother. Mom will be upset if I don't, and despite my extreme doubt over her whirlwind romance, I don't want to spoil things for her. She has always been there for me, and I can't remember the last time she was this happy and giddy about everything.

My makeup is light and natural around my green eyes, my red hair is soft and straight past my shoulders, and I have on a nice pair of jeans, a plain black T-shirt, my leather jacket, leopard booties, and a few dainty pieces of jewelry to complete my look. I'm as ready as I'll ever be. I do one final pass through the room to make sure I have everything before I make my way downstairs to check out. I have enough time to grab some coffee. Fuck knows I need it.

After sailing through the drive-thru at Caribou, a fresh iced coffee in hand, my brain feels more prepared to be functioning. I check out the stores and restaurants I pass while I drive toward the house, and I'm surprised at all the variety. At our old house, we were kind of far from all these types of places, so I can't help but have some excitement bubble up over having access to these places on the regular. I make a mental note of some cute boutiques as well. I could use a couple of new things before I start school in a few days.

My nerves get the best of me, and I basically inhale my iced coffee. It's long gone by the time I pull up into the winding driveway of my humble new abode. I curse in my head as I take in the gigantic house before me. It's made of massive stones, set in the middle of nowhere. There's a fountain in the center of the driveway that circles around in front, and even the grass seems greener here than everywhere else I drove by. I can't imagine what the inside is going to look like.

I park right in front of the house, so it will be easy to unload the bags I have with me. I text my mom that I'm here before shoving my phone in my purse. I get out of the car, rub my palms down my jeans, and grab one of the easier bags to carry. I hear the front door open, and my mom's unmistakable squeal hits my ears.

"Oh, my darling daughter has finally arrived! I've missed you so much, baby!" I turn around and step into my mom's arms.

We stand there like that for a moment before a distinctly male chuckle can be heard behind us. "I assume this is the incredible Sutton I've heard so much about. Welcome home!" I pull away from my mom and look at the man standing in front of us. He's tall, has dark brown hair with bits of gray near his ears, and he has kind blue eyes. He reminds me of someone, but I can't put my finger on it. Either way, he's handsome, and the way he's looking at my mom has me hopeful that everything she's been spewing at me about her instant connection with this man is true.

"Hi, yes, that's me. It's so nice to finally meet you and put a face to the man that my mom hasn't stopped gushing about." I extend my hand as we all chuckle, but he pulls me in for a hug.

"Please, call me Sam or Samuel, I'll answer to either. We're family now, and I'm so glad you're here. Your mother and I have been worried about you making the drive on your own, but now the fun can start. We thought we could all spend the day together and get to know one another better, after you get settled, of course. How does that sound?"

"That sounds like a great idea. I won't take too long if someone could just point me in the direction I should go." I bend down to pick up the bag I set down and hoist it back onto my shoulder.

"I'll help you," a sexy and familiar voice says from the door.

"Ah, there's my son. I was wondering where you had disappeared to. Come meet your new sister. Sutton, this is my son, Landon. You'll both be attending Brighton together.

He'll be able to show you around and give you the scoop about everything. Isn't that right,

Landon?"

"Absolutely. I can't wait to show you all the things you'll need to know about your new life." He smirks and marches over to me. My mouth is still resting against the driveway when Landon, my new fucking stepbrother and most recent man to enter me, steps closer and gives me a hug. He licks my earlobe, and a shiver runs down my spine. "Close that mouth, little sister.

I'd hate to have to show Mommy and Daddy what it's good for right here in the driveway."

I jump back like I've been electrocuted, and Landon keeps that million-dollar smile plastered on his face as he starts unloading my bags from the car. I try to play it off for my mom and Sam, but she frowns at me.

"Thank you, Landon. You're so sweet and helpful." My mom

walks over to where Landon stands with the rest of my stuff hanging off his shoulders.

"Oh, it's nothing, Lauren. I'm happy to help. Come on, Sutton. I'll show you to your room, so you can get settled." He looks like a fucking boy scout, and my mom and Sam are beaming at him. Fucking great.

"Isn't that so sweet, Sutton?" There's an edge to my mother's voice that I'm sure wouldn't be there if she knew that Saint Landon fucked me twice in my hotel room last night.

"The sweetest. Thanks, Landon." I manage an awkward smile, and he winks at me.

"No problem, sis. Let's go." I reluctantly follow him.

"Find us in the kitchen or on the patio out back when you're ready, baby!"

"Okay, Mom. See you in a bit." I offer a wave, but she doesn't even notice because she's wrapped in Sam's arms, giggling.

Landon is waiting for me in the foyer with a wide grin. I roll my eyes at him and follow him up winding stairs, down a long hallway, past what feels like a hundred doors, and finally stop before the last door on the right. Landon pushes the door open, and we walk into a massive room, complete with an en suite. It's brightly lit with lots of windows, and everything is in white and cream, waiting for me to step in and personalize all of it.

I realize that as I'm taking in my new room, Landon is taking me in. "Thanks for helping me bring this stuff up. I appreciate it. And it probably goes without saying, but can we please keep what happened between us last night, you know, between us?" He sets all my stuff down before closing the distance.

I take a few steps back, but I find myself trapped against a wall, boxed in by his arms on either side of my head. "I'll keep it between us for now, sure. There are a few things you need to understand though. For starters, don't get too comfortable here because you'll be sleeping in my bed. I'll happily show you around your new school, with the understanding that you are to do as I say. And today? We'll play nice and not alert our parents to any funny business. We'll wait for that until they're ready."

What the fuck? No, no, no. "Listen, Landon. Last night was fun, but I'm not going to be sleeping in your bed and doing anything you tell me to do from this point forward. So thanks for your help, but you can leave now." I try to push him away, so I can start unpacking, but he pins me to the wall with his hips and laughs.

"You don't understand yet, but that's okay; you will soon. I'll leave you alone to get settled for now, but this isn't over. The sooner you accept what's right in front of you, the better off you'll be." He pushes off the wall and takes a step back, and I can finally take a breath.

"Whatever. Get out of my room. Bye." I start to walk away, but he pulls me into his chest.

"You don't tell me what to do. I'll be back in a little bit to get you, so we can meet up with our parents together." He squeezes my chin and slams his mouth onto mine.

It's so fucking annoying that my body instantly remembers what he did to me last night. I'm already soaked between my legs, and everything inside me wants him to throw me down on the bed and give me a replay. I melt into him as he dominates the kiss, but he backs off.

"I'll be back in a little bit. Be a good girl, little sister." He winks and strides out of the room, closing the door behind him. *Shit. I'm so fucked.*

CHAPTER 4

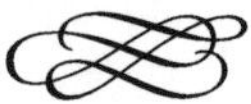

LANDON

My dick is so hard it hurts, and all I want to do is go back into Sutton's room and fuck her against the wall. I'll just have to remember to do that later. I'm not planning on giving her too much time to settle in; she doesn't need it. I meant what I said about her being in my bed; she will be, whether I have to drag her kicking and screaming into it or not. Maybe I should mention something to Dad, so he can help run interference with his new wife while Sutton... adjusts.

My dad is a tough businessman who worked his way up from nothing and created an empire with his all-encompassing digital security firm. He started small out of his college dorm and now employs hundreds of people. I've always admired him, but he's a romantic at heart, and that's just not the guy I am. Or at least I thought I wasn't.

When he told me about meeting his "soulmate" at this wellness retreat, I was positive she would be a twenty-five-year-old gold digger that loved spandex. I was pleasantly surprised when he introduced me to Lauren. She's this free-spirited, kind woman, and it was annoyingly clear how much they were already in love. I thought he was being stupid for making such a big decision so quickly, but it's his life. Then, a few weeks later, I turn around and basically do the same fucking thing. With my new stepsister, no less. Like father, like son.

My room is always fairly clean and well organized, but I take a pass through it and my bathroom to make sure it's presentable. Of course, nothing is amiss. I fuck around on my phone for a few minutes before my thoughts turn back to Sutton. I remember how that sassy little mouth looked wrapped around my dick, and how she moaned in pleasure when I made her come. Fuck, I'm never going to be able to get anything done when I know she's right next door. Why bother, then?

I march out of my room and straight back into Sutton's without warning. "Hey! What the fuck do you think you're doing?" She has her hands on her hips and looks adorably angry.

I stop directly in front of her, grab her wrists, and pull her into my chest. "Initially, I thought I'd give you some time to warm up to all this. Then, I was thinking that if I give you time to sit around and think, you'll try to talk yourself out of a good thing. So I've decided not to wait."

"Get the fuck off me, Landon. I swear to fucking god, I'll scream." She tries to push me away but can't with the way I have her wrists trapped in my hands.

"Oh, baby, I hope you do." I slam my mouth over hers and devour her protests.

The bed is right behind us, so I only have to guide Sutton a few steps before we're steady. With one hand still holding both of her wrists, I bring the other one in between us, so I can undo her jeans and my own. It takes some work, especially with Sutton being uncooperative, but I get her underwear and jeans down far enough that I can slide them off her feet. She rips her mouth away from mine and tries to push at me again, throwing her body weight into it.

"No, Landon, I said no. We're not doing this again. Ah!" I thrust into her, and it's perfection.

Despite all her talking about not wanting to do this, she's soaked for me. "See, little sister? I knew you wanted it." Her body clenches around me at my words, and I chuckle.

"F-fuck you," Sutton's breathy voice stutters on a moan.

"Do you still want me to stop?" I have one finger circling her clit as I push back inside.

"Oh, god, Landon." Her body writhes underneath me, and it's the sexiest thing I've ever seen.

"That's right, Sutton. Me. This is mine. Every inch of it. Do you understand me?" I've released her wrists, and my hands trail up and down her body before I wrap one around her neck and apply light pressure.

She smiles up at me, a wicked glint in her eye. "I don't understand any of that." She laughs.

I shake my head at her. "Oh, baby, you will."

My hand flies to cover her mouth as she lets out a little scream when I pick up the pace of my thrusts. I take one of my fingers and work it in alongside my dick to get it lubed up.

Without warning, I slide it out of Sutton's dripping pussy and slide it directly into her ass.

"What the fuck are you doing?" She impales herself on my dick to get away from my finger, and it feels so fucking good I need a second.

"I have every intention of fucking your ass at some point soon, so there's no time like the present to get you warmed up. Now, hush. You don't want your mother to hear you, do you?" Her pussy clenches, and I laugh. "Is my little sister a freak? Do you want us to get caught?" I slow my thrusts down as I work my finger into her ass.

"N-no, you can't tell them. My mother would kill me. Oh, fuck, oh god." She goes nonverbal as my dick pounds into her while I finger her ass and play with her clit.

"Look down here, baby. Look at what a good job you're doing taking me like this. Doesn't this feel good?" I watch her slowly open her eyes and look down at where we're connected.

"Fuck yes. Please don't stop, don't stop." She lets her legs fall completely to the side, and we're as close as we can be.

I lean down over her and take her mouth too. She was hesitant when we first started, but now she's kissing me back with everything she's got. I continue the delicious torment on her clit until she's pulsing around my dick and screaming into my hand covered in her juices. My rhythm falters, and I spill into Sutton with long languid strokes.

I lean into her and whisper, "Admit it or don't, I don't fucking care. You. Are. Mine." Then I move over and kiss her again.

After a moment, I gently slide myself out of her and pull myself together. She lies on the edge of the bed and stares at me. "You're insane." She shakes her head and slowly moves up the bed as she pulls up her pants.

"You don't even know the half of it. So don't test me. Now, I'm going to go have a quick chat with my father. I better see your ass downstairs in the next ten minutes."

"Or what?" I have to turn around to see her smirk.

I close the distance between us and grab her chin. "Try it and see. Please, Sutton, keep pushing. This is fun for me." I give her a gentle kiss, then turn and head down to my father's office.

I know my dad well, and if he can sneak off to his office to check on things at work, or grab an extra glass of scotch, he will. I push open the door, and he's there, staring at his computer with a freshly poured drink to his left.

"Hey, son. What's up? Did Lauren notice I went missing?"

I sit down across from him. "I don't think she's noticed yet, but she probably will when everyone else sits down to eat and you don't. I need a favor though."

"You actually need something? Well, I am all ears, son. How can I help?"

"I know you just got back from your honeymoon, but I need you to take Lauren on another trip. For at least two weeks, but anything more would be preferred."

Dad laughs. "Okay, and why is it that you need this?"

I blow out a breath. "Listen to everything before you interrupt or have faux outrage. Last night, I ran into Sutton at a bar. She didn't know who I was, but I figured out who she was when she said her name. Anyway, we fucked. I'm not going to pretend I'm sorry. I want her, and I'm going to do everything in my power to make her mine. So don't pretend you have fatherly feelings for her. Sutton is reluctant in returning my affection, but I think if we have time alone while she settles into her life here, it will make all the difference. The time away will make it easier for Lauren to accept things when you guys get back."

Dad takes a deep breath and releases it before speaking. "Well, that is not at all what I was expecting. I don't think this is what Lauren had in mind when she looked at you and said she felt like she was gaining a son." He laughs and rubs the back of his neck. "I'm not going to stand in your way. I can work from anywhere, and it's not like it's a hardship to take a luxurious trip with my new wife. I'll have arrangements made, and Lauren and I will be off tomorrow. Now, I love you, but don't fuck this up. I may not have fatherly feelings for that girl, but I have loving husband ones for her mother, and I will kick your ass if you make her cry. Got it?"

I reach my hand across his desk, and we both stand and shake. "Don't worry about it,

Dad. I've got this handled."

Enjoy your last moments of freedom, Sutton.

CHAPTER 5

SUTTON

It sets a bad precedent when you give in to a dictator; as such, I will be waiting longer than ten minutes to go downstairs. Landon doesn't scare me. The fact that I only waited an extra couple of minutes doesn't mean anything. I'm just really hungry and anxious to see Mom again. As I reach the bottom of the stairs, a door in the far corner opens, and Landon strides out with a smile. When he spots me, that smile only gets wider, and I don't like the dangerous twinkle in his eye.

"Oh, Sutton. I'll let it slide this time, but you better start picking up on the rules of your new life quickly. In case you haven't noticed, I'm not a patient man. Now, let's go sit down. Our parents have news." He tries to drag me along with him, but I rip my arm away.

"Excuse you. I don't have to do anything you tell me, and keep your fucking hands to yourself. You do not get to touch me anymore for any reason. Do you understand me? I will tell our parents exactly what is happening, asshole. Don't push me." I storm in the direction of the kitchen, but an arm wraps around my waist, another around my mouth, and I'm being dragged through the living room down a hallway.

I'm shoved into what looks like a library, and I catch myself on the back of a chair. Landon closes and locks the door, storming in behind me. I try to back away from him, but I'm unfamiliar with the layout of the room and find myself against the wall next to a large stone fireplace. Landon's body towers over mine, and I realize I have nowhere to go now that he's boxed me in.

"Listen, I want to have a nice dinner with our parents tonight, so I need you to lose the attitude. You don't give in easily; I get that, but neither do I. And I promise you, I'm going to win in the end. Instead of making this harder for yourself, give in, and let me keep you. Otherwise, the result is going to be the same, but you won't like the method of getting you there. It's up to you." Before I can answer, he covers my mouth with his and forces his tongue past my lips.

I hate that he's such a good kisser. He grips the back of my neck, holding me in place as he grinds his already hard dick against me. I refuse to acknowledge the spark of desire he's igniting in me. He literally just assaulted me minutes ago, but my body is ready to betray me all over again. He pulls away and smiles like he knows exactly what I'm thinking.

"Get the fuck off of me." He kisses the tip of my nose and backs up with his hands held up in surrender.

"I'm only giving in because we're late for dinner. Be good, Sutton. I mean it." He gives me one last forceful look before he straightens his clothes and leaves the door open behind him when he exits the library.

My thoughts are a jumbled mess. Ordinarily, if a super sexy guy was showing this much interest in me, I'd let him. Well, I'd probably let him. The fact that he's my new stepbrother and he's acting like he owns me is where the problem lies. My mom can't ever find out about what has happened between us. She'll blame me, and it'll cause problems with her new husband, which I don't want. She does deserve to be happy if she truly is. I guess sitting down to dinner will help me see if she really is or not. Maybe she's kind of miserable, regrets her decision, and is looking for a way out. I could certainly help with that. With a hopeful skip in my step, I walk toward the door.

I turn around and take another look at this dark and cozy room with bookshelves against every wall. I'm definitely coming back here to read. My eyes linger on the spot where Landon had me trapped against him, and my heart rate picks up again. No. He's an asshole, and my body is only reacting because I need to get laid more regularly. With a new determination, I head off to find dinner.

Something smells absolutely divine as I make my way onto the back patio where a large table is covered in food. Mom is setting pasta salad down next to steak, corn on the cob, Caesar salad, and a variety of chips. It looks delicious, and my mouth waters at the steak. My mother is a wizard with the grill, so I know they are going to be incredible.

"Do you need help with anything else, Mom?" She offers me a warm smile and walks over to wrap her arm around me.

"No, I think we're all set now. I made your favorite. I hope you like it. Why don't you sit down right there?" She points to one side of the table, and I'm relieved to see that we'll all be sitting on our own sides so that I won't be too close to anyone. "I'm just going to run in and grab the wine."

I take my seat and sip on the ice water that has already been placed at every seat. It's a gorgeous and warm afternoon, but my body is still a little flushed from everything. As I'm debating how rude it is to start eating before everyone else has sat down, there's a soft breeze and a low voice.

"This won't do at all." Landon is suddenly standing across from me, looking down at the spot set for him.

Before I can even relish the moment, Mom comes back out with two different bottles of wine, and Sam trails after her. "Honey, I know you prefer white, but you should really try the red with the steak you made."

"Listen up, buddy. I know you're all fancy with the big house and the grill of my dreams, but I will not adhere to stupid rules about what kind of wine I'm allowed to drink with my dinner. Rich people, damn." Sam playfully swats my mom's butt, and she giggles.

I can't help but smile at their playful interaction, but when I notice that I'm being studied by Landon, I adopt a blank expression. He narrows his eyes at me for a split second before he grins. I watch as he picks up his plate and utensils and moves them next to me.

"Sorry, Lauren. You did a beautiful job with the table, but I'm staring into the sun on this side. Mind if I join you on that side, sis?" I refuse to vomit and ruin my appetite for steak, so I glare at him.

"Oh, Landon, I'm so sorry. I didn't even think of that. Of course, move next to Sutton." Mom doesn't notice my expression, and I don't want her to think I'm not trying, so I softly smile but say nothing as Landon sits down next to me.

We all enjoy easy banter as we dish up our plates. Everything becomes quiet for a few minutes as we dig into our food, but the conversation easily rolls into the start of school and the fact that it's only days away.

"Listen, sweetie. I have to come clean about something." My stomach fills with dread as I look over into the pleading eyes of my mom. "I made your favorites as kind of an apology. Sam surprised me with another trip, can you believe it? Our honeymoon was tropical and amazing, but Sam has organized a mini art tour of Europe. We're going to be gone for about a month, but I figured you wouldn't mind. You'll be so busy getting used to classes and making friends I figured it might even be nice to have a parentless house to come home to and hang out in. But if you're not comfortable with it, just say the word. We can postpone or shorten our trip, I promise. I don't want to leave you if you're not okay with it." I want to scream that no, I'm absolutely not okay with this, but before I can, Landon starts talking.

"I know I can't officially speak for Sutton, but I can assure you that we'll be just fine here without you guys. I promise I'll take very good care of Sutton. You guys should definitely go. You deserve more time to yourselves and to enjoy your newlywed bliss for longer. Don't you agree, Sutton? Don't they deserve time to be happy?"

"Oh, Landon, you are such a sweet young man." My mother practically coos at him before looking at me hopefully.

"Yeah, Mom. I'll be fine. You should go and enjoy yourself. Well, both of you." I fake a smile and laughter.

"Oh, sweetie, thank you! I promise I'll bring you back something amazing, and we'll talk all the time!" I nod my head at Mom's placating words.

She and Sam start going into detail about their trip and itinerary while I try to smile and show interest. Landon's hand, which was sitting on his armrest, slowly makes its way over to my leg. I try to pull away, but he clamps his fingers around my thigh and prevents me from moving it anywhere. I give in for now, only because he's not trying anything else and I don't feel like spoiling the evening or the good mood my mom is in.

Eventually, the sun lowers, and the evening starts to turn chilly, so we all pitch in to clean up. Mom and I say our goodnights and goodbyes because she and Sam have to leave early in the morning. I really want to point out that she's leaving a day after I arrived, but I can tell how excited she is. I'll be fine. I wish Sam well and tell him to take care of Mom before I decide to head to my room to continue unpacking.

When I get to the top of the stairs, everything is dark. I can only make out the outline of my door because I left the light on in my room. I kind of wish I'd made my mom come up here with me, so we could talk for a while before she leaves. I don't see or hear Landon, so I decide to quickly and quietly make a run for it. I release a breath as I start to close my bedroom door, but a foot stops its movement.

Landon steps into my room and pins me against the wall next to the door. I try to push him away, but it's like he barely has to put any effort into holding my hands above my head. The rest of his body weight pushes into me, and I can feel his cock resting against me.

"You get tonight, little sister. Enjoy it." His tongue sweeps into my mouth so quickly that I have no time to block him out.

He grinds me into the wall as I take everything he's giving me. He pulls away suddenly, and I'm left feeling horny and cold. He winks at me and leaves. I hear his door close quietly next door. I shut mine before I slowly sink to the floor against it. *Shit.*

CHAPTER 6

LANDON

Dad stopped in my room at five this morning to say goodbye and to remind me not to fuck up my situation with Sutton. I happily and easily reassured him, and he went on his merry way. I had decided to stay in bed, but the excitement of the first day with Sutton all to myself makes it impossible to go back to sleep. With her mom gone and me in control for the next month, I'm not worried about getting Sutton on the same page as me.

I roll around for a solid hour before I can't take it anymore. I was going to let Sutton sleep in, but I feel like a kid on Christmas morning. I'll just go in and look. The way my dick pulses as soon as I see her sprawled out on her bed makes it impossible for me to only look. I quietly shut her door behind me, even though we're completely alone in the house. I stand there, taking in her perfect body as she lies on her back, that gorgeous pale skin, her red hair fanned out around her, and her barely covered pussy, hidden from me by the edge of her long T-shirt.

I slowly walk over to the bed and look at her. My dick is already hard and begging to be released. I have no idea if she's a heavy or light sleeper, but it feels like the perfect time to find out. I trail a finger up her leg, starting at her ankle. When I reach her thigh, she mumbles something but doesn't wake up. With my other hand, I push her T-shirt up her stomach and skim my finger over her clit before sliding it all the way down her other leg. She doesn't move an inch, and I can't help but wonder what else I can do without waking her up.

The easiest thing is to push her shirt all the way up, so I can see her glorious tits. They're too perfect. I suck on each nipple, swirling my tongue over it before biting down a little. Still nothing from Sutton other than a soft whimper. There's no point in beating around the bush, then. I stand up and slide her underwear down her legs, unhooking them from each ankle and tossing them on the floor. Her legs are slightly more parted now, but I push them open even more, so I can lie between them.

Sutton's tight little pussy is already glistening, and I run my tongue along her sweet slit. She lets out a sigh, but there are no signs that she's aware of anything. I groan when her taste explodes across my tongue. I keep up the sensual assault on her clit, and her body grinds into me, seeking release. My eyes are locked on Sutton's, waiting for her to wake up. She's writhing beneath me, moaning, but she isn't awake yet. I continue licking and sucking on her, then push two fingers into her wet heat.

It only takes a moment, and Sutton's pussy is clamping down on my fingers, riding out her orgasm. I fully expect her eyes to open and for her to discover what I'm doing to her, but other than a lot of moaning and moving around, they stay closed. Now it's a challenge, and this is the perfect example of how badly Sutton's body needs and wants me, but she's too stubborn to admit it. I'll show her. When her body slows down and rests, I pull my fingers out and lick them clean.

My dick is rock hard, and my boxers are wet from the precum leaking out of the tip. I stand up and push them down my legs. Now that we're both basically naked, all I can think about is burying myself inside her.

"Come on, baby, it's time to wake up," I whisper into her ear before I place a kiss on her neck and trail my lips down.

Her body shudders, but she still doesn't wake up. I continue my path down her body, paying extra attention to her nipples and clit before I start rubbing the tip of my dick through her silky wet folds. It's exquisite torture, and I can only hold myself back for a moment. I guide my dick to her entrance and fully sheath myself inside her in one thrust. She startles awake and tries to sit up.

"Shh, I've got you, Sutton. Let me take care of you." She struggles against me as I keep pushing in and out of her.

"What are you doing? No, get off me—" I cut her off with a kiss.

She pushes at my chest for a few more seconds before her body slowly melts into me. I've been keeping a steady rhythm up until now, but once Sutton starts kissing me back, I unleash all my desire for her and fuck her into the mattress.

"Why do you keep fighting this? I know you feel how fucking good we fit together." I grind into her, and she moans into my mouth.

Her hands claw at my back, and I can't wait to show those off later. Her hips thrust up, meeting me blow for blow, and I can't think past her delicious heat wrapped all around me. Her pussy throbs around my length, and her whimpers and moans get louder. I keep the same rhythm, fucking her with long deep strokes.

"Oh god, oh, fuck. Landon, I—" Her words are cut off by a series of moans that make my entire body tingle.

With her tight little body wrapped around me and still pulsing with pleasure, I lose myself, filling her up with my cum. She's still shuddering and moaning underneath me, and I take the chance to shift to my side, pulling her with me, and run my hand up and down her body. I roll her nipples between my fingers, breathing in her small sighs. My fingers trace swirls across her belly until they find her clit.

She stirs with a gasp. "No, I can't again. Please, no."

I silence her with my mouth as my spent cock comes to life inside her again. I move in and out of her slowly, dragging her pleasure from her. Sooner than we both expect, our orgasms pull us under. We lie there for a while, catching our breath, and I lift up to hover over her. She looks exhausted.

"Good morning, little sister. It's time to get up and get ready. We have things to do today." I take my time kissing her.

When I pull back, she looks dazed, like she isn't sure if she's awake or dreaming. I use it to my advantage and slide out of her to stand, then carefully help her to her feet. She leans on me as I swiftly guide her into the bathroom and turn on her shower. Once we're both under the water, I lather up a loofah and run it over Sutton's body. When she starts to push me away, I back her into the corner, crouch down to my knees, lift one of her legs to rest over my shoulder, and eat her out until she's screaming my name.

After we finish, I help her out and get her dried off. "What are we doing today?"

"We're getting some last-minute things we need for school, and I'm going to get some new clothes for you."

She looks confused before she turns and walks out of the bathroom. I follow after her and watch as she pokes around in her bags before pulling out a simple black T-shirt dress. She hesitates to drop her towel with me standing there and watching her, but when she realizes I'm not moving, she does. She grabs her bra and puts it on, then reaches for the panties. I snatch those out of her reach with a smile.

"You don't need these."

She lets out an annoyed huff and slides the dress over her head. She grabs sandals, and I tug on her arm to pull her into my room while I get dressed. I'm not ready to let her out of my sight yet. It's going to be a long day, and she isn't going to know what hit her.

CHAPTER 7

SUTTON

It's like I'm in a fucking daze. Every time I start to get annoyed or tell Landon to go fuck himself, he's on me. He kisses up my jawline, devours my mouth, reaches under my dress, and plays with my pussy until I'm a writhing mess and my irritation floats away. He's fucking with my head, and right now, it's working. He steals my breath away, and it works very well to shut me up while we shop.

We stopped to get stuff for school first, and Landon made sure I got all the notebooks and pens I prefer along with the other less exciting accessories like highlighters and other boring stuff. When we stopped for clothes, I picked out several cute tops and a couple pairs of jeans. Landon then proceeded to pick out the rest of the store and arranged to have everything delivered to the house later, so we don't have to carry anything. I will concede that this is one time when his money and charm pay off. Not that I'm going to breathe a word of that to him.

"Are you hungry?" We're walking back to his car, and Landon is guiding me with a hand on my lower back.

"It's basically one of my personality traits." I offer him a side glance and hate the fact that he looks so sexy in jeans and a plain black T-shirt. It's bullshit.

"I've noticed." He chuckles and helps me into the car before getting into the driver's side.

"I know a really great place if you like soup dumplings." Well, fuck.

"I fucking love soup dumplings." He takes in my serious expression and bites back a grin.

"Consider it done. It's close by." He doesn't expect conversation, and I'm not going to give him one.

We pull up to the restaurant a few minutes later, and I scramble out. My stomach started growling as soon as food was mentioned, and I must be fed. We walk in, I tell the hostess two before Landon can, and he frowns at me. The big guy must like ordering everyone around. The place is buzzing with a late lunch crowd, but we're seated at a table near the window and afforded a small amount of privacy.

"Groceries are being delivered to the house later if we get hungry, but I couldn't pass up the chance to stop here. It's one of my favorite spots." He's looking around at the other people here, pretending not to be paying attention to me after sharing a piece of personal information.

"Soup dumplings are one of my weaknesses. I'm excited to see how they are here." I can tell that my response isn't what Landon was expecting, and it rubs me the wrong way. "You know, I'm actually a very nice and reasonable person, so you shouldn't look so surprised." The waitress chooses this moment to step up to our table, so I drop the attitude to prove my point.

After we order, Landon clears his throat. "I know you are nice and can be reasonable. I also know you're intelligent. That's why I'm confused on why you're fighting me so hard. Just stop, then we can spend our time doing the fun stuff." He winks at me like I don't know what he could possibly mean by that.

"You don't understand why I'm not going to just roll over for some guy that I barely know, who wants to take over my life and keep me all to himself? Right after dealing with my mother suddenly remarrying and having to uproot my entire life, then starting college? Yeah, I mean, it definitely feels like an unsolvable mystery. Weird." He reaches for my hand, but I pull back out of his reach.

Landon's eyes flash with anger for a moment before he looks away and takes a breath. "I wasn't expecting you either, you know. I'm about to start my last year of college, and then it's on to Dad's business to learn the ropes and one day take over. I planned to work hard, let loose with my friends, and see what came along. Then you happened. You're not the only one adjusting here, baby." He leans back in his chair and crosses his arms across his chest.

"This is crazy. You should still follow your plan. Study hard, get drunk with your friends, and have fun. You should be living it up for your last year of college. Sow those wild oats before the reality of adulthood crushes your soul. I'll happily be an oat." I smile at him, hoping that using his own words makes him realize how ridiculous he's being.

"No."

"No? What do you mean, no? No to what, exactly?" I lean across the table to look into his eyes, and all I see is fire.

"No, you aren't an oat. No, I'm not going to ignore this connection we have. You might be able to lie to yourself, but I know you feel it too. From the moment I saw you, I knew I had to have you. If that moron hadn't shown up, I'd have made my move shortly. It all worked out for the best though." He runs a finger back and forth across my wrist in a hypnotic rhythm.

"You call assaulting your stepsister 'working out for the best'? Eventually, you're going to come to your senses and realize I'm right. You're going to regret all this shit you've pulled." I slide my wrist back, but he grabs it and yanks it closer to his side of the table.

He lifts my wrist to his lips and gently kisses it. "You're wrong, little sister. There might be some things I regret about this life, but the best decision I've ever made was to fuck you." He leans all the way across the table, so he whispers the next part. "And it will continue to be the best part of every day, baby." He kisses me below my ear and sits back just in time for our food to arrive.

He smiles as he watches the emotions he's brought out in me dance across my face. I'm pissed that he thinks he can control me. I'm even more pissed that his bullshit keeps turning me on. What the fuck is wrong with me? I'm not giving in to this raving lunatic because I don't believe in rewarding bad behavior. I ignore the way my pussy throbs at his words because she cannot be trusted. Our waitress finishes setting everything on the table and leaves with a smile.

The two orders of soup dumplings in front of me are an amazing distraction. I don't know what the fuck to say to Landon's crude—and incredibly hot—words. Burning my mouth by shoving an entire soup dumpling into it seems like the only logical choice I can make. It's so fucking delicious, and I'm not even mad about the roof of my mouth peeling off. I wonder if this place does delivery because I can obviously never come here again and give Landon the satisfaction.

Thankfully, Landon must be hungry enough that he lets the conversation pause to focus on eating. I don't even look at him while I have many intimate moments with my dumplings, promising them filthy things if they never leave me. When I'm finished eating every last bit, I lean back in my chair and close my eyes with a sigh. Fuck, that was good. I realize that Landon is staring at me, and I roll my eyes.

"What?"

"Watching you eat is like a theatrical experience." If I hadn't just rolled my eyes, they'd be rolling again. How cliché.

"Why? Because I'm so beautiful, and watching me put my lips around things is arousing?" I inject as much sarcasm into my voice as possible.

Landon laughs. "Not quite. Each dumpling had a name and a different voice. Then there was that bit at the end where you were apologizing to them before eating them. The eulogies were surprisingly moving, given that your mouth was full."

I clear my throat and ignore my warm cheeks. "Yes, well, some of them deserved more of an explanation before leaving for Tummy Town."

Landon's laughter is sexy, and that shouldn't be a thing. "You're adorable, baby."

"I am not adorable. Shut up." I push my chair away from the table as soon as Landon signs the receipt.

He quickly stands and grabs my waist, pulling me into him. "You are absolutely the most adorable thing I've ever seen. And you're going to look just as adorable bouncing up and down on my cock when we get home." A shiver runs down my spine, and he notices with a satisfied smirk.

"No, you can't tell me what to do." I stomp away from him and walk to the car.

CHAPTER 8

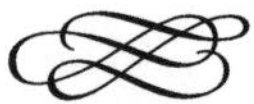

LANDON

It turns out I can tell her exactly what to do. We get home, and as soon as we're inside, I drag her to the dining room. She's letting me lead her, but I'm sure she'll try to bolt any second. I let her hand go when we're standing next to the long wooden table where we eat. Where I'm going to eat now.

"Lie back on the table. Now."

She squares her shoulders as she looks from the table to me. "No." She shrugs and starts to walk away.

She barely makes it two steps before I have her pinned to the table with me on top of her. "There, just like that. You need to work on listening."

"Fuck you, Landon. Get off me." She tries to push me off her, but she doesn't stand a chance.

"We'll get to that, don't worry." Her dress rode up during our struggle, and I can see how wet she is.

I move quickly, so she doesn't have time to react. I'm sitting in the chair at the head of the table, my arm holding a struggling Sutton down while my mouth descends on her clit and my other fingers work their way into her pussy. I groan at how tight she is, and my cock is already begging to be let out, but it's going to have to be patient.

Sutton isn't even attempting to pretend she doesn't want it anymore. She's moaning and writhing on the table as I work her over with my tongue and fingers. When I feel her start to clench around me and her moans get louder, I press on her clit more firmly, and she explodes. I keep going as she rides out her pleasure, and I lick up every drop of her release. I'm still gently licking and kissing her while she comes down from her orgasm.

"Oh fuck, that was so... fuck." She breathes heavily, then pushes at me to stop. "I'm not done eating yet." My tongue thrusts in and out of her, making her gasp.

"Landon, I can't—"

"You can, and you will."

My focus returns to her clit, and I have her screaming her orgasm again in minutes. I do the same thing as before. I slow my rhythm, give her time to catch her breath, then start again. She didn't even try to push me away this time, but her movements are languid, and she is practically melting into the table now.

"Please, Landon, please." Her request is followed by a moan.

"What do you need, little sister?" I suck her clit into my mouth, and she bucks beneath me.

"I don't know," she whispers as pleasure pulses through her.

"I can't help you if you don't tell me." I push my fingers inside her again and watch as she rolls her hips, welcoming them in. "That's it, baby. You look so beautiful all laid out for me like this. Take your dress all the way off."

Sutton doesn't even fight me on it. She slowly pulls the fabric up the rest of the way and slides it over her head where it falls to the table. My dick is so hard it's painful at this point, but she's lost in pleasure, and I can't let that go to waste. Speaking of, Sutton comes with a groan as her hips chase my mouth to milk the last wave of her orgasm.

"Landon, please, no more. I need you inside me."

My name is practically a moan on her lips, and my cock is begging to be let out to play. Not yet. I give her a minute to catch her breath, and I start to lick and suck on her clit all over again.

"Please, please, Landon." She's gripping my arm that's pinning her in place, and I know I'll have claw marks from her nails digging into me.

"That's more like it, little sister. Beg me to fuck your pussy." I smile darkly before swirling my tongue inside her.

"Fuck, please. Landon, I need it." I scoop her up and throw her over my shoulder.

It takes me no time at all to run up the stairs and get her into my room. I don't bother closing the door because I'm the only one here that will hear her screams. I toss her on the bed and pause to admire how fucking sexy she is. Her red hair fans out around her, and her pale skin is so soft and smooth that I could lick every inch of it. Her green eyes latch onto me, and for the first time, I only see her lust and desire. Finally.

I get undressed and join Sutton on the bed. She watches me closely as I sit, leaning against the headboard with my cock standing at attention. I look at her pointedly.

"If you want my cock, come and get it, little sister." I wrap my hand around my length and stroke myself while she licks her lips.

Before I have to tell her again, she's crawling toward me. Once she's straddling me, she raises up and guides my throbbing dick to her entrance. As soon as I feel her wet heat, I want to thrust all the way into her, but she's going to have to take it. She lowers herself slowly, pausing a couple of times before I'm fully inside her. I close my eyes and revel in the way she fits around me so perfectly. Her rhythm starts off slow, and it feels like fucking heaven.

"That's it, ride me, baby. Fuck, you're so perfect." Her head is thrown back, and she's got her hands firmly planted on my chest to keep herself steady. It's so fucking hot.

"I hate that your dick feels this good," she whines while her eyes roll back into her head.

I've proven my point for long enough. I grab onto her hips and thrust into her roughly. Sutton screams out in pure satisfaction as her orgasm hits. I roll us, so she's on her back, her body still writhing beneath me, and I pound into her with a growl.

"Get used to it, baby. This dick is the only one you're ever going to have again. You. Are.

Mine." I punctuate each word with a hard thrust that has her pussy gushing around me.

She doesn't answer, but she could be reciting the world's greatest poem right now and no one would be able to understand her. Everything comes out as a moan with an occasional 'fuck' thrown in. I lean down and kiss her, absorbing every cry and whimper, and she doesn't even try to fight me for control. It's a small act of submission, but it's enough to trigger my own release. I growl her name as I finish, filling her up with every last drop of my cum.

"Fuck, I could live in this pussy." I gently pull out of her and lie down beside her.

"It feels like you basically do." There's no fire in her words, and I smile.

"Stay here," I instruct her.

Sutton looks at me but doesn't say one way or another if she'll do as she's told. Let's see. I get up and go into my bathroom and get a warm wet towel to clean her up with. The sight of my cum leaking out of her gets me hard again, but I'm going to give her a little break. She doesn't push me away or complain as I clean her up. When I'm done, I toss the towel in my hamper, pin her with a look, and head downstairs.

I grab some bottles of water and some fruit before I head back up to Sutton. She's lying in the exact same position as before and warmth spreads across my chest. She eyes my erection, but I get under the covers and hand her the water and set the bowl of fruit between us on the bed.

"Scoot up and have a couple of pieces of fruit. Relax." I grab the remote and turn the TV on.

Sutton does as she's told and grabs some grapes out of the bowl. I land on reruns of *The Office*, and eventually, Sutton actually starts getting comfortable and laughs at the show. We finish off the fruit, and I pull Sutton to me. She puts her head on my chest, and I hold her while we continue to watch. After a little while, I realize she's asleep. I don't want her to nap for too long and be unable to sleep tonight, but the feel of her against me, comfortable, relaxed, trusting me, is incredible, and I'm going to enjoy it for a little while longer.

CHAPTER 9

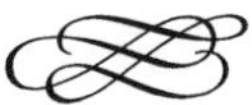

SUTTON

Landon spends the next couple of days fucking me on every surface in the house. I still fight with him and try to spend some time alone, but he's clearly figured out that if he's touching me and I'm coming, I am malleable. I don't know anyone here yet, so I'm hoping that time out of the house at school and having other things to focus on will cool things between Landon and me. Maybe we can even get to a place where one day we'll laugh about the time he bent me over the kitchen island and fucked me while feeding me warm croissants with butter. What silly hijinks, you know?

These are my thoughts as I pick out what I'm wearing on the first day of school. Although, why I ever thought I'd be allowed to do such a thing is beyond me. Landon storms into my room and stares at me standing in my walk-in closet in my towel, and his gaze darkens.

"If it wasn't your first day at school, I'd fuck you against the wall right now. You'll wear this today." He smiles as he pulls down a cute black midi dress that would be both comfortable and look nice and put together for my first day.

Unfortunately, his enthusiasm has ensured I can't wear it. "No,

I'm going to wear jeans and a T-shirt. You will not dictate how I dress. Get over yourself." I toss the dress at him and walk out with my outfit in hand. I don't know why I expected anything other than him tossing me on my bed and pinning me there on my back.

"I don't remember asking. You'll be comfortable all day, and your ass will look amazing in this. Put it on. Now. If I have to say it again, it's going to be hard to focus on all the information of the first day when said amazing ass is throbbing from the beating I give it." He smiles, and my pussy throbs as I struggle to swallow.

"Fine. Get off me." I push at Landon, and he bounces back to his feet.

"I'll go get breakfast ready for us. We have to leave in thirty minutes." With that, he's gone, and I take a deep breath.

I'm hot and bothered, and it's so fucking annoying I could scream. I'm no prude, but I've had more sex in the past week than all of my life combined, and it's like he's fucking conditioning me to crave his dick. That's probably exactly what he's doing. Goddamn motherfucking asshole. It is *not* working.

I grumble as I put the dress on but can't deny that it basically feels like I'm wearing pajamas. It looks so nice though. I do my usual tinted moisturizer and mascara routine with a little blush, so I look alive, and call it good while slipping ChapStick into my bag. I've got everything I need, and I have a moment where I'm appreciating Landon and his help making sure I had everything for today. That's enough of that.

After a quick breakfast of toast, eggs, bacon, and juice, we're on our way. I've got those first day jitters that are a combination of excitement and absolute dread at the actual things I'll have to do now, but I let it hold my focus, so I don't have to make conversation.

"It was impossible to get any classes together because of where I'm at in my degree, but we have a couple of breaks at the same time. I'll be waiting for you at the end of your morning classes, and we can grab lunch before you have to head to your afternoon stuff. We'll meet in front of the library at the end of the day, and I'll drive us home. Understood?" He's focusing on pulling into a parking space, and I take a deep breath before I answer.

"What if I meet people in my classes? I'm here to get an education, make friends, build a life, and have fun. Not to mold my life to yours. I'll agree to lunch because it's the first day and I don't know anything around here, but I'll keep you posted on everything else."

Landon finished parking a moment ago, so his entire focus is on me as I tell him how today is going to work. He has that sexy smirk on his face that makes me want to simultaneously punch him and let him throw me down on the nearest flat surface.

"You're adorable. You will do as I say. I want you to have all those things if they'll make you happy, but you're also in a relationship so you can't be entirely selfish with your time. We'll find our groove after a couple of weeks though." He gets out of the car as if the matter is settled.

I exit the car after him but storm off ahead. He catches up to me in seconds, and my irritation grows. He doesn't try to get me to talk to him as we make our way to my first class of the day, but I resent the fact that he's walking me all the way there. Even though if he weren't, I'd probably have to stop and ask someone for directions. I don't care. I'm carefully reading the room numbers as we enter a long hallway, but right before we reach the room where my English class is, Landon shoves me through the door next to it.

His lips land on mine, and he consumes my brain. The way he's so in control, his body pressed firmly against me, it all feels so good. I can't help myself as I grind against him. He chuckles darkly, and even that has my pussy pulsing.

"I'm going to take such good care of you later, little sister. I promise. Be a good girl for me, and pay attention in your classes this morning. I'll see you soon, okay?" He caresses my cheek so softly before planting more kisses along my jaw and lips.

"Yeah, okay. Have a good day." I'm caught up in too many emotions to fight with him at the moment, so I let him kiss me again and watch the way his delectable ass flexes as he leaves.

I walk next door to my English class and take a seat in the second row. It's close enough to see everything, but I don't have to worry about potential professor spit. As I pull out my textbook, notebook, and pens, the seat to my left is pulled back, and a handsome man sits next to me.

"Mind if I sit?" He drops his bag on the table.

"Doesn't matter if I do, but go ahead." I organize my stuff and ignore the man.

After he sits and pulls his stuff out, he angles his body to face me. "Are you hoping to major in English, or are you knocking out the general classes too?"

I need to remember not to pick early classes next semester. "I have no idea what I want to do, but it's definitely one or the other."

"Well, maybe you can tutor me if I run into a rough spot. Reading isn't exactly my favorite thing to do, but I have other strengths. I'm Cole, by the way."

"Hi, Cole. I probably will never ever be able to tutor you for anything, so let the little guy down easy now."

"What little guy?" Cole faces me head on, so I mirror his position.

"The one in your pants. I'm never touching that. Ever. If you're genuinely a good dude, I wish you all the best and lots of happiness. If you're not, get fucked by a cactus. Pick your poison."

"That's rude. You don't even know me." His surprise is clear.

"You're right, I don't. That's why I gave you two options. It looks like you're option two guy now though. That's a bummer, Cole."

Cole mumbles under his breath, then ignores me for the rest of class. I'm actually interested in English, but my heart isn't in this today. I'm annoyed, and I don't know why. I'm already hungry, there's a tickle in my throat, and I want to leave. When time is finally up, I write down the reading that is due for the next class and pack up. I'm not in a rush because I have a bit before my next class, but I'm the last to leave.

As I'm about to step out, I'm shoved back into the room, and the door is slammed shut.

Cole is standing there with a wicked glint in his eyes.

"I can still make this good for you if you don't fight me." He rushes at me and shoves me into the table and podium at the front of the class.

I fall into it, and he pounces. Cole shoves me down on the table and stands between my legs.

"Impress me, and maybe I'll even keep you." I'm kicking and clawing at him, but he presses his weight into me, and it's hard to fight him off.

"You'll regret this. I'll make sure of it. Get the fuck off me, you rapist fuck."

He laughs at my words and thrusts into me. We're fully clothed, so it doesn't accomplish anything other than to further irritate me. Before I have a chance to say anything, the classroom door bursts open, and there stands Landon, looking like the Devil himself.

"You're so fucked." I laugh as Landon roars and pulls Cole off me.

I can't deny the relief and safety I feel with Landon's presence. Maybe there are some perks to this situation after all.

CHAPTER TEN

Landon

I got to Sutton's classroom right as people started leaving, so I know there is no fucking way she evaded me. When no one else comes out and I haven't seen Sutton, I pull my phone out and text her. I slide it back into my pocket and push open the classroom door to make sure she isn't taking her sweet-ass time. It takes less than a second for a violent rage to take over.

Cole Stevens, the guy who should be graduating this year with me but hasn't been able to pass most of his general education classes, is holding my Sutton down on the table, looking like he's going to try and hurt her. Cole Stevens is a dead man. Without another thought in my head, I dart forward and rip Cole off of Sutton. I toss him into the white board next to the table, then grab him before he has a chance to recover and pin him to the wall.

"What the fuck is your problem, dude?" Cole looks so confused by the sudden turn of events.

"What the fuck do you think you're doing?" I slam his body against the wall again, and he grimaces.

"What do you care? I thought I'd have a little fun with the snotty bitch freshman. You could get a piece too if you let me fucking go." His voice raises at the end like he thinks I'm going to take him up on his fucking offer.

I lean in close and whisper, "She belongs to me. No one touches what belongs to me." I drop him to his feet, then punch him in the face.

He slides down the white board at first, then stands up, swinging at me. I land another punch on his nose, and a third across his eye. He's bleeding a little bit, and his face is puffing up. Sutton has straightened up and is standing next to the door but isn't making any moves to leave.

"Are you okay?" Her eyes snap to me, and my gaze sweeps her from head to toe, looking for any injuries but thankfully not seeing any.

"I-I'm okay. Thank you."

She looks as surprised to be saying it as I am at hearing it, but I nod. "You're welcome. I meant what I said."

Cole finishes wiping the blood from his face and lunges at me again. This time, I dodge his fist and meet him with my own. He falls back to the floor, and I punch him a couple more times before it's lights out. I'm not trying to kill the guy, unless he touches Sutton again, so I let him lie there. His chest is moving, and there isn't a lot of blood. He'll be fine.

I slowly approach Sutton as she stares at me with wide eyes. She's seen my angry and possessive side, but not like this. Before I get all the way to her, Sutton runs at me and throws her arms around me.

"Are you sure you're okay, baby?" I wind my arms around her and kiss the top of her head.

She leans back, so we can look at each other. "You saved me. Thank you, Landon."

I want to say something funny, but before I can, she's yanking my face down to hers and kissing me. My hand cups the back of her head, and I help her wrap her legs around my waist.

My fingers tangle in her hair, and I pull her away from me for a moment. "I will always keep you safe. You're already mine, admit it. Admit it, and I'll make sure everyone knows, and you never have to worry about anything ever again. I'll always take care of you."

She moans into my mouth as I kiss her and trail my fingers between us. I easily push the dress up and groan into her mouth when I feel her bare pussy, no underwear to stop my progress. She's already wet, so I gently rub circles on her clit before I plunge my fingers inside her, keeping my thumb on her bundle of nerves. She rocks into me, riding my hand, and she looks absolutely stunning.

"That's right, Sutton. Let me give you what you need." I kiss along her jaw and down her neck, and her body shudders.

She's squeezing my arms for support before she lets out a muffled scream. I'm absorbing her cries with my kisses, and my dick is trying to claw its way out of my pants to get to her. I set her down on the table for a moment, so I can free myself from my pants and boxers. As soon as my dick is out, she's wrapping herself around me again. I lift her up and spin us, so I can press her into the wall.

I line up at her entrance, and she impales herself on me. I look down at her in wonder as she rides me this way. I can't help the smile that overtakes my face. I grab her hands so she can't hold herself up and pin them above her head. I pull out and slowly thrust back inside of Sutton. Her eyes roll into the back of her head, and she arches off the wall.

"You're mine, Sutton. It's time to admit it. Say the words." I pound into her, knowing her body already knows what I'm saying is true.

"Landon, I don't... oh, fuck." Her body tightens around me as her orgasm rips through her.

"See, baby? You belong to me. Your body already knows it. It's time to hear you say the words." I keep thrusting, determined to get her to come once more before I finish.

I release her hands from above her head, so I can play with her clit. My lips ravage her, and she pulls away to catch her breath. I keep fucking her, leaning my forehead against hers, reveling in the feeling of her sexy body wrapped around me everywhere.

"Landon?" My name leaves her lips on a gasp, and it pushes me that much closer to my release.

"Yeah, little sister?" She bites my lower lip and sucks it into her mouth. "Oh, fuck, baby."

"Oh god, don't stop." Sutton is digging her nails into my back, and I pinch her clit as I drive into her.

"Tell me you're mine. Now. This pussy belongs to me. Only me." My words come out on a growl as my breathing turns ragged, my orgasm so close.

Sutton comes with a shout, and I fuck her through it as I chase my own orgasm.

"Say it."

She locks her ankles behind my back and holds on for dear life. "I'm yours, Landon. I'm

yours."

My orgasm hits as soon as the words leave her lips. I keep pumping into her as I fill her with my cum, triumph coursing through my body. I cup her face in my palm, her smile matching my own. I claim Sutton's lips and revel in the feeling she's pouring into our kiss.

"There's no going back from this, baby girl. You're mine, and I'm never letting you go. Do you understand that?" My hand tangles in her hair as I stare into her eyes.

"Like you were going to let me go before anyway?" She teases, a glint in her eye.

"Good point. I meant what I said, Sutton. I'll always take care of you."

"I know you will. I've fought you every step of the way, but for what? It's fucked up, people are going to say shit, I have no idea how I'm going to explain this to my mom, but you worked your stupid arrogant self into my heart, and I guess that's where you're going to stay." She gives me a soft kiss.

"Stupid, arrogant self, huh? Better that than a stubborn, little sister that doesn't know what's in her best interest."

"I guess it's a good thing I've got an overprotective big brother to look out for me, then." She winks, and my dick gets hard again.

"I always look after what's mine." I ease out of Sutton's pussy and thrust into her again.

"I have to get to my next class." Sutton's whisper ends on a moan.

"Shh, it can wait. I can't, and I don't think you can either."

"Fuck, you make me feel so good, Landon." Sutton's pussy flutters around my cock. "I know, baby, and I always will." And I do.

The end, for now. Landon and Sutton will return in future stories.

ABOUT IRIS JAMES

Iris James is a perpetually tired, impressively pale, lover of books. When she isn't writing or reading, she enjoys binge-watching shows, eating nachos, and spending as much time as possible with her husband and two small children somewhere in Minnesota.

Join my Facebook group for exclusive content and shenanigans!

Group: Iris' Ravishing Darklings
Facebook: /irisjamesauthor
Instagram: @irisjamesauthor
TikTok: @irisjamesauthor
Linktree: /IrisJamesAuthor

ALSO BY IRIS JAMES

The Sundown Series

Splintered

Irreparable

Annihilation

The Kuramordere Mafia Series

Lust & Blood

Loss & Blood

Love & Blood

TARNISHED EMBERS

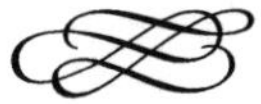

ROSA LEE

TARNISHED EMBERS

Instead of two ugly stepsisters, I get four gorgeous stepbrothers.

Caspian, Oct, Kit and Prince.

The twins and their older stepbrothers. All more beautiful than the last. All as dark and depraved as demons. All with wounds that run so deep, there's no way to heal them.

Sounds like a fairytale right?

Wrong.

I do get the wicked stepmother, and when my father dies not long after their marriage, everything changes and suddenly all their secrets come to light and I'm in the middle of something that nightmares are made from.

There's no fairy godmother coming to magic me a pumpkin coach and a pretty dress. No Prince Charming to rescue me from a life of torment and punishment.

Just four wicked boys with black souls, and dark pasts who are just as trapped as I am.

Tarnished Embers is a dark whychoose stepbrother fairytale retelling, where our girl (and the guys) will end up with more than one love interest. If you love broken bad boys, a FMC who's not afraid to take what she wants and don't mind a whole load of heartache then this is the book for you! Be warned, love hurts.

***Warning: 18+ Please be aware that this book may contain graphic scenes that some readers may find upsetting or triggering, so please read the author's note at the beginning. ***

Disclaimer: Please note. Rosa Lee cannot be held responsible for the destruction of underwear of any kind. She recommends you take adequate precautions before reading to avoid any sticky situations.

PROLOGUE

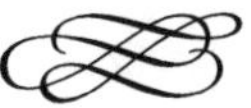

EMBER

Pain.

I'll never breathe again, never feel at peace now that she's gone. I stare at her place in the woods, the place where she wanted her body to be buried, surrounded by the nature that she so loved, and all I feel is pain ripping my heart in two.

How will I go on? Now that the woman who gave me life breathes no more? How will I navigate the world without her gentle guidance, her love that protects me from all the monsters that hide in the shadows?

Her death wasn't easy, it was quick, too quick as the cancer we thought had gone ate away at her. I watched as she wasted away, her life slipping through my fingers and there wasn't a fucking thing I could do about it. I couldn't hold on to her, and the way her last breath rattled out of her chest will haunt me for the rest of my days.

"Come on, my little Spark." My father's deep voice sounds broken and rough as he places a hand on my shoulder and squeezes gently. "It's just you and me now, kid."

Tears drip down my face, the sunshine of the late autumn day a mockery of the hurt that surrounds me and the despair that's trying to pull me under.

But, it's not just me that's lost her. I tear my eyes away from the spot under the old oak tree to look up at my father. Dark circles ring his eyes, and although his suit is wrinkle-free, his hair and light beard neat, the sadness in his blue eyes matches my own. Maybe even surpasses it.

"O–okay, Dad," I whisper, my voice sounding hollow to my ears like I've wandered into a cave and can't find my way to the light.

CHAPTER 1

EMBER

FIVE YEARS LATER…

"Dad! I'm home!" I yell before kicking the heavy wooden door closed behind me as I walk through it. I sigh heavily, taking in the mansion we now live in with a slight grimace.

Dad threw himself into his work after Mum passed, and turns out he's really fucking good at business and made a shit ton of money. So we left our perfectly reasonable, Victorian townhouse in North London for this McMansion in Chelsea. Don't get me wrong, it's nice. Just not home. There's no soft, colourful furnishings that Mum loved, no sense of chaos with pictures and letters stuck to the fridge. It's too…clean, almost like it's a showhome, cold and empty of life. Or maybe that's just me.

"I'm in here, little Spark," he calls from the living room. Well, the yellow living room because this place is so big that we have to define our reception rooms by fucking colour.

I dump my bag on the hall table, smile at Smithers—*yes, we now have an honest to fuck butler*—and head to the yellow room. I chose the colour when we moved in because yellow is my favourite. It's soft, like freshly churned butter, and I spend lots of time drawing in here as the lighting is fantastic.

"You won't believe what happened today—" I come up short, pausing in the doorway when I see a woman standing next to my dad, his arm wrapped around her waist as they both look at the doorway expectantly. "Um, hi?"

"Honey, this is Odette." My dad beams at me, his smile wide as he turns his face away from me to gaze down at her. My heart pounds at the look he's giving her. He's practically glowing with hearts in his fucking eyes.

"It's so lovely to finally meet you, Ember," she gushes in an American accent that I can't quite place while stepping out of my father's embrace and rushing towards me. She's pretty, like really pretty, and maybe a little younger than Dad, although for all I fucking know she's got a talented surgeon. Her dark brown hair is styled to perfection, falling in waves around her heart-shaped face. Her hazel eyes stare into mine as she grabs my hands, squeezing them before pulling me in for a hug.

I freeze, my arms hanging at my sides, my eyes wide as I look over at my dad. His smile is indulgent as he stares at us, his face all soft lines, and I must admit that he looks happier than I've seen him in a long time. It eases me enough to gently embrace Odette back. She pulls away but keeps hold of my hands in her soft, manicured ones. Heat touches my cheeks when I see the paint under my own short nails.

"Silly me! You have no idea who I am, and here's me already celebrating the fact that I've finally got a daughter." She titters, and I find the back of my teeth hurting with the sound.

"W–what?" My pulse rushes past my ears at her words, and I can't help but blink rapidly as if that will help to make sense of her words. *Daughter?*

"Honey," Dad starts, walking over, deep laugh lines at the corners of his eyes as he once again wraps his arms around Odette's waist. "I have some exciting news. Odette and I—"

"We got married!" Odette interrupts loudly, letting go of one of my hands to flash her left hand at me. There on her ring finger sit two rings. Both silver and one with a fucking massive diamond in the middle.

My stomach plummets, my skin going ice-cold as I look at the bands, then slowly back up into their faces. Both have huge grins, and I just stand there, barely able to breathe, let alone say anything.

"Aren't you going to wish your father and I congratulations?" Odette questions, her smile looking a little forced the longer I remain silent. Her grip on my hand becomes almost painful, and I have to swallow the wince that wants to escape as she practically crushes my fingers in hers.

I lick my dry lips. "C–congratulations."

I have to widen my lids, moisture threatening to gather in my eyes and spill down my cheeks at the fucking shock of it all. *He's married?*

"Hey, little Spark," my dad says soothingly, reaching around and placing a hand on my shoulder, squeezing gently. I'm reminded of the day we stood by my mother's grave, but this couldn't be further from that reality. "I know it feels like a big surprise, and I'm sorry I didn't talk about it with you sooner, but I'm happy. Odette makes me happier than I've felt since..."

Since Mum died. I know that's what he means, and suddenly I feel like the worst bitch alive. I take a deep, shaking breath, plastering a smile on my face that only wavers a little and blinking back the tears. I'm mostly successful.

"If you're happy, then so am I. It's a surprise," I tell them both, noticing the way Odette's smile drops slightly as she looks at me, a frown threatening her Botoxed brow. "Welcome to the family, Odette."

Her face instantly smooths as my dad stares down at her, and I wonder briefly why she hid her annoyance from him.

"That means so much, Ember, and I really can't wait to spend more time with you, just us girls together. Lord knows I need it after being surrounded by the boys these past few years." She giggles, the sound making me inwardly wince as it's like nails on a chalkboard, high pitched and just fake as fuck.

"Boys?" I ask, my forehead wrinkling as I hear the front door opening followed by the sounds of several people talking, and by the low timber of their voices, it's several boys.

"Ember, these are your new stepbrothers," my father introduces, a gleam of yearning in his tone. He has always wanted a son, yet I ended up being his only child. Sweat makes my palms slick and my stomach clenches once more. How can I share after all this time? After all these years of it just being us? And now it's not only with another woman, but who knows how many boys too? My breathing rasps as panic looms at the edges of my vision.

I turn, letting go of Odette's hand, and once again am rooted to the spot as four boys step through the door. Though, perhaps boys is the wrong descriptor. Men, or maybe even gods would be more accurate as Jesus fucking Christ they are unlike any boys I've ever met before.

Four pairs of eyes lock onto me, four gazes that somehow make me feel like a deer caught in headlights even though not a word is spoken.

"Hello, little sister, nice to meet you."

His voice is deep, American, and has a low drawl that sets my nerves tingling and my core clenching. My chest tightens and my breathing becomes shallow as a guy with walnut-coloured hair steps forward from the group. It's longer on the top and has that artful bedhead look I know took him some fucking time to master. I can't move as he steps so close that my breasts brush his chest, my nipples stiffening at the light contact, and I have to crane my neck in order to look him in the eyes. Irises the colour of bright copper stare back at me, and they're such an unusual colour that I'm captivated, unable to look away from the intensity of his stare.

He reminds me of when the clocks go back and suddenly it's

darker than it was the day before, leaving you fearful and out of sync, wondering where the time has gone. A shiver cascades across my skin and his lips lift in a devastating smirk.

I take a stuttering inhale through my nose and am flooded with the tart scent of crisp apples mixed with the sweet smell of caramel. My eyelids close reflexively as he leans in, a large hand landing on my waist and heating the skin underneath my school shirt before he presses his lips to my cheek in a barely-there kiss.

"Fucking delicious," I think I hear him say in a deep, gravelly whisper, the hand at my waist tightening ever so slightly and letting me know I didn't imagine his touch. He pulls back but his palm remains there, warming me in a way that I don't hate. "I'm Caspian." His American accent is different than Odette's, and if I had to guess, it sounds like maybe he's from New York, but as that's based solely on films and endless reruns of Friends, I could be wrong.

I swallow once. Twice. "N–nice to meet you."

"Hey, quit hogging her, big bro!" another low voice cries out, also with a US accent but different again to Odette and Caspian's. Caspian is shoved aside to be replaced with one of the others whose hair is lighter than his brother's, a honey brown, and he screams surfer vibes with it falling in soft waves framing a gorgeously handsome face. My lips want to tug up to match the beaming smile of his own but I keep the impulse in check, not wanting to give that part of me away just yet. His eyes are a beautiful clear blue, like a tropical sea shining under a sun-kissed sky, and everything about him calms my frantic pulse. That he puts me at ease with such little effort is a huge red flag. It's always the most charming devils that will take your soul. "We've always wanted a little sister."

I let out a squeak as I'm abruptly wrapped up in a tight hug, my feet dangling off the floor when I'm lifted off the ground. *Damn tall bastard.* I position my hands on muscular shoulders as another kiss is placed upon my cheek, which is now tingling, and I'm feeling pretty hot suddenly, sweat beading down my spine as he sets me on my feet again. A distinctive floral scent fills my nostrils, and it reminds me of rolling around the wild meadows back on Hampstead Heath in North London as a child.

"You never were good at sharing, Oct," a third voice teases with the same accent as Oct, and then I'm torn from Oct's embrace, my head spinning as I stare at the same man who just had me in his arms. But no, his eyes are a darker blue, like a stormy sea ready to swallow any unfortunate souls sailing on it. His hair is the same honey shade as Oct's, but it's shorter and far less tousled. He holds me at arm's length, his eyes raking over me, burning a path across my body, and I shudder. "Well, aren't you a pretty little thing?"

My cheeks heat and I take a deep inhale, getting a faint whiff of lime, mimosa, and cedar which does strange things to my insides.

"So pretty," Oct answers, crowding next to the newcomer whose hands still grasp my upper arms in a firm grip. "But where are our manners, brother? I'm Octavious or Oct, and this is my twin, Christopher or Kit."

"P–pleased to meet you both," I stutter. "I'm Ember."

"Oh, we know all about you, Pretty Thing," Chri—Kit purrs, elongating my name and sending another tremor along my nerves.

"Y–you do?" My brows dip because until they walked in, I knew fuck all about these guys.

"We do, Sugar," a last voice informs me, and hoe my gods his deep, southern drawl has my kitty cat up and purring, which is highly fucking inappropriate given that they're my stepbrothers. The twins part, Kit's hands dropping as another sinfully gorgeous guy steps towards me. His hair is pitch black, so dark that it almost has blue highlights. His eyes are a bright, sparkling green that leaves me gasping for breath, filling my nose with the intoxicating scent of rum, leather, and spice. "We know *everything* about you, Ember." I swallow as he, too, steps into me, forcing my head up in order to maintain eye contact. They're all taller than I am, not difficult at my five foot five and a half, but this one is taller than the others. Maybe a little older too as there's an air of maturity about him that the others don't have, like he has more responsibilities than them somehow.

There are swirls of colourful ink that peek out from his collar, and a spark of electricity runs through me. I'm a sucker for tattoos on a guy. "I'm Prince, the eldest one."

"N–nice to m–meet you, Prince." Fuck, I'm so pissed at sounding like a simpering damsel, but give a girl a break. A lot has happened in the past ten minutes. He leans closer, dipping his head to place his lips against my cheek in a lingering kiss and I swear to all that is holy, fucking sparks fly from where he makes contact.

"It's nice to finally make your acquaintance too, Ember," he replies while taking a small step back, and I would laugh at his old-fashioned way of speaking but I can't look away from his eyes which are locked on mine. They sparkle and shine like the green sapphires I saw once in a jewellery store in Hatton Gardens. Then he reaches down, takes my hand in his, and brings it up to his pillowy lips, brushing my knuckles with a barely-there kiss and sending my pulse skyrocketing.

"Well," my father states, breaking the spell that Prince has me under, and I look towards my dad as he walks over to us and claps the twins on the back. "You boys must be tired after travelling today. Ember, can you show them to their rooms?"

I cast my eyes over the guys to see that they look like they've been on a journey, their T-shirts are wrinkled and there's an air of tiredness about them all that only travel gives you. I don't recall Odette being the same, but maybe she arrived earlier, which would have been strange. Or maybe she's just not the type of person to allow a wrinkle anywhere near her. My father's words hit me then.

"Their rooms?" I ask, biting my lower lip as I frown. I swear I hear a soft growl from nearby, which can't be right as we don't have a dog, much to my disappointment.

"Of course, little Spark. Where did you think they were going to stay? We're a family now," my dad answers, his smile so wide that it reaches his eyes and leaves them sparkling.

A family. *I thought we already were a family...*

"Silly me." I give a small huff that I mean to be a laugh, but it sounds strained instead. Fingers give my hand a squeeze, and I startle, looking down to see Prince still holding it. "W–where are their bedrooms?"

"We thought it would be best if they were in your wing, Ember," Odette informs me, coming over and wrapping her hands around my father's bicep. She reminds me of a possessive snake, claiming its prize and warning off any others. The thought sends unease running through me. Plus, it's strange that she's not greeted the boys, her sons, isn't it? Although, there must be a story there given how close all the boys look in age.

"Oh–um–sure," I reply, back to the stammering idiot as my dad and Odette smile at me. "Do you guys want to follow me?" I look back at them, their beauty stealing my breath for a moment.

"Lead the way, Pretty Thing," Kit tells me with a smile that should really be illegal because my brain short-circuits and I can't remember my own fucking name, let alone what we were about to do.

"The bedrooms, Sugar?" Prince adds after an embarrassingly long moment, and I blink several times, heat colouring my cheeks again.

"Right, yep, um, this way then." Please, for the love of all that is holy someone either smite me now or stop me from sounding like such a fucking twat.

I take a step forward, then pause when my hand tugs, and I glance over my shoulder to see Prince still clasping it. He gives me what I can only describe as a smouldering smile—whoops, there goes my knickers—and then raises his brows as if I'm the one holding us up again.

Narrowing my eyes at him, I spin and lead us out of the room towards the staircase, gorgeous stepbrothers in tow and Prince still holding my hand like he owns it.

Fuck. My. Life.

Only I would get cursed with four hot-as-hell stepbrothers. Fate clearly thinks that she's a funny bitch. Well, I'll be sending her the bill when my vibrator breaks from all the overuse it'll be getting from now on.

"Oh, you won't need a vibrator now that we're here," Oct's teasing voice says far too loudly as we walk up the stairs. My body jerks to a halt as I realise I must have spoken aloud, and Prince bumps into me, his hand clinging to mine while his other comes around me to hold me steady. Fire races from every part of me he touches, and once again my brain has up and left, leaving my pussy in charge who's rolling over and waiting for belly rubs.

"He's right, Sugar," Prince whispers in my ear, and I can't take a single inhale as his warm, rum-scented breath washes over me like a soft, teasing caress. "After all, what are brothers for if not to take care of their sister in times of need?"

Lightning races across my entire body at his words, and I can't fucking breathe. It's just so much to take in. A new stepmother, and four gorgeous stepbrothers that my body craves even though it's all kinds of fucked up and wrong. Add the fact that they talk like this, like they might want me as much as I seem to want them...

"Breathe, Little Cinders." Caspian's copper eyes fill my gaze, his warm palms cupping my face, and I take a gasping inhale, the flood of oxygen filling my lungs and leaving me lightheaded. "That's it, good girl." My eyelids flutter at the praise, and his thumbs stroke my cheeks, soothing me. "These assholes didn't mean to overwhelm you, we're just excited is all. You're more than we could have ever hoped for."

"I–I am?"

"So much more," Prince murmurs against my ear, and I sink back into him, despite my mind screaming that this is so wrong. It seems like my body is giving her the middle finger and taking what it wants right now.

"You're so fucking beautiful, Pretty Thing," Kit says from next to us, and my head turns slowly, as if it's underwater, only to be caught in his stormy stare.

"Gorgeous," Oct adds from the other side, and I swing my gaze to him, letting myself get lost in his sparkling, blue eyes.

"Boys..." Caspian warns in a dark tone, and they all step away, even Prince. I'm suddenly left feeling bereft while moisture threatens to fill my eyes, and I want to hide but Caspian's grip on my cheeks won't let me, and his face softens the longer I stare at him. "Let's get to the rooms, okay?" I nod, a single tear escaping me and I don't know why I feel like bawling my eyes out, but the lump in my throat won't go away. He leans in, kissing the tear away and my body relaxes the moment his lips make contact. "It'll be okay, Little Cinders. We'll make sure of it."

His words give me the strength that I didn't know I needed, and my hand reaches up, taking one of his off my cheek and tangling our fingers together.

"Okay." A long exhale falls from my lips and the smile that he gives me is the stuff that poets dream about. "This way."

~

CASPIAN

Fucking captivating.

Ember Jane Everly is utterly spellbinding and I can see my stepbrothers are just as affected as I am.

I didn't exactly lie when I told her we would look after her, that we would make sure everything was alright, but Odette promised us a plaything of our very own, a gift for being such good and dutiful sons, and we intend to indulge all of our darkest fantasies.

I just didn't expect to find her so...addicting. I clutch her hand in mine, Prince giving me the stink eye even though he knows that I'm the best one out of us all for calming her down. I've got just the right amount of command and care.

Prince, on the other hand, wants to devour her and infect every part of her until she doesn't know who she is anymore. He may come across as a Southern gentleman, but he craves the ultimate control that only comes with ownership. The twins are tricksters, they'll play with her until she doesn't even realise that she's been broken. Oh, she'll enjoy every moment, but she'll be destroyed by the time they're through.

And me? I want to take care of her, wrap her up and smother her until she doesn't see anyone else, until she can anticipate my every desire and is desperate to fulfil it.

We've had years to dream about what it would be like to truly be in charge for once. To get what we crave most. For too long we've had to obey, and while it's been fun, it's also been a mind fuck that has threatened to destroy us. So to finally have control is a heady feeling that none of us will give up anytime soon.

Ember just happens to be the only one, the only thing, that we have ever had control over.

And we plan to keep a tight rein on her.

CHAPTER 2

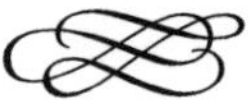

EMBER

With a slightly racing heart, I lead the guys to my wing. There's something about having my own wing in a house that makes me feel icky, like I'm one of the many entitled, rich bitches at Morley College expecting everything to be handed to me. But, if I'm being honest, it'll be nice not to be all alone in this part of the house anymore. Caspian still has a firm grip on my hand, and even if tingles race from the place where we touch, there's a comfort in it that I'm not looking too deep into. I don't have the mental capacity to examine why my new stepbrother affects me this way or why I feel so settled in their presence, yet at the same time a maelstrom of lust, want, and need ever since they walked into the room.

My room sits in the middle of this hallway, overlooking the extensive formal gardens, and I hadn't realised until now, but there are four other bedrooms, two on either side of mine. Fate strikes again, fucking bitch.

"Mine is the middle," I tell them, pausing at the first door we come across and pointing at my door. "The bedrooms on either side are unoccupied."

"I like that you'll be in the middle of us," Oct purrs, his hand skating down my arm, making all the hairs stand on end even though I'm wearing a long-sleeved shirt. I've the impression that he's talking about more than the room, but before I can comment, he grabs the door handle and turns it, throwing open the carved, wooden door to reveal a room in the exact shade of blue as his eyes. Well, fuck me sideways.

No! No fucking your stepbrothers, Ember!

Again, my body disagrees as Caspian pulls us into the room, my entire body flooding with warmth at Oct's words.

"This one is mine," Oct states, striding over to the French doors that open out onto a balcony. *Oh shit, the balcony.* I feel the blood drain from my face at the realisation. "A balcony that connects all the rooms, how convenient." His voice is a low purr as he stalks back towards me like a jungle cat, just waiting to pounce. I clear my throat and chew on my lower lip, my thighs clenching together trying to ease an ache that I'm refusing to admit is there.

"Yep, and they all have en suite bathrooms too. I'm sure you can change anything you don't like," I tell them in a slightly choked tone, looking around and trying to picture Oct's enormous frame inside the space. They make these vast rooms feel small, they're just so fucking big, and I don't hate it. I love my room but have often felt a little lost in the enormous space. I have to swallow past the sudden lump in my throat before speaking once more. "Shall we see the others?"

Cas's hand squeezes mine as we leave Oct's bedroom to open the next door, the room next to mine, and I'm stunned to see that it's also blue, only a darker, moodier version with navy accents. *What the actual fuck is going on with my life?*

"It's almost as if you knew we were coming," Kit teases, walking around and eyeing the huge four-poster bed. Each room has one, complete with drapes that can be pulled shut to create an intimate sleeping space. Heat colours my cheeks at Kit's words, and the bastard notices as he turns back to glance at me, a feline smile drawing his lush lips upwards. "What are you thinking about that has you blushing, Pretty Thing?"

"S–shall we move on?" I squeak out in a rush, turning on my heel and hurrying to the door. Of course, I'm slowed down because Caspian won't let go of my fucking hand.

"I want to see your room, Sugar," Prince purrs, and it's not a request. No, there's a note of command in his voice that renders me unable to deny him. *Fuck, this is not good. Why can't I resist them?*

Against my better judgement, I stop in front of my door, Caspian beside me and the others a furnace at my back. My free hand trembles as I reach out and grasp the handle, turning it while sunlight spills out of the room, filling me with sunshine and a lightness like it always does. For what feels like the first time since I walked into the house today, my lips pull up into a genuine smile.

"Fuck me, Little Cinders," Caspian breathes out next to me, and I turn to look at him with raised brows. "We need to get you smiling like that more."

I can feel the blush that seems to be a permanent fixture on my face deepen, my pulse pounding as I look away, unable to hold his adoring stare any longer.

"This is me," I tell them softly, inching into the space and trying to block the door as if I'm afraid they'll somehow taint it with their... overbearing manliness. It's a lost cause, Caspian not letting go of my hand and using his grip to move me aside.

"It's perfectly you," Prince declares, striding past me and inside, looking around. I try to see what he means, to take it in as if for the first time. I was drawn to the soft yellow walls and the large windows that let in so much light it's an artist's dream. Suddenly, my eyes widen, my stomach filling with damn butterflies as I catch the corner of the room in front of the windows that has my easel set up, my paints and charcoals strewn messily on a table beside it.

Caspian finally lets go of my hand, only to casually stroll over to the art space, something that no one else has ever seen, and his eyes take in the half-finished painting and then the others tacked onto the wall beside it.

"You're an artist?" he questions, his tone soft and almost reverent. The others join him while I'm rooted to the spot, wanting to bolt and scream at them to leave all at once. I can't see their faces fully, only the side of them, so I don't know what they're thinking. "Little Cinders, these are amazing."

He turns to face me and then his eyes lock onto mine, something unreadable in the expression, and I still can't move, trapped as my soul is laid bare for these strangers. Something inside me warms, liking his praise.

"I'm taking this one," Prince states, reaching over to pluck a drawing from the wall. It's an ink and watercolour of a phoenix in flight, the bright orange and yellow colours dripping down the page, the ink splattered across it. I made it recently, feeling like after five years I was finally rising from the ashes that were left after Mum passed.

"Is that okay, Little Cinders?" Caspian asks seriously, and in that moment I know that Caspian would tell Prince to fuck off if I said it wasn't okay. I've somehow gained a protector in the past half an hour, and it's enough to almost bring tears to my eyes. I swallow hard, my eyes flicking back to Prince who still holds my drawing, his expression unreadable, though his brows are lowered like he's waiting for me to deny him.

"S–sure," I say, licking my lips, and for a moment they all stare at me with molten fire in their stares, their eyes shining like jewels. Prince's lips kick up in a half smile that leaves my knees weak, and I'm sure I'd give him all my drawings if he smiles at me like that every time.

"Then I want one," Oct declares, his eyes leaving mine to roam over the wall. "That one." He points to another of my watercolours, this one a pink, purple, and turquoise octopus, and I see it suits his surfer vibe. I made it recently too, after a lovely day when Dad took time off work to take us for a weekend away by the sea in Cornwall.

Oct carefully takes it off the wall, then reaches for another and pulls that off too. "This one can be yours, Kit."

Kit takes the painting, also of an octopus, but this one is in shades of deep violet and navy with galaxy stars down its side and spilling out of it in an ink spill across the page. This image makes my chest tight because I painted it a few years back when I was in a bit of a dark place. My hand rubs over my shirt sleeve, over the scars that litter my forearm from that time, the reason I wear long shirts even on the warmest of days. Kit's lips lift, and he looks up at me.

"You are exceptionally talented, Pretty Thing."

"T–thank you," I reply in a rasping whisper, feeling like I'm too raw. To most, these are just pictures of animals, but each one holds a special meaning to me, as if they're a part of me.

"Will you choose one for me, Little Cinders?" Caspian pleads, and my gaze flies to him, my heart suddenly pounding. "Please?"

He holds his hand out, and the others stand back a little. Slowly, reluctantly, I inch towards him, my palms sweating and I'm not even sure why. I let him take my hand, and he pulls me in front of him, wrapping his arms around me from behind and engulfing me in his scent of caramel apples. It calms me, even though I know it shouldn't because we're effectively strangers, and I let myself sink into him just like I did with Prince on the stairs. A contented rumble sounds from his chest and he pulls me even closer. I let my hands rest on his arms, his muscles tensing and proving that he's every bit a man who could pin me down right. *Dammit, Ember! Not the fucking time for dirty thoughts of your stepbrother.*

My eyes roam over the drawings, noting the gaps now that the others have taken their paintings. Then my vision snags on a dragonfly in shades of red and bronze, and I know that this belongs to Caspian.

"Did you know dragonflies symbolise change? Transformation?" I tell them, leaving the warmth of Caspian's embrace to reach for the picture and take it off the wall. "It reminds us to open our hearts to change and encourage us to feel relaxed, even when situations are difficult." I turn and look at Caspian as I say the last part, his copper eyes so intense that they're practically glowing. "This is the picture I think you should have, Cas."

His irises flare brighter at the nickname that slips out from my lips, and his smile stops my heart altogether.

"Thank you, Ember."

Oh lordt, when he says my name like that, like I'm something precious to be cherished and looked after, I can't think of a single response.

"Why don't you show Cas and I our rooms, darlin'?" Prince drawls from behind Cas, and blinking as if coming out of a daze, I look over at him and nod.

"Of course, you guys must be exhausted."

"Not too tired to—oomph." I look at Oct, seeing him rub his side and giving Cas a death glare. A small giggle bursts from my lips, even as my cheeks warm, wondering what Oct was about to say. Surely he can't have meant...

"Add that sound to the 'noises we need Ember to make every day' list," Kit declares, striding forward and grabbing my hand before pulling me towards the door, the others following behind.

"I've another sound I'd like to he—fuck, dude!" Oct curses, and I know that Cas, who seems to have become my protector, has once again stopped Oct from saying something that might be a little too much for me right now.

I barely repress a groan when we reach the room on the other side of mine and open the door. Shades of green greets us, from a deep, almost black to a bright emerald and I know by the way that Prince saunters into the space that he's already laid claim to this one.

"I like the idea of being next door to you, Sugar," he purrs, and again, all the hair on my body stands on end as his gaze slides up and down me. I just hope the walls are thick, the idea of him being able to hear every noise I make is enough to have me in cold sweats.

"Can you show me my room, Little Cinders?" Cas gently asks,

stepping in front of me and once again diffusing the situation. I could kiss him for that. *Fuck! No kissing your stepbrothers.*

Taking my hand in his again, he tugs me to the door. Kit keeps hold of my other hand, and I can't say that I dislike being between them, both of them refusing to let me go.

We come to the last room at the end of the corridor, and before Cas even opens the door, I know just how wide his grin will be. I've never enjoyed the colour brown before, but when he looks back over his shoulder at me, his copper eyes twinkling, I know that fate really is some kind of masochist.

"These rooms were all decorated like this before we moved in," I rush to tell them, feeling the need to justify how perfect these rooms are for each of them, but Cas's grin just gets wider.

"Of course they were," Oct says, his voice light and teasing, his fingers brushing the back of my neck and sending a tremble over my muscles. Cas pulls me into his room, and as Kit refuses to let go, he comes too as we look around.

"Sirs, Miss," a male voice interrupts us, and I jerk my hands out of their grasp, my fingers gripping each other tightly as I spin, looking at Smithers from across the room with wide eyes. I can just make out the three guys around me, Oct still at my back, all with completely nonplussed expressions on their faces, the bastards.

"Yes, Smithers?" I ask, my voice higher pitched than usual. My stomach churns, as if I've been caught doing something I shouldn't have.

"I've instructed the staff to bring up the bags. We just need to know which room is whose?"

"Oh, of course. This is Cas's—I mean Caspian's room. The one next to this is Prince's. Then Kit's is on the other side of mine and Oct's is next to his."

"Thank you, Miss. I shall get the bags into their rightful places shortly," he replies, giving us a small bow which still makes me cringe even though he's been doing it since we moved here two years ago. If he saw anything before he spoke, he doesn't make any kind of reference to it now, just turns and leaves like the professional he is. My shoulders rise and fall with a deep inhale, and then turning back around, I face the guys, my new stepbrothers, once more. I have to take a step back, Oct smirking at me as he stands close.

"I'll leave you to settle in. I have some homework I need to catch up on anyway. Dad has some plans for dinner, I'm sure, so I'll see you then?" I don't mean it to sound like a question, to sound so fucking desperate, like I need them more than I really ought to. I meant to be firm, confident, but I guess that ship has fucking sailed.

"Wouldn't miss it, little sister," Oct answers first, and I blink at the nickname. They've each given me one and although I always thought they were cheesy, I secretly have always wanted a guy to give me one. Admittedly, one I was dating and not my new siblings, but this seems to be my life now so I may as well roll with it.

He strides towards me, leaning in to place a kiss to the corner of my lips, leaving them tingling and me desperate for a little more. I know the placement is completely intentional as he gives me a wink and then saunters out of the door.

Kit is next, kissing the other side, and I'm sure his tongue flicks out just briefly to taste me. A shuddering exhale leaves my lungs, but all I can do is stand still and flex my fingers at my sides as his hand ghosts across my hip. "See you soon, Pretty Thing." And then he's gone.

Prince stalks over to me, and something inside me recognises him as a predator, but my fight-or-flight mode is firmly stuck on freeze because I just watch, my heart pounding in my ears as he gets closer. His hand captures my chin, his jewel-green eyes tracing over my face as if he's memorising every line. He lowers his face until his lips are a hair's breadth from my own, and if I take a big inhale, I know that the distance will close. A part of me wants to do it too, and my lids lower over my eyes in preparation, his intoxicating, spiced rum scent making my head spin.

Cold air hits my lips as his warm breath moves to my ear. "Until dinner." His voice is a low, husky whisper and sends shivers cascading down my spine with the promise in his words.

I blink, and he's gone, leaving me chilled and feeling empty. Then there's just Cas left, standing a few feet away and watching me with an intense stare.

"Are you okay?" he asks gently, and my lips tremble as the past hour comes crashing down around me, a small whimper leaving my throat. "Oh, baby." He rushes over, sweeping me into his arms and pulling me so close that the front of our bodies mould together. "I know that this must be so fucking crazy for you, and I'm sorry to add to any kind of heartache that you're going through," he tells me, placing a kiss on the top of my head. "But I won't apologize for wanting you just as much as my brothers do. You are perfect, Ember. We will take care of you, whatever you need, you only have to ask and I swear it will be yours. There is just one thing we won't do."

I pull back, my neck craning even as my fingers clutch at his already wrinkled T-shirt. "What's that, Cas?"

"We won't leave you alone. You are now ours, you are the first thing to ever truly belong to us, and we will never let you go."

CHAPTER 3

EMBER

Pleasure shoots up my spine, my eyelids fluttering as I have the most intense sex dream I've ever had in my life.

"That's it, little sister. Come all over your brother's face," a deep, husky voice whispers in my ear and shivers tickle my nerve endings as I struggle to drag myself awake.

But the sparks flying from my core are all-consuming, and I'm lost in the depth of just how fucking good it feels. How incredible his tongue feels on my pussy, licking and sucking and sending shockwaves all across my body like he's running a live wire over my skin.

"Fuuuuck," I groan, my fingers tangling in the hair of my lover, pulling him closer, urging him deeper. His low rumbles of appreciation vibrates across my pussy, adding to my building orgasm and I'm a slave to this euphoric feeling he's giving me.

Another set of hands caresses my breasts, lips sucking my nipples, and fucking hell... It's like they both know exactly how to play me because I'm soon alight, my entire body going rigid as a pleasure so decimating I know I'll be useless afterwards sweeps me under.

They don't stop though, determined to wring out every last drop of my climax until I'm a twitching hot mess, whimpering and pleading for a reprieve.

It's the sound of my voice in my ears that has my eyes snapping open, noticing the soft light that fills the room, highlighting the very real men in my bed. My heart stops beating as I lock eyes with Kit, his lips and chin glistening, his face between my splayed thighs as he looks up at me with a sinful look in his stormy blue eyes. My fingers release their death grip on his hair, leaving it mussed and far too sexy looking.

"You're magnificent when you come, Ember," he says, his voice low and seductive. "You climaxed so beautifully on my tongue." As if to prove his point, he leans in and licks a long line from my opening to my clit, and electricity races up my nerve endings, my toes curling in pleasure.

"W–what are you doing here?" I stammer, finally getting my tongue to work.

"I thought that was obvious, little sister," Oct drawls from beside me, and a shiver raises all the hair on my body as he circles his finger around my damp, peaked nipple. "We were taking care of you, like you needed us to." His tone suggests that this is completely normal, having my two new stepbrothers in my bed, playing my body like a musical instrument, and giving me the most intense orgasm of my life. I'm suddenly very aware that my tits are out and Kit is still between my legs. *What the fuck happened to my pyjamas?*

"Y–you can't be in here," I whisper, afraid if I say it any louder that my dad will come rushing in and catch us. "This is so not okay." I bring my hands up to my face, covering my eyes and nipples, wondering how in the space of twelve hours my life became such a shitshow.

I'm lying practically naked in my bed, wearing just my long-sleeved sleep top that has been pulled down so my breasts are exposed, two of the most gorgeous men in existence with me, giving me pleasure like I've never known. Only they're my new stepbrothers and this is just so so wrong.

"Hey," Oct says softly, his hands grabbing mine and pulling them away from my face, lightly pinning them on the bed either side of my head. He leans over, and all I can see is the blue tropical waters in his irises. "Don't hide from us, Little Sis. You were so wound up last night, and now you feel better, don't you?" His bright, turquoise eyes are just so fucking earnest, like he's talking about having made my favourite cake and not the fact that his brother just made me come.

"I–that is–um–yes. Yes, I do feel better." It's not a lie, my muscles are relaxed for the first time since I walked into our house yesterday afternoon. His sudden smile is like the clouds parting and the sun bursting through, warming me all over and adding to the feeling of contentment that my orgasm has left me in.

"See? So there's nothing to worry about," he tells me, brushing a kiss to my temple.

"It can be our little secret, if you want?" Kit offers as I squirm, trying to get Oct to release me so I can pull my sleep top back up to cover myself a little. I'm completely naked from the waist down and I've no idea where my fucking shorts went.

"T–that might be for the best. If my father finds out..." I trail off, dread making my stomach churn and my movements freeze at the thought of what my father would do if he were to discover us. Whatever it would be, it wouldn't be good, and he's only just found happiness after all this time. I can't ruin it for him.

"Then that's just what we'll do," Kit says, pushing up to kneeling. He's only wearing a pair of deep red boxer shorts, which showcases every one of his mouth-watering abs, as well as some dark and moody tattoos across his pecs and down his arms. They also don't hide the hard length of him that pushes at the fabric. I flush as he chuckles, catching me ogling him, but before I can look away, he's lowering himself over me, Oct releasing my hands, and that very solid member is nestling against my slick folds. "Like what you see, Emmmber?" He elongates my name, making it something sinful and decadent like rich, hot chocolate on a winter day.

He gives me no chance to answer, slamming his lips onto mine in a kiss that short-circuits and hot-wires my brain all at once. I gasp, his tongue invading my mouth and giving me a taste of myself as well as him. He tastes just like his eye colour; stormy seas and wild winds, and I'm unable to stop my arms from wrapping around his neck, my fingers once again in his hair as I pull him closer and kiss him back with a ferocity that scares me.

Who is this person who kisses her stepbrother so wantonly? I barely recognise myself, but I don't stop. Instead, I grind my pelvis against him, fire pooling low in my stomach when he groans and pushes back, his fabric-covered dick sliding between my wet pussy lips in a way that's driving me wild.

He pulls back with a low growl, his eyes just as wild as a maelstrom.

"If Cas hadn't ordered us not to fuck you yet, I'd be balls deep inside you right fucking now, Pretty Thing." His voice is a deep rasp, there's colour on his cheeks, and every hard inch of him presses against my softness.

"Don't forget Prince has first fuck," Oct reminds Kit from beside us, and I tear my gaze away from Kit to look into his twin's eyes. His pupils are blown out, the bright blue almost completely swallowed up.

"First fuck?" I question, my voice breathy but with a sharpness to it that has both boys chuckling.

"Oh, you're gonna give him hell, Little Sis, aren't you?" Oct says, leaning down and capturing my lips. A deep groan sounds in his chest, his tongue swirling around my mouth in what I assume is a bid to capture the taste of my pussy that Kit left there.

My anger melts, my thoughts scattering as Oct fills me with sunshine and laughter, his kiss teasing and everything that is best about a summer's day. I keep one hand on Kit, the other gripping the back of Oct's head and pulling him closer, a small whine-like sound falling into his lips from mine when Kit starts to suck and tease my neck.

There's no thought about how wrong this is because it doesn't feel wrong. To be in between the twins feels just right, and my body is screaming to take it further, to let them bury themselves inside me so deeply that they'll never leave.

A sharp rap on the door has me pulling back, my heart thudding in my chest. Neither boy so much as moves an inch, and my eyes go wide when my father's voice sounds on the other side of the door. Thank fuck he started knocking as I got older.

"Little Spark? You up, honey?"

I have to swallow hard past the sudden dryness in my throat in order to get the words out.

"Y–yes, Dad. I–I just woke up."

The last of my words end on a slight gasp when Kit licks a line up the side of my neck. Fuck. These two are bloody dangerous.

"Well, when you're ready, can you join us for breakfast? There's a couple of things Odette and I want to discuss."

Discuss? What more is there to talk about?

"S–sure, Dad," I answer, distracted from my thoughts and the conversation when Oct suddenly sucks my earlobe. "I–I'll be down soon."

"Great, little Spark," he says, and my body sags as I hear his footsteps retreating down the hall.

"Fuck," I breathe out, trying to break through the lust haze that the twins have put me in, are still putting me in. I take my hands off them both, my fingers immediately itching to get back on them. "I–I think you guys should go. I need to get ready."

They both pause, heads slightly tilted as they study me with a banked heat in their stares and suddenly I'm itching to hide as they train their eyes on me.

"As you wish, Pretty Thing," Kit purrs, placing a soft kiss on my lips and leaving them tingling. He pushes up, the slight chill of the spring morning air hitting my feverish body as he gets out of bed and stalks towards the balcony doors. Of fucking course that's how they got in.

"We'll be back tonight, Little Sis," Oct promises, copying his brother and kissing my lips, though he lingers longer, peppering me with small kisses until my breath is panting from my chest. "Don't bother locking the doors."

I watch through half-lidded eyes as he gets out of my bed and stretches, showcasing all of his glorious muscles and the fact that like Kit, he's in just some boxer briefs, a gaudy orange pair that tugs my lip upwards. *He's definitely my sunshine.* He has random tattoos decorating his body, bright bursts of colour in a patchwork that suits him in its chaos. There's a clock face on his forearm, a bird swooping low on his hip, and a teal butterfly in the centre of his chest.

He gives me the cheekiest smile known to man when I catch his eyes, then saunters to the balcony doors, his hard-on bobbing with each step, before going through and softly closing them behind him.

I flop back onto the sheets—the damp fucking sheets—and a huff of air leaves my lungs as I try to decide if I want to cry or giggle like a fucking schoolgirl. I want to call them back, but I have to physically grip the duvet to stop myself from reaching for them even though they're gone.

How is this my life? How did it go from moving on from my mother's death to...this? I'm not even sure what this is, but I think I just agreed to let the twins back into my room tonight. I didn't tell them no...

And what did they mean by Cas ordered them not to fuck me yet? And that Prince gets first fuck? My head spins trying to decode what it all means, and I've got sweet fuck all. Add in that my dad wants to discuss something and I can feel the tension building, itching to give me a headache.

My fingers twitch in the covers, and the thought that I know what will help to ease the pressure slams into me with such force that I'm up and out of my bed in an instant, heading to my bathroom with a desperate need that won't be ignored.

Reaching into the back of the cabinet, I take out a small pouch, the sound of the zip loud as I drag it across the teeth. Anticipation leaves me feeling giddy as I pull out a freshly wrapped blade, and take off the paper, the light gleaming off the silver surface.

My hand is steady as I roll up my sleeve, my eyes darting over the mixture of silver and pink scars that litter my forearm.

"Just four cuts," I murmur, smiling when I realise the sudden significance of the number. "One for each of them."

The rush as the blade slices across my skin rivals that of the orgasm Kit just gave me, and my eyes flutter closed for a second as I let the feeling wash over me, bringing peace in its wake.

Opening my eyes, I repeat the move three more times, my muscles relaxing with each slice, the beauty of the crimson blood that drips down my olive skin—the same tanned hue of my mother's—captivating me for a moment.

Wrapping the blade back in its packet and then some tissue paper, I drop it into the bin and turn on the shower, feeling like I'm floating and finally able to just fucking breathe. It may not be a healthy coping mechanism, but it's all I've got, and it works to calm me when everything feels too much.

And my new family, my new stepbrothers, definitely qualify as too much.

CHAPTER 4

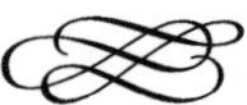

PRINCE

We wait for Ember in the dining room, sitting down with plates piled high and still feeling jet-lagged as shit. The twins look fresher than Cas and I, and I don't even need to guess where they were this morning having heard Ember's cries of pleasure through the wall between our rooms.

My dick was so fucking hard imagining what they were doing to her that I came in my sheets like a horny teenager at the whimpering sounds she made, thinking of her making them while I'm buried deep inside her, my hand wrapped around her throat.

Fuck. Now I'm hard again, and with her dad sat at the table, inappropriate doesn't even begin to cover it.

Then she walks in, shoulders back and breasts thrust forward, her long-sleeved, white shirt and high-waisted jeans clinging to every mouth-watering curve. It's not helping my dick, but I'm just as entranced as my brothers as she strides in, pausing when she sees us all staring. A flush warms her cheeks pink, and I love the colour on her.

"G–good morning," she greets softly, her big, blue eyes wide as she tries to work out where to sit.

"We saved you a seat," Caspian tells her, rising and gesturing to the place between him and I. The pink in her cheeks darkens when she catches my gaze, and I know that I'm giving her a predator's smile, but I don't give a fuck. Cas might want to fool her into thinking he's a good guy, but I have no such qualms.

The way I see it, she doesn't have a choice so why sugar-coat it?

"Oh, thanks," she replies in a surprised whisper, slowly making her way around to us. She pauses once more as Cas pulls out her chair, and I can see the rapid rise and fall of her chest as she lets him push it in under her.

"I got you a plate," he tells her, motioning to the very full plate of food that's in front of her. She licks her lips, blinking owlishly at it.

"I usually just have some muesli," she informs him quietly, not looking up from the plate of food, but he just smiles indulgently down at her.

I lean over, placing my lips next to her ear.

"Be a good girl and eat your breakfast, Sugar. Then maybe later you'll get a treat." I fucking love the way she shivers, her hands grasping each other in her lap.

"How kind you are, Caspian," Odette coos sweetly, giving Cas a wide smile. "Although, I agree Ember will need muesli in the future if she wants to keep her figure. Us women can't afford to eat pancakes every day." She titters, and I see Ember flush deeply, but this time I suspect she's embarrassed as she rubs a patch on her forearm and looks down at her lap.

My brows dip at the clear barb in Odette's words; I don't like that she made Ember feel any less than gorgeous, which she is. Yes, she's not rail thin like Odette, but personally, I like something to grab hold of when I'm making a woman scream my name, and my sister is soft in all the right places.

"You're perfect, Little Cinders," Cas assures her under his breath, and I see her swallow, rubbing that patch on her arm again. "Eat a little for me, please?"

She heaves out a breath, biting her lower lip, no doubt uncomfortable that we're all looking at her. "O–okay."

I murmur an appreciative noise when she takes her first bite, envious of the fucking fork that disappears into those lush lips of hers. I can see meal times will be a challenge from here on out.

"Little Spark, Ember, honey," Richard, Ember's dad says, and she looks up at him, those baby blues giving him her entire focus. There's a burning in my chest when she continues to stare at her father. I want her to focus on me, no one else. Well, maybe I'll make a concession for my brothers. "Odette and I have been talking, and we think it's best if you stay at home and we bring in tutors from now on, just like the boys have."

The clatter of her fork hitting the plate sounds like a gunshot in the room, her mouth falling open as her breath hitches, and my hand goes to her thigh, rubbing soothing circles on it.

"What did you just say?" she questions in a trembling voice, her body quivering. "What about college? My friends there?" Her face is lined with confusion, her voice a little wobbly, and my chest aches at hearing the hint of her upset. I want her here with us, fuck letting any other dickhead even look at her, so I'm all for this suggestion. Though a part of me feels the need to make it right, to take away any slight pain she may feel.

"Well, you'll have the boys, and I'm sure you can still see your friends from time to time," Odette adds dismissively, tilting her head to the side. She pauses in cutting up her sliced avocado while Richard just stares at Odette with such adoration it makes me feel queasy. She doesn't deserve it, not by a long shot. "And having one-on-one tuition is the best type of education. You want the best education, don't you, Ember?"

Odette's tone leaves me feeling uneasy. She's spoken to us like that, like we're being so unreasonable for wanting something other than what she has decided. Like we're stupid. My palm tightens on Ember's leg, and I only ease up when she hisses. I don't like Odette talking to my darlin' like that.

"O–of course I do, but I've only just started my final year, isn't this a bit disruptive? And you know I wanted to go to Goldsmiths so I can't afford to let things slip." She's looking at her dad, her dark brows lowered over her sparkling eyes, so she misses the pinch of Odette's brows. The guys and I don't, all of us stiffening in our seats.

"Well, it's a good thing that your father secured you an alumnus from Goldsmiths as your art tutor isn't it?" Her tone leaves a sour taste in my mouth, and I can see how Ember's shoulders slump when she gives in. Suddenly, I don't want her to. I want her fire, I can see it simmering just below the surface and I want it to burn us all.

"W–when do I leave?" she asks quietly, and I grind my teeth at the sound of defeat in her voice. I fucking hate it.

"Your tutors will start on Monday, same as the boys, so you have the weekend to relax and all get to know each other better." I move my hand up higher on her thigh, watching the way her breath hitches when my fingers brush just below the apex of her thighs. Maybe I can get that fire some other way, distract her a little. "You'll share some sessions with Christopher and Octavius, and you'll all take riding lessons together in Hyde Park. Trust me, Ember, this is for the best." Odette, clearly finished, goes back to her coffee and sliced avocado, talking with Richard.

"It's not all bad, Sugar," I whisper, inhaling her scent of lavender and rosemary. I love the sharp perfume and want to coat myself in it, in her. "This way we'll get to spend more time together." My fingers coast higher, and her chest rises and falls rapidly as her cheeks brighten.

"I thought you knew everything about me, Prince?" she questions in a slightly sassy tone, tipping her head towards me, and fuck, her eyes are like the purest sapphires, drowning me in their brilliance. Then her words and brattiness register and I find I like it, my lips splitting into a wide grin. I like it a lot.

"Oh, I know almost everything," I say, inching my fingers up higher until I'm stroking over her jeans-clad pussy. I bite my bottom lip at how warm she feels and how wet I know she is underneath those pants. "But there is always more to find out, don't you think?"

Her eyelids flutter when I apply pressure just over her clit, her hands clenching the edge of the table and I don't let up, seeing how far I can take her. I've learned to read a woman and her reactions like a book, and the sweat that breaks out on her brows tells me she's close.

"Ember?" her father queries, and she jerks so suddenly, the plates rattle.

"Y–yes, Dad?"

"Odette and I have plans today, why don't you give the boys a tour of London, if you're all not too jet-lagged?" He looks around at us, completely oblivious to where I am touching his daughter.

"I'm sure we'll manage, especially if Ember is there to take care of us," Kit answers, and I know his words are nowhere near as innocent as they sound, his eyes travelling up and down Ember's torso, pausing on her luscious tits.

Fuck, I love the way her cheeks colour when we say shit like that. My cock jumps in my pants at the sight of her all flushed and needy. I press a little against the seam of her jeans again, and she coughs before drawing both lips between her teeth, her fingers gripping the table so hard that her knuckles turn white.

"Splendid!" Richard beams. "That's settled then. Take Davis," he instructs, then takes out his phone, his thumbs flying across the screen. "And I have topped your account up, so just have fun and don't worry about anything, okay, Little Spark?"

She lets out a slow breath, her hand finally coming to grab mine as she tries to pull me away. I do like her fight, it's cute that she thinks she can control what I do to her. We'll teach her she has no control real soon.

"Okay, Dad." I let her pull my hand away from her core, but quickly flip my hand so that my fingers tangle with hers. A zap of electricity lights up my arm, and I catch her wide eyes as she looks back up at me.

"Best finish your breakfast, Sugar," I tell her, rubbing her knuckles with my fingertips and liking the feel of holding her hand in mine. It's so small, just like she is. "Looks like we've got a busy day."

~

EMBER

As instructed, we take Davis—our driver—and the Bentley, which is a seven-seater so it can fit all of us, and head into the centre of London. The boys all jostle to be either side of me, but Prince and Cas win when they point out that the twins had me to themselves this morning. My cheeks must be flashing neon red because I had no fucking idea that it was common knowledge.

"Where to, Miss Everly?" Davis asks, his eyes darting to mine in the rearview mirror. He's around my father's age, early fifties, and is handsome in a silver fox kind of way. He's been with us for the past couple of years since Dad decided we needed a full-time driver—in part, I think because he's too worried something will happen to me if I learn to drive myself. I would have liked the option, but I never wanted to make an issue out of it.

"We'd like to see the sights, so, um, maybe Trafalgar Square?" A rush of genuine excitement enters my veins when I think about going to the National Gallery and showing them some of the wonderful artwork inside.

"Of course, Miss," Davis replies, and then the privacy screen comes up between us and him, leaving me with them. My new stepbrothers.

"What has you smiling so beautifully, Little Cinders?" Cas questions in a husky voice as we pull onto the main road.

"Why do you call me that?" I counter, twisting around to look into his beautiful, copper eyes which sparkles in the light when the spring sunshine hits his face every so often. I'm itching to capture them on paper, my fingers twitching with the need for my charcoal.

"I asked first," he replies, and I take in a sharp breath when he reaches out and tucks a piece of my hair behind my ear.

"I thought maybe we could go to the National Gallery, and I'll show you some of my favourite paintings, if you like?" I'm useless to resist his commands when he touches me. Now that the words have left my mouth I feel almost shy, sucking my lower lip under my teeth and nibbling it. He *tuts*, his thumb pulling my lip out and lingering for a moment before he pulls it away.

"That sounds perfect, Little Cinders," he says, his lips quirking up in a half smile and I can't help mine doing the same. "And I call you that because you remind me of Cinderella with your long, blonde hair and big, sad, blue eyes."

My brows dip when he says the last bit. "I have sad eyes?" I have to swallow past the lump in my throat as his face softens and he palms my cheek. For a moment, for a single space in time, I forget that he's my stepbrother and I lean into the touch, my breath easing out of me in a sigh of pure bliss. Cas calms me in a way that I've never experienced before, and I'm quickly becoming addicted to the feeling.

"There's a world of pain in those blues depths of yours, Little Cinders, like your heart has been broken and you're not sure how to put back the pieces."

How does he see me so clearly? How does he look into my eyes and understand the pain of my mother dying and my father pulling away to lose himself in business, as if it's plain for all to see?

Tears sting my eyes and he offers a deep sigh, his hand tugging me closer until our foreheads touch. It feels so intimate and leaves me taking a shuddering breath that fans across his lips. My eyelids close, the tears spilling down my cheeks in a warm river, but I don't wipe them away. I can't move as I breathe him in, his tart, toffee apple scent a balm that I need more of.

"Like recognises like, Little Cinders. We share the same pain of losing a loved one, we all do. Your sorrow is ours and ours is yours. It's what connects us, Ember."

My hands come up, fisting his soft jumper, and a small sob falls from my lips, my eyes open and drowning in his copper ones.

"W–who did you lose?"

He takes a shuttering inhale, and the sound is so raw that it breaks my already fractured heart a bit more. "My mom had a miscarriage when I was nine and she fell into a deep depression. She couldn't get over the loss. One day, we couldn't wake her up, she'd OD'd on sleeping pills." A soft noise escapes my throat, my hands tightening in his jumper until my fingers go numb. "Dad wasn't able to cope, all alone with an angry and hurting nine-year-old boy. He jumped off Manhattan Bridge two weeks later."

"No—" My gasp ends on a muffle as I pull him to me, burying my face in his neck and sobbing against his skin. "Cas, I—" My chest tightens at the memory of what I'd done earlier, the way I'd cut myself. I'd never go that far, to take my own life. Well, not anymore anyway.

"Shhhh, baby. It's in the past now, and I never would have met these guys, or you, if it hadn't happened, so it's not all bad." He pulls me closer, rubbing my back to soothe me when I should be the one comforting him. I soak in his embrace for a few moments before I drag myself away from him.

"Shit, Cas, I should be comforting you, not the other way round," I say, my voice thick as I pull back.

"Don't apologize for being sad for me. I don't think anyone has ever cried for me before," he tells me, and the crack he's unwittingly caused in my heart grows bigger. "I'm sorry I stole your smile, Little Cinders. I don't like to see you cry."

Warmth presses against my back, the smell of rum, leather, and cedar surrounding me as Prince wraps his arms around me and pulls my back so that it's flush against his front. My arms stretch, my fingers still gripping Cas's jumper, and his copper eyes burn as they look at me and Prince.

"I only ever want to see you cry when you're begging me to stop, and you will beg, Sugar," he purrs in my ear, and it's as if my body flashes with heat, burning away the sadness from moments before. He rubs his nose up my neck, shivers following in his wake, and I can barely catch my breath with the change from desperate sorrow to molten lust.

"Seems like you're the one begging, Prince," I rasp, my filter blown to smithereens, and my eyes widen at the brazenness of my comment when he pauses.

"Oh, that's fighting talk, Little Sis," Oct comments from beside me, and I'm frozen, cursing myself as one of Prince's large palms glides up my shoulder, his hand wrapping around the front of my throat in a way that has dampness soaking my knickers.

"Is that so?" he questions, his other hand skimming down my side, slipping around the front of me and stopping just above the button of my jeans. Cas brings his hands over mine, holding them captive against him as Prince slowly undoes the button, then the zipper of my jeans.

His fingers slide inside my cotton knickers, and the thought that perhaps I should have worn lace flits through my mind before he fries all my fucking brain cells when he makes contact with my slick folds.

"Prince…" I moan, pushing my hips up in a bid to seek more friction.

"I told you that you would beg me, darlin'," he breathes in my ear, the warmth of his breath making my nipples pebble. "And you proved me right in less than thirty seconds. Now, why don't you add a please to that and I'll let you come all over my fingers."

Fuck. Me.

I lick my lips, contemplating not saying a word, but I'd be kidding myself if I thought that I'm going to do anything other than what he commands.

"Please, Prince," I beg in a cracked, desperate tone, not even recognising the wanton, husky sound of my voice.

"Fuck, Little Cinders," Cas groans, and he looks down at Prince's hand between my legs.

"Good girl," Prince praises, and I just fucking melt as he begins to swirl his fingers and tease my clit. "She's so fucking wet." Three deep groans sound in the enclosed space and more wetness seeps from me at the sound.

"Oh, fuck, Prince," I gasp, his touch driving me crazy, all my previous sorrow forgotten as I grind against his hand.

"Take her jeans off, I need to get my fingers inside her," Prince orders in a low drawl that teases across my skin and leaves me panting.

"Lift, Cinders," Cas orders, and I comply, unable and unwilling to stop chasing the high that is just out of reach.

He pulls my jeans and knickers down, leaving them around my ankles. Pushing my thighs apart, he widens my legs, and the twins groan from the back.

"Such a pretty pussy," Kit purrs from next to my ear, and my head falls to land on Prince's shoulder as I open wider, encouraging him to go lower with his hand. I roll my gaze to look at Kit and Oct in the back seat, matching looks of lust written over their faces and lips parted as they stare at my cunt.

"Use your words, Sugar," he commands, sucking and kissing my neck.

I'm going straight to hell because I don't even think about disobeying my stepbrother.

"Please fuck me with your fingers, Prince. Please make me come."

"Jesus fucking Christ, Cinders," Cas rasps, and I gasp when he pulls his hard cock out of his jeans. Fucking hell, that's a gorgeous dick, thick and long, and my eyes widen when I see the glint of metal at the end.

"She just got wetter looking at your dick, Cas," Prince informs him just as he lowers his fingers and slams two of them inside my aching cunt.

"Prince!" I cry out, so wound up that I'm coming already, wetness squirting out of me as I grip Cas's jumper so tightly I'm surprised it doesn't rip.

"Shit, she just squirted everywhere," Oct moans, but I can't concentrate on anything other than Prince's fingers as he keeps thrusting in time to Cas pumping his dick. I come again when Cas goes rigid, his hips thrusting forward and spurts of cum hit my pussy and lower stomach.

I expect Prince to pull back, but he doesn't. Instead, he scoops it up and thrusts Cas's cum inside me, sending shockwaves throughout my entire body as he stuffs me full. As the waves of pleasure subside, my hands drop from Cas's jumper to rest at my sides, and I slump against Prince as I bask in the glow of two epic fucking orgasms.

"Such a good fucking girl for your brothers," Oct whispers, and I roll my head to the side to see him looking at what Prince is doing, his blue eyes almost black and his pupils blown.

"She clenches around my fingers when you call her that, Oct," Prince murmurs, keeping his fingers inside me as though he wants to keep Cas's cum there. "You like it when he reminds you he's your brother, don't you?"

I look straight into Oct's eyes, having no energy left to fight whatever it is that's going on between us. Not that I want to. "Yes."

My answer doesn't even shock me anymore. I've always liked sex, but with these guys, it's like I've never experienced anything like it before. I've had the two best orgasms of my life today, and neither was with a dick inside me.

Not to mention both were with two people to whom I definitely shouldn't be sexually attracted to. They're my new brothers for fuck's sake. My family. *What the fuck am I doing?*

I must stiffen a little because Kit is suddenly there, my sweat-damp face in his palms.

"Our secret, remember?" My breathing calms as I look deep into his stormy eyes, nothing but acceptance and reassurance in their depths. "Nothing that feels this good is bad, okay?"

"O–okay." I nod like a fucking idiot, but there's something about just following their lead, doing as they say, and letting them take control that puts me at ease.

It's as if I can finally let go and leave someone else in charge of my life. Which is strange as I felt so out of control after Mum passed that it's all I've craved since, but I'm just so tired.

"Let us take care of you, Cinders," Cas urges, pulling some wet wipes from somewhere and nudging Prince's fingers from inside me. I moan as Prince withdraws while grumbling. Then I hear more than see him lick and suck his slick fingers.

"He tastes good on you, Sugar," he groans, bringing his fingers to my lips. I hold Cas's stare as I part my lips, allowing Prince to slide a long digit inside my mouth. A musky saltiness bursts on my tongue and my eyelids flutter as I greedily clean every inch of his finger, my hands holding his wrist so I can start on another.

"Fuck, I'm hard again," Oct groans from the seats behind me, and I hear the others murmur their agreement, but if I'm doing this, I'm fucking doing this.

Letting go of Prince's hand, I lean forward towards Cas, my jeans and knickers around my ankles but I don't give a shit. Cas looks up, and I swoop in, pressing my lips to his and sliding my tongue into his mouth when his lips part in surprise. I want to give him a taste of us too, and I've been wondering what those lips would feel like ever since I met him yesterday.

Fuck. Was it only a little over twelve hours ago that these boys came strolling into my house, into my life? And now I'm making out with one, his cum leaking out of my pussy while the other three watch.

"I do taste good on you, Cinders," he mumbles against my kiss-swollen lips, his voice a husky purr that has my core clenching again. "But we should probably finish getting you cleaned up."

I give him a nod, sucking my lower lip under my teeth and running my tongue along it to catch the last taste of him.

I'm in so much fucking trouble with these guys and I'm not sure that I care.

CHAPTER 5

KIT

Ember is mostly presentable by the time we reach our destination. The flush on her cheeks just makes her look so damn beautiful, it takes more effort than I possess not to grab hold of her when we leave the car. So I don't bother, earning a growl from Prince—possessive bastard—as I spin her away with me and towards the monument.

"So this is Trafalgar Square, huh, Pretty Thing?" I coo in her ear as I tuck her under my arm. I fucking love that she doesn't hesitate, after all, no one knows us here, and she wraps her arm around my waist. Oct snags her other hand, and I know the others are close behind us as we stare up at the tall column.

"The one and only," she answers in that soft voice of hers. I pull her closer, letting the warm, spring sun shine down on us.

When Odette said we'd have a new stepsister, a plaything for us for being such dutiful stepsons, Oct and I thought we'd quickly break her with everything that we've craved to do after all these years. But after this morning, after she came on my face, filling my mouth with her pleasure, and then kissed me...fuck. Something clicked into place, and catching Oct's eye, I knew the same was true for him.

We still want to play with her, shit, we still want to break her, but for the first time in my life, I want to put her back together again. To remake her and then bask in her fucking glory. She's exquisite, so goddamn beautiful that it almost hurts to look at her, and there's something about her soul that's so pure and shines so bright. I'm drawn to her like a month to a fucking flame and I don't give a shit if my wings get burned.

And she wants us. Hell, she cried for Cas and he was right when he said no one has ever cried for him, for any of us. I want to tell her our sorry tale just to see if she cares enough to shed a tear like she did for him. Something tells me she would, and fuck if it doesn't make my soul crave her tears just to know someone cares.

"Would you like to see the gallery?" she asks eagerly, and my chest warms at the eagerness in her tone. I look down at her, my breath catching at her exquisite features.

"I wouldn't want to do anything else, Pretty Thing," I reply, and her cheeks flush so easily at the compliment that I resolve to use the nickname more. "Show us your favourites first."

Her blue eyes fucking sparkle, and I can't help it, I swoop down and place a kiss on her plush lips, one of her hands coming to rest right over my black heart that I'm wondering if she owns now, the other clutched tightly in my grip. Our eyes close and I get the faint hint of Cas's musk, and fuck if that doesn't make my dick hard again. When Cas whipped his cock out in the car, Oct and I followed suit, and watching her fall apart was the hottest fucking thing I think I've ever seen in my life.

Reluctantly, I pull away, her lids fluttering open and she locks those stunning eyes on me again.

"What was that for?" she asks, her voice low, and fucking hell, the sound makes me even harder.

"For being you, Pretty Thing," I say, placing a light kiss on her nose because I just can't help it. "Lead the way." I sweep my arm out, instructing her to take us in the direction of the gallery.

She blinks twice, her eyes unfocused and it's too fucking

adorable. I love the way I can affect her so much that she loses herself when I touch her. Then she takes a deep inhale and heads towards the massive columned building that seems to be pretty busy with people coming and going, pulling me along with her.

"You all have different accents," she comments, and I smile as I see the dip in between her brows. "Are you not from the same place?"

"Nah, we didn't grow up together, well, not really," I tell her, stepping into the cool interior of the building. The outside is fucking magnificent with towering stone columns, but the moment we step foot inside, a shiver works its way up my spine. Red marble columns hold up the impressive, painted ceiling and glass dome, and huge wooden doors lead into the galleries at the top of more steps. Shit, it's pretty old and there's a feeling about it, like the building itself has its own presence and is weighing us as we step through its doors. I think I would like to study architecture, perhaps now we can follow our own interests rather than—I stop my train of thought, not wanting to think of anything bad today. Not with the sun on my arm.

"What do you mean? Where are you all from and how did you meet?"

"Curious, ain't you?" Oct teases, and she blushes, but he just brings her hand up to his lips and kisses her knuckles to let her know that he's not serious.

"Oct and I are from California," I tell her as we stroll through the crowds. "We were the last to join the crew."

"Join the crew?" She has the cutest fucking frown on her face, but if I kiss her again, I just won't stop, and I want to get our story out. I need to tell her about us.

"Well, Prince was the first, then Caspian was adopted when he was nine, and Odette married our dad when we were eleven." I can see the puzzled frown tugging her brows down and I know her next question before she even asks it. "Our mom died when we were young. I don't really remember much about her but apparently, she got sick and it was all over quickly."

Her gasp pulls us up short, her steps faltering and her hand clenching around mine as she turns to face me. Oct is beside us and Prince and Cas surround us so that the crowds part around us, like a river parts for a boulder.

"M–my mum died of cancer five years ago," she tells us, her blue eyes already swimming and it's fascinating to watch such emotion fill someone so completely. The centre of my chest pulses with an unfamiliar ache, enough that I want to rub it away but resist the urge, completely captivated by our stepsister in her pain.

"I'm sorry, Pretty Thing," I murmur, surprised to see that I am sorry for her. For years it's felt like I have been numb, going through the motions but not feeling much of anything, and yet, here she is, making me almost burst with emotions that I thought were long buried. I don't like her heartache. In fact, I fucking hate it.

"What happened to your dad?"

At her question, the ache in my chest grows, a flash of pain burning hot and bright enough to steal my breath for a moment. My jaw clenches hard, my vision blurring as memories of that time try to resurface and break free from the box that I keep them in.

"He was coming to collect us from a friend's party," Oct interjects next to us, and his eyes have a redness to them they always do when he talks about that night. "It was stormy, and we'd begged him to use the Camaro earlier to come and get us." Another sharp sting in my chest has my teeth grinding. *It's all our fault.* "And the brakes failed or some shit because he came off the road and wrapped the car around a tree. He didn't make it." Oct's shoulders are slumped, the last words barely a whisper over the loud crowds that are here at the gallery.

But Ember hears him alright, and I watch as the tears track down her cheeks Fucking hell, to have someone cry over me, to feel my pain as if it were theirs is unlike anything I've ever known. How the hell did Cas let her go earlier?

"It's okay, Pretty Thing," I assure her in a hushed whisper, reaching out and cupping her cheek with my free hand, then rubbing my thumb across the smooth surface, feeling the track of her tears carving a path down her skin. "It was five and a half years ago."

The tears drip down her cheeks, and I know by the sorrow in her eyes that she realises just how similar we are, just how much we have in common.

"But it still hurts you, like it hurts me."

I freeze, my heart pounding in my chest so hard that I wonder if the whole fucking gallery can hear it.

She knows. She sees me, and I'm not sure how to feel about that. My knees feel weak, my chest tight, as I look at this young woman, barely eighteen, and marvel at how she got so fucking wise.

"Yes." That's all I can say. It's a small confession that hurts with the force of a punch to the gut. I watch as another tear trails down her pale cheek, glinting in the gallery's lowlight. She nuzzles into my palm, then steps closer, resting her face on my chest, releasing Oct as her arms come around me in a comforting embrace. Oct comes closer too, burying his face against her neck and inhaling deeply.

"I'm so sorry, Kit, Oct," she breathes out, and I pull her closer, absorbing her fucking light like I can't get enough.

"See, they made us for each other, Little Sis," Oct tells her, and I couldn't agree more. She knows our agony and feels our pain like no one else.

She shivers as we press her between us all, Prince and Cas also moving closer until we're in our own bubble and each touching her. I look up, catching each of their eyes and they all give me a nod.

We're keeping her. She belongs to us now whether or not she wants to be. She's more than just a toy to be tossed aside when we grow bored. She's ours and no fucking one will take her from us.

~

EMBER

How can my heart feel heavy yet lighter than it has in years? These boys, my new stepbrothers, understand me on a level that no one else ever has before, and although I've not heard Prince's story yet, I can see in his green eyes that it's as devastating as the others. As all of ours. We've each lost a parent, or in the twins' and Cas's case, both parents and that's something that rocks your very foundations.

"Will you show us your favourite paintings?" Oct asks softly from next to me, and my cheeks heat knowing that we've just been standing in the middle of the National fucking Gallery, hugging and seeking solace from each other as if we were alone and not surrounded by people.

"I'd love to," I reply, my voice only a little thick from the sorrow that seems to surround me, while looking up at Kit. Before I second-guess myself, I press my lips against his, tasting the salt of my tears as he kisses me back.

Kissing Kit is like coming home and finding everything changed. It leaves my head spinning and my pulse racing but not necessarily in a bad way. We part after several moments, only for Oct to spin me around and plant his lips on mine.

I melt into him, what else can I do when he kisses me like I'm the oxygen that he needs to breathe? He's like a fairground ride, terrifying and yet exhilarating and my hands clutch his jumper as he deepens our kiss, giving no shits that we're in public.

Just as quickly as he started, he pulls back, his eyes alight with mischief.

"I needed another taste after this morning," he tells me with a wink, taking my hand and stepping to the side. My heart thuds in my chest, my stomach dipping at his words.

Prince is there, and my eyes dart to his lips, wondering what it's like to kiss him. He's the only one of them who I haven't tasted yet, and my body leans towards him in an unspoken plea. He gives me a smirk, a devilish expression that destroys my already damp panties.

I watch, barely breathing as his hand comes out and wraps around the front of my throat before he steps closer. It's a soft touch, his thumb stroking my racing pulse and his eyes tracking over my lips. My tongue comes out to trace them, an obvious invitation, and heat flares through me when his green eyes become the colour of emeralds; dark and sparkling.

He leans in so close that my eyes close waiting for his lips to land on mine.

"When I kiss you for the first time, Sugar, my thick cock will be buried so deep inside you that you'll feel me for the rest of your life."

My heart fucking stops, but a second later, cold air hits me like a slap to the face and my lids blink open to see him standing a few feet away, his gaze locked on me and a smirk on his pillowy lips. Fucking bastard.

"Ready, Cinders?" Cas asks, a slight note of teasing in his tone. I narrow my eyes at him in a glare and he laughs, the sound making butterflies swarm in my stomach. "Don't be salty," he says, taking Prince's place and darting in to press a quick kiss to my lips, "and he's not lying. Prince likes to fuck hard and deep and he's got the weapon to back up his promises."

My eyes widen, my mouth dropping open at his words.

"How do you know that?" The question blurts out before I can stop it, but something tells me I can guess the answer and I am not ready for it.

"We told you, we're family, and family takes care of each other."

Oh, my motherfucking god.

My brain just shuts the fuck down, lust roaring through me as I stand in the middle of the National Gallery and try not to melt into a puddle on the polished, marble floor.

"Come on, Little Sis. Show us those paintings," Oct urges, his voice full of laughter as I try to reboot all my systems, his hand sliding into mine, his palm warm and enough to get my brain semi-functional again.

He pulls me towards one of the galleries, Kit holding my other hand. I try to ignore the slightly shocked expressions on some of the people around us, having clearly caught the kisses and possibly Oct's nickname for me. It mostly works, though I can feel their curious stares like an itch across my skin.

"Mummy, I thought you said we can't marry our brothers?" a little girl asks as we pass, and my cheeks flare, my entire body going blistering hot.

Fuck my life.

CHAPTER 6

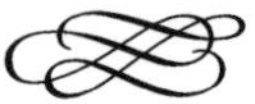

EMBER

We spend the rest of the morning strolling through the galleries, and I point out all of my favourite pieces. They all seem interested, especially Kit who it turns out has an interest in art and architecture.

We stop for lunch at the Hard Rock Cafe, which the guys declare is their new favourite place to eat after enjoying the rock-inspired vibe and the yummy American-style food. Afterwards, I take them to see the sights of London, a whirlwind tour of all the major buildings, and by the afternoon even I'm flagging.

The twins snagged the seat either side of me for the drive back, and the movement of the car soon lulls me to sleep, my head drifting to Oct's shoulder.

"We're home, Little Sis," he whispers what feels like minutes later, and I blink, trying to focus my blurry vision. The sun is setting and the car is indeed pulled up outside of our front door.

"Maybe I should call you sleeping beauty," Cas teases from behind me as the door opens and a blast of fresh spring air hits me in the face, waking me up.

"What's the time?" I ask, my voice thick, and I swallow against the dryness in my mouth. *Shit, what if I snored? Or dribbled on Oct?* I glance to the side to check, not seeing any obvious wet patch on his shoulder, then let out a slow breath, aware of their eyes on me.

"It's about five-thirty, I think," Kit says, getting out of the car and holding his hand out for me. "Maybe an early dinner and then bed?"

Heat pools in my core, his storm-filled eyes looking me over as he helps me out of the car. My fingers grip his tightly and he pulls me close, his scent enveloping me until it's all I can smell.

"Sounds good," I reply, all my tiredness disappearing as lust fills my veins, and I wonder who the fuck this brazen girl is. I know he had a double meaning, that he was hinting at the promise he and Oct made this morning, and rather than shy away like I know I should, like my mind tells me I should, I'm agreeing.

"Sounds more than good, Little Sis," Oct whispers in my ear and a shiver has my nipples pebbling and goosebumps covering my skin.

"Come on, you two, let's get Cinders inside and then we can see what happens later," Cas says, ever looking out for me, and he pulls me from the twins towards the house. "Odette texted, she and your dad won't be back til late, so it's just us tonight."

Oh god, my mind goes in all the wrong directions after he says that, dinner utterly forgotten as I imagine all the other things we could get up to. Seems like my new stepbrothers have turned me into a horny mess, and the worst part? I don't even care.

I vowed to myself this year that I'd start living, that I'd embrace whatever life throws at me, and stop letting the death of my mother colour everything in shades of sadness. I wonder what she'd think of me and the guys. I think maybe she would've been happy, maybe even proud regardless of the taboo nature of the things that have happened between me and the guys so far.

She always used to tell me that life won't wait around and that the only thing you can do is live.

"I could make something to eat, if you'd like?" I suggest to them as we enter the dark house and I lead them down the hallway towards the kitchen.

"You can cook?" Cas asks, his brows raised, and I huff out a laugh.

"What? Because I live in this big house there's no way I know how to cook?" I question, pausing in the doorway to the kitchen, hand on my hip as he clasps my other in his warm palm. "I'll have you know, Cas I-don't-know-your-last-name, that I make a mean omelette," I tell him, flicking the light switch on as we enter the room.

"Scott. Caspian Rudy Scott and I'm from New York. My favourite food is pizza or pasta and my favourite colour is red." I giggle as he spins me, pulling me into his body in a way that has mine lighting up and leaving me breathless. "I love walking in Central Park, or any Park or green space really, and I play the guitar."

I squeal as I'm torn from his embrace, and Oct is suddenly there standing in front of me. "Octavius Dante Johnson and, as you know, I'm from the Sunshine Coast itself. I love walks on the beach, surfing, ice cream, and playing video games."

"Pleased to make your acquaintance," I tease, my smile wide as he grins boyishly back at me.

There's a warmth at my back and Oct turns me slowly until Kit is in front of me.

"Christopher–much prefer Kit–Adam Johnson, also from California. I like history, discovering where we came from, and who walked the earth before us fascinates me. I also enjoy going to the beach, sailing, and watching sunsets with pretty girls." He swipes a piece of my hair behind my ear, and I feel the heat of a blush staining my cheeks.

I'm tugged from between the twins and then Prince is standing in front of me. He's the most mysterious to me, I barely know a thing about him and I'm desperate for any scraps he gives me.

"Prince–I will never tell you my real name–Marshall Brown." He yanks my hand again and I land against his chest, my palm splayed across the soft, wool jumper he's wearing. My heart thuds loudly in my chest, anticipation leaving me giddy and breathless. "I enjoy getting new ink and giving people tattoos." My eyes widen at his words, my mouth parting in delighted surprise. He's an artist too?

"That's right, Sugar, I can draw too. I gave these assholes all their ink." He smirks and the others chuckle. "And I'll happily give you some, *if* you're a good girl for me." I take in a sharp breath, his jewel-like eyes roving over my face, drinking me in. "But I'll choose the design."

My spine snaps straight then, my lids lowering in a glare.

"It's my body, Prince. If I want a tattoo, I'll be the one to choose the design." His nostrils flare and then his lips tilt up into a grin that shouldn't be attractive but somehow is.

"Oh, darlin'," he purrs, one hand coming up and lightly circling my throat, effectively scattering any brain cells I own to the four winds. "It may be your body, but it belongs to me, to us, so what happens to it is our choice." I shouldn't be turned on right now. He's just taken my autonomy away, I should rage and be spitting mad, but the anger just won't come, and the thought that maybe it would be nice to let someone else take control for once seems to settle into my bones. I feel myself relax in his hold, my body sinking into him, and his smirk turns into a wolfish grin that leaves my core clenching. "Exactly so. Now let's see if we can't rustle up something a little more exciting than an omelette for our girl, shall we?"

Our girl.

I can't even register that he's being offensive about my cooking skills. He called me their girl, and on top of all the other things they've said, the way they've claimed me so quickly, I'm starting to believe that maybe I do belong to them.

Does that mean they belong to me? That I own them back?

OCT

"Hey, stop thinking so hard, Little Sis," I say to Ember as the others get to work on making our dinner. I've never been much of a cook, but

Prince is a fucking genius in the kitchen, and Kit and Cas enjoy helping so I'll keep our girl entertained.

Our girl. I like the sound of it, like having something that truly belongs to us.

"It's just, I only met you guys a little over twenty-four hours ago and now..." she trails off, and I take her hands in mine, rubbing her knuckles. I love touching her, can't get enough of it.

"And now?" I prompt, finding that I'm curious about where her mind is at. I want to know everything about her, all of her secrets and fears, her hopes and dreams...I want it all.

*She doesn't know everything about you...*a small voice in the back of my mind reminds me, a flash of guilt making my stomach churn, but all of that's behind us now. All that shit is best left in the past.

She huffs a breath and glances at the others, who have paused in whatever it is they're doing to look over at us, then she turns back to me. "And now it's like we've known each other all our lives."

My heart stutters in my chest because she's just described exactly what I'm feeling. It's so comfortable with her and it takes no effort to be around her. She slots in as if she's been with us forever.

"We were just waiting for each other, baby," I tell her, using my grip on her soft hands to draw her closer until our bodies touch.

"You can't say stuff like that, Oct." She sighs but snuggles closer into me and my body heats at her contact, my dick twitching in my jeans.

"Why not? It's the truth," I reply, brushing my lips across the top of her head and breathing her in deeply. She smells of lavender and rosemary, of something that I've not dared to hope for in such a long time; home.

"And what happens when you leave? Or when my dad and Odette catch us?" Her body is stiff, her hands fisting the back of my jumper, and her rapid breaths speak of a panic that stirs in my chest when I think of anything happening to her to take her away from us. I pull away slightly, just enough to look at her perfect face.

"Look at me, Ember," I command, my tone brokering no other option. My cock fills when she obeys immediately and without question, keeping her arms around me but pulling back enough to tip her face towards me. "We are not going anywhere, we're family now and that shit's for life," I tell her, earning a small smile even though her brows are still furrowed. "And as for the other stuff, don't worry about it. We're not letting you go."

She nibbles her lower lip, in a way that makes me want to do the same, her eyes flicking between mine. "How can you be so sure, Oct? It's been, like, a day. We're practically strangers."

"I've known you for months," I inform her, my voice firm as I hold her suddenly wide stare. "I know about the time you snorted a wasp up your nose at age seven. I know that your favourite colour has been yellow since you were little and that you like to sleep with the curtains open so you can wake up with the dawn." Her eyes are even wider now, and it takes some effort not getting lost in their blue depths. "It may feel like only twenty-four hours to you, but it's been fucking months of waiting for us, and to have you finally here, finally in front of us...fuck, Ember."

I press my lips against hers, needing to taste her more than I need my next breath. Everything I said is true. Odette told us about her months ago when she first started seeing Richard, and we've been obsessed with her ever since, trying to find out everything we can about her. We've the resources and I've the hacking skills to discover all her skeletons. All her secrets.

I deepen the kiss, basking in how she melts for me. Her mind may only think she's known us for less than a day, but her body knows who it belongs to.

"You know you sound like a stalker, right?" she asks when I pull away, her voice breathless, and I'm seconds away from saying fuck it, hoisting her up on the table and eating her for dinner.

"Oh, baby," I say, pulling her towards the kitchen island where the others are setting out steaming bowls. "A stalker has nothing on the depths we went to."

She swallows hard and blinks quickly, but I just give her a peck on the temple, then help her onto the stool in front of one bowl.

"Chicken stir-fry...how did you know it was my favourite?" she asks, her forehead creased while she looks up at Prince, Cas, and Kit as they take their seats.

"How did we know it was one of your favourite dishes?" Kit teases, one of his brows raised.

"Fine, point taken," she grumbles, and we all chuckle at her ire. The moan that she lets out a moment later has us all pausing, chopsticks halfway to our mouths as we each stare at her with matching expressions of hunger in our eyes. "These are the best fucking noodles I think I've ever had," she gushes, taking another bite and groaning again.

"You keep making those noises, Sugar, and I won't be held responsible for my actions," Prince warns her in a dark tone, and I don't miss the shiver that falls across her, chopsticks frozen midway to her mouth. She takes an unsteady breath, blowing it out through pursed lips, and my rapidly hardening dick twitches in my pants once more.

"I think she wants you to show her, Prince," I say, and her cheeks bloom in that way they do.

"Well, she can eat her dinner like a good girl and then I'll show her," he replies, not taking his stare from her. The colour on her cheeks spreads down her neck at his words. Oh yeah, she enjoys being told what to do by Prince very much. Not that I can blame her, he's one fucking hella persuasive Dom. "And don't forget to drink your water, darlin'. You haven't drunk nearly enough today to stay hydrated."

"How do you know how much I've been drinking?" she quizzes, her spine snapping straight as she glares at him. It's cute as fuck to watch her try to top him from the bottom, and by the twitch of Prince's lips, he feels the same way. Like a kitten that sinks its teeth and claws into your hand when you rub its belly.

"Because, Sugar, I'm always watching you," he deadpans, taking his chopsticks and grabbing a whole load of noodles, yet never taking his gaze off her.

"You're all crazy fucking stalkers, you know that?" she sasses, looking at each of us with an accusing stare.

"Good, you finally understand," Prince drawls, and I have to bite my lip at the bark of laughter that wants to escape at her incredulous look. "Now eat your noodles and drink your water like a good girl."

She holds his stare for a second longer, her nostrils flared. Huffing a breath, she picks up her chopsticks and places more noodles in her mouth, still giving Prince the stink eye.

"Happy?" she asks around a mouthful of noodles, the word muffled. Then swallowing, she reaches for her water and downs half the glass.

"Ecstatic," he replies, finally looking away from her and at his meal.

Well, fuck me sideways, the tension between these two is something else and I can't wait to be there when they explode.

CHAPTER 7

EMBER

My eyelids are drooping again by the time we finish dinner, my stomach full and a contented feeling wrapping around me like a soft, snuggly blanket. I don't even realise that my head has drifted to land on Cas's shoulder and I'm slumped in my seat, my hands in my lap until he nudges me awake.

"Come on, Cinders, let's get you to bed," he suggests gently, and before I can even protest that it's too early, a yawn cracks my jaw almost in half.

"O–okay."

Cas leads me from the room, the others clearing our dishes as we head down the corridor and upstairs, turning down our wing. I pause before my door, Cas behind me. His warmth is like a balm, and I know that this is too fast, that I shouldn't be feeling so comforted by his nearness, but the part of me that was broken five years ago doesn't care. I feel more awake than I did moments ago, my pulse loud in my ears as I work up the courage to ask for what I really want.

"Will you stay with me?" I don't turn around, just speak into the door, my hand on the door handle, and wait, my heart thudding in my chest. Part of me knows that I'm not just asking about tonight, that I want him and the others in my bed from here on out, regardless of how wrong it is.

"If you want me to, Cinders," he replies softly, his front pressing to my back in a way that has me shuddering and leaning against him, wanting more of the intoxicating comfort he gives me.

"I want you to stay more than anything," I confess quietly, stilling as his arm brushes my side, his hand grasping the door handle over mine.

"Then I'll stay all night."

He pushes down, swinging the door open, and his other hand lands on my lower back and urges me forward. We step into the darkened room, and he flips the switch, filling the space with the soft glow of my lamps. I had it rewired when we moved in so the main light never comes on, only the small lamps that dot the room.

"I need a shower," I mumble, wincing when I remember I haven't washed since the car ride this morning, when Cas covered my pussy with his cum. I can't say that I've hated having it on me all day, but I really ought to wash it off.

"Let's have a shower then," he suggests, taking my hand in his warm palm and leading me towards my en suite. Again, the light switch only turns on soft lights, nothing too bright, and for the first time, I realise how intimate this type of lighting is. Being in here with Cas is a vastly different experience to being on my own and I'm aware of each beat of my heart as it pumps blood through each of my veins.

Letting go of my hand, he heads over to the large shower, leaning in to turn it on. The sound of running water fills the room, and several moments pass then steam swirls from the shower as he shifts to face me. His copper gaze trails up and down my body, and I can barely breathe under his heated scrutiny.

He pads towards me, a swagger in his step, and my heart pumps in overtime, but I don't move, just wait. I'm trapped in the stormy spell he's weaving, unable to do a thing as I let him take charge like my mind and body craves.

"Up," he orders, his hands skimming down my arms and taking my hands in his once he's in front of me. He brings them over my head, then untucks my shirt and pulls it off. My arms drift down, my skin pebbling as he takes me in. His eyes snag on my forearm and go wide, his body freezing, and all too late I realise what he's looking at; my cuts from this morning.

As though ice water has been thrown over me, I try to hide them with my other hand, my shoulders caving in as my feet shuffle beneath me. I can't look at him, worried about the judgement I may see in his eyes.

"Don't hide from me, Cinders," he says firmly, a slight rasp to his tone, and my eyes dart to his face before he clasps the wrist of my scarred arm and my hand covering them drops away. "These are fresh." It's not a question, but a statement as he looks down at the red-scabbed lines. "But some are old?"

My mouth opens, yet no words come out, not immediately anyway, and tears fill my eyes in relief and shame at finally having someone else know my secret.

"Your research didn't tell you this then?" I ask, my tone bitter. His gaze snaps to mine, the copper bright, and his muscles rigid. It hits me again that his parents took their own lives and I open my mouth to apologise but he speaks before I can.

"There is still so much we don't know about you, Cinders, but nothing, fucking nothing, will make any of us want you less," he tells me, his voice unwavering as he steps right into my personal space, his hand tight on my arm. A shiver cascades over my skin where it brushes his soft jumper. His free hand grabs my chin, forcing me to keep eye contact, just as I was about to stare beyond him, unable to face the heat of his passion. "But you come to us for pain if you need it, okay? We will give you what we need, but you stop doing it to yourself right now. Yes?" There's an edge of pleading, of panic to his tone and wild eyes, a slight tremble in his muscles that speaks volumes about how important this is for him.

I take in a shaky exhale, sudden tears sliding down my cheeks as the tension drains out of me. I want to agree, if nothing else but to see the panic that lurks in his copper eyes disappear, but what would it be like to give up that part of myself? I've been seeking relief in this way for five years. It's a comfort, a release, and I felt the need this morning because of Cas and the others. Though maybe it would be nice to have someone else help when I feel overwhelmed.

"Yes." My lips form the word even before I've completely committed to the idea, and I'm surprised with how okay I feel about it, my body loose and my muscles weak with relief.

"Swear it, Cinders. Promise me you won't cut yourself anymore. That you trust us to give you the pain you need." His voice leaves no room for argument, his jaw firm and eyes intense. So I look into his metallic eyes and agree.

"I swear." His touch on my chin softens, the slight throb of his grip a reminder of my promise. His entire body relaxes as though he was terrified of my refusal.

"Good girl. Now let's get you cleaned up and into bed."

He strips the rest of my clothes with a reverence that no one has ever shown me before, like I'm something to be cherished, something to be worshipped and adored. I'm not sure anyone else has ever shown me such devoted care and attention in this way, and my skin flushes from the way he worships me with every touch.

Then he does the same, taking off his clothes and leaving me incapable of coherent thought. Like the twins, his body is muscular, but he's a little more stacked than they are. His body is covered in beautiful works of art, one image flowing into another, all black and devastating in their beauty. My eyes spot crosses, heavenly light, a beautiful Madonna mixed in with flowers and death head moths, and two bars shining in his nipples. But he's pushing down his jeans before I can study all these images properly and when he straightens my eyes go straight to his thick cock, standing hard and proud and with that glint on the end.

He just smirks, taking my hand and pulling me into the shower after him. I let out a groan and close my eyes, the water the perfect temperature when it falls over my aching muscles. A sharp gasp falls from my lips when large hands glide over my breasts, and I open my lids to find Cas washing me, his hands covered in the suds of my favourite lavender and rosemary shower gel.

He keeps everything PG, which doesn't stop my clit from pulsing, and by the small half-smile he's giving me as his eyes follow the path his hands take, he knows exactly what he's doing.

Well, two can play that game, arsehole.

I grab the shower gel, squirting a large dollop onto my palm, and then rub my hands together, creating hundreds of sudsy bubbles. He drops his arms to his sides in simple invitation, daring me to do my best.

Giving him a teasing smile, I sweep my palms over his rock-hard pecs, toying with his nipples ever so slightly and tugging on the bars, eliciting a deep moan from him. His hands come up to grip my waist, his fingers digging in.

"Cinders," he growls out as my hands travel lower, tracing the line of each muscle and the V that leads to what I'm really after. Unlike Cas, I decide that the time for teasing is over, and having decided to take what I want, to live my life to the fullest, I grasp his dick in one hand, my fingertips barely brushing around his wide girth. "Fuck!" he rasps, and I'm inclined to agree.

He feels like velvet steel in my palm, and I slowly pump his shaft up and down, my thumb toying with the piercing in the tip, a desperate need making my vision waiver.

"You said that you'd give me whatever I want, whatever I need," I remind him, my voice low and husky as I continue to work my fist up and down his length. "I want you, Cas. I want this,"–I squeeze my hand and he hisses a breath–"and I want you inside me right fucking now."

"Prince will fucking kill me," he groans, but he hoists me in his arms, his hands under my thighs, and my arms come up to wrap around his neck. He presses my back against the tile wall and it's my turn to hiss as the cold hits my overheated skin. "But you make me not give a shit about any of that, baby."

Before I can utter a single word, he's pushing inside me and my eyes roll at the feel of his hard cock stretching me to full capacity.

"Cas!" I cry out, my nails digging into his shoulders as he fills me more than anyone ever has before. "Fuck, Cas."

"I know, baby. Shit, you feel so fucking good wrapped around my dick, letting me in like you know I own this pussy." A rush of wetness floods my cunt, allowing him to slide in the last couple of inches, and we both groan and pant at the feel of him fully seated inside me. "Tell me you need me, Cinders," he breathes out, his forehead pressed to mine, an edge of vulnerability in his tone.

"I need you so bad it hurts, Cas. Please," I beg, shifting my hips. I'm not lying, I need him to move, to show me I'm owned by him. And even though I know that I'll never be the same, not after fucking one of my stepbrothers, I couldn't stop this if I wanted to. "Please."

"Always, baby," he whispers, pulling almost the entire way out and then thrusting back inside me so hard that I scream. "I will always take care of you, Cinders. Always give you what you need."

He fucks me hard and fast, just like I've been craving since I woke up with Kit's tongue in my pussy, and I hold on as my body accepts every punishing thrust, every shock wave that he sends shooting through me.

"Fuck–Cas—" I open my eyes, my eyes catching on the dark green sapphire of Prince's gaze and with a gasping cry, I shatter, my inner walls clenching around Cas as my entire world rearranges itself.

"Fuck, baby, you're strangling my dick," Cas grits out, thrusting his hips harder, prolonging the pleasure that is rendering me speechless, unable to breathe as I hold Prince's intense stare. Cas stills, a deep, rumbling cry leaving his chest as he buries his face in the crook of my neck and bites down.

The sharp pain sends me spiralling again, lights flashing before my eyes as another orgasm hits me full force. My body is not my own, taken over by pleasure until I'm just a vessel, filled to the brim and overflowing.

We stay together for a few moments, and my skin tingles the entire time. I didn't realise how much I needed that, and when he pulls out, letting my feet drop to the tiles, my legs almost buckle and he has to grab my waist to keep me from landing in a heap on the floor.

"Cas–that was–Jesus," I mumble, looking away from Prince and into Cas's beautiful eyes. He chuckles, the sound low and deep, making my nerves prickle.

"You're incredible," he whispers, placing his lips against my own and giving me a kiss that has tears filling my eyes. "What I ever did without you, how I managed, is something I'll never know." His lips brush mine with every word, my body shuddering in response.

"Cas..." I reply, my voice thick with the lump that fills my throat.

"It's okay, Cinders. Let's get you to bed, it's been a long day." He grabs the shower gel, my legs only trembling slightly as he steps away, washing me again, then himself before shutting off the shower.

He doesn't even pause when he turns around and spots Prince, arms crossed over his chest, leaning in the doorway, his brows lowered and jaw tight. Cool air rushes over my body when Cas opens the door and steps out, holding out a hand to help me out too.

Prince twitches like he wants to rush at Cas, so instead, I hurry to him, pressing my wet body against his and gripping his face in my palms. He doesn't complain, just straightens up, his hands pulling me closer.

"I needed him, Prince, so badly," I tell him, and then go up on my tiptoes, pressing a soft kiss to his lips. "Please don't be mad, I couldn't bear it." My voice cracks on the last word and his arms wrap around me, uncaring of my dripping skin soaking his clothes.

"It was probably better it was him first," he murmurs against my lips, and I'm shaking my head but he stops me with his next words. "I like to hurt when I fuck, Sugar, and I'm not sure you're ready for me yet."

My exhale flutters over his lips, and I pull away, letting go of his face with my left hand and using my right to turn his stare in the direction of my forearm. "I need the pain too, Prince."

I watch as his eyes widen and then go hooded, his tongue coming out to trace his lower lip.

"She promised to come to us if she feels the need to cut again," Cas adds, pulling me away from Prince and wrapping a warm towel around me, tucking it so that it stays up. "She swore."

Prince's eyes flit up to mine, our gazes locked. There's so much swirling in those green depths of his; hunger, lust, and a need that takes my breath away and leaves my chest aching.

"Where are your razors?" he asks.

"Bathroom cupboard, in the pink pouch at the back, third shelf," I answer immediately, holding his stare.

I hear Cas open the cupboard, the sound of things moving, and then he's next to us, holding the small pouch out to Prince who takes it and looks it over. It's so pretty, yet so innocent looking, the kind of thing that would hold a few items of make-up.

"You come to me when you need these," Prince commands, shaking the pouch slightly.

"Yes, Prince," I answer with a nod and watch as the green in his eyes darken to the colour of ivy leaves.

"Good girl. Let's get you to bed." He takes my hand, guiding me out of the bathroom and into my bedroom. He pauses at the foot of my bed, turns, and lets go of my hand. In a move that shouldn't be sexy but is, he pulls his black T-shirt over his head.

My breath leaves me in a whoosh at the sight of him. Like Cas, he is covered in ink, but unlike Cas, Prince is a riot of colours. It travels up his neck, framing his jaw, and glides down his arms, over the back of his hands and down his fingers. His designs are incredible; a tiger hiding in grass with its mouth open in a roar, blue, purple, and green elephant heads across his pecs and upper chest, and an orange butterfly resting at the base of his throat.

He's stunning, and I want to catalogue every piece of art, but he doesn't even give me the chance to speak, tugging on the towel until it pools at my feet. The green of his irises grows even darker for a moment, then darkness covers my eyes, my nose full of the scent of rum and leather as he pulls his T-shirt over my head.

I instantly want to snuggle into the garment as I put my arms through the sleeves, wrapping them around myself in a hug as I take a deep inhale.

"You'll stay too?" I ask, a slight hint of panic in my tone as my breaths catch. I'm not sure when the idea that I needed them both here with me became crucial, but now that I thought of it, I know I won't be able to sleep without them.

His entire face softens as his hand reaches out, cupping my cheek. The comfort that slight gesture gives me is visceral, instantaneous, and should leave me worried, but I'm not. How can I be when it feels so right to be with him, with them like this?

"Of course, darlin'." My shoulders slump, the panic gone as quick as it came, and my eyes close for a moment as a small smile spreads across my lips. "Get into bed, darlin'."

Opening my eyes, I give him a small nod, crawling into bed from the end and my smile widens when matching groans sound out behind me.

"That was mean, Cinders," Cas grumbles, getting in beside me, wearing only his grey boxers. He tugs me towards him and my body instinctively curves around him, my leg draping over his.

The bed dips behind me, and then Prince presses against my back, his hard, very much naked cock pressed against my arse.

"Sleep now, Sugar," he orders, his arm wrapping around me as he presses even closer.

I don't think I'll be able to, not sandwiched between these gorgeous men, but I find my eyelids drooping, and soon I'm embracing the darkness like an old friend, safe knowing that my stepbrothers will keep the nightmares at bay.

CHAPTER 8

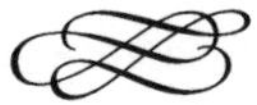

OCT

Kit and I are sitting on his bed, playing video games where—as usual—I'm beating the fucker's ass. The sound of Ember's cries of pleasure filtered through the wall earlier, even over the shower, and both of us are sporting semis in our shorts that we don't bother to hide. Why would we? We've seen enough of each other's dicks in the past few years that it doesn't even phase us anymore.

The door opens and in strides Odette, our stepmom and the woman who rules our fucking lives with an iron fist. Her clingy, silk nightdress hides fucking nothing, and a slight chill lifts the hair at the back of my neck, my semi shrivelling at the sight of her. She's always been open with us, but as we got older, we realised that walking in on us showering and wearing low-cut, provocative things around us wasn't the normal behaviour of a parent or guardian.

"Where are your brothers?" she questions, her eyes trailing over my bare chest, then pausing at my crotch. Her tongue comes out to lick her lower lip and I have to swallow the bile that hits the back of my throat, the feeling of ants crawling over my skin making goose-bumps erupt over my flesh.

"Looking after Ember," Kit says, pausing the game and drawing her attention to him like he always does. There may be only four minutes between us, but somehow he thinks that because he's older, he has to protect me. I cut him a glare, but he misses it and my stomach roils when Odette's eyes light up.

"Excellent. I'm so glad that you're enjoying having a new sister," she purrs, sashaying closer to us. "I want you to take such special care of her, she's been through so much and I know you can make her feel better."

Her eyes linger on Kit's abs, also on display as he didn't bother with a shirt either. My hands grip my controller tighter at the predatory look in her eye, and the plastic cracks, her snake-like stare swinging back to me. She smiles, but it's not a nice one, instead, it's full of a smug satisfaction that I want to swipe off her botox face.

"Well, I'll say good night, boys." She leans over, brushing her fake tits up against me as she presses a kiss to my cheek. I have to hold my breath to stop from breathing in her overpowering, sickly sweet perfume. It reminds me of dying flowers; cloying and sticks to the back of your throat. I don't know how Ember's dad stands it.

I breathe a quiet sigh of relief when she pulls away, my teeth gritting when she does the same to Kit. I see his body shudder, his jaw clenched as he tries to hide his revulsion. She's a fucking spider, but she's all we have, all we've known for so long.

We're quiet for a long moment when she closes the door behind her. I can't help the maelstrom of toxic thoughts from swirling around my head; could we have tried harder to get away from her? Put our foot down a bit more? And most worrying of all; what is her fascination with our new stepsister? I toss the controller onto the bed, flopping back and covering my eyes with my hands.

"We should just tell her to fuck off, take Ember and leave."

Kit sighs. "We can't, not yet anyway. It's not the right time. Prince said—"

"Fuck what Prince says!" I leap from the bed, my nostrils flaring as I pace beside it. I'm so fucking done being used by her. "Do you not see her interest in Ember? She's fucking up to something, and I swear to god if Ember gets hurt..."

The thought of Ember having to do what we've done...my fists clench at my sides. No, she has her dad, he'd never let that happen, and he's loaded, so it's not like we're short of money anymore.

"She won't get hurt, Oct," Kit says, coming to stand in front of me, forcing me to stop pacing like a caged animal. He grasps the back of my neck, bringing our foreheads together. "She has us, and we won't let Odette or anyone else hurt her."

"I know." I close my eyes and try to let the rage drain from me, taking several deep breaths until my tightly coiled muscles relax. "I'm just so tired of not being able to have a life, Kit. It was fun and games when we were younger, but I want to do what I want for once."

"We will. We're set up here, money isn't an issue anymore, look at this place." He pulls back, using his grip to turn my head and look around at my room. He's right, it's the nicest bedroom I've ever had, and the one back home wasn't bad. We were okay money-wise, we weren't loaded like Ember and her dad, but we had everything we needed. My shoulders loosen further as his logic sinks in and pushes the panic and anger away.

"What are you going to do when you grow up?" I ask him. It's the question that we have asked each other ever since we were little. It's become more of a comfort over the years, something to keep us from going crazy as our control was slowly taken away.

He chuckles, letting me go and sitting back down on the bed, hand running through his hair as he stares into the distance, thinking. "I think I'd like to study architecture. The gallery we went to today? It was incredible, and I'd love to work with old buildings, maybe. Not sure I'd be any good at it, but I'd like to try." He looks up at me, his deep blue eyes calmer than I've seen them in a while. "You?"

Musing, I chew my lip, looking around at the plush room. "I'm pretty good with computers," I say slowly, churning the possibilities around in my head. "I think maybe game design." I'm warming to the idea the more I think about it. I like the creative element and I enjoy the challenge of playing them. "Or become the most sought-after hacker in the world." I catch the pillow that Kit throws at me, and then I flop back onto the bed, picking up the controller again, my thumbs playing with the controls. "The fuckers stole our night with her."

"Yep. They sure did," Kit replies, picking up his own controller and resuming the game. "We'll have to be quicker tomorrow night."

"Amen." The thought of our new little sister has my dick twitching again. She's a shining beacon we've all needed for far too long, a light that calls to our darkness.

She doesn't know all your secrets though, she'll probably be disgusted if she finds out...

I shut down that fucking cunt of an inner voice, not allowing my fears and worries to take root. We'll just make sure she never finds out about all of that. It's all in the past, and that's where it's going to stay.

CHAPTER 9

EMBER

I wake up to delicious warmth, the combined scents of rum, leather, and toffee apples mixed with that undeniable musk of man filling my nose and leaving me feeling calm and desperate all at once.

It's still early, the sky outside is just turning lilac with the rising sun, and ignoring my lust, I wiggle from between my sleeping stepbrothers and head to the bathroom to pee.

After washing my hands, I stare at my reflection, at the way my eyes sparkle for the first time in years and the way my cheeks are slightly flushed, trying to recognise myself. This is the girl who had sex in the shower with her new stepbrother, someone she's only known for a little over a day. One who wants to have sex with the other three too and has every intention of making it happen.

Who feels so comfortable with the new men in her life that she's not quite sure how she lived without them before.

"You weren't living, Ember. You were surviving," I whisper to myself, watching my lips move and knowing that I'm speaking the truth.

Ever since cancer stole my mother five years ago, I've been lost, my anchor gone, and my father becoming almost like a stranger as he threw himself into work to escape his grief. My stomach tightens, my eyes misting at the thought that I'm moving on without her. I know she would have wanted me to, would be ecstatic that I am, but I can't help the flash of guilt that she's not here and I am.

The need to paint suddenly overwhelms me, and I follow the urge, leaving the bathroom and walking over to my nook by the large windows. Taking a fresh sheet of paper, I clip it to my easel and pick up a pencil, closing my eyes for a moment as I just breathe.

Opening my eyes with renewed purpose, I grab my headphones and then open Spotify, selecting one of my favourite songs. The deep, seductive tones of Austin Giorgio singing "You Put a Spell On Me" caresses my ears, making my nipples pebble, and my hand flies across the page, the lines taking the shape of three figures, limbs tangled.

Grabbing my watercolours, I mix up copper and green, letting the paint drip down the page. I add yellow in the middle, my breaths coming in pants as my fingers practically throw the colours onto the paper, my thighs becoming slick as I lose myself to the fantasy in front of me.

Strong hands grasp my upper arms and I gasp as I'm spun around, Prince's green eyes so dark that I fall into them headfirst. My brush darts out, painting a strip of yellow across his chest, claiming him as my own. His lush lips split into a wide, feral grin, then his hands travel upwards, the sensual song filling my ears as he grips the neck of the shirt I'm wearing, his shirt, and he yanks.

The fabric rips down the middle, my brush hitting the wooden floor with a clatter, the sounds muffled by my headphones. My body jerks with the force, my heart pounding as his emerald eyes devour me. Reaching past me, he takes hold of the brush that's covered in the exact shade of his eyes and brings it between us.

The first stroke of the bristles has my entire body lighting up, the cold wetness of the paint doing nothing to cool my fevered skin. He trails it down my breast, around my nipple, and then moves to the other side, repeating the movement until my body quivers with every touch of the brush. My fists clench and unclench at my sides, the touch of the brush more sensual than I ever knew it could be.

His eyes snap to mine when a small whine leaves my chest, and I feel it vibrate inside me, my need for his fingers to touch me so strong that I can't stop from pleading with my eyes.

Touch me.

Fuck me.

He drops his brush to the hardwood floor, his fingers push the rest of the ruined T-shirt off me until I'm just as naked as he is. My gaze darts down to see his tattoos really do cover every inch, just his thick, hard, massive cock untouched. My eyes widen as I wonder how on earth that beast will fit inside me.

The music stops, and I look up just as Prince takes my headphones off, placing them on the table behind me.

"Don't worry, Sugar. I'll make it fit."

Oh lordt. My thighs clench, more wetness sliding between them at his filthy fucking words.

"Please, Prince," I whisper, my voice shaky as fuck, but the need to have him fill me is unlike anything I've ever felt before. The dark look in his eyes promises me it will hurt so good, and I'm desperate for his brand of pain.

"Such a good girl for me, begging for my dick at just the sight of it," he purrs, his fingers trailing down my side. God, even that small touch has fire racing through me, and I sway towards him, wanting whatever he will give me. "Up on the table."

I cast a glance behind me, seeing my table full of art supplies, but he gives me no more time to think, crowding me until my arse touches the edge. Then he bends, grabbing my thighs and lifting me onto the top as if I weigh nothing. My hands cling to his powerful shoulders, feeling the flex of his muscles as he settles me to his liking, my legs open and my pussy pulsing with his nearness.

He steps back slightly, just enough so that he has a clear view of my body, and when he sucks his lower lip between his teeth, I almost lose it completely, a wanton moan falling from my lips before I can stop it.

"Prince..." His name comes out on a whine, a plea for him to put me out of the misery that he's created.

"Shhhh, darlin'. I've got you," he tells me softly, spitting into his palm and slicking it over his dick. That shouldn't be so hot, it's saliva for fuck's sake, but I can feel the slick wetness coating my folds at the sight as he gives himself a couple of leisurely pumps.

Closing the distance between us, he uses his tip to rub up and down my slit and it almost blows my fucking mind. My nails dig into the wood either side of me, my hips thrusting forward, desperate for more.

"More, please, Prince. I need more," I beg, close to tears at this point.

"Such a needy little sister, aren't you?" he muses, teasing me with the glide of his hard tip.

"Please, please, please, Prince," I beg, my words like a prayer as my body tightens, an orgasm just out of reach.

"As you beg so prettily, darlin'."

With no warning, he snaps his hips forward and thrusts inside me so hard that the table rattles and the crash of art supplies accompanies my scream. His mouth covers mine as my world explodes in vibrant colours, my hands gripping his shoulders as I come around him so hard I'm shaking and my vision blurs.

He allows me a single moment to bask in the glow of one of the most intense orgasms I've ever had, and then his hands grip my thighs and he fucks me so hard that I know that I'll be sore. The bite of pain has me crying out his name over and over again, my body trembling as orgasm after orgasm hits me until they all meld into one and I can't fucking breathe with how good it feels.

I open bleary eyes to watch him, his lips pulled in a tight grimace as he watches the place where our bodies connect, then his head snaps up, his jaw tight.

"You're going to come for me again, Sugar," he grits out, and I'm shaking my head before I can even formulate the words.

"I–I c–can't, Prince," I moan, my voice a cracked whisper.

"You can and you will," he commands, taking my left arm in his hand and bringing my forearm up to his lips. He doesn't stop his brutal thrusts, and he watches me as he opens his mouth, right over my scabbed cuts, and then bites down hard.

My pussy walls clamp down on him, my entire body tensing as the pain heightens the pleasure, and then I'm screaming as I fall into rapturous agony once more. Wetness erupts from me, coating Prince, and I hear his roar of ecstasy, feel him bury himself so deep that he practically invades my womb as he fills me with his cum.

My chest heaves, my body slick with sweat and paint, tingles racing across my skin as I hold him to me with my free arm and just try to breathe again. My mind is a blur of sensation, reduced to mush by his massive cock and the orgasms that he just gave me. I'm floating, surrounded by a blissful cloud that I know I will crave for the rest of my life. He stays inside me, his own back rising and falling, his face buried against my neck. My left arm hangs limply at my side, his fingers brushing over the skin and sending flutters all across my body. When I finally bring it up to inspect it, blood drips from the cuts, the shape of his teeth marks indented into the skin. It throbs, and he lifts his head, looking at me and then my arm.

Leaning over, he presses a light kiss to the wound, and then his lips are on mine, his palms cradling my face as he kisses the shit out of me, the copper taste of my blood coating my tongue. Prince decimates me with his kiss, he owns and possesses me with his lips and tongue, allowing no other option than to bow to him. I open for him, letting him take as I drink him in, my hands tangling in his black hair and pulling him closer.

He pulls away slowly, and I love that his lips look bee-stung, that he looks just as dishevelled as I feel.

"Fuck. That was..." he trails off, his Adam's apple bobbing, and he presses his forehead to mine. "You're incredible, Ember."

We both groan when I clench around him, the sound of my name on his lips exquisite.

"How can it be like this, Prince? How can it feel like this?" I ask him, my fingers still gripping his hair. My heart feels like it's too big for my ribs to contain, my muscles twitching as I'm overwhelmed by my need for this man. For them all.

"Because we were always meant for each other. I'm just sorry it took us so long to find you."

The warmth of tears slides down my cheeks, and he kisses each one as a hot body presses up against my side.

"Don't cry, Cinders," Cas soothes, his hands gliding over my body, pulling himself closer to me even as Prince refuses to let go or slide out of me, his cock still semi-hard as if he doesn't want to leave the comfort of my body as much as I don't want him to go. "We're here now, and you'll never be alone again."

A sob rips through my chest at his words. How did these guys see right to the heart of my loneliness when I've never admitted to them how alone I've been?

One hand leaves Prince to grasp Cas around the neck, pulling him in for a kiss which he gladly gives me.

"Thank you," I whisper against his lips, my limbs feeling shaky and a little sore now that my high is settling into a warm glow.

"Always, baby," he answers. "Now let's get you cleaned up and fed."

I gasp when Prince finally pulls out, his eyes darting down to my bright pink, abused pussy, to his cum which trickles out a little.

"You're going to be so full of our cum, darlin', that we'll always be with you wherever you are."

I shiver, my mouth suddenly dry. How does he have the power to turn me on with just a sentence?

Placing a last kiss on my lips, he saunters to the balcony doors, letting in a blast of frigid air when he opens one and slips out, heading towards his room next door.

"Come on, baby," Cas murmurs, helping me off the table and

then supporting me when my legs almost give out. He chuckles. "He does like it rough. I know from experience how much that bastard enjoys using his monster cock as a weapon." My eyes widen and I lick my lips.

"Do you guys..." I trail off, unsure how to phrase it exactly, Cas's warm arm wrapped around my waist.

"Do we fuck each other, Cinders? Is that your question?" His copper eyes shine in the morning light, and my whole body goes hot at the thought.

"Yes, that's my question," I reply in a barely audible whisper.

"We're family, we take care of each other, remember?" he says, leading me to the bathroom, his arm supporting me on my shaky legs. "And we enjoy pleasure in all its forms, especially when it's with someone you're already close to. The twins aren't with each other in that way, but we all know what the others like in the bedroom. Does that bother you?"

We've stopped walking, just outside the bathroom doors, and he turns to look at me, the light of the dawn behind him now and creating a halo effect.

"N–no. It doesn't bother me," I tell him, my heart fluttering in my chest at the thought of them pleasing each other and of me being in the centre of all that.

"Does it turn you on?" He waits, his copper eyes boring into mine, even though I'm pretty sure he knows my answer already if the smile playing around his lips is any indication.

"Yes. It turns me on." I don't hesitate with my answer, my voice clear and the wide grin he gives me tells me that was the right response.

"I'll make sure the others know that too. I'm sure they'd be happy to indulge any fantasies you might have. You are family, after all." He has a wicked gleam in his eyes and he resumes our steps to the bathroom. The idea of them together has me weak at the knees, and not for the first time, I wonder how I got so lucky to have them drop into my life.

CHAPTER 10

EMBER

Cas helps me to the shower, leaving me to it after saying that he couldn't trust himself and I definitely need a break after the pounding that Prince gave me. His words, and I blushed like a giddy schoolgirl when he said them.

He wasn't wrong though, it's not just the freshly opened scabs that are throbbing. There's a dull ache between my thighs that makes me smile every time it pulses as I walk down the stairs and to breakfast.

"Little Spark!" my dad greets, getting up from his chair and striding over to me as soon as I walk into the room. "I take it by your smile and glowing complexion you had a good day with your step-brothers yesterday?" His face is wreathed in smiles, and he pulls me into a giant bear hug that reminds me of my childhood.

I hug him back, casting a panicked look over at the guys as my cheeks flame, all of whom are smirking, the fuckers.

"Um, yes, it was lovely," I reply, Oct's oomph sound letting me know that he probably said something to either Cas or Prince and got a kick under the table for it. "We went to the National Gallery."

"I'm so pleased to see you having fun, and with people of your own age." He pulls away, studying me, and his brows dip slightly, his blue eyes so like my own dulling a little and I worry I didn't school my features quickly enough to hide exactly how much I've been enjoying my new brothers' company. "I've been worried about you, Ember," he adds, his hand squeezing my upper arms as his eyes rove over me. "But I think having brothers suits you."

Oh, my god, can the floor open up and swallow me whole now, please?

"Having a little sister certainly works for us," Kit comments, coming over and taking my hand in his. I give him wide eyes and suck in a sharp breath, but a flick of my eyes to my dad just sees an indulgent father looking at his daughter and her new stepbrother. Can he not see the way Kit looks at me? Like he plans to devour me whole? Can he not feel the tension between us, that unfulfilled promise from the other morning?

"Let's eat. Odette and I have some exciting news for you all," my father announces, and my stomach swoops as I wonder what bombshell he will drop on me next. A bitter taste fills my mouth, anger at my father who's been so absent for the past five years pulling me up short on my way to the table.

I'm happy for my dad, glad that he's finally found someone to share his life with, but was he so blinded by his own grief that he couldn't see mine?

"You okay, Pretty Thing?" Kit asks me quietly, and I take a stuttering breath, noting that the others are staring, a mix of concern and worry on their faces.

"Yes, sorry," I mumble, letting him lead me towards the table. I try to see things from my dad's point of view, it must have been unbearably hard for him to lose the love of his life. My muscles tense at the thought of losing even just one of the guys, and I've known them for far less time than my dad and mum were together for.

"We're all here, Pretty Thing," Kit whispers in my ear, and I realise that I've got his hand in a death grip, my breathing grating in my chest.

"How did you know that's where my mind went?" I ask under my breath as he leads me to my chair, in between him and Oct this morning. He lets go of my hand to pull out my chair, bending down to speak in my ear as he pushes it in for me.

"You looked as panicked as I feel at the thought of anything taking you away from us."

My heart gives a solid thud in my chest, the pulse reverberating across my entire body like a gong has been struck, and I let out a trembling exhale. This is just so fast, too fast for me to keep up with it. One minute I'm alone, getting through each day as if wading through a thick, grey fog, and the next, my life is filled with the bright colours of four boys who have taken me as their own and are carving their way into my heart.

"Morning, Little Sis," Oct greets, his hand landing on my thigh, his palm warm through my cotton tights. It's enough to jolt me out of my panic. I've opted to wear a long-sleeved, flouncy mini dress with a blue, floral print and some knee-length, brown leather boots. "You look beautiful this morning, and so thoughtful of easy access for your brothers." His voice is a low whisper, but my eyes still dart to my father to check he didn't overhear. He's oblivious, leaning down to listen as Odette murmurs something in his ear.

Kit sits down as Oct's palm coasts upwards and I squeeze my thighs together, blood making my cheeks heat and the pit of my stomach tingle as his fingers brush my apex. My eyes close, my hands clenched in my lap as I try to breathe through the heady rush of desire that floods my veins. It doesn't matter that I have cotton tights and knickers on, he may as well be touching my rapidly soaking core.

"Now that you're all here," my father begins, and I snap my attention to him, even as my legs part slightly of their own accord. "Odette and I have decided that we ought to go on honeymoon, now that we're married and all." My father looks over at Odette, and she simpers in a way that I can't help feeling is a little false. Do I look like that when one of the guys look at me? I fucking hope not. "So we're leaving for the Cayman Islands first thing tomorrow for three weeks of sun and sea."

Oct's hand pauses, and I stare wide-eyed at my father and Odette as the realisation hits me smack in the face; I'll be at home, alone with the guys for three weeks. No dad. No Odette. Just us.

Fuck.

"That sounds fantastic," Cas says, but I can't look at him, at any of them, and I can feel their eyes burning a hole in the side of my head. I won't be able to hide the excitement, the raw fucking desire that's coursing through my body this very moment, sore cunt notwithstanding.

"Your tutors will still come Monday to Friday, starting tomorrow," Odette tells us, and I can't decipher the look she gives the guys. It's almost as though she knows what's going on, and I catch Prince's slight nod in Odette's direction as I quickly glance at him. "Don't worry, Ember. My boys will take good care of you."

I don't realise I've been worrying my bottom lip until she speaks to me and I go to answer. "I–I'm sure I'll be fine. It'll be nice to have some company for once. You guys just have a great time."

"Oh, we will have the best time, won't we, Richard darling?" She turns her hazel eyes on my father, and I can practically see heart eyes emojis in his. My chest aches fiercely as a sense of loss washes over me.

He's happy, Ember. That's all that matters.

"Let's have breakfast, then we can have a lazy day all together," Dad suggests, and I go to reach for a bowl and some muesli.

"Oh, Ember, honey. I had the kitchen prepare you something special," Odette says, and there's just something about her tone that feels disingenuous.

Sally, one of our staff, places a tall glass in front of me, full of what looks like green sludge.

"What the fuck is that?" Oct exclaims, his nose wrinkled, and I'm inclined to agree with him.

"Octavius Dante Johnson, you watch your language at the table!"

Odette scolds, her face full of a rage that seems far too extreme given the situation. Oct looks down, his ears reddening.

"It's okay, darling. He's just a passionate young man," my father assures her, trying to keep the peace. I watch as he strokes her hand, and she shakes her head slightly, her face transforming back into its serene beauty.

I ignore the alarm bells that ring in my head at just how quickly her face can morph from rage to normalcy, instead, placing my hand over Oct's that is still on my upper thigh and squeezing it. He gives me a small, grateful smile, and I wonder what hold she has to make him feel so bad about a single swear word.

"As I was saying before I was so rudely interrupted," Odette continues, and I grind my teeth at the way Oct shrinks back a little. "It's a wheatgrass smoothie and is a great antioxidant plus aids in weight loss."

I can feel my cheeks burning, my body frozen as I stare at the glass of green goop. I've heard of wheatgrass and decide it looks fucking revolting even if it is good for you.

"How thoughtful of you to help Ember, honey," I can hear my dad say. "I didn't know you were on a diet, Little Spark."

Tears sting my eyes at his words and I don't know what to say. Sure, I'm not supermodel thin like Odette, I mean, who the fuck looks like that, really? But I didn't think I needed to lose any weight.

"Oh, us girls just know these things, don't we, Ember?" I slowly bring my gaze upwards, refusing to let the embarrassed tears fall. Odette just looks at me like she really is helping me out, and I'd believe it too if there wasn't a spark of something in her hazel irises, a malicious sort of pity perhaps? Oct's hand squeezes mine but I barely feel it, and all my mind can focus on is that Odette basically just called me fat, and no one called her out on it.

"Um, yes. I–I think I might take this upstairs if that's okay? I'm feeling a little tired." Not waiting for an answer, I just rip my hand away from Oct's and grab the glass, ignoring the concerned call of my father as I rush from the room.

***

CAS

I watch Ember flee the dining room, the glisten of tears in her beautiful, blue eyes, the pounding of a war drum sounding in my ears. My fists are clenched so tightly around my knife and fork that I'm not even surprised to see that I've bent them a little, and I count backwards from ten just to calm myself down enough not to launch myself at Odette.

"I hope she's okay," her pathetic, fucking clueless father says, but to give him some credit, he looks genuinely concerned, his brows pitched low.

"It's probably her time of the month, Richard," Odette titters, and I know her cycle has nothing to do with why she left in such a hurry. We know from her medical records that she's got a coil so she doesn't have periods particularly, not that I'm convinced her not being on birth control would have stopped either myself or Prince coming inside her.

"Perhaps one of us should check?" Kit asks, and I see her father soften as he stares at Kit. I get he has always wanted sons, or so he told us the many times we met him back in New York, but maybe if he spent less time travelling for business and more time with his daughter then she wouldn't have been so alone. So lonely.

"That would be great, Kit. Thank you."

Kit immediately gets up, even though he's not eaten anything, and rushes out of the room. I don't miss the croissant he swiped and hid in his pocket before he got up. We may not be able to stand up to Odette how we would like to, but we can do something to mitigate her vile fucking behaviour.

I push my plate away, my appetite gone when I think about the look on Ember's face as she fled and what she must think of us for not standing up for her. For not telling Odette to go fuck herself because surely no one else would want to stick their dick in a bag of bones like her.

Fuck, Cinders. It's only the second day and we've already failed her.

We'll just have to work extra hard to make it up to her.

CHAPTER 11

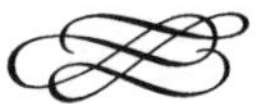

KIT

I could fucking kill that bitch! As if what she's put us through over the years isn't enough, she has to pick on Ember who has been nothing but welcoming ever since we stormed into her life.

The things we've done over the years to help, to keep us all afloat would make most people sick to their stomachs. Sure, sometimes it was fun, but lately...I shudder, swallowing down the self-disgust, and hurry after the one light to come into our lives.

Her door slams, the distinct sound of a lock clicking shut sounding as I reach it. Then her sobs follow and my heart cleaves in two.

Fucking Odette. Jealous cunt.

"Ember, Pretty Thing, let me in, baby," I say, my palm and forehead pressed against the wood as I beg her.

"Go away, Kit." Her voice is thick with tears, and my palm clenches into a fist on the door.

"Never, Pretty Thing," I promise, leaving the door and heading into my room next to hers. I stride to the French door that leads to our shared balcony, opening it and walking out into the still-chilled morning air. The sun is halfway up, not quite warm yet, but it looks like it might be a beautiful day, and I won't let our girl spend another moment steeped in sadness.

The crack in my heart grows when I look through her window to see her curled up on the bed, her arms wrapped around herself and facing away from the window, those sexy leather boots in a heap on the floor.

The cold metal of the door handle gives way as I push it down, and I breathe out a sigh that she didn't lock this too. I would have been able to break in, but I'd rather not have to explain why we needed to fix the glass.

"Baby," I greet softly as I shut the door behind me and rush over to her. "Ignore that jealous bitch, you're fucking perfect." She huffs a laugh that's so bitter it stings as it reaches my ears.

"Right, you say that now, but not fucking one of you stood up for me when she effectively called me fat downstairs." She shuffles away from me, still refusing to look at me, so I toe my sneakers off and get on the bed, placing the pastry on the side table and kneeling behind her. Her lavender and rosemary scent washes over me, and it goes some way to calming the simmering anger that's bubbling away inside me. "I'm just a plaything for you all, something to fuck until someone better comes along."

"Look at me, Ember." My voice comes out harsher than I intend, and I hate the way she flinches slightly. "Please, baby."

Slowly she turns around, uncurling like the most beautiful flower, her eyes and nose red, but fuck she looks pretty when she cries. Though only if I'm the one causing the tears to fall and only when she's begging me to stop giving her pleasure.

"You are fucking perfection, fuck what anyone else thinks or says," I insist, leaning over and grasping her chin, not allowing her to look away from me. "And if you were just a toy, something to play with and discard, we wouldn't have spent months obsessing over you, finding out every minor detail about you." *Lies*, a whisper flits through my mind, but I ignore it. She may have been nothing more than a shiny new toy before we met her, but as soon as we saw her, we all knew. "You. Are. Ours."

I move around her, forcing her to her back, making her legs part as I gaze down at her from my knees.

"Kit—" She cuts off with a yelp as I reach underneath her dress, grab her tights, and yank them and her panties off in one harsh move.

"I wouldn't crave you with every fibre of my fucking being if you weren't something special, Pretty Thing," I tell her, shifting so that I'm settled on my elbows, my face hovering above her sweet, pink pussy. It's swollen and looks well-abused and blood roars towards my dick so fast that I go a little lightheaded. "Oh, baby, Prince fucked you good and hard this morning, didn't he?" I don't give her time to answer, just dip my face and lick her slit. "Shit, you taste so fucking good, you know that?"

She moans as I dip my head and lick her again, her sweet musk bursting on my tongue in a flavour that I know I will crave every fucking day for the rest of my days. She's already dripping for me, probably in part because of Oct's attention under the table before everything went to shit.

I dive in, showing her exactly how fucking beautiful she is with my tongue, sweeping it across her slick folds and lapping up every drop of pleasure she bestows on me like the gift it is.

"Fuck, Kit..." she groans, her hands coming to tangle in my hair, and I smile against her pussy. She pulls me closer, and not a man to argue when a feast is presented, I set to work again, my tongue dipping inside her heated channel, my dick so fucking hard that it's a miracle it's not snapped off with how I'm grinding it against the bed.

But this is all about her, all about showing her she is more than I ever could have dared hope for, and I'm never letting her go.

"Come for me, Pretty Thing," I command, feeling the tremor in her thighs as I force them wider and go deeper with my tongue.

Her pussy flutters against my tongue, a deluge of pleasure soaking my chin and filling my mouth as she cries out her orgasm.

She's so fucking responsive, and she comes so beautifully that I keep going, needing every fucking last drop she'll give me.

When she's a trembling, twitching mess, I finally let up, pushing up and crawling over her. She blinks up at me, her eyes half-lidded and her cheeks flushed with her golden hair a mess, and she's never looked more beautiful.

I lower down, pressing my lips against hers, and just like that first morning, she opens to me, kissing me back with a passion that she hides most of the time.

"Don't make me fall for you and then leave me, Kit. It would break something inside me that could never be fixed," she whispers against my lips, and I'm shaking my head before she's even finished.

"There is no world where that would even happen, Pretty Thing," I assure her, settling more of my weight on top of her and pushing her body into the mattress. My jeans-covered dick is pressing into her hot core, and it's taking almost more willpower than I possess not to open my zipper and slide inside her swollen cunt. "You are it for us. There is, and never will be, anyone else."

She stills, eyes darting between mine as she whispers, "You barely know me."

I chuckle, brushing my lips across hers. "I've known you for a lifetime, Ember. I know you feel it too."

"It scares me," she confesses so softly I almost miss it, would have if I wasn't staring at her lips, and I hold her tighter.

"I know, baby, but the best things usually are fucking terrifying."

EMBER

We get up, and Kit gives me another kiss before leaving me to shower —again—and change. I strip the bed too, placing the now wet things in the laundry basket and getting out fresh sheets and my spare duvet. My cheeks heat at what the staff will think. They'll know what the stains are from, surely? I make a mental note to go on Amazon and buy a sex sheet.

"How did this become your life?" I ask myself as I look in my mirror, seeing the blush spreading across my cheeks. I went for another short dress with long sleeves, the first being such a hit earlier, but opted for my furry, slipper boots as we will stay at home.

A sharp rap on my door has my head snapping upwards.

"Cinders?" My shoulders sag as Cas's voice filters through the thick wood, and I rush over to unlock and pull it open. His pinched forehead smooths as he takes me in. "You okay?"

"Yes," I answer, feeling my cheeks heat even more—does he know what Kit did earlier?—and wondering when the reaction will lessen as it's all I seem to do around these guys.

Aside from coming harder than you ever had before...

"Look, I'm sorry about breakfast. I should have said something, but, fuck, no excuses." He looks me dead in the eyes, his full of remorse. "I apologize, Cinders. I should have told Odette to fuck off. You're the most beautiful woman I've ever met, the best fuck of my life—"

"Cas!" I whisper shout at him, grabbing his arm and tugging him into the room, slamming the door behind us. "Someone might hear you!"

"I don't give a shit," he says, his tone a low growl that has my nerve endings tingling. He spins us, crowding me until my back is pressed against the door, his arms bracketing me in, and I can't seem to draw a full breath as his copper eyes engulf me in metallic flame. "I want the world to know how fucking incredible you are. How fucking mine you are."

The last part is said right against my lips, and the brief touch leaves me reeling and light-headed.

"Cas..." It's a moan, a prayer, and I'm not even sure what I'm asking him for. My hands fist his shirt, the soft, light green cotton making his eyes pop and spark as he rakes them over me.

"If I hadn't watched Prince fuck the life out of you earlier,

Cinders, I would be buried deep inside that beautiful cunt right now," he tells me and my knees feel so weak that I'm not sure how much longer I can keep standing. "But you need a rest, so come downstairs and watch the movie with the rest of us."

It's like a bucket of ice-cold water has just been poured over me, and even the warmth of his body pressed against mine can't warm my suddenly chilled skin as I swallow hard. "Is–Is Odette going to be there?"

He heaves a sigh, then presses a tender kiss to my temple, and my eyelids flutter at the touch. "Yes, but you'll be sitting with us, and I promise if she says anything, I will call her out on her bullshit."

"You would do that, for me?" I press my face into his chest, inhaling the toffee apple scent that will forever remind me of Cas.

"I would burn the fucking world down for you, Cinders. Standing up to that bitch is nothing." My heart stills in my chest, and a question bubbles up before I can stop it.

"Then why didn't you earlier?" I feel sick asking it, the thought that I really am nothing but a plaything for them makes something inside me shrivel and die. His chest expands beneath my hands, his exhale ruffling my hair, his forearms either side of my head. The skin bunches around his eyes and his jaw clenches as he takes a shuddered inhale.

"A lot has gone down in the past, it's fucking messy and complicated but this is a fresh start for us. I forgot that for a moment, and I will apologize for the rest of my days for letting you believe anything other than that you are a fucking goddess, Ember."

My name on his lips has a similar effect as when Kit used it earlier. It makes my breath quicken, my entire being flooding with warmth when they use it.

"Will you tell me about it? About what has you all so scared of her?" I don't think he's going to answer, his body so rigid I can feel the tension thrumming through him.

"One day, Cinders," he says after a long pause. "But for now, come watch a movie with me?"

"Okay."

His whole body sags, and then his lips are against mine and I'm fucking lost. He's like a poison, a drug that I'm still not sure won't kill me, but I'm powerless to resist. I melt into him and his hand cups my face as he deepens our kiss, almost as though he will steal my very soul from my lips, and I know now that regardless of the fact I've only known these guys for a short time, I'd let any of them take it.

CHAPTER 12

EMBER

We spend the rest of the day in the family room watching films and relaxing. After a delicious lunch of homemade pizza, Odette and Dad go off to pack their last few bits, and I snuggle between the twins, my body relaxing fully as the huge screen plays the opening credits of Deadpool.

Oct drags a blanket over us, and I rest my head on Kit's shoulder, breathing in his lime, mimosa, and cedar scent, letting it wash over me in a soothing wave.

"Are you sniffing me, little Pretty Thing?" he asks, a teasing note to his voice, and I freeze, my nose firmly buried in the crook of his neck.

"Is that weird?" I ask, realising how weird it sounds that I even have to ask. Of course it's fucking strange to go around sniffing hot guys.

"Not when you do it, Pretty Thing," he assures me, and my chest swells when he angles his head so I can take in another lungful. A wicked idea comes to mind then, and I dance my fingers down his soft T-shirt and over his muscular abs, which clench and ripple as my hand heads lower. "What are you up to, Pretty Thing?" There's a hitch to his tone, a breathiness that makes my core heat up.

"You made me feel good earlier," I tell him in a low whisper, and he hisses a sharp breath when I pop open the first button of his jeans. "I'm just returning the favour."

He widens his legs, and a rush of power flows through me at having him following my lead for once. Having opened all the buttons, I slip my hand underneath his boxers and wrap it around his hard length. His nostrils flare, his skin flushing as I pull him out, pausing when I feel something unexpected running down the underside of his impressive shaft. My fingers tease down what feels like metal bars, counting them.

Holy. Shit.

He has a Jacob's ladder with eight fucking rungs on it.

"You found my accessories then, Pretty Thing," he murmurs in my ear, his hand coming over mine and taking my fingers up and down the bars. "I can't wait for you to feel them inside you."

My poor aching pussy clenches, my centre flooding with heat.

"That needs to happen soon," I tell him, and he laughs, a deep husky sound that has my thighs squeezing tightly together.

"As you command, Pretty Thing..." The last syllable of my nickname trails off into a masculine groan that I know the others hear when I once again fist him and pump slowly.

"What are you doing to my brother, Little Sis?" Oct asks, pressing against my back, the heat of his body leaving me shuddering.

"Making him feel good, as a little sister should do," I reply, and four growls fill the room.

The rush of knowing that I affect these stunning men so much goes straight to my core, drenching my knickers, and I tighten my grip on Kit.

"Fuck, baby," he moans, his hand dropping away from mine and letting me truly take over. I skirt my thumb over the tip, swiping up the pre-cum and swirling it around the head. His hand lands on my thigh, his fingers digging in as I shift to have better leverage, giving Oct more of my back.

"Twist your fist, Little Sis, he likes that," Oct breathes in my ear, and I follow his instruction, my breath quickening when Kit curses. "See."

Oct sweeps my hair to the side, kissing and nibbling my neck as I move my fist, watching Kit with half-lidded eyes. His head is resting on the back of the sofa, his eyes closed as a pained bliss covers his face.

"Shit, I will not last long at this rate," he groans, his hips thrusting forward, and the blanket slides down so that I can see him fully, see the piercing glinting in the film's light, my fingers not meeting as I hold his shaft and pump it faster.

My tongue darts out, licking my lips, and all I can think about is how I want to taste him, how I need his flavour on my tongue.

"Oct?" I breathe, my voice a huskier version of my normal one.

"Yes, Little Sis?" he says, pausing in his attention on my neck.

"Hold my hair, please?"

"Why would he—fuck!" Kit swears as my lips close over his head, and I moan at the salty, musky flavour of him.

I take him deeper, breathing through my gag reflex as he hits the back of my throat. His metal is an unfamiliar experience, the hard material contrasting the soft skin of his cock. Oct gathers my hair up in his fist and then uses his grip to pull me up before forcing my head down until Kit is buried in my throat and I can only take in a sliver of air.

My thighs are soaked with how fucking hot it is, my fist still holding the base of him as he's just too big for me to fit in completely.

"That is beyond hot, Sugar," Prince moans, and I open my eyes, sliding my gaze over to the other sofa to see him palming his own monster cock as he watches us.

"You take him so well, Cinders," Cas praises from next to Prince. He gives me a wink, then shuffles around and takes Prince's dick into his mouth. The moan that leaves my throat vibrates down Kit's shaft, and his hips jerk, burying himself deeper in my throat.

I couldn't breathe even if I had the room. The sight of Prince's cock disappearing down Cas's throat has rendered me utterly incapable of coherent thought.

"You like that, huh, Little Sis?" Oct whispers in my ear, finally pulling me up, and I take a huge, rasping breath. He keeps Kit's dick in my mouth so I can only murmur my agreement, sucking Kit's head harder the more I watch Cas.

"She's so fucking perfect for us, isn't she, brother?" Oct asks, and then he's pushing me back down, making me choke and gag on Kit's cock.

"Fuuuuck..." Is all Kit can say, his fingers stroking my jaw as I bob up and down, saliva and tears dripping down my hand and making his cock even slicker. "I'm gonna fucking—"

He groans long and low, burying himself so deep in my throat that all I can do is swallow the cum that he pours into me.

"Don't worry, Little Sis, I got you," Oct purrs, and then his fingers are darting into my knickers, toying with my clit. I'm so worked up that I explode within seconds, my cries muffled by Kit's dick which is still buried to the hilt in my mouth.

I pull off him just in time to see Prince thrust his hips up and Cas's head down, his head thrown back in exquisite agony as he comes, and another smaller orgasm trembles over me, leaving me shaking and floating.

Popping off Kit's dick with an audible sound, I slump back into Oct, who wraps his arms around me and pulls me close, brushing my sweaty hair off my forehead and peppering kisses all over my temple.

"That was... Shit, I can't even think right now you made me come so fucking hard, Pretty Thing," Kit gushes in a breathless whisper.

He leans over, his palms cupping my hot cheeks, and presses his lips to mine, uncaring that my mouth must taste like his cum as he kisses me slowly and so deeply my heart aches. I've never felt as treasured as I do by these guys. They make me feel like I'm worth something that cannot be replaced.

He slowly pulls away, rubbing his nose against mine before he slouches back and tucks his now soft dick back into his pants. I shuffle on the leather, my tights completely ruined, and my nose wrinkles.

"I need to clean up," I tell them, Oct helping me to my feet. My legs feel like jelly, and we all laugh when I wobble.

"Come here, Cinders," Cas orders, and I make my unsteady way to him and Prince. Leaning up, he cups the back of my head, dragging my face down to his and giving me a kiss that has my toes curling. The taste of Prince is still on his tongue, and I lap it up, my hands gripping his shirt. "Such a good girl for your brothers," he praises as he pulls away.

"Always," I breathe out, butterflies taking flight in my stomach as I straighten up and release my hold on him.

A smile splits my face as I open the door, closing it quietly behind me. Turning around, I come to a stop, my heartbeat thrashing in my ears as I come face-to-face with Odette.

"I'm glad to see my boys are taking such good care of their sister," she remarks, and my brain whirls. Did she hear us? Or is this just an innocent remark? "Oh, don't look so scared, Ember. They're passionate boys, it was only a matter of time before they convinced you to get into their beds."

"It's not like that," I blurt, my hands flying to cover my mouth as if that will stop the incriminating words that have already escaped, but it's too late, her Cheshire cat grin tells me that.

"Well, either way, I'll keep your little tryst to myself as long as you don't make my life here difficult. With my boys or your father." Her face is serene, probably on account of all the Botox, but her eyes are sharp, cutting into me and leaving me feeling raw.

"Why would I make things difficult?" I choke out, lowering my hands to my sides, still keeping my voice low so as not to alert anyone to our conversation.

"Oh, honey," she coos, reaching out and tucking a strand of hair back from my face. I flinch, and bile fills my throat at her touch, at the way she appraises me as if I'm something to be used. "Things can always get difficult when there's only ever been one woman in a man's life and now there are two, but we understand each other now, don't we? So there's nothing to worry your pretty little head about."

My jaw clenches, my lips pressing into a flat line, but she has me over a barrel. I don't want my dad to know what's happening between me and the guys. He might send me away. He might send *them* away, and the thought of not seeing them again has my pulse racing and my stomach knotting.

"There'll be no trouble from me, Odette." My voice is monotone as a numbness fills my limbs and tears prick at my eyes.

"Good. Now, why don't you go and change out of those clothes and join them for more movies? Your father and I are going to get an early night, having such an early start tomorrow." She leans in, placing a light kiss on my cheek, and I don't miss the way she takes a deep inhale, no doubt smelling what just went down in the living room. "Good night, Ember. Make sure to give my boys all they need while I'm away."

A shudder works its way through me, and I swallow repeatedly as I try not to throw up all over her red, silk robe. As soon as she pulls back, I flee, racing up the stairs and to my room, slamming the door behind me.

I press my back to the wood, in the same place that Cas had me earlier, but unlike then, my heart is racing for an entirely different reason.

There is something not right about all of this. Something big that I'm missing.

And I'm afraid I won't find out what it is until it's too late.

CHAPTER 13

EMBER

I wake up alone, and the emptiness that fills me has my breath catching and a lump in my throat forming. I shouldn't feel this way after only two days with them in my life. Shit, it really has been just over forty-eight hours since I've met them. A shiver runs through me at the thought of how close I've let them get, how much I already depend on them for comfort.

I'd locked my door after coming upstairs last night, and I just got ready and crawled into bed, not able to face the guys after my run-in with Odette.

There's a heaviness in my limbs as I lie there, thinking about what she said, what she didn't say, and what it all means. Though the puzzle pieces just aren't fitting together, and with a heavy sigh, I get up and head to my bathroom, screeching when I glimpse a dark figure outside on the balcony.

"Fuck! Prince!" I gasp, heading over and unlocking the door. I'd locked it too after the last time when Kit came in that way. The sky is grey, an oppressive cloud covering it, and the wind is biting as it wraps its icy fingers around me. I pull him in, hissing when my hand makes contact with his bare skin. "Shit, you're freezing."

My heart thuds painfully in my chest as I take in his expression. It's intense, his green eyes travelling over me, even as his body shivers.

"You didn't come back last night," he states, and I swallow hard, tugging him into my room, slamming the balcony door shut, and pulling him towards the bathroom. Leaving him just inside the doorway, I reach in and switch on the shower.

"Have you been outside all night?" God, what if he's got frostbite? It's only February, it can still get below freezing overnight. "What were you thinking?! You're only wearing a fucking T-shirt for Christ's sake and you could get sick or—" Panic makes my chest tight, and it's suddenly hard to breathe, my eyes darting over him, looking for any sign that he might be ill.

"Sugar, hey, baby, breathe." He's there, his frozen hands holding my face as my vision wavers. "In and out, follow me." One hand grabs mine, placing it on his chest and I suck in a desperate breath when his chest expands. "That's it, good girl."

My head clears and the sound of the shower behind me replaces the sound of my racing heart that was all I could hear moments ago.

"D–don't you ever do something so stupid again, Prince," I tell him, my voice thick and my throat full of glass. "If anything happened—"

"I'm sorry, darlin'. I was worried about you. *We* were worried about you, but the others said to give you space. I just couldn't leave you so alone." His own voice is rough, and I see the deep etches in his brow, see the way he traces my face as if cataloguing every movement. He was scared too. I don't know his full story, but I know that, like me, he's lost someone, and it's left a mark on his soul as deep as my own.

"I won't lock that door again. I won't shut you out, Prince, I'm so sorry." Using my hand on his chest to pull him to me, I bite the inside of my cheek when his frozen skin touches mine. "I'll tell you why I did it, but right now, I need to get you warmed up, okay? I need to take care of you."

A deep shudder runs through him, and I wonder if anyone has

ever cared for Prince before or if he's always been the one to look after people. I see the way the others defer to him, look to him for leadership, but we all need to be looked after every so often.

Stepping back a fraction, I tug at the hem of his T-shirt, lifting it up and encouraging his arms to rise. I bite down on my lip hard to stop the panic from rising when I notice how pale his usually golden skin is underneath all his ink. He must have been outside all night.

We don't speak as I undo his jeans, pushing them down his hips, but there's no time for me to admire his beauty, my need to make sure he's okay is enough to leave my hands shaking as I pull my sleep shirt off—a T-shirt I stole from Kit—and then grab his hand and lead him into the shower.

He hisses out a curse when the warm water touches his skin, and my breathing picks up when I try to recall the signs of hypothermia. Fuck, maybe a warm shower isn't the best option, maybe he needs to be seen by a doctor, or go to hospital or—

"Ember!" I blink, gasping a breath when his now warm hands are on my face. Wide, bright green eyes stare back at me, his brows deeply furrowed. "Sugar, I'm okay, I don't have hypothermia, I wasn't out there all night. Fuck, baby, I'm so sorry I worried you."

I burst into tears and he pulls our bodies flush as I sob loudly against his chest, which is already warming up. He holds me, the hot water pouring over us as he rubs soothing circles over my back and whispers assurances quietly in my ear.

"I–I don't do well with people I care about getting sick," I confess after what feels like forever, my arms wrapped tightly around him. "N–not after what happened with Mum."

"I'm so fucking sorry, Ember. I shouldn't have worried you like that. I just wanted to make sure you were okay, and I lost track of time, but I'm okay. I've the constitution of an ox." I huff a small laugh, the sound unconvincing, but he just pulls my face away from his chest and brings our lips together.

He kisses me sweetly, and it's so unlike the Prince that is dominating but is exactly what I need right now.

"Let's get washed up. Can't be late for the first day of homeschool," he teases as he pulls away, and I pause when I remember what day it is.

"I'd forgotten about that," I confess, twisting to grab the shower gel and squeezing some into my palm. "What will you be doing today?"

I don't even know my timetable, but I'm sure I'll find out soon enough. A pang goes through me when I think about my friends back at Morley College. I still don't really see why the guys couldn't have joined me there. It's one of the best private colleges in the country.

"Oh, the usual," he says, his eyelids fluttering as I rub my hands over his torso and down his arms. I love the feel of his skin underneath my fingertips, the way his muscles twitch and flex. "Sugar, you keep touching me like that and we'll definitely be late."

"Sorry." I chuckle, heat lighting up my body as his dick hardens between us. Not cold anymore at least.

"Never apologise for touching me, baby," he replies, reaching past me to grab the bottle and squeezing some shower gel into his palm. "I love that you want to take care of me, that you want your hands on me as much as I want mine on you." He glides his soapy hands all over my body, paying me back for my teasing touch moments before, and when I try to arch into him, he *tsks* and shakes his head. "Later."

Frowning, my core on fucking fire, I let him turn the water off and watch his biteable arse as he gets out, wrapping a towel low around his hips and then grabbing another and holding it out for me.

We head back into my room and all the while my mind tries to think of ways of getting him back for leaving me with blue ovaries.

"I'll see you downstairs," he says, kissing me on the lips and then heading back out of the balcony door.

Sighing, I turn to my walk-in wardrobe and contemplate my choices, a smile tugging my lips upward when I see my old college uniform still hanging there.

Fucking perfect.

~

I'm the last one to enter the dining room for breakfast, and four pairs of jewelled eyes swing my way, heat making the colours shine brighter as they trail down my body.

"Fucking hell, Little Sis," Oct rasps, his eyes burning as he takes in my outfit. I tucked my white school shirt into my plaid mini skirt, and knee-high, white socks, chunky-heeled Mary Janes, and two French braids complete the naughty schoolgirl look I was going for. Looks like my efforts have paid off too.

"One should always try for the first day, don't you agree, Prince?" I question, my eyes locked on Prince's green ones. He swipes his thumb over his lower lip as he studies me, and I'm glad my father or Odette aren't here because the sexual tension in the room is off the fucking charts. Turning to Kit who's closest to me, I catch his gaze. "I bumped my hip on the way down, can you check there's no bruise for me?"

I keep my expression all wide-eyed innocence as I lift the side of my skirt, and I have to bite the inside of my cheek when four groans sound as they realise that I'm not wearing any underwear.

"What the fuck did you do, bro?" Cas grumbles just as the door handle rattles and I drop my skirt, twirling to face the door I just came through and flashing my bare arse as the material lifts a little.

"Miss, the first of the tutors is here," Smithers announces with a small bow. Gosh, I wish he would stop doing that.

"Thank you, Smithers. We'll be along presently," I reply, and he gives a nod, leaving the room and shutting the door with a quiet snick.

"Not until you've eaten, Sugar," Prince commands, his voice slightly strained and I mentally high-five myself.

"Of course, sir," I sass back, and the growl that vibrates from his chest has my thighs clenching. He clearly enjoys being addressed like that. The chair between him and Cas is free, but I decide that I'm not quite done playing the brat, so instead, I turn back to Kit. "Is this seat taken?" I indicate his lap, and he gives me a boyish grin that has wetness coating my inner thighs.

"No, miss." Scooting his chair back, he pats his knee and I lower myself to sit on it, biting my lips between my teeth when my bare pussy rubs against his jeans. His arms wrap around my waist, and he pulls me back until our upper bodies are flush. "Remind me never to piss you off, Pretty Thing," he whispers in my ear, and this time a peal of laughter rings out from my lips.

I haven't felt this...free in so long; the feeling goes straight to my head, leaving me almost dizzy with the rush of how much fun it is just to not be serious and mess around a little.

I eat whatever Oct feeds me, Kit's hand resting on my upper thigh but going no further, his form of payback. I'm just glad his jeans are dark, perhaps the damp patch I'm leaving won't be so obvious then.

After a few minutes, I quickly finish up.

"We should probably get going. What's our first class?" I ask, annoyed that Odette didn't even leave a timetable, never mind letting me choose what subjects I'm doing. I'm sure a one-on-one tutor is better than a class situation, but I can't help feeling like I'm losing all control over my life.

"We all have English first," Oct tells me, settling his arm across my shoulders as we head in the direction of the library, where our lessons will take place. "Then maths." He laughs when I make a face. "And after lunch, you'll be doing art while we do fencing and other sports."

"What about the subjects you guys want to study?" I ask, and he pauses, all of us stopping just outside the library doors. "And shouldn't Prince and Cas be at university by now?"

"We'll talk to Odette once she and your dad get back," Cas says from the other side of me, and I look at him, seeing the way a flush creeps across his cheeks, the way the others won't look at me but down at the floor instead.

"It's always been this way, us being home-schooled, we get a better education," Oct adds, but his tone is uncertain. Like he's trying to convince himself as much as he's trying to me.

"You have to fly the nest sometime," I tell them gently, all of their faces snapping towards me and can't help wondering why she's kept them at home for so long. "I'm sure Dad will be happy to help you guys with anything if you want to go to uni," I tell Prince and Cas.

"You are too good for us, Cinders," Cas replies, a slight rasp to his voice as he cups my cheek in his palm and kisses my lips softly. I should worry that someone will see, but with my father and Odette away for three weeks, and no one else around, I can't find it in me to care right now, so I enjoy the feel of his lips against mine. "We should go inside," he whispers against my mouth, and reluctantly I nod, pulling away and taking a deep inhale.

"Let's go to school?" I say, but it sounds more like a question, and the guys laugh as they open the door and we walk inside.

THE MORNING GOES by faster than I thought it would, Our English tutor, Mrs Brown, is engaging and animated. I enjoy the discussion she starts on how a recent study found only six narrative plots which pretty much every story fits into.

I struggle a bit more with maths, having bid that subject good riddance a long time ago, and fully intending on never studying it again. Mr Green isn't a poor teacher, he's good and with his moustache, round glasses, and waistcoat, he looks every inch the old mathematician. Kit, Oct, and Cas all are really fucking good at maths. Prince is like me, hopeless at sums, and I whisper to him it's our creative brains that make the subject difficult after Mr Green asks him a question that he can't answer. Poor Prince's cheeks bloom in embarrassment when he fumbles for the answer. It's nice to see one of them blush for a change.

The grateful smile Prince gives me is enough to make me not hate maths so much, but I vow to chat with Odette when she and my father return, telling her I won't be continuing with the subject.

We have a quick lunch, then the guys head down to the gym in the basement that I've never used, and I head into the sunroom, squealing when I see an easel set up and a table full of art supplies laid next to it.

"I'm glad to see your excitement, Ember," a deep, feminine voice says from my left, and I turn my head to see an older woman, her grey hair up in a messy bun, wearing the brightest dungarees I've ever seen. "I'm Mimi, and I'll be your art teacher."

"Hi," I reply, giving an awkward as fuck finger wave, even though she's stood right there. Ugh, sometimes I wonder about how I ever managed around people. She just chuckles, holding her hand out to indicate two of the wicker chairs.

"Odette mentioned that you'd like to attend Goldsmiths?" she asks, tucking her legs up under her. I cross mine, slightly regretting my life choices right about now as I'd love nothing more than to get comfy but I'm not sure Mimi wants to see my clam-shell.

"That's the goal, yes," I tell her, my fingers toying with one of my pigtails. "I'm not sure if I'm good enough though." I suck my lower lip in between my teeth, worrying at it.

"Hey, from what your previous tutors sent over to me, you are very talented, Ember. We just need to make sure you've got all the things they'd like to see in your portfolio. Can you bring that next time?" I nod eagerly, the need for Mimi's approval after such a compliment making my heart beat faster. "Fab. For today, how about we just let go, and you show me what you enjoy doing best?"

"Okay," I say, excitement flooding my veins as I get to my feet and head over to the table. Everything is in neat rows, unlike my table upstairs which is organised chaos. My fingers itch to rip open all the packets and I hear a soft laugh.

"Feel free to use anything on there, Ember. It's all yours to do with as you see fit."

Reaching out I snag a pencil, an idea already beginning to form in my mind of what I'd like to draw. I touch the tip onto the fresh piece of paper. So white. So bare and ready to take whatever I give it.

Taking a deep inhale, ignoring the fluttering in my stomach, I drag the lead across the page and make my first mark.

Hours drift by, and when I come back to myself, the page is no longer a pristine white. A portrait stares back at me, one half a young woman, her gaze fierce and unyielding, yet colourful flowers tangle in her long hair on one side. Her face morphs into the head of a lion, his mane a riot of jewel colours, a look of protection about his features.

"Absolutely stunning, Ember," Mimi says, coming up behind me and placing a hand on my shoulder. "You were so lost in your creativity, as happens to many eminent artists. I adore the use of colour, the way the ink drips down. It's beautiful. What does it mean to you?"

I trace the lines of the piece with my eyes, my heart rate slowing as the adrenaline from simply creating wears off.

"That sometimes your heart knows things that your brain refuses to acknowledge."

CHAPTER 14

PRINCE

The rest of the week goes by quickly, English and Math in the morning, some sort of physical activity; fencing, squash, and boxing after lunch. Our PT—Andy T—is an ex-marine and his training is brutal as fuck, but I welcome the burn as I push my body to its limits. It helps me to forget the guilt that is an ever-present weight on my chest.

Guilt that we are still under Odette's thumb, that I've not got us out yet. I want to be independent as much as I can see the others do, but until now, it's not been an option. We have nothing of our own. No money aside from what Odette gives us, no real qualifications, and I didn't see just how much she was controlling every aspect of our lives until it was too late. Until we were in so deep that I didn't know how to get us out.

The worst guilt, the thing that keeps me up at night, is the simple fact that I've not protected my brothers from the toxic shit that we've done which I know eats away at them as much as it does me.

Yeah, it used to be fun and games, but after a few years, it got old, and it made my stomach turn when the twins got involved a little over five years ago. Sure, they didn't mind, but I fucking did. I know how much it eats away at you, how dirty you feel afterwards, and no amount of washing will ever get you clean.

"Motherfucker!" I yell, my head snapping to the side with the force of the blow that Andy delivers, pain shooting up the side of my face.

"Head in the game, Prince," he replies as I swipe at my lip, a smear of crimson on my arm when I pull it back.

I give him a vicious smile, then throw a punch that he blocks, only to catch him with a swipe of my leg, taking his feet out from underneath him. He lands with an oomph on his back just as the door to the gym slams closed.

I look away from him to see Ember catching sight of me, her eyes widening when they take in my busted and bleeding lip.

"Prince! Watch—" I don't hear the rest as I'm suddenly feeling the mat beneath my back and all the air leaves my lungs.

"What did I tell you about paying attention?" Andy grins, holding out his wrapped hand for me to take. I smile back, grasping his palm and letting him help pull me up. Before I know what's happening, Ember is right there in front of Andy, pushing him in the chest.

"Why is he bleeding, arsehole?" She shoves him again, but of course he doesn't move and I can see him biting the inside of his cheek in a bid to not laugh at the small, blonde firecracker trying to take him on. "Are you fucking laughing at me?" Her voice is like ice, and even Andy grimaces at what must be the death glare she's giving him.

"Hey, Sugar, we were just sparring, and I wasn't paying attention," I assure her, grasping her shoulders and spinning her to face me. Her gaze immediately softens, her hand coming up to palm my cheek, her fingers tracing my lip.

"But you're b–bleeding," she says, a slight wobble in her voice, and I realize that maybe this is like when she found me outside her room on the balcony, shivering from the cold.

"I'm okay," I assure her in a soft voice, my chest tightening. Fuck, no one has ever really cared whether I'm hurt. I mean the guys, my brothers, don't want to see me seriously injured, but a few scraps or a busted lip? "I'm okay."

I pull her towards me, and she comes willingly, clearly forgetting in her concern that Andy is there, and wraps her arms around my waist, resting her face on my bare, sweaty chest. Warmth suffuses my limbs at the fact that she's here, worried about me and in my arms, and I look up at Andy with a narrowed stare. He holds his hands up in a 'not my fucking business' kind of way, then turns to go help the twins with their session.

"I don't want any of you hurt. Ever," she breathes, and my heartbeat races, drumming in my chest at how we got so fucking lucky.

We both jump when the gym door slams open, and I pull her closer, my shoulders tensing when Smithers, their butler, comes hurrying in. His usually put-together appearance is in complete disarray, his bow tie askew. The hair lifts on the back of my neck as his eyes scan the room, resting on Ember in my arms.

"M–Miss E–Ember?" he stutters, and as he comes closer, I can see the unshed tears in his eyes.

"Smithers? What's wrong?" She turns in my arms, but I don't let her go, the pit in my stomach telling me that his news is not good.

"I–it's Mr E–Everly. T–there's been a–an a–accident," he can barely get the words out, and I feel Ember going rigid in my arms.

"What happened, Smithers?" The way her voice is barely above a whisper breaks something inside of me, and I don't want to hear what's next, but there's nothing I can do to stop it.

"H–he, Mr Everly, went fishing just off the coast. T–there was an unexpected swell, and he was swept overboard. He..." His face is so pale, and his hands tremble when he holds them out, as if to help ward off the blow he's about to give.

"He what, Smithers?"

My eyes close, unable to look at Smithers as I know what's coming, have experienced this news too many times.

"I–I'm so sorry, Miss. He's dead."

~

EMBER

My knees buckle, but there's no pain because I don't hit the floor. Instead, I'm swept up into powerful arms that pull me close. Rum, leather, and cedar surround me, and I nuzzle into Prince, blocking out everything else.

He's dead.

Two words that have the power to change everything.

How can he be gone? He's always been there, even when he withdrew and buried himself in work, he was still there.

"Breathe, Cinders, come on, baby."

A gasp of air hits my lungs, burning as it gives me the oxygen I didn't realise I was denying myself. Bright, copper eyes creased in concern, stare back at me.

"Cas—" My voice doesn't sound like me. It's a broken, agony-filled sound that hurts as it leaves my throat.

"I'm here, baby. We're all here." Toffee apple fills my nose, and as I pull him closer, the softness of my bed registers, a warm body pressed behind me, arms holding me close. When did I end up in my room?

"Tell me this is a nightmare, please, Cas," I beg, knowing that I wouldn't have them with me if I was in one of my nightmares.

"I wish I could, Cinders. Fuck, I wish I could." His voice is rough, and I bury my face against his chest, hearing the rhythmic thump of his heart, and mine fractures into tiny pieces.

A wail shatters around us, a sound like that of a wounded animal, and it takes me a moment to realise that it's me making that noise. That I'm the one screaming and crying as if it will make a difference. As if it might bring back my dad and I won't be an orphan.

"Please calm down, Little Sis," Oct's broken voice sounds in my ear, but I can't stop, the pain inside me is too great to hold back.

"This will help her sleep," someone new says, a voice that

features in the blurry time after my mother's death, when I was lost to grief and had to be sedated more often than not. A voice that is always present in my nightmares, even if the doctor meant no harm.

"No..." My plea is ignored when I feel a sharp prick in my neck, and then nothing but blackness.

CHAPTER 15

EMBER

I don't know how many days I spend in the dark, surfacing briefly, only to dive back down into the black because it's easier to face than the agony of my reality.

"I won't fucking get her sedated again." Prince's angry voice floats into my mind, and a deep sigh leaves my chest.

"Prince?" My voice sounds cracked and bleeding, raw, and the pain in it has my breath stilling.

"I'm here, Sugar." A warm hand strokes down my face, and I lean into the touch, trying to absorb all the comfort that it's offering me. "Can you open your eyes for me, baby?"

The effort to lift my lids is almost too much, but slowly, I blink them open, and his green irises are all I can see. I hiss a breath as the ache in my soul pulses, his image turning watery as tears mar my vision.

"It hurts so much," I confess in a hushed whisper, and his brows dip, his palm holding my cheek tighter.

"I know, darlin', but I can help take the pain away for a little bit, without the meds, if you want me to?"

Blinking the tears away, my eyes dart to his other hand, holding my pouch, the one that contains my razors. I feel the tension drain from my body at the sight, a lump forming in my throat.

"Please."

He nods.

"Prince—" Cas's voice is full of pain, full of an agony that I'm struggling to make sense of right now. All I can focus on is the bliss that the slice of a blade can offer me, and I don't trust myself to deliver the cut right now, don't trust that I won't take it too far, but I do trust Prince.

"We'll make sure it doesn't go too deep, Cas. She needs this, look at her."

I twist my head slightly, the softness of my bed underneath me as Cas comes into view. He's sitting on the other side of me, and I can see the fine tremor in his limbs as he stares at the pouch as if it's poison.

"Please, Cas," I beg him with every fibre of my being, I need the release from all this torment that's threatening to drown me. His jaw is hard, his copper eyes locked on mine. He takes a deep inhale, then gives a sharp nod, and my eyelids flutter closed for a moment. "Thank you."

The bed shifts underneath me, and then I can feel his heat pressed against my back as he wraps his arms around me and pulls me close.

"But you come back to us after this, okay? Fuck, we've been so worried about you, Cinders." His voice cracks at the end, and my chest tightens as I reach for his hand and tangle our fingers together, pulling him closer.

"I won't do your arm, Sugar. I'm going to do the outside of your thigh, so you know whose cuts these belong to," Prince tells me, moving the blanket off me and letting the cool air of the room caress my skin.

I look down to see that I'm only in shorts and a tank top, and I wonder how long I've been out because I'm sure I wasn't wearing this the last time I was awake.

"How long have I been..." I'm not sure how to finish the sentence; since I've been asleep? Sedated?

"Four days, Little Sis," Oct replies in a pained tone, getting onto the bed in front of me, Prince moving further down and letting Oct slip next to me. Oct's hand cups my jaw, his head dipping and he takes a huge inhale, which given that I haven't showered in several days, can't be hugely pleasant, but a tension leaves his body as he snuggles closer, and I place my hand on his chest, feeling his steady heartbeat through his cotton T-shirt.

"Four days, sixteen hours, twelve minutes," Kit corrects from beyond Oct, his voice sounding choked, and there's a pain in the back of my throat at how much they've suffered over the past few days too.

"I'm sorry," I tell them, holding Kit's stormy stare. His blue irises are so dark that they're almost black, and there are purple smudges under his eyes as if he's not slept a wink in all that time. His features soften, and he, too, climbs onto the bed, scooting up so that he's behind Oct, who shuffles lower, my hand slipping from his chest as he rests his head over my heart, between my breasts.

"No apologies needed, Pretty Thing," Kit tells me, taking my hand and placing a kiss on my palm. "We know what it feels like to lose someone."

I flinch, and they all tighten their grip on me, the crinkle of paper attracting my attention back to Prince. A small, silver razor blade glints in his fingertips, and my heartbeat picks up, adrenaline making me feel a little giddy.

Prince looks from the blade to me, his green eyes sparkling as he stares at me. "You ready?"

I feel breathless, anticipation making me tingle all over. "Yes."

The fingers of his other hand trail down my outer thigh, goosebumps following in their wake. "Four cuts, one for each of us." A small smile tugs my lips upward, remembering that's what I thought the last time I cut myself.

I watch, transfixed, as he lowers the blade, holding my breath when he places its keen edge against my skin. Cas's grip tightens on me, and my fingers clench his as Princes draws the blade across my skin, the flesh parting and a wave of euphoria washes over me. A deep groan leaves my lips.

My eyelids flutter closed as the sharp sting melts into bliss, all of my pain trickling away like the crimson droplets that drip down my thigh.

"You doing okay, Cinders?" Cas asks in my ear, his voice a husky whisper.

"Yes," I murmur, and I mean it. I feel the fog receding from my mind, the agonising heartache lessening. I moan when Prince makes another cut, and the bliss this time is sharper, making my core ache.

"Little Sis," Oct growls, rubbing his face over my breasts, his hot breath fanning across my nipples even through the tank top, and my breath catches when I feel Cas's hard length pressing into my arse.

Prince makes another cut, deeper this time, and my fingers grip Kit's and Cas's hands, my eyes rolling as pleasure explodes across my skin in tiny pinpricks. It's never felt like this before. Yes, there's always been the bliss of release when I cut myself, but never this desire, this desperate need to have them inside me at the same time.

"Please," I beg, my voice a needy whine, my thighs clenching together.

"You want Cas inside you the next time I cut you, Sugar?" Prince asks in a low, rasping tone. I open my eyes, the thought of his suggestion flooding my core with so much heat that I can barely breathe. "You want us to help you forget?"

"Yes." I hold his stare, the others taking in sharp breaths as my answer settles over us. "I want you all."

"Take her shorts off, Oct," Prince commands, and I tingle all over as Oct complies, hissing when the fabric touches the fresh wounds on my thigh.

"Fuck, she's already soaked for us," Oct comments, swiping his finger through my folds and my hips jerk as pleasure fills my veins.

Oct grabs my thigh, draping my leg over Cas's hips and I can feel

Cas's hard length, his piercing teasing my entrance and making me feel so fucking desperate.

"Please." I sound like a broken record, but I can't help it as I try to get Cas inside me, though Kit and Cas refuse to let go of my hands, so I can't guide him in.

"Shhhh," Prince coos, and I settle a little at his tone of command. "Cas is going to push inside that sweet pussy at the same time that I'm going to give you your last cut." My body quivers at his words, my breath coming in short pants as I try to hold still.

"Good girl," Cas murmurs in my ear, and then he sucks in a breath between his teeth. "Fuck, Oct."

I look down to see Oct stoking Cas's dick, his hand wrapped around it and he pumps slowly up and down. Heat sears my insides, leaving me full of such a powerful lust that I think I might explode.

"You like it when I touch him like this, don't you, Little Sis?" Oct asks, and I look up to see his pupils blown, just a fine ring of turquoise around the black.

"Yes," I breathe out.

"You'll like it even more when my dick rubs alongside his inside that sweet cunt of yours," he adds in a low tone, and I swear my inner thighs grow slick with how fucking turned on I am.

A small voice tries to tell me that this is wrong, that I'm grieving and shouldn't be seeking pleasure so soon, but I shake my head, ignoring the doubts and knowing that I need this if I'm to face what's coming.

"You ready, Cas?" Prince asks, and Cas mumbles an affirmative against my neck, sucking the flesh there and making my nipples harden to fine points. "Now."

Before Prince has finished speaking, Oct has lined Cas up and he's pushing inside me just as the fire of the last cut races across my skin.

It's too much. Too much sensation for me to hold inside myself, and I shatter with a cry, stars bursting across my vision as I come so hard my entire body goes rigid.

"Fuck, Cinders," Cas growls in my ear, fighting my clamping inner walls and pushing deeper. "You're like a fucking vise around me right now."

I can't reply, and another wave hits me when Prince lowers his head and traces the fresh cuts with his tongue. I can't breathe because it feels so fucking good, my mind fractured into a thousand pieces as I continue to climax.

"Little Sis, you still with us?" Oct's amused voice asks, and I open bleary eyes to see him smiling at me.

"Shit," I mumble, and they all laugh, Cas's still very much hard dick jerking inside me. "That was..."

"We're not done yet, beautiful. You said you wanted all of us," Oct reminds me, his blue eyes full of a fire that I want to consume me. My heartbeat thuds in my chest as I nod.

"I need all of you, Oct."

Prince hands him something, a clear bottle of lube by the looks of it, and he pumps some in his palm. I watch as he pushes his shorts down, his long, hard length springing free. My mouth waters at the sight, at the slight curve I know will have me screaming in no time.

Wrapping his hand around the base, he slides his fist up and down his dick, making it glisten as he coats it with lube.

"You just tightened around me, Cinders," Cas murmurs in my ear, and I shiver with the lust in his tone. "You enjoy watching him stroke his cock, seeing what you do to him, to us."

My eyes dart up as my fingers are wrapped around a velvet cock, the ridge of metal on the underside letting me know that it's Kit's.

"You make us crazy with need, Pretty Thing," he tells me, covering my hand with his and pumping both at the same time.

A gasp falls from my lips when I feel Oct push against my already full pussy.

"Relax, Little Sis," he instructs in a rasping tone. "That's it, baby, let me in."

I breathe through the sharp burn as he pushes alongside Cas, my nails digging into Cas's hand and my grip tightening around Kit's dick the more Oct sinks inside me.

"Fuuuuck," Cas moans behind me, and I want to say the same, but I'm so full, my nerves in shreds as Oct bottoms out and we lie there, connected. Sweat breaks out across my skin as they let me adjust to having them both inside me.

"You take them so beautifully, Sugar," Prince praises, and I clench around Cas and Oct, who groans with pleasure. I twist my head to see Prince kneeling at the end of the bed with his fist around his rock-solid shaft. "Can you take Kit in that pretty mouth of yours too?"

My mind blanks, but then my hand is released from Kit's cock, and someone grabs my hair in a fist and tips my head back. Kit is there, towering over me on his knees by my head, his dick right in front of my mouth.

I open for him, wanting to taste him again, and as he slides inside my mouth, his musky flavour bursting on my tongue, Oct and Cas move and I am lost to the feel of having them all here, three of them inside me.

I let them use me, the pleasure they're giving me in return the stuff of dreams as another orgasm fast approaches, my core tightening as my nerves tingle.

"She's close," Cas grits out, thrusting hard inside me and making me moan around Kit's dick in my mouth.

"So am I," Oct replies through clenched teeth, his fingers digging into my hips as he matches Cas's hard and fast pace.

Fingers find my swollen clit, and at the first brush, I'm spiralling, my pleasure squirting out of me as I let out a muffled scream and once again, my body tightens as sheer fucking bliss drags me under.

I hear the yells of Cas and then Oct, both thrusting so far inside me that another orgasm hits me before the last has even finished. I can't think, can't breathe, and can only feel as I'm consumed by pleasure, my body clinging to them like it never wants to let go.

Kit pulls out of my mouth, his ladder piercing clinking against my teeth as he withdraws, still rock-solid. I gasp when Oct and Cas withdraw, the rush of wetness between my thighs obscene, but before I can miss them too much, Kit is taking Oct's place, pulling me on top of him.

"I–I can't, Kit," I beg, my limbs refusing to obey as I drape myself over him, my knees either side of his hips, and he just chuckles darkly.

"You still have two brothers to please, Pretty Thing," he teases, lifting me slightly, and then he's at my soaked opening, thrusting inside me.

A pained moan escapes me at the same time as he groans the sexiest sound I've ever heard. His piercings drag along my inner walls and fuck, they feel amazing. I lie against his chest, my face buried in the crook of his neck, my fingers digging into his pecs, unable to move much but that doesn't seem to deter him. He grabs my hips and moves me up and down on his shaft, waves of bliss flooding me once again.

I gasp when slick fingers toy with my puckered hole, one pressing inside me in a way that has my limbs trembling.

"Anyone ever fuck you here before, Sugar?" Prince's low drawl caresses my skin and I shake my head against Kit.

"N–no, n–never."

"Good." He adds another finger, pumping them in and out in time with Kit thrusting his dick inside me, and I can feel another climax building.

"Shhhit," I moan when Prince withdraws his fingers, the wide head of his dick pressing against the tight ring of muscle.

Kit pauses, and a whine escapes my chest when Prince pushes past the barrier, slowly sinking inside me, inch by inch. Fuck, it hurts, but it feels so good at the same time too.

"Fuck, darlin'. Your ass is so fucking tight." His fingers dig into my arse cheeks, his grip tightening the further he goes until his hips meet my backside, and we all take a moment to just breathe.

"I can feel him inside you," Kit groans, one of his hands coming between us, his fingers rubbing around my clit in maddening circles. "They made you to take us, Pretty Thing."

A deep moan leaves my throat when Prince withdraws, and I scream when he pumps back in, hard. Once again, I lose myself to the rhythm of our dance, my body a vessel to hold these gorgeous men, and the noise of our fucking fills the room, accompanying our cries and heavy breathing.

"Come for us, Sugar," Prince orders in a strained tone, his thrusts becoming harder and more erratic. His fingers tease along my thigh, finding the cuts and pressing down at the same moment that Kit pinches my clit, and I explode.

I scream their names, the waves of ecstasy drowning me in a way that leaves me boneless and utterly spent. I feel them sink deeper inside me, both filling me up with their own climaxes as they groan my name, but I'm lost in the bliss that's holding me captive.

My body is boneless, weightless, and I barely make a noise as they leave it. I hear the shower running, and feel myself lifted in muscular arms, but can't open my eyes, even when the warm water cascades over my skin.

I let them take care of me, my stepbrothers looking after me as though I'm the most precious thing in the world to them. Soon, I'm back in bed, the smell of fresh sheets enveloping me as I sink into the soft mattress. It dips behind and in front of me, the wild, floral scent of Oct and the lime, mimosa, and cedar scent of Kit telling me it's the twins who have joined me.

"Sleep now, Little Sis. We'll keep you safe," Oct whispers in my ear, and I drift off knowing that they will keep the nightmares away. That I can hide from my new reality for just a little bit longer.

CHAPTER 16

OCT

My brother and I watch Ember as she sleeps, holding her soft body close to ours. Fuck, I was worried that we were losing her for a moment; she was so lost to grief that we had to keep her sedated for four fucking days. I hated every minute, seeing her pain and being unable to rip it out of her has been one of the hardest things I've ever had to do.

"What do we do now?" I murmur into the darkness. The sun has set since we came to bed with her, Prince and Cas going to sort some shit out, giving her more time before she has to face it all.

My arms tighten around her, pulling her even closer to me. Kit grumbles then shuffles so he's pressed against her back again.

"I don't know," he admits softly, his hand stroking down her arm. She sighs, and I could live off that sound, the contentment in it has my chest aching.

"Do you think we'll have to..." I trail off, bile filling the back of my throat at having to go back to that.

"I don't know." Kit grits out quietly, sounding frustrated, then brushes a kiss on Ember's head. "Her dad was pretty loaded, so we should be alright." He doesn't sound convinced, and if I'm being truthful, neither am I. Odette spends money like it's going out of fashion, and even we've gotten accustomed to a certain lifestyle, although Kit is right, Ember and her dad are—were—rich as fuck.

"I'm not sure I can, after Ember," I tell him, my voice barely a breath in the darkness. I can't voice what we've done, can't let the disgust sink in any more than it already has. It coats me like a second skin, never washing away no matter how hard I scrub. Since meeting our new sister, the feeling of being suffocated by it has lessened, and I'd hoped that one day, I'd be able to take a full breath and not taste loathing.

"Me neither," Kit answers, and we stay quiet, digesting what this means.

"We may not have a choice."

And there it is, the thing that I'm most terrified about. It's not like it was before, where it was just us and our rapidly growing aversion to the parties. The idea of Ember finding out, of hurting her in that way... My stomach churns, and I bury my face in her hair, breathing her in to calm my racing heartbeat.

Kit breathes out heavily. "Don't worry about it now, Oct. We don't even know if it will be something we'll have to do again."

But my dry mouth and constricted throat won't listen, and as we go back to silence, I can't help wondering what will happen next. I may have only known Ember in real life for less than two weeks, but I know I can't be without her. The last four days have shown me that. We almost went out of our goddamn minds.

She's essential to me, to us, as much as the air that fills our lungs.

And I won't let Odette take that away.

~

PRINCE

Sick.

I feel fucking sick to my stomach, and no amount of deep

breathing can calm the roiling of the organ. History is repeating itself, for a third time, and the feeling in my gut tells me that something is not right. Hasn't been right for a long fucking time and I've been too cowardly to look too closely.

I stare at the screen on my laptop, at the weather reports from the Cayman Islands for the past three weeks, including the day that Richard Everly went fishing.

No reported swells or unusual sea activity aside from the one incident that took Ember's dad's life. The boat returned with no damage, all the rest of the crew were fine.

My phone vibrates on the desk next to me, and seeing the caller ID, I pick it up and bring it to my ear.

"Thank you for returning my call. I hear you can unearth secrets that people want to keep buried?" I say into the device.

"We can do anything, Prince Brown. The Fallen have unlimited reach. It just depends on if you can pay the price."

A favour. That's the price for the help of The Fallen. You will owe them a favour that they will collect at the time and place of their choosing. It could be gathering intel. It could be murder.

I heave a heavy sigh, looking out into the darkness of the night, the moon shining bright as I think about how close we came to losing her, our sister.

Our soulmate.

"You have yourself a deal, Lucifer. We'll owe you whatever you need. In exchange—"

"In exchange, we will find out whether your mother killed Richard Everly, Brant Johnson, and Michael Scott."

The line goes dead. Hearing someone say my suspicions out loud is like a fist to the gut. I can't breathe for a second, the guilt making my chest tighten until I want to claw at my insides.

A knock at my door has me gasping a breath.

"Prince?" Cas's voice comes through the wood, and I have to clench my jaw to stop the bile from spilling. I've kept so much from them, from my brothers, taking on the mantle of protector and keeping my suspicions to myself. It would hurt them, and thus far I've never had any concrete evidence to support the theories I have about my mom. "You coming down for something to eat?"

"I'll be there in a minute," I reply, no hint of the turmoil that plagues my soul in my voice. I'll tell them when Lucifer gets back to me, but until then, I'll let them live in ignorance for a bit longer. It's kinder this way.

I close my eyes as I listen to his steps getting further away. My hands clench into fists, and not for the first time, I hate the universe for giving me a mother who is no mother at all.

~

The End...or not quite...

If you want to find out what happens next with Ember and her stepbrothers, pre-order Tarnished Embers the novel now!

ABOUT ROSA LEE

Rosa Lee lives in a sleepy Wiltshire village, surrounded by the beautiful English countryside and the sound of British Army tanks firing in the background (it's worth the noise for the uniformed dads in the local supermarket and doing the school run!).

Rosa loves writing dark and delicious whychoose romance, and has so many ideas trying to burst out that she can often be found making a note of them as soon as one of her three womb monsters wakes her up. She believes in silver linings and fairytale endings...you know, where the villains claim the Princess for their own, tying her up and destroying the world for her.

If you'd like to know more, please check out Rosa's socials or visit
www.rosaleeauthor.com
https://Linktr.ee/RosaLeeAuthor

ALSO BY ROSA LEE

Highgate Preparatory Academy

A dark whychoose romance

Hunted: A Highgate Preparatory Academy Prequel

Captured: Highgate Preparatory Academy, Book 1

Bound: Highgate Preparatory Academy, Book 2

Released: Highgate Preparatory Academy, Book 3

Dead Soldiers Vs Tailors Duet

A dark whychoose enemies to lovers romance

Addicted to the Pain

Addicted to the Ruin

STANDALONES

A dark whychoose Lady and the Tramp(s) retelling

Tainted Saints

A Dark whychoose stepbrother Cinderella retelling

Tarnished Embers

A dark whychoose mafia romance Co-written with Mallory Fox

A Night of Revelry and Envy

FAR AWAY

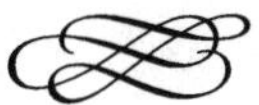

A STEPBROTHER ROMANCE

M. BONNET

ABOUT FAR AWAY

Six years ago, Theo Woods held my heart in his hands. I thought it would be safe with my best friend—the man I loved and trusted since we were children—but I was mistaken. He promised to love me forever, then crushed me into a million pieces when we suddenly became step siblings. I couldn't bear to look at him anymore, and as soon as I graduated high school, I ran far away from him.

My new life has no room for him or the pain he caused me. Unfortunately, fate has other plans for me. An emergency forces me to come back and face the lumber-jacked, scowly ex best friend of my past. He makes it clear he has no intentions of ever letting me leave him again.

Too bad, Theo Woods. I hate you. And as soon as I can, I'm running far, far away.

Themes & Content Warnings: Friends to enemies to lovers, stepsiblings, Virgin FMC, unprotected sex, betrayal, miscommunication, forced proximity, playful and hateful banter, mention of a severely injured parent, secrets, lies, and groveling.

PART I

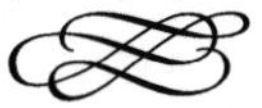

CHAPTER 1

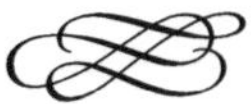

STELLA

"Give me a few more minutes," I say, shoving a bathing suit in my weekend bag for the hot tub. "I just need to finish packing."

"Take your time, Stell Bell. I told everyone to get to the cabin an hour after us, so no rush," Theo reassures me as he stretches out on my bed, nose in his phone. "Do you need help?"

"No, I'm almost done," I reply.

I rush around my bedroom, grabbing clothing from the closet and shoving them into my bag, not even bothering to fold them. I'm too excited to waste time folding clothes. My best friend, Theo Woods, and I are meeting our friends at my late father's cabin off Lake Kennebago. The four-bedroom cabin is the definition of serenity, sitting a couple of miles off the lake in the woods near the mountain. There are no neighbors, noise, sirens, or crowds of people. Only silence. I can actually hear myself think when I'm walking around the spruce, oak, and maple trees. It's like stepping into a fairytale compared to the busy suburb we live in outside of Augusta. Especially in late autumn, when all the leaves start to fall and the air gets crisper. Theo always packs a s'mores kit for our bonfires, making sure to include a hazelnut chocolate bar for me.

Ever since I turned sixteen, my mother has let me go to my late father's cabin with my friends on the weekends or during school breaks. She thinks it's healthy for today's youth to *get off their phones and enjoy the fresh air*. Add in some beers, board games, and good times, and it's truly the perfect getaway. We don't go as often during the school year, but this weekend is a special occasion. Theo and I are turning eighteen.

Our birthdays are a few days apart, November 13 and 16, so we've always celebrated together, ever since we were in diapers. Our moms were best friends since childhood. Each year, they took photos of us to mark the occasion. In one, we're toddlers smashing cake on each other's faces. In another, we're a little older, sitting on our mothers' laps showing off the giant leaves we found. In my favorite one, we were ten. Our dads had a business trip in Boston and took us with them to see a Patriots game. We were bundled up from head to toe, hugging each other in the stands with the field behind us.

Theo's mom passed away right before the start of freshman year, so we keep the tradition alive. Every year we sit and page through our mothers' albums. Then we add new photos and talk about what we want to do next year. I'm sort of nervous about that conversation this time around. This is the last birthday we'll spend together while we're in high school before life takes us in what could be completely opposite directions. Theo wants to study architecture. He wants to build beautiful buildings in hopes of one day making his mark on a city's skyline.

I want to study art history. My dream job would be curating and restoring fine art, so people all over the world can appreciate them in museums. There's something truly unique about art–it represents the human experience. A room full of people can look at the same painting and each person can glean a different meaning from it. Art is subjective and personal to each viewer. My father and I would visit museums whenever we traveled, and he'd always ask me what I saw.

How did the painting make me feel? Whenever I look at art, I always think of him, and it makes me feel closer to him in some way, even though it's been almost five years since he passed.

I'm not naïve. There's a slim chance either of us will stay in Maine to accomplish our goals. Both of our families have been pillars of the Briar's Creek community for generations. They're the definition of old money and expect to be treated as such. The Woods made their fortune in lumber, eventually branching out to developing real estate. My dad's ancestors invested money somewhere, using the returns on their investments to start a commercial fishing trade. The business provides most of New England's seafood. Things like finances or practicality didn't limit people with our backgrounds. We could afford to go anywhere to pursue our passions. Our families' connections can get both of us jobs in our intended fields. The likelihood of us ending up in the same country–let alone the same city–isn't great. But I hold out hope that our paths will cross and that even if they don't, distance won't lessen our connection.

Because I'm in love with Theo Wood. I have been since we were children.

I turn toward the bed, allowing myself to get a quick eyeful of Theo's tall, muscular frame. His arms are behind his head on my pillow, his phone forgotten on his stomach. The plaid shirt he's wearing defines the carved tone of his biceps. Following the buttons to the waistband of his jeans, I notice his legs stretched out, one ankle crossed over the other. His body reminds me of a Hellenistic Greek statue–all planes and sharp lines. He caught me looking this past summer and teased me mercilessly, but I couldn't help myself.

He lets out a relaxing sigh, and my gaze swings to his face. I've spent hours drawing it and could do so from memory now. It has an oval shape with a strong jaw and prominent brow. His dark blond hair is mussed as if he raked his fingers through it like he always does when he's in thought. Deep dimples cap his lazy smile. That smile lights up my heart, especially around our birthdays, when I inevitably think of my dad and how much I miss him. As if he can read my mind, he cocks his head in my direction and flashes me a winning grin, filled with perfect, straight teeth and mischief.

"Chop, chop, Stell. Stop daydreaming and keep packing! We have a moose to meet in the woods," he mockingly orders me, tapping on his imaginary watch.

"Oh yeah, we can't keep Bullwinkle waiting," I snark.

I walk to my dresser to get a few pairs of underwear, my last items to pack. As I put them in the bag, I notice him tracking me across the room, and my face heats. I don't want him to see them...I mean, I do, I think? Just not like this. I always imagine the first time Theo sees my underwear as something romantic and sexual, not him peeping them while I pack for a weekend trip.

I cram them in the bag in an effort to hide them from him and save myself from any embarrassment, holding the edges of the zipper together so I can close it. It catches halfway through, refusing to glide the rest of the way because I overpacked. Something is stuck in there. I yank it a few more times without success. A warm body presses against my back as strong arms come around from both sides of me. Large, veiny hands gently knock mine away. My knees almost touch the mattress, but I feel anything but trapped; Theo has always made me feel safe. I can feel his body heat seep through my knit sweater and black jeans. His breath hits the shell of my ear as he breathes.

"I got you," he rasps as he deftly parts the offending fabric from the zipper line, like he's a superhero who's been training his whole life just to address this problem.

Theo makes everything seem so easy. I see the familiar fabric in his hands. My entire face turns red as my body burns from the inside out. *No. Please no. Anything but that.*

He holds my black lace thong out in front of us over the bag, from end to end, so we both have a decent view.

"Do you wear these..." he whispers in a low, raw voice. He runs his thumb over the gusset, the only opaque, solid fabric on the whole garment.

I stay still, caught between his arms, with nowhere to go. I can't lie, because why would I have them if I don't wear them? His mouth brushes my ear, so I can't pretend I didn't hear him.

"Yes," I breathily reply, unsure of what else to say.

His nose skims the shell of my ear, then runs down my neck, leaving warm breath in its wake before stopping where my neck and shoulder meet. He places a feather light kiss there and my heart pounds so hard against my chest, I'm sure he hears it. He kisses my neck once, twice, and a third time, moving up until he bites my ear. I die standing. I'm a fucking ghost floating around the room now. This feels like an out of body experience.

I was never sure if Theo felt the same way about me. I know he cares about me; he's proven that time and time again. When I was bullied in elementary school, he always had my back. When my father died and I fell apart, he picked the pieces back up and helped me put them together again. When Keith Jacobson cheated on me last year with half the cheer squad, Theo beat his ass.

I never knew if he cared for me as more than a friend. And I was always too scared to find out because I didn't want to lose him. But I guess I'm finally getting my answer.

He presses into me harder, and I feel something solid dig into my lower back. *Oh my God, it's his dick. I made my best friend hard...*

"The thought of you wearing these..." he rumbles, with an edge to his voice. "The things I'd do if I ever see you in them..."

I hold my breath, shocked to hear him say such things to me. I've imagined him saying things like that before, at night when I'm alone. He's been the fodder for my dirty, private thoughts for years, occupying my mind the way no man ever has. He loops the thong around his wrist, letting it slide to his elbow. His hands slide under my sweater, trailing up my sides at a glacial pace, as if he's waiting for me to say no or stop him. I risk turning my head, and our lips brush. His inner palms graze the side of my breasts as his thumbs caress my hard nipples through my bra. My panties dampen, and I'm lost in the sensation. I kiss him again, but this time it's deeper, more consuming. His tongue slides into my mouth and a garbled whimper breaks free.

"STELLA ROSE!" my mom yells up from the foyer. I can hear her climbing the stairs and realize my door is wide open. Theo quickly unzips the front pocket of my weekend bag and stashes the thong there. Then he smoothly steps back, sitting on the Queen Anne chair in the corner like he's been there the whole time. I will my body to stop shaking and plaster a smile on my face as my mother walks into the room.

She and I are almost carbon copies. We both have the same heart shaped face and hazel eyes. The same mouth, lips, and chin. The only difference is that my nose has a slight curve from when my cousin accidentally threw a football at it when we were little. And she has straight ginger hair, whereas I have wavy brown hair like my dad. She's been looking so glum lately. Almost as sad as when Dad died. I feel guilty for leaving her alone for the weekend.

"You two are going to be late if you don't leave soon. You don't want to get caught in Saturday traffic." She forces out a chuckle, but it sounds hollow. Not like the way she laughed when I was younger.

"We're leaving now. Are you sure you're going to be okay?" I press. If she isn't, I'm not leaving her no matter how badly I want to spend time with Theo alone in the woods. "I can always stay behind."

"Yeah, Mrs. Cunningham. We can always stay here and have a movie night," Theo adds. I turn and smile at him. He knows how sad my mom can get sometimes. His dad is widowed too, so he understands how lonely it can be...how the absence of a parent can feel like a giant, gaping black hole. Knowing he'd give up our weekend to stay with her is everything. "We can order some takeout, eat some junk food. Play Monopoly. We can let Stella win this time if you're feeling generous."

Ha ha ha, very funny. That game is ridiculously hard and there are too many rules. I'm not ashamed in the slightest to say I'm no good at it. Really, I just play so I can be the cute little dog game piece.

"No. No, you kids go on. Have fun and please be safe. The forecast says it will rain on your way home."

"Don't worry. I'll take care of Stella," Theo says, a shimmer of heat passing through his gaze. I never saw such a hungry expression before, especially one aimed toward me.

"You always do, Theo. I wouldn't be half as comfortable with Stella Rose going to that cabin if you weren't with her," my mom says.

We both hug my mom, then Theo grabs my bag and hauls it downstairs. He opens the door for me like he always does, offering a hand to help me into his Land Rover, then places my bag in the back before climbing into the driver's seat. He checks that my seat belt is secure before reversing into a K-turn. My mom waves us off from the front door, and I catch Theo staring at me. His bright green eyes penetrate me in a way they never have before, like he's able to see the parts of me I've never shown him before. The wetness I felt earlier comes back, and I rub my thighs together, trying to calm myself down. He smiles again, cocking his brow like he knows something I don't. He most likely does, as he's always been harder to read than me.

I have a deep gut feeling that this weekend is going to be different. Our past birthdays will pale in comparison to our eighteenth.

Theo and I arrive before our friends. As soon as we settle, I work on getting the food in the cooler he packed into the fridge. He builds a roaring bonfire in the fire pit in the backyard. Then he gets all the outdoor furniture ready before he comes back inside.

He sits at the kitchen island as I prepare a marinade for the chicken we'll grill later, his hand brushing against my arm. "Do you need any help?"

"Can you get the peppers and zucchini out of the refrigerator for me?"

He puts them on the counter, then leans against it as he watches me chop the top off the pepper. I pull the seeds and pith out. As I cut it, I see him move in my peripheral vision.

"You're going to cut your fingertip off," he says as closes the distance between us.

He stands to my right, wrapping his arm around me. I'm nestled right into the crook of his arm, and can smell his cologne. It's woodsy, with a hint of musk. Gently taking my left hand off the pepper, he replaces it so that my fingertips and thumb are curled under. His other hand closes over my right hand that holds the knife, and he chops with a rocking motion. The sound of the knife slicing through the pepper and hitting the cutting board reverberates through the room until neat Julienne strips sit in a pile at the other end of the board.

"That way, your fingers are protected from the knife, and you can cut more accurately..."

"Thank you." I take another pepper from the bag. He still stands so close to me, and I try not to tremble as a frenetic heat runs through my veins. It's not like Theo hasn't touched me before. We've hugged and snuggled as we watched a movie...but he's never been close to me like this. "It's so much easier now."

Looking up from the cutting board, I turn to him, and heat hits me like a brick. His green eyes look molten as they pierce me in place. I put the knife on the counter, and he grasps my jaw, angling it up. He kisses me again, but this time it's more insistent. He's not exploring like he did the last time. This time, he conquers my mouth, owning it with every slide of his tongue against mine. His kiss screams mine, as if he's trying to claim me. Little does he know, he's always had me. I'm already his.

His hand moves to the back of my neck as his other arm wraps around my waist, holding us together. He nips my lips, then bites and sucks his way down my neck. His tongue soothes away the stings. The mix of pleasure and pain sets my nerve endings alight, and I feel as if electricity is coursing through my body. I'm swept up in him so completely that my brain goes offline.

"Theo," I gasp as he nips my earlobe. His name is a plea. I need more from him.

He grabs my ass, a cheek in each hand, squeezing so hard his fingertips will leave indents through my jeans. I hear him push the cutting board and knife away before he lifts me onto the counter. I am not a small woman by any means, yet he handles me like I weigh nothing. His tousled hair feels so soft as I wind my fingers through it, pulling slightly as he lifts my sweater. He pulls my bra cup down, sucking my nipple into his mouth. The wet, hot feeling of his mouth on such a sensitive part of my body sends shivers down my spine. I moan as he scrapes his teeth along the stiff peak.

"I love the sounds you make," he rasps in my ear. His voice is deep and smooth, and it feels so...intimate. Like an audible caress. My heart beats so fast as he kisses along my jaw. "I want to hear what you'd sound like if I was inside you."

He runs his hands up my thick thighs, then unbuttons my jeans, grinning like a wolf as he reveals another pair of fancy undies. A wine-colored satin cheeky cut pair that matches my bra. He pulls them and my jeans down to my knees, my ass hitting the freezing counter. I spread my thighs, silently willing him to touch me between them. No one aside from myself ever has–I just never felt comfortable enough with anyone to let them. I want him to be the first.

He breathes in deeply, licking his bottom lip and he eyes my bare sex. His hand slips past it, as two fingers rub my folds. I can hear the slick sounds of him moving through my arousal.

"You're *so* wet. So fucking soft and warm. Did you get this wet for me? Did you shave this pretty, pink pussy hoping I'd see it?" Hearing the word pussy come out of his mouth as he dips his finger inside me renders me speechless. I try to answer his questions, but nothing comes out. "Come on, Stell Bell. Use your words and tell me. I want to hear your beautiful voice."

"Yes, I shaved it for you," I whine as he slides his finger in all the way, rubbing my inner walls as he stretches me. "I'm wet for you, only you. You're the only man who's ever touched me...*there*."

He sharply inhales, then puts another finger inside me. It burns, but not painfully. After a moment, it feels so good, especially when he thrusts them further up and hits this place inside me that sends a blissful feeling all the way to my toes.

"No one's ever touched you..." he repeats in awe. His voice has a gravelly edge laced through it that sounds like music to my ears. I want to hear him speak to me like this all the time. "You saved yourself for me, my beautiful girl?" The pad of his thumb circles my clit as he moves inside me, and I feel like I'm going to explode. I've never felt this way when I've touched myself. "You're all *mine*."

The new possessiveness in his voice washes over me like a baptism. I'm his. Not just his best friend... but *his*. I've wanted this for such a long time, and for it to finally happen is like a dream come true. He pulls his fingers from me, and I whine at the feeling of emptiness. But then he circles them around my clit in fast, firm motions. My orgasm barrels through me like a bullet, hitting me so hard that a scream tears from my throat.

Theo unbuttons his pants, pulling them and his boxers down just enough that his cock is free. It's so much better than I imagined. Long, thick, and curving slightly to the right, the head glistens with pre-cum. The itch to hop off the counter and drop to my knees so I can taste it is strong, but I'm distracted when he starts to stroke himself in front of me. He fists his length with a firm grip as his breathing increases. His ferocious pace coupled with his intense, hungry stare turns me on so much I think I could come again.

"You drive me crazy. Look what you do to me, beautiful. You've been doing this to me for years," he grits through his teeth.

He's felt this way the whole time...

He steadies himself with his free hand on the counter, leaning into me. Our foreheads touch as he continues to pleasure himself in front of me. It's the dirtiest, most intimate thing I've ever seen.

"Later tonight, when all our friends are asleep, I'm going to show you exactly how crazy you make me feel. I need you, Stella Rose."

Something about the way he says my full name is so soft and

romantic—a complete juxtaposition from the carnal, masculine way he comes with a groan into his hand. We stay still for a long moment, breathing in each other's air, until we hear the front door open and slam closed. A chorus of *happy birthdays* for us rings through the house, breaking the spell, and Theo rushes to zip up his jeans. I fix my clothes and meet our friends at the door to give him time to wash his hands.

By the time we all walk into the kitchen, Theo sits at the table, leaning back in his chair with his legs spread wide. He greets our friends, but his eyes are on me the entire time. They track me across the room and my cheeks heat. My best friend fingered me on the kitchen counter... then he touched himself. The whole thing is too surreal. I've wanted Theo for so long, and he wants me too. It's finally happening.

We spend the day grilling, hanging out by the bonfire, and enjoying each other's company until nightfall. Someone brought alcohol, but neither of us drank any. I think both of us know what's going to happen and want to be fully present for it. I shiver at the thought of Theo touching me again. A warm, syrupy feeling settles at the bottom of my stomach as I imagine him undressing me, kissing me, and making me feel good. Somehow, my quiet dreams have gone from fantasy to reality.

Theo scoots over, then drapes his coat over my shoulders and wraps an arm around my waist. "Are you cold?" He's offered me his coat before, but our friends must sense the change between us, because they watch us out of the corner of their eyes.

"Not anymore, thanks." I put my arms through the sleeves and breathe in the coat's woodsy, smokey scent. It's all the best things about my favorite season. I lean in to whisper in Theo's ear, "I was just thinking..."

"Thinking of what?" he asks.

I shake my head, too embarrassed to say what I'm really thinking to him around all of our friends, even if we are whispering.

"Come on," he coaxes me. He takes my chin with his finger and thumb, tipping my head up and kissing my cheek. "You can tell me anything, birthday girl."

I turn my head so I can whisper right into his ear. "Will you... will you k-kiss me down there?"

"I'll do more than kiss you." His words wind around me, gripping my heart and sensibilities, leaving me breathless. "I'm going to spread those creamy thick thighs and bury my head between them until I can't breathe anymore. Until you're begging me to stop. I've wanted a taste of you for such a long time and I'm going to get my fill."

"*Oh*," I reply, more like a moan than an actual phrase.

I sit next to him in stunned silence as he rubs my back, my mind racing a marathon as unbidden thoughts crash my thoughts.

What if he doesn't really like me, and he's taking pity on me? What if he sees me naked and thinks I'm disgusting? What if I'm awful my first time?

I didn't stay a virgin on purpose. There was never anyone I felt comfortable enough baring myself to in that way. Keith constantly pressured me while we were dating, but the more he pushed, the firmer my refusal became until he sought sex elsewhere. While we were still dating. Theo had such a negative reaction to Keith that I didn't really talk to him about dating or any of that stuff until he found me sobbing in my car after my very public, humiliating breakup. I know he dated around and was in a short relationship with Candy Bergman, but I have no clue if he's had sex before. He must have because he knows what he's doing when he touches me.

What if he compares me to the other girls he's been with?

"I can hear you thinking," Theo states. He takes my hand in his and kisses the back of it, then each knuckle. The feeling of his lips on my skin chases away all my intrusive thoughts, like a light pushing away the darkness. "You're the most beautiful, funny, compassionate woman I know. If I had known you felt the same way about me that I feel about you, I would have told you way sooner."

"I could have told you...but I thought we were just really good friends. I was going to tell you over the summer after we had that movie night and fell asleep in each other's arms on the couch. I thought that was a sign. The next day, I saw you talking to Candy in front of your house. You were so close to her, and it seemed like a private discussion."

"No, I broke up with her because I can't stand her. She was texting me constantly for a week and I ignored her. Then she showed up at my house. I want you, not her," he admits. His words go straight to my heart. "That explains why you were so frosty toward me after that night. I thought maybe you regretted it, or I made you uncomfortable."

"Theo, I trust you more than anyone else in the whole world. You never make me feel uncomfortable. You actually make me feel really good." He smirks, and I sigh. "Not just physically. You make me feel so safe, like you're always there for me. You're my favorite person."

Theo is silent as he stares at me. Why did I word-vomit all of that? I probably freaked him out. When he lets go of my hand and gets up from the bench we're sharing, my heart cracks. I won't blame him if he decides to drive all the way home to get away from me.

"Get up," he says. When I stand on shaky legs, he grabs my elbow and steers me inside the house, away from our friends, who are still drinking and partying. They don't even notice we left them.

"Theo..." I try to get his attention as he leads me up the stairs to the master bedroom I stay in when we're all here. "Theo, what are you doing?"

Once we're inside, he slams the door shut, locking it. *Oh no.* He's going to break my heart and there's no way I can escape. He takes my head in his hands before I can say anything, holding my head still as he kisses me with so much passion that I melt on contact. This isn't a regular kiss. It's demanding. A claim. My knees buckle as my hands claw at his chest for purchase so I don't fall. He drives his tongue so far down my throat that I can't breathe. I'm too wrapped up in him to inhale. He's everywhere all at once and I never want it to be any other way again.

He backs me up until the back of my thighs touch the foot of the bed. I sit down to quell my trembling legs, and he kneels in front of me. He's so tall that we're nearly at eye level. When Theo captures me in his stare, it's as if the entire world stops spinning. Sometimes it's unnerving. I hold the hem of my sweater, twisting it between my fingers while waiting for him to say something.

"Stella, look at me," he commands in an unwavering tone. He takes my sweater from my hands and holds them in his. "You're *everything* to me. I want to be everything to you. Your best friend. Your protector. Your confidant. Your boyfriend. I want to always keep you close to me..." he says as he runs his hands up my jean-clad thighs to the button of my jeans. He touches them but doesn't unbutton them yet. "I want to stay in your room tonight."

"I want that too... I want you."

He unbuttons my jeans, and the feeling of the rough fabric sliding down my skin sends tingles through my body. I imagined this moment so many times, pondered over every detail. No matter how it happens, I know reality will be better than my fantasy because I'm with Theo. He said I'm his everything–he feels the same way about me and this feels right.

He tosses the jeans behind him, spreading my thighs wider and taking a moment to look at my panties. I changed into the black lace thong he put into my bag before the bonfire started. He hooks his thumbs under the sides and slides them down my legs. Bringing them to his face, he inhales deeply, then puts them in his back pocket. He presses down on my shoulder gently, until my back hits the bed. Then he positions my feet so they rest on the edge of the bed, spreading my legs as wide as they can go. He rubs my inner thighs slowly, soothingly.

I squirm in place, trying to convince myself that I have no reason to feel self-conscious over my thick thighs and stretch marks. He peppers every inch of them with soft kisses, working his way down one and up the next, skipping where I really want his mouth to be. Then he leans over me, so he can see my face.

"Stell Bell, I'm going to be as gentle as I can, but this may hurt. If you need me to stop, tell me. I won't be mad. Do you understand me?"

"Yes," I answer, nodding my head.

"I'm going to take care of you," he reassures me in a low, raspy voice.

"I know, you always do, Theo."

CHAPTER 2

THEO

"I'm going to take care of you," I promise her. Little does she know, I've always taken care of her. Since I became aware of the world around me, I've always protected her from it.

On some level, I've always been in love with Stella Rose Cunningham. When we were toddlers, I followed after her like a puppy, constantly keeping watch over everything she did. I wouldn't let any boys sit next to her in elementary school, and even forcibly moved a few of them so I could take the seat instead. I hated the thought of them sitting near her, breathing the same air as her. They didn't even deserve to be in the same room as her.

Right after my mom passed away, we moved into the house across the street from the Cunninghams. My father couldn't stand to be in a home surrounded by her memories anymore, and I spent a ton of time at their house, anyway. The proximity only brought us closer together. Through middle school, I walked her to every class and escorted her home, carrying her backpack the entire way. We did our homework together and spent every spare moment we could in each other's company. Every year, my feelings grew, evolving into a love that ran so deep it bordered on obsession.

. . .

In high school, it got stronger. Stella grew into the most beautiful woman I had ever met, and I never took my eyes off her. I knew the way I felt wasn't *normal*...or healthy. I may have beaten a few guys up that talked about Stella like she was a whore. She wasn't a whore; she was *mine*. My dad got involved, and made me go to therapy to *sort myself out*.

The Woods have a reputation to uphold, son. So do the Cunninghams. We're the lifeblood of this town, and you can't get yourself into fistfights over shit lesser people say. Your behavior reflects on this family. Stella won't want a man that suffocates her, anyway.

My therapist told me I had to let her grow into her own person, and that my actions were a result of codependency and abandonment issues from my mother dying. She didn't understand...I felt this way about Stella when my mom was still alive. Regardless, I tried to give Stella some space. When she dated Keith, I sat back and let him fuck it up, even though I knew he'd only hurt her in the end. I even tried to date someone, Candy Bergman, because admittedly, I wanted to make her jealous. She needed to feel as untethered and out of control as I did. But ever since her dad passed away, Stella became much harder to read. I was never sure if she felt the same way that I did, and I wasn't about to risk ruining our friendship if she didn't. I'd rather have her in my life as a friend than as nothing at all.

But now I have exactly what I've always wanted. Stella wants me...and saved herself for me the same way I did for her. It's a sign that we belong together. I slowly peruse her perfect, naked body spread out before me. Her thighs are spread wide–her wet, tight pussy and rosy pink nipples are on display for me and only me. Her soft stomach and creamy skin feel so right beneath my touch.

Fuck unhealthy feelings and abandonment issues. Fuck reputations and being pillars of the community. I realize that this woman is my destiny. We were always meant to be together, no matter what anyone else has to say about it. Tonight, I'm making Stella Rose mine.

I'll spend my days by her side and my nights inside her, and she'll want it just as badly as I do. She'll never know life without me. She'll never need or love another man, and God help any man who thinks he can change that.

She asked me earlier if I was going to kiss her. I almost laughed. I plan on doing so much more than kissing this pretty, glistening pussy. I'm going to devour it until she's screaming my name so loud the world can hear her.

I place my hands on the back of her thighs, gripping them so she doesn't move, then lick her from her slit to her clit. She inhales sharply, her entire body tensing. I lick over and around her clit, sucking on it until it becomes hard and swollen. Her breathing turns into panting, and she winds her fingers through my hair, holding my head in place. She pushes herself toward my mouth as she bucks her hips off the bed. I open my eyes, gazing at the way she bites her bottom lip, trying to stifle her moans. That won't do.

I lean back, taking my mouth and her impending orgasm with me, breaking her hold on my hair. She looks confused at first, then pouts in frustration.

"Stella Rose..." I say as I cover my middle finger in her juices and sink it deep inside her. She gasps as I move, opening up her impossible tightness. "Why are you holding back my beautiful girl?"

She doesn't answer me at first until I pick up my pace. I graze a spot that makes her loosen her lips, and a keening, desperate noise escapes. Adding another finger, I do it again, hitting it over and over until her thighs start to shake. A tear runs down her face and her moans turn into unintelligible ramblings.

"Theo, *please*. Oh, oh fuck. So good. Oh! Theo!" she shouts.

"Yes, baby girl. Fuck yeah, that's it, say my name so loud all of our friends downstairs hear you. Tell me what you want. Use your words," I encourage her. "I love the sound of your voice."

"I-I want you to make me come. *Please*, Theo, make me come!"

She's so lost in her own pleasure, she's practically screaming now. Her head thrashes from side to side, and I lean back down, licking and sucking on her clit until she gushes down my fingers and palm. Her arousal coating me makes me lose my shit. I push her further back onto the bed and kneel between her thighs. I stroke myself with my wet hand, spreading her juices all over myself so no drop goes to waste.

The need to ram myself inside her–to claim her in the most basic, primal way–is so strong that I have to take a few breaths to rein myself in. She looks up at me with such wide eyes and blind trust. She trusts me not to hurt her or take advantage of her, and I can't cause her pain on purpose, even if I've been fantasizing about doing it for years.

"Are you ready?" I ask her as I line myself up. I swipe my cock through her wetness, hoping it's enough to make this tolerable.

"Yes. I want you, Theo," she whines.

I take one last look at my beautiful girl, committing her flushed cheeks and glazed over eyes to memory. This is the last moment of being her *'best friend'*. Because once this is over, I'm never holding back again. I'm going to be her everything. Damn the consequences.

"I love you, Stell Bell." I push inside her in one thrust and tears stream down her face. I can't tell if they're happy or sad tears, and that makes me nervous. I drop to my forearms and weave my fingers through her curls. Our faces are so close now, I can kiss her tears away.

"Talk to me, baby girl. Are you okay? Am I hurting you?" I ask, trying to keep any franticness out of my voice.

"No..." she says through deep breaths, her voice raw. "You're not hurting me. I'm just so happy. You're the best birthday present I could have asked for."

Fuck. My brain short circuits, and I can't respond to her with words. I brutally kiss her, consuming her mouth as I roll my hips in short thrusts until I can go deeper. She wraps her legs around my waist, tilting her hips up. I tighten my grip on her hair, and drop my forehead to the mattress as I drive inside her deeper, slower.

"*Stella,*" I groan into her ear. "Fuck! You're strangling my cock, baby. I need to change positions, or else this is going to be over way too soon."

I roll us over and sit up so we're face to face, not wanting to miss a single second of this. Her eyes widen at the change in angle. I rest my back against the headboard and push her hips down as I thrust up. I can get deeper this way, and see her tits bounce as she moves. I take one of her hard nipples into my mouth and suck, watching as the heat behind her eyes turns into a full blaze. I feel a tingle at the base of my spin and lose control over myself, driving into her harder. She matches every thrust, slamming onto me as she scrapes her fingers down my back.

"You're mine, Stella. Forever, always. I love you."

"I love you, too," she moans as she clenches around me. I come so hard I see white for a few seconds.

She rests her head on my shoulder, and I move us so we're laying under the covers. I hold her the whole time; I'll never let her go. Her legs tangle in mine, and I rest my chin on top of her head. After her breathing evens out, I kiss her forehead.

"Happy birthday, Stell Bell."

I WAKE up the next afternoon exhausted. The feeling of Stella's ass rubbing against my cock in the middle of the night was too good to ignore, so I took her again, lazy spoon style. I want to wake up next to my baby girl every day. If we live here in the cabin, we could look out the bedroom balcony at the acres of wilderness and the mountains beyond. We'd have our breakfast every morning on the patio outside or by the fire pit. Then we could take long walks amongst the trees, down to the river. We'd be alone out here, just the two of us far away from civilization. The urge to kidnap her and make that a reality is strong, but I know I'd never get away with it.

One day, I want to make that dream-life a reality.

The cabin is quiet and our friends have left, so I start cleaning up the bottles they left behind. The firepit is trashed, with crushed beer cans littered all over the place. Just as I clear the last of the trash, I get a call from my dad. I hesitate to answer it.

I don't hate my dad. He tries to be a parent, but running a huge business takes up a lot of his time. Ever since Mom died, he's drowned himself in work. I can't blame him; watching your wife suffer from cancer for three years has to be difficult. Sometimes he spends days at the office or on-site, and I won't hear from him for days. I was mostly raised by a nanny and Mrs. Cunningham and her staff. He knows I'm up here for my birthday, so the call must be urgent.

"Hey Dad," I answer, trying to sound normal. He may just want to chat or wish me a happy birthday, but I highly doubt that. It's just not his style.

"Happy birthday, son," he says. "Are you and Stella enjoying your trip?"

"I always enjoy spending time with Stella," I reply. It's the truth. And now, I can have all the time I want with her, whether it's *unhealthy* or not. "I actually have some news."

"Same, but I should go first, though. Mrs. Cunningham and I got married this morning."

Excuse me? The mountain air or the lack of reliable reception must be causing some static, because I swear, I heard him say he married my girlfriend's mom.

"You what?" I ask. "I think I misheard you."

"Constance Cunningham and I got married this morning," he repeats. I almost drop the phone from shock.

"Why?!" I shout. "You know I'm in love with Stella. Why would you marry her mother and make her my stepsister?"

"Because there are extenuating circumstances. When Constance's first husband died, he left her sole ownership and proprietorship of his company and assets. The company is run by a board and CEO, who updates Constance monthly. Her mother-in-law, Barbara, contested the will, citing that Constance is mentally unfit to run a company. She also thinks that because she invested some of the initial start-up money and owns a small percentage of shares, she has a legal claim to it," he explains, as if any of that answers the question.

"Okay, and how does marrying you come into play?" I snap, quickly losing my patience with him.

"Merging her assets with mine offers her protection from that shrew. I have a legal team that will wipe the floor with her...and other methods of keeping her quiet. If Barbara wins this lawsuit, The Cunninghams may lose everything–their company, money, investments, assets, properties. Stella won't get an education, and they could lose their home. Barbara will keep them wrapped in legal suits until she's in the grave. They're practically family, and I genuinely care for Constance. We've examined this situation for a while now, and getting married and taking over the company from her, at least on paper, seemed like the best solution."

"Wow, Dad, what a knight in shining armor you are," I deadpan, unable to believe the bullshit happening to me right now. I finally have the woman of my dreams, the only woman I'll ever want, and he marries her fucking mom. "So I'm dating my *stepsister* now?"

"You certainly are not. Anything going on between you and Stella needs to end, *now*. The press will have a field day if they catch wind of that. Both your reputations and your families' reputations are on the line, son. You need to man up and make the right decision."

"Fuck no! I've waited years to have Stella to myself, and last night I made it official–she's *mine,* Dad," I snarl, unable to control the rage coursing through my veins. If it were physically possible, I'd strangle him through my phone. "She belongs to me, body and soul. *For life.* I'm not letting her go, so you can fuck off and shove your fake marriage up your ass!"

I've never talked to my father this way before. The rare times we spend one-on-one time together are so stilted these days that we usually just make small talk or sit in silence. He clears his throat, then waits a few moments before responding.

"Theo, use your head. The scandal of a relationship between you and Stella can ruin your futures. You're a man of means, so most people will write off your behavior. Eventually, you'd move on...but Stella will be treated differently. Women always are. The press will drag her name through the mud and she'll be ruined, the whore who fucked her stepbrother. No college. No status, no job. She would be blackballed. Do you want that for her?"

I take a minute to weigh his words, and he makes a good point. All I ever wanted was the best for Stella. I've only ever wanted to protect her and give her the best of everything. I want her to follow her dream of traveling the world and restoring beautiful art. But how will she do that if she's blackballed? I've heard our fathers and their associates say enough times, *"You're only as good as your name."* I can't ruin her life because of my own selfishness.

"No, I would never hurt her. I love her, Dad."

If you truly love her, you'll let her go so she can find someone more appropriate. First loves are always the hardest, Theo. Eventually, the pain will fade, and you'll find another girl. The best thing you can do is end things now and help me secure her future. You can't tell her anything about this. She shouldn't have to stress over money."

"We can't keep it a secret?" I'm desperate for any kind of solution that will let me keep her, even though I know none exists.

"She deserves a man who will publicly love her, Theo. She deserves a beautiful home, children, photographs, and memories. There's no way a secret affair can satisfy her. She's a wonderful girl worth more than that."

His final words are the nail in the coffin to any hopes I had of a life with Stella.

CHAPTER 3

STELLA

I*t's already two thirty?!* Theo let me sleep in way too late. As I stretch, I feel subtle aches and pains, evidence of what transpired last night. I ease out of bed, rushing to get dressed in leggings and a slouchy sweater, leaving my panties and bra behind. If today is anything like last night, I won't need them. I'm only wearing clothes because I'm not sure if it's just us here.

Us. Theo and I are an us. Not two best friends, or family friends, or people that share classes together. We're a real couple. For years I had heart eyes for Theo Woods. He's been the star of all my fantasies. I can remember way back when we were little kids, maybe six or seven, and he used to follow me around. I would purposely run, just so he'd chase me. There was one time, in particular, I ran all the way to the park, and he chased me the whole way. I climbed up the slide and found out I was afraid of heights. He spent what felt like forever coaching me down, never once judging me for being afraid or getting myself into such a predicament. When I apologized, he said, "*No need to be sorry. I'll always be there for you, Stell Bell.*" I think that was the moment I fell in love with him.

Now I get to spend the rest of my life showing him how much I love him without constantly worrying about whether or not he feels the same way. I'm no longer afraid of him not wanting me the way I want him anymore. He's my boyfriend now, although the term boyfriend sounds a bit juvenile, considering how adamant he sounded when he said, *"You're mine, Stella Rose."* I feel like the first book of my life is finished, and the sequel began last night the moment he told me he loved me.

I walk downstairs and peek out the window, only spotting Theo's car in the driveway. He isn't in the cabin, so I throw on my Uggs. I find him sitting outside by the fire pit, his head hung low, and he wrings his hands together. He seems...tense, angry. His jaw is clenched so hard I fear he may crack some teeth. He pops his head up as I approach him, giving me a blank expression I've never seen before. It's emotionless.

"Hey... are you okay?" I hesitantly ask.

He leans back, reaching out for me with a flat palm. I give him my hand, and he tugs me down into his lap. Instead of answering me with words, he surprises me with a slow, passionate kiss. When I slide my tongue against his, it builds from a low simmer to a rolling boil. There's a desperate, frenetic feeling that wasn't there yesterday. Somehow we go from passionate kissing to him grasping my hips, pulling them down so my sex slides over his jean-covered length. The friction of the fabric against my sensitive clit sends little waves of pleasure through me, and I moan.

He grips my ass, using it to hold me up as he rises from his seat. I wrap my legs around him, and he walks us to the side of the house, laying me down on one of the lounger chairs. He strips my leggings off, throws them on the ground next to us, then pushes my sweater up. My nipples pebble in the cold autumn air, and he straddled my hips, leaning over to lave one with his tongue. He moves with an urgency he didn't have last night. I feel like he's everywhere at once, and it overwhelms me in the best way.

"Mmm," he murmurs, sucking it until it reaches a stiff peak. He alternates between rolling the other one between his thumb and finger and pinching it.

He moves down, his fingers skimming down my stomach until they find my pussy. They glide through my wetness and he sinks one in, then two. He's moving so fast that my body struggles to accommodate him. The burn is almost painful, but it eases as he moves inside me.

I moan as he hits the same spot deep inside me. When our gazes meet, he seems disconcerted. He repositions me so I'm on my hands and knees, then runs his hands over my ass cheeks, gripping them in his palms. He kneads them, his fingers digging in hard enough that I'll feel their marks in the morning. He eases himself inside me and starts with an intense, pounding rhythm. There's no buildup or gentleness like there was last night. He doesn't say a word the whole time, but his grunts and groans let me know this feels as good for him as it does for me. He reaches around to play with my clit, giving me an unexpected, shuddering release.

This position is different from the last time. I don't like that I can't see his face or his reaction to what we're doing. He picks up more speed, and his thrusts become arrhythmic. His hands grip my shoulders on the last few punishing drives, and he comes inside me.

"Theo..." I test his name out because my gut is telling me something is off. He doesn't respond.

I turn around and sit down next to him. He's buttoning up his pants, pointedly not looking at me. I reach for his hand to get his attention, but he shrugs it off. It hits me then: I'm sitting here naked on a sun lounger in the cold outdoors, and he's fully clothed. I'm not worried about anyone seeing us, as the closest house is a few miles away, but the glaring difference makes me uncomfortable for some reason...

What's going on?

"Is something wrong?" I ask.

His face floors me. Gone is the smile from last night and the soft, bedroom eyes. His scowling face is hard as granite. I'm not sure how, but I think I angered him in some way.

"Stella, put your clothes on and get your things. We're going home." His tone makes it clear–that wasn't a request.

"Theo, we have a few hours at least until we have to travel back. Let's eat something and go for a walk," I suggest.

"I'm leaving in thirty minutes, whether you're in the car or not." He gets up and gathers my clothes off the ground. "You're outdoors, for fuck's sake, get dressed."

He stomps off, leaving me naked and confused. I don't understand what's happening. Last night he told me he loves me, but now he's clearly angry at me. I put my clothes on, immediately regretting the decision as his cum leaks out and dampens my leggings. I go up to my room to get a change of clothes and find Theo sitting on the bed, hunched over, with his head in his hands. His elbows on his knees show off his strong forearms, but I don't let that distract me. He's obviously going through something.

"Theo, please tell me what's going on. You're acting strange. Did I do or say something?"

He ignores me as he gets up and moves around the room. He retrieves all of our things and throws them onto the bed. He's never ignored me before or treated me this way. I'm not sure how to handle it. I place my hand on his arm, hoping to get his attention, and he glares at me.

"You're not going to get the hint, are you?" he derisively asks.

"What?" I croak. His voice is dripping with contempt and the tone alone is sharp enough to cut me.

"Stella, last night and this morning were fun, but we're better off as friends," he grits out. "I don't want a relationship with you."

His words make me flinch. He could have physically hit me, and it would hurt less than the crack spreading through my heart. "But you said you loved me. You wanted to be my everything..."

He sighs like I'm some idiot and not his best friend of almost eighteen years. "Yeah, and I changed my mind, obviously."

I sit on the bed before my knees give out. Everything was amazing last night. I thought he felt the same way I do. How can everything go from cloud nine to flaming garbage so quickly?

"I don't understand...what made you change your mind?" I'm trying really hard not to cry, but I can feel my tears rolling down my cheeks as I take a deep breath. "Was it something I did...something I said? We've been best friends for years..."

"Stella, I'm a man. We fuck, then move on. Sorry to break your dumb bitch bubble, but you're not special just because we're friends."

The crack in my heart doesn't matter anymore–he just shattered it. I can't breathe because I'm crying so hard. My throat feels as if it's closing up. I don't understand why he's being like this. Hugging my knees to my chest, I rest my head on them, tilting my face away from him. I can't look at him right now. If I could move right now, I'd run far away from him.

"Pack up your shit, we're leaving in a half hour." The door slams closed a few seconds later.

I lay under the covers, pulling them all the way over my head and plunging myself into darkness. Squeezing myself into a ball, I try my best to control my breathing. The therapist I see at school told me these are called panic attacks, but I can't remember what she said to do. Theo usually walks me through them, but now I have to deal with it alone. I can't stop crying. It feels as if my whole world is crashing around me, and I'm helpless to save myself. I love Theo Woods...and he just wanted to *fuck me and move on*? How can he take advantage of me like that...He lied to me. Did our friendship mean that little to him?

I'm not sure how long I spend under the blanket, but I cry myself into a light sleep. I'm sure when I wake up, this will all go away. It's just a nightmare, probably from stress. Except it's not. The blanket is ripped off me. Theo stands above me, glowering at me like my mere presence here offends him. His flannel shirt, leather jacket, and black jeans give him an edgy, bad boy vibe, and he looks like a totally different person. The whole vibe fits because

I'm not sure who this man is. He's not my Theo Woods, that's for sure.

"I told you to pack up." His voice is low, commanding. I'm not sure how to respond, so I don't. I lay there, hoping he leaves without me like he said he would. Spending two hours trapped in a car with him is something I cannot do. "Quit crying, pull yourself together, and pack your stuff."

"Please leave without me." My nose is stuffed from crying and my throat hurts, so I try to speak as clearly as I can. "I can call my mom for a ride later."

"Don't burden that poor woman with your bullshit, Stella. Grow the fuck up."

This has to be a parallel universe. How can someone I've loved my whole life just flip on me like this? What did I do? I hear him rustling around, then the closing of a zipper. Before I can ask him to leave the room, a hand closes around my ankle and I'm dragged to the edge of the bed. Theo throws me over his shoulder and we move toward the door. I beat my fists on his back, screaming at him to put me down. He ignores me, even when I flail and try to kick his face. Somehow we make it down the stairs, and I see my Uggs on the floor by the front door. He bends, scoping them up before we make our way to the car. He places me in the passenger seat. When he reaches for the seat belt, I try to push him out of the way, but he's too big. I try to slap him, but he swats my hand away. All I want is to run far, far fucking away, and never see Theo Woods again.

"Calm down," he growls. My seatbelt clicks into place, and he pulls the strap tight. "I'm taking you home."

I'm too distraught to fight him, so I give up. He throws my boots, bag, and his bag in the back and peels out of the driveway. I spend the entire trip home staring out the side window, watching the white line on the highway trail ahead.

How did my happily ever after turn into a fucking nightmare? However it happened, I know one thing for sure. My friendship with Theo Woods is over. Things between us will never be the same.

~

A SLAMMING car door wakes me up. We're parked in front of my house. I turn around to grab my Uggs and weekend bag, but find that my boots are already on my feet. Theo stands outside the car with my bag. Taking it from him, I make my way to the door. I want nothing to do with him anymore. He follows me to my front door, and I spin on my heels.

"Go home, Theo," I snap. He has no right to come into my home —he's no longer welcome here.

"My dad is inside. Our parents want to talk to us." He opens the door, letting me in first. Good to know that even though he's a total asshole, he still believes in chivalry.

Our parents sit at the dining room table with glasses of wine. There's a full dinner spread, with four plates. The very idea of eating food at the same table as Theo makes me feel sick. I'm too emotionally wrung out to be around people.

"Hey, Mr. Woods. Mom, I'm not feeling so well. I'm going to rest upstairs." It's not a lie. I don't feel well. My entire life just fell apart, and I want to be alone right now.

"We have some news, Stella. Why don't you sit at the table for a few minutes and see how you feel?" she asks. I humor her, because for once she seems happy. I don't want to ruin that.

Theo sits on the other side of the table next to his dad, and I thank the universe for small mercies. Mr. Woods takes my mom's hand, running his thumb over her knuckles. The contact is weirdly intimate, but my mom doesn't seem uncomfortable. They're both smiling, but Theo isn't. He seems extremely disgruntled and angry, like he did at the cabin.

"We got married yesterday," my mom announces, her voice cheery.

My entire body tenses up. I know for a fact I didn't mishear that. She married Theo's father...which means he's my stepfather. Theo Woods is my stepbrother. I feel like I'm going to vomit, but I hold it back. My mom looks so joyous. The light from the chandelier above her is soft, creating a halo around her head. It compliments her beaming smile. I look at her ring finger and see a diamond band that she wears on top of Dad's ring. This is real...it's actually happening. The room is quiet, and everyone looks at me.

"Um, congratulations. That's great," I manage to say. My mom knows something is up, but she's graceful enough to let it slide and not ask questions. Or she doesn't notice. I hope it's the second one, because Theo's whole rejection just became so much worse. Not only did I give my heart and my virginity to my best friend, but after he smashed it to fucking pieces, he became my stepbrother.

Theo doesn't look surprised at all... He may be a bit more reserved than I am, but I know he'd usually react to a surprise like this. Did he know already?

Did he know about this before what happened between us?

"Stay with us to celebrate, Stella. The cook made surf and turf, your favorite!" My mom's excitement only makes me feel more nauseous.

"Oh, that's something I have in common with my stepdaughter," Woods Sr. says.

His new stepdaughter. Theo's stepsister. I'm going to be connected with him for the rest of my life. I'll have to see the man who broke my heart every single day. Spend holidays with him. Eat meals with him. They may even live here.

I get up, waiting until I leave the dining room to bust into a run. When I get to my room, I close my door and sit on my bed. Even my bedroom isn't safe. Memories of Theo are everywhere–of him lying in my bed watching movies with me, doing homework with me at my desk, building me a custom shoe rack. Reliving the memories must have summoned him. He lets himself in my room, locking it behind him.

I'm trapped now. That's the only way out of my room, short of jumping out a window. He paces, rubbing the back of his neck. When our eyes meet, he looks away from me.

"Please come back downstairs. Our parents are really looking forward to celebrating with us." His tone has completely changed, again. Now he sounds like he's asking a completely reasonable question.

"No. Please leave my bedroom. I want to be alone." He stands there, staring at me. I used to think Theo was so handsome. Tall, muscular, and a face any woman would swoon over. Now I just see disappointment and pain. "Leave my bedroom, now," I manage to say in a firmer tone.

"Stella, don't be like this. Just go downstairs, eat dinner with us." He sounds exasperated. It amazes me how he has the fucking audacity to act like nothing happened between us. "Don't ruin this for your mom. She seems really happy for once."

"If they sent you up here to try to coax me down, tell them you tried. I have no interest in dining with you, seeing you, talking to you, or being in your general presence."

I'm so angry that I'm past the point of yelling and screaming. In eighteen years, I don't think I've ever been this...ruined. I didn't even know I could feel such emotions. Theo stands there, and I can see his wheels turning.

"Did you know? Before you fucked me, did you know we were stepsiblings?" The question surprises him, and he sits next to me. If I didn't want the answer so badly, I'd kick his ass out of my room.

"No. I didn't know until my dad called me this morning," he admits.

"You broke up with me because we're stepsiblings?" It would make sense as to how he could go from one extreme to the other so quickly.

"No, Stella. We'd have to be together to break up. You're my best friend, and you've been throwing yourself at me since we started high school. I figured I'd throw you a bone. Don't make it out to be more than it was," he snarks in a cocky tone.

"Well, good news, Theo. We're not friends anymore. Don't feel like you have to go out of your way for me. Act like I don't exist, because I'm *done* with you. Outside of being stepsiblings, I want nothing to do with you. As soon as I graduate, I'm moving far away, so you won't have to see me again."

He pauses, scanning me up and down. If he's waiting for me to back down, he'll be disappointed. I meant every word I said. I get up, unlock the door, and open it for him.

"Good, there are other girls I can fuck. You weren't the first and you won't be the last." His words are so painful that I don't even feel them right away. I file them away for later when I'm not trying to be brave.

"Have a great life, see you around," I announce as I open the door and gesture for him to leave.

He walks through the door, but turns at the last minute. Before he can say anything, I slam the door in his face. I'm done with Theo Woods. I'll never let him inside my heart again.

PART II

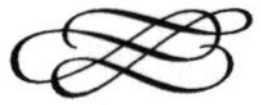

SIX YEARS LATER

CHAPTER 4

STELLA

"*Carissima,* your phone is ringing, answer it," Valentino murmurs in my ear as he presses his hard length into my back, pulling me further away from the nightstand and erasing any space between us. He kisses and bites at my neck, acting like the animal he is in the sack.

"Noooo," I moan, rubbing my ass against him. "I can call them back *after* our alarm goes off."

"It's 4 in the morning. Who would call you at such an early hour, hmmm? You have a boyfriend I don't know about?" he mockingly asks.

Absolutely fucking not.

He does make a point, though. I rub the sleep from my eyes, wondering who thinks it's a great idea to call someone at such an hour. I should ignore whoever it is and call them back at a decent hour. It's not the tour company, as they usually send itinerary changes via email. Some of the coordinators will send a courtesy text too, if they like you enough. I highly doubt it's any of my friends–none of us are early risers. A sour feeling settles in my stomach and sends distress signals to my brain. I learned not to ignore my gut feeling over the years–it's never led me astray. *Something is wrong.*

I pick up my iPhone, gasping at the name on the screen. *Woods Sr.* What reason does my mother's husband have to call me at ten at night, his time? The phone rings out; it's the fifth missed call from him, with no voice messages. It starts up again. I answer it after the first ring, my teeth chattering from nerves.

"Stella," he says as a way of greeting.

I don't dislike Woods Sr. as a person. I just dislike the situation he and my mom put me in all those years ago… a situation I try to force out of my mind whenever it pops in uninvited. He's always been nice to me, but he does come off short sometimes. This is not one of those times. His voice sounds exhausted, devoid of any happiness or energy.

"Hey, what's going on? It's four in the morning in Florence…" I remind him. Maybe he just forgot the time difference and is calling to wish me a happy new year a couple of days early?

He clears his throat, and I automatically know that whatever he's going to tell me will be devastating. "Stella… Your mother got into a car accident driving home from a friend's house tonight. She was badly injured, and she's in critical condition in the hospital. The doctors aren't sure she's going to pull through. We need you to come down here…"

I roll to my back and stare at the ceiling, unable to blink. *This can't be happening. My mother never drives, rarely goes anywhere. How did this happen? What if she doesn't make it? What if she does, and she's incapacitated? She's all I have left. I'm supposed to visit her next week…*

"Stella? Did you hear me?" he asks, interrupting my spiraling thoughts.

"Um…yeah. I'll get on the next plane and be there as soon as I can." Tears cloud my vision, threatening to overflow.

I am not going to cry. I don't cry. Get a goddamn grip, Stella.

"Call me as soon as you get to the airport, and I'll send a car over.

No matter what happens, Stella, you're not alone. You'll always have Theo and me. We're your family."

If only he knew how wrong he was. "Okay."

I end the call. Valentino is talking, but I don't hear what he's saying. I take a few deep breaths to gather myself, enjoying the feeling of his hand trailing up and down my spine.

"What did you say?" I ask as I take in his dark, bed-rumpled hair and chocolate brown eyes. His plush lips frown at me.

"*Bella*, what's happening? You're so pale like you've seen a ghost," he says as he gets out of bed and grabs my suitcase. He starts piling my things onto the bed for me. "Where are you going?"

"Uh...my mom. My mom w-w-was in an accident. I n-need to go home." I barely get the words out as my body shakes. Hearing it from Woods Sr.'s mouth and saying it myself are two very different things. It's more real now.

"Okay, pack your bags. I'll take over your tour and combine it with mine until the central office can make more permanent arrangements. Then I'll drive you to the airport."

"I don't need you to take me anywhere–I can manage," I say in a clipped tone as I rush around the hotel room, gathering the last of my things.

"*Carissima*, don't be ridiculous. You're in shock. You can't possibly think it's safe for you to drive?" Valentino cages me in his arms, using his size to block me. "Pack your bag, grab your coat. I'm driving you to the airport, end of discussion."

He grabs my jaw and kisses me, but I wriggle out of his hold. I bolt across the room, throwing on panties, a sports bra, leggings, and a hoodie. I can't have a conversation with this man naked and expect it to go my way.

"Valentino... please stop. You're my friend, not my boyfriend. My safety isn't your concern. You're going to have a long day with two tour groups, so rest up while you can." I keep my voice neutral and my cadence slow, so maybe he'll understand me this time.

"Don't you dare say that to me. We've been more than friends for quite some time now and you know it. You're mine, *la mia anima.* Stop throwing these walls up between us and let me take care of you. I want you, and everything that comes with you. You have me, Stella. Just give me a chance, and I'll show you how good we can be together."

His angry, passionate plea plays at my heartstrings. Any woman would consider herself lucky to have a man like Valentino throw himself at them. They'd literally stab someone to hop on this Italian Stallion and ride off into a pasta and dick-filled sunset. But something inside me is broken. *It's been broken.* He may not know it now, but eventually, he'll see me for what I truly am. He'll want someone better, someone whole and untarnished. He'll hurt me like men always do. I just can't stand any more heartache in my life.

I'm not a moron, though. After 20,000 steps around wineries and the city during the day and a bottle of wine and marathon sex at night, I'm too exhausted to focus, let alone drive. "Fine. You can drive me. We'll talk about this–" I say, gesturing between us, "when I come back."

He hops out of bed with a smile on his face and a pep in his step. The smug bastard.

"Whatever you say, Stella."

After a tense goodbye with Valentino and a stressful plane ride, I find myself wandering from baggage claims to the pickup area at Augusta State Airport in Maine. This is the closest to home I've been in a couple of years, and I can't shake the itchy, foreboding feeling slithering through my body. I thought about my mom the entire trip here. We FaceTime a couple of times a week, but I barely see her in person. I'm so scared of running into Theo that I've barely come home to visit for more than a week or two at a time since I left for college. The rare times I do come home, I make sure to ask mutual friends of ours if he'll be there so I can avoid him.

What a fucking coward–I've missed time I could have spent with my mom–my only living parent–to avoid some prick who broke my heart in high school. Disappointment seeps into every fiber of my being, as I call Woods Sr. to let him know I'm in the pickup line.

"Good, you're here in one piece. Theo's there waiting for you. He'll take you straight to the hospital," he says, like his words haven't shot through me like a bullet. *What the fuck.* Why is he picking me up?

"He texted me that he sees you. I'll see you soon, Stella," Woods Sr. says, ending the call before I can protest his son picking me up.

I barely have a few seconds to get my bearings before a shiny red Jeep appears, pulling over and parking right in front of me. A tall, handsome lumberjack-looking man hops out of the driver's side, complete with a plaid shirt, worn jeans, and work boots that have seen better days. His dark blond, slightly shaggy hair is swept away from his face. His thick beard is in need of a good trim, but that doesn't detract from how handsome he is. Pale green eyes, a strong nose, a hard-set mouth, and a square jaw are the prominent features on his stoic face.

Wait, no, that man is not a lumberjack. That's Theo...*my stepbrother*. I sigh, and he gives me a weak smile. He looks so... different. Gone is the youthful, smiling face I remember from my childhood and the glacial glares from the months we lived under the same roof. This face is as hard as marble, as if Michelangelo carved it himself. He clears his throat, then makes his way around the hood of his car, leaving a few feet in between us. He reaches for my suitcase, but I grip it harder until my knuckles turn white as I roll it closer to me.

"*Stella...*" Only he can make me hate the way my own name sounds. "Give me your suitcase."

"I can put it in the car myself." I refuse to say his name or even look at him. It's too painful to see him...to remember what he said to me and how he betrayed me.

You were a convenient fuck. You're not special.

He steps up to me, and I feel the soft, worn fabric of his shirt graze my bare, gloveless hand. His hand curls over mine on the suitcase handle. I flinch at the contact, and he frowns at me. I would almost think my reaction hurt his feelings, but I know better. This heartless asshole has none.

"Give me your suitcase, *please*, so I can put it in the car for you. I'm sure you're tired after your flight," he grits out between clenched teeth, as if it physically pains him to have to act like a decent human being.

I walk around him, open the door, and climb into the passenger's side. I hear his shuffling around outside and feel the cold wind rush into the car as the trunk door opens. It's easier for me and my own sanity if I don't engage. Anything he says or does will just hurt me, if he can even hurt me more than he already has. I thought I had moved on with my wonderful life, traveling the world, seeing new things, and meeting interesting people. But the sad truth is, I haven't. As soon as I saw his face, all my old wounds reopened. His words sliced me open like a knife to my jugular vein, releasing the emotional mess I never dealt with. All the excruciating pain from six years ago that I pushed down and avoided is inescapable now as my stepbrother climbs into the driver's seat and pulls out of the pickup line.

Even though commuters have long since arrived at work, traffic is still awful in the city. The first several minutes of our ride are silent. What can I even say to him? *"Hi, how have you been since you professed your undying love to me while taking my virginity, only to turn around and date one of my closest friends because I was, in your words,* just a convenient fuck." doesn't seem to cut it. I also don't care to know how he is. Whenever my mom brings him up in conversation or asks why we grew apart, I change the subject or shut down the conversation. Any part of me that gave a flying fuck about Theo Woods is dead, along with my *'girlish naivety'* and hope of a fairytale ending.

He finally breaks the silence. "How are you?"

Like you care...

"I'm fine," I reply, keeping my gaze firmly on the rearview mirror on my side of the car. Watching the lines pass behind us is the only thing relaxing me.

"You don't seem fine..." he points out.

Congratulations, Captain Obvious. I'm glad your critical thinking skills and keen powers of observation are enough to tell you that a woman whose mom might die is, in fact, not fine. Not one fucking bit.

"Well, people can be deceiving," I reply. His face cringes, and I don't hear from him for another couple of minutes. Yeah, that shut his ass up.

"What did you do in Tus–" my ringtone cuts him off, and I jump at the chance to answer it, even if it is Valentino. I'd take possessive male bullshit from him over a conversation with Theo any day.

I pick up and see that he's in a hotel room. The television is on in the background. He immediately bombards me with questions.

"*Carissima,* did you get my texts? Did you arrive in one piece? You know how to make a man worry," he croons. His accent sounds so thick after spending time at an American airport. It reminds me of the picturesque Tuscan sun. I would much rather be there than in Maine, where there's currently six inches of snow on the ground.

"Hey, Val. Yeah, I'm on my way to the hospital now. I'll be okay. Don't worry about me."

The car swerves slightly, and I glance over at Theo. His face is red, and his jaw is clenched so tight his teeth may break. His brows are slashes on his face, like an angry cartoon character. What the fuck is his problem? He didn't have to drive me. I would have rather traveled in an Uber, honestly.

"I will always worry about you, *bella mia.* The central office is combining our tours, and they reassigned your next one, so you'll have a couple of weeks at least to spend with your *mama.* They sent you an email with all the information. How are you traveling from the airport to the hospital? Are you safe?"

"My stepbrother is driving me."

"You never mentioned a stepbrother..." Valentino is all about family. They live in Tuscany and Rome and I've met them on multiple occasions during our tours and off-time. It boggles his mind that I'm not closer with mine, let alone have a stepbrother he's never met.

I hear Theo's exasperated huff next to me, and can't help but feel elated that my never mentioning him annoys him. *Sorry, stepbrother. I have way more important things to talk about than you.*

"We're not close, and don't have a ton in common."

Theo glares at me, and I roll my eyes. If he didn't want it to be this way, he shouldn't have made it this way.

Valentino, either by choice or sheer male obliviousness, changes the subject. "I'm going to miss not seeing your beautiful face all the time, *luce della mia vita.* You make my days sparkling and my nights bright. You're a strong girl, you'll get through this. Call or text me if you need me, okay?"

"*Grazie.* Knowing I have your support helps. You're so good to me..."

Val and I end our call, and the car is silent again. The tension between us is like a flame, burning through all the oxygen in the room and leaving a thick, suffocating smoke behind. There are so many things I wanted to say to him, and he wouldn't let me. As soon as he took my virginity, he discarded me like I was a used tissue he blew his nose in. Right after it happened, I wanted to tell him. I wanted to rage on him and unleash all the fucked up, angry feelings I had and tell him how much he hurt me. The feeling didn't lessen once I went away to school. I even called him when I was drunk once, to tell him just how awful a person he was with the most colorful language I could. Thankfully, my friends took the phone before I could leave a voicemail.

But now, I don't even care. If anything, I should thank him. He taught me a hard, quick lesson early on–don't love and trust lightly. Don't give your heart away, because eventually, it will break.

When we finally pull up to the hospital's visitor parking lot, my anger is replaced by fear and sadness. My mom could be dying in that building... This may be one of my last few moments with her. I take a deep breath as I open my door and walk to the front lobby. Boots thud behind me, and I don't have to turn around to know they belong to Theo. He has the same gait and heavy footfall he did when he was eighteen.

He catches up to me, walking by my side and holding the front door for me. I breeze in, walking straight to the check-in desk.

"We're here to see Constance Cunningham. She was admitted yesterday evening," Theo says in the same collected, confident tone he had when we were kids. He gives the woman our names for the visitor nametags and vouches for me when I can't find my identification. I left it in the car.

"She just got moved to a room in the Intensive Care Unit. Third floor, room 309."

I walk toward the elevators, with him hot on my tail. He's so close, I can feel him moving behind me. I hear him existing, and it puts me on edge. When the elevator door opens, I opt to take the stairs, needing some space from him. I don't think I can do this. The stairwell door never closes behind me, and I glance over my shoulder to see him standing at the bottom of the stairs. Apparently, he can't take a hint. He waits until I'm halfway up the first flight before he starts, and I thank the world for small mercies. At least he won't be up my ass.

I try my hardest to shake his presence and use my limited time on the stairs to prepare myself. Woods Sr. didn't say how bad it was, or what exactly was wrong, but in our text exchange earlier, he said she sustained life threatening injuries and needed surgery. That can mean any number of things. Part of me wishes I'd asked more questions, but I'm not sure I can handle knowing ahead of time. Not knowing gives me a sense of hope. Her condition may not be as bad as he's making it out to be.... He could be exaggerating.

Right before we get to her door, Theo takes my shoulder to stop me. I turn around to tell him not to touch me, but the way he leans into my space and the serious look on his face give me pause.

"Stella, I saw Constance after she got admitted to the ER, and she doesn't look good. Maybe you should take a few minutes to prepare yourself," he suggests.

"Seriously... You give a shit about my feelings now? All of a sudden, you want to play knight and shining armor again, and warn me how awful my mom looks after a near-fatal car accident? If I want your opinion on how to handle myself or my mom, I'll ask for it," I whisper-shout, trying so hard not to explode right here in the hallway. Our parents can't hear us arguing. I won't put that stress on Woods Sr. or my mom...if she can even hear me. They're dealing with enough right now.

He pulls me toward him, the stern look on his face cracking just a bit as he sighs. "I'm just looking out for you, Stell. I know you're strong, and you're putting on a brave front, but this can't be easy for you."

This guy needs to take up acting. For fuck's sake, this is some Oscar-level work.

"Don't pretend to be anything other than what you are, especially for my or my mother's sake. You stopped caring about what's easy for me six years ago." I remove his hand from my shoulder before I walk in, unable to deal with his bullshit right now.

Woods Sr. rises from his chair upon seeing me, wrapping me in a hug. Again, I don't dislike the man–he's always been good to me, even before I was his stepdaughter. But he's not one for overt displays of affection or hugs, for that matter. His out of character behavior cannot bode well.

"Now that you're here, I'm going to get the doctor so she can explain our options," he says, swiftly leaving the room.

Theo's gaze hits me like a physical touch. The hair on the back of my neck and my arms stand up, but I ignore it. He's like a looming specter that's always haunting me, reminding me of past mistakes.

I get closer to the bed and gasp. My mother looks *awful.*

I don't think she's awake... She may not even be conscious. Her face is so bruised and bandaged, I barely recognize her. Both of her eyes are black and her lips are split. An angry red seatbelt lash stands stark against her pale neck. She's hooked up to so many beeping machines, their noises layering over one another. Her right arm is in a cast, and her leg is hanging from some kind of traction system. As I take in her numerous visible injuries, I think about the ones I can't see. If she survives this–no, *when* she survives this–she'll never be the same. Whether she suffers from PTSD, fear, depression, or a combination of the three, she'll need time to mentally heal.

A middle-aged black woman walks into the room in a white lab coat, followed by Woods Sr. She holds a clipboard and a pen. She seems nice enough, but doctors always make me nervous, especially in situations like this.

"Ms. Cunningham, I'm Doctor Williams. Your mother was found unresponsive at the scene of the accident. The car's alert system notified emergency services, who brought her to us. She's in a coma. Her body's impact on the airbag and steering wheel caused severe internal bleeding, and we had to remove her spleen because of damage to the organ. She's also had surgery on her leg, which broke in three places. The nerve and muscle damage is concerning, as it may impede her ability to walk," she says, pausing momentarily to look at me.

When she's satisfied I have no follow-up questions, she continues. "Our two main concerns are the internal bleeding and her coma. We aren't sure if the bleeding will stop. We did all we could on that account, but it's too early to tell. Her coma is concerning because we aren't sure if she'll wake up. The longer she stays in a coma, the less chance she has of waking up, and if she does wake up, she may not have the same level of functioning as before."

Woods Sr. grabs my hand, squeezing it. His tight grip keeps me grounded.

"Another concern we have is her not having a spleen. The spleen plays an important role in one's immune system, so if your mom survives, she'll have to take certain life-long precautions. She may have to take regular rounds of antibiotics for the rest of her life. She'll have a higher risk of illness and infection, and won't recover as quickly from them."

I nod, trying to absorb the torrential amount of information she's throwing at me. "What are the chances she'll survive this?"

"I would say they increased to fifty-fifty after her surgery. Unfortunately, it's a waiting game right now. We won't know for at least a few days yet."

"Okay..." I murmur, unable to form a coherent sentence. Doctor Williams stands there for a couple of minutes but then checks her watch.

"I know this is a lot to take in. Here's my card if you have any questions. My on-call number is on the back. Please don't hesitate to reach out to me." She leaves the room, and I sit on the edge of my mom's bed.

Taking her hand in mine, I cry as my fingertips move over the cuts and abrasions on the inside flesh. I feel hollow. Numb. There's a real chance my mom could die within the next few days, and I can't handle that.

"Stella, we need to talk about a few other things," Woods Sr. tells me as he sits on the chair across from the hospital bed.

"Dad, now isn't a good time. She's in shock. Maybe that can wait until tomorrow after she's had a good night's rest?" Theo cuts in.

Even though he's most likely right, he has no right to dictate my life. He doesn't have a say in concerns to me, not anymore. I ignore him and focus on his father. "What's on your mind?"

"Constance has a living will. I'll email you the entire document, but to paraphrase it: she doesn't want to live hooked up to machines. If there's not a good chance she'll come out of a coma on her own, she wants us to pull the plug. She also has a DNR clause. That means if she dies, no resuscitation. A living will is a legally binding directive, so I have to follow it."

Mr. Woods is one of the most intimidating men I've ever met. The man runs a multi-million dollar lumber business and can fell a tree by hand like a true lumberjack. He's always taken the world head-on, but tonight, he's shaken. Seeing the fear in his eye while he explained my mom's last wishes drives home the severity of this situation.

My mom may die tonight.

"I also wanted to let you know that there are certain things we need to discuss if Constance passes..." Woods Sr. trails off when his eyes meet Theo's.

"Dad, enough," Theo says with a forceful tone. "You can have that discussion if and when the time comes, but not now. Why don't you go to the hotel and shower? I'll take Stella home when she's ready."

I want to protest, to beg Woods Sr. to stay so I don't have to be alone with his son right now, but I'm unable to move or say anything. Everything in my life is falling apart. The decisions I've made in the past, the ones I was so passionate about, seem wasteful and cowardly now. The room is spinning, and the one person I could always count on to be there for me–my only family–could be ripped away from me. It's not fair. She has so much more life to live. She finally found happiness in her life again.

I grip her hand a little harder, silently refusing to let her go. Death can't have her yet.

CHAPTER 5

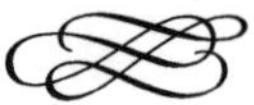

THEO

Stella sits on the edge of her mother's bed. Her mouth is turned down into a frown, and there's a furrow between her eyebrows. She's been here so long that she fell asleep sitting up. Her soft breathing and the rhythmic beeping of medical machines are the only sounds in the room. I stand by the door, giving her space. It pains me to keep distance between us when she's so close–I could literally touch her if only I'd take a few steps forward.

What a metaphor for the two of us. So far away from each other, even if we're standing together.

I hate that it's come to this. The woman sitting in front of me is a complete stranger to me, filled with anger, spite, and sadness. She's just like the priceless artwork she presents on her tours–a pretty picture behind a glass case that no one can touch. She's not the Stella Rose I knew as a child... I destroyed that girl and her trusting innocence a long time ago.

I'm not the same Theo either. Losing Stella fucked me up so badly that I abandoned my father and leadership position in his company. Had I stayed on that path, he'd expect me to play the part–giving a shit about profits, getting married, having kids to carry on the Woods legacy. *What a fucking joke.* I refuse to live a life where there's no room for Stella. No other woman can compare to her.

Instead, I moved to a simple two room cabin in the woods. I built it with my own two hands on Constance's land and can see the Cunningham's lodge-style cabin from my window. I guess you can say I'm a glutton for punishment. I wake up every day to the view of her favorite place, waiting for her to return, knowing I can't have her. I would rather be alone with my thoughts and crippling guilt than spend time with people pretending that everything is okay. My remote job and the forest surrounding my home keep me busy enough, so I don't need them, anyway.

Stella slumps over, breaking me from my melancholy thoughts. Her sitting here feeling sad and beating herself up over her mom won't help anyone. She's going to fall off the bed and hurt herself if she stays any longer. It's time for her to come home.

No, not home. She hasn't considered this town home in a long time.

Lifting her bridal-style, I carry her out of the room and down the hallway to the elevator. I get a few odd looks from the nurses on staff but ignore them. It's been a long time since I gave a shit about what anyone thinks. As soon as I press the button, the elevator door *dings*, and the doors slide open. I step in and press the button for the ground floor, setting off another *ding*. The sound rouses Stella from her slumber. Her face brushes against my chest and she wriggles slightly, reminding me of a time before she hated me. When she was on her period, she'd take a nap after school. Sometimes I'd stay and watch television until she woke up. I loved to watch her sleep; she was always so peaceful. I knew when she was going to wake up because she'd rub her face against the pillow right before her eyelids fluttered open.

Fuck, she's about to wake up in my arms. This isn't going to end well.

Before I can think of a way to cover up my behavior, she's wide awake. She glares at me as she punches my chest. I momentarily lose my grip from under her knees and her feet fall to the ground. She stumbles a bit as she wrenches free from my hold, but overall she's graceful. Another new quality, as she used to be a walking disaster zone. Her hand cracks across my face in a stinging, unexpected slap.

"Don't fucking touch me, asshole!" she shouts at me. It may have been six years since I broke her heart, but the pained expression on her face is fresh. Her heart is still bleeding and knowing I caused her that pain makes my blood boil. I hate myself every day for what I put Stella through. Sometimes the anger gets so overwhelming that I can't control it.

I whip around, smashing my fist against the stop button. She bristles at my impulsiveness, standing ramrod straight and glowering at me with a burning hatred. I've never seen such a fire in those green eyes. She's beautiful when she's angry at me.

"Who the fuck do you thi–" she starts to say before I grab her arm and push her against the elevator wall, pinning both her arms above her head in one of my hands.

She struggles in my hold, but I grip her slender wrists harder as I shove my thigh between her legs. She's pinned to the wall, trapped like a cornered animal. The rage pouring off her makes me feel reckless and stupid, but I don't give a fuck anymore. I crush my mouth against her lips, and our frantic collision is all teeth and tongues. She kisses me with six years of pent-up hatred for what I did to her, which I match with my own loathing for myself. Her body shivers at the sensation of my calloused hands gliding over the soft, warm skin underneath her hoodie. I reach where her bra should be but she isn't wearing one–just some flimsy scrap of lace that barely contains her tits. Her hard nipples could rip a hole through it. She gasps as I flick one and roll it between my fingers, gripping my hair so hard my scalp stings.

We break apart, and she starts talking again, but I'm not listening. All I can think about is how good it feels to touch her again, to hear her voice, even if she's yelling at me or making scathing comments. Both of which I deserve after what I did to her.

"Shut up," I snap at her. "Shut the fuck up and listen to me."

She frees herself from my grasp and tries to slap me again, but I'm paying attention this time and grab her hand, bringing it to my mouth and kissing her palm. I tug her close to me again, determined not to let her get away. Banding my arm tightly around her waist, I hold her jaw, angling her head up so she sees me.

She cringes as if the idea of being this close to me is disgusting to her. For all I know, I'm the shit on the bottom of her boots. Her Italian *lover* is probably a way better choice than me. Maybe he takes her to fancy pasta dinners with wine and tiramisu, then strolls under the moonlight with her. They travel the world together, taking tourists on adventures and showing them the time of their life. He sounded like he cared for her on the phone earlier. But I don't give a flying fuck about him, or how fucking wonderful he is, or whether or not she gives a shit about him. He can be her dream guy, but the perfect man for her will always be me. We have a history. I've loved this woman since we were toddlers before I even knew what love was.

Yes, I did and said some horrible shit to her, but it was for her own good. At least I thought it was. Constance told me multiple times how she feels like Stella pulled away from her over the years. How even though she smiles and laughs over FaceTime, the smiles never reached her eyes. Her laughter always felt hollow. She's just as torn up over us as I am, even all these years later. I'll bet money she hasn't moved on, and I'm not going to let her slip away again.

"I'm sorry, Stella Rose," I say before kissing her again. I don't want to give her a chance to say anything until I've said my piece. "I should never have let you go. I thought I was doing right by you, letting you have your reputation and eventually find the love you deserved. But I was wrong."

She breaks free again, storming to the other end of the elevator and pressing the button again so it moves. Her face is bright red.

She's sniffing, like she's on the verge of breaking into anger fueled tears.

"Too little, too late, you stupid, arrogant prick. I didn't need my reputation. I didn't need you to make decisions for me. *I needed you!* My father died, my mother was depressed, and my entire world changed when our parents got married. I needed my best friend, the man who I *thought* loved me unconditionally. You took the love I deserved away from me and made me face everything on my own. You paraded Candy Bergman around like a dipshit poodle at Westminster to what...create space between us? To break my heart so I could move on?"

"*Stella Rose,*" I cry, my throat agonizingly tight with guilt and shame over what I did.

"No. Don't you dare call me that. All you did was prove to me how little I meant to you...how replaceable I was. You proved to me I was a stupid, naive girl who was dumb enough to serve you my virginity on a silver fucking platter. You said it yourself, I was a convenient fuck. You may not have felt that way–or fuck, maybe you did–but you made me feel like I didn't matter to you, and that hurt worst of all."

The doors open on the ground floor halfway through our argument, and a group of people is gathered in the hallway, watching with horrified expressions as she takes her pound of flesh. I'd let her flay me alive if it could heal all the damage I caused. She's shaking with anger, sobbing because I'm an ass. I don't know what to say to her. When I reach out to hug her, she bolts, rushing toward the front door.

I follow her but lose her when a security guard corners me, asking about a disturbance near the elevator banks. By the time I'm able to shake him off and get out the front door, she's gone. Where would she go? She doesn't have her luggage or a car. She could have used one of those rideshare apps. The closest rental place is miles away, so I doubt she rented a car. I still have her number, even after all this time. I only called her once since she left, in a moment of weakness my freshman year of college, and she didn't pick up, or return the call.

I call the number, but it was disconnected. *She changed her phone number...* I immediately call my dad.

"Theo, what's wrong?" he asks, his voice groggy. "Is Constance...?"

"No change in her status, Dad. Sorry. I'm calling about Stella. She ran away from the hospital. I can't find her. Do you have any clue where she is?"

He exhales a deep, tired sigh. "Hold on," he clips out before hanging up.

I'm so used to my dad's brusque behavior and know not to take it personally. It's just how he's wired. After several minutes of me pacing, he calls me back.

"She's on the highway, heading in the direction of the cabin. There's a blizzard with high winds coming in soon, Theo. They're predicting two feet of snow. You have to catch up to her and make her come home."

"How do you know that? What if she's visiting friends?"

"When she got her job with EuroTrot Tours, Constance worried herself sick over Stella's safety, so I asked a friend to track her phone. I know she's going to the cabin, because that's her place. She doesn't know you live on the grounds, so she still thinks it's safe."

Ha, fucking hilarious. "You're the one who made me break Stella's heart, so don't rub my nose in the fact that she avoids me. She *hates* me. I'm still in love with her–I always have been–and she can't even stand for me to touch her." I'm yelling now, unable to stop myself from purging all the feelings I've been too ashamed to say. "Stella should be traveling the world with *me*, wearing *my* ring. We should have a child on the way. We should be building a life together, but we're both miserable and hate our lives, so we don't tarnish our families' reputations. I gave up my dream for a man who couldn't even find the time to be a father to me? No wonder she hates me, I'm a fucking moron!"

My father is silent. I expect he's gearing up to rip me a new asshole, or at the very least make a derisive comment about how disappointing I am.

You need to stop going down this self-destructive path and get help. Why did you drop out of college? If you leave the company, you leave your trust fund behind. Who's going to carry on my legacy? Why can't you be thankful for everything I'm handing to you?

"I didn't know you still felt that way about Stella and assumed you got over her a long time ago. I thought you were acting out because you didn't want to take over the company." He sounds sincere, solemn almost, as if he's a child who's been chided for stealing cookies before dessert.

"Let's get something straight. When I catch up to her, I'm fixing the damage between us by whatever means necessary. She's mine, Dad, and I never should have let my girl go."

"You're right," he agrees. "I should have known back then what you felt for Stella was real. You're more like me than you want to admit, Theo. We're men who know what we want and make it happen. I'm sorry that I played a part in making both of your lives miserable."

I'm caught off guard. I've never heard the great Theo Woods Sr. apologize. Sorry, until recently, wasn't even part of his vocabulary. "Thank you... I'll keep you updated," I awkwardly say before hanging up.

I hop in my Jeep and hightail it up to the cabin. Turning on the weather station, my heart leaps into my throat when the announcer cautions people about the oncoming storm.

Winter Storm Janis is estimated to leave behind anywhere from twenty seven to thirty three inches of snow. Wind speeds upward of forty miles an hour and ice particles in the precipitation will severely limit visibility. Authorities caution everyone to stay off the roads except for emergencies. The damage Janis leaves behind may leave the greater Augusta area, surrounding suburbs, and more rural areas without power...

Groaning, I hit the steering wheel in frustration and switch to a rock station. If I don't reach her in time and convince her to come home, we could get stuck up there for days without power. My cabin has a good supply of food, but we'll only last so long without heat and electricity.

I push those thoughts to the back of my mind and hit the gas pedal. I'm coming for you, Stell Bell. Everything is going to be okay.

~

It's already snowing by the time I reach the halfway point to the cabin. This storm hit like a lead weight, with inches of snow and ice piling up at light speed. The winds are so high, I can barely see the road. Stella could be out there with some stranger in a rideshare or driving a car on her own. Is she safe? I pray to a God I'm not sure I believe in that Stella makes it there in one piece. This whole situation is my fault. I broke her heart in the worst way and doubled down on it. I should have been honest with her and found a solution with her the day we found out. We could have tried sneaking around. Or I could have been a man and told my dad to fuck off right from the jump.

If I knew how much Stella suffered after she left–that she would still have feelings for me all these years later–I never would have let her go in the first place. I was such a dumb fuck. She needed me and I abandoned her. Every day I pushed her further away when she was already suffering out of some warped sense of doing the right thing. I paraded other girls around to drive her away.

Well, I got my fucking wish. And now she's still running away from me, even if it could kill her.

When I reach the cabin, I'm forced to park at the mouth of the driveway. The fresh snow on top of the soil doesn't give my car's wheels enough traction. I don't see any tire tracks or cars parked near the house. If she is here, she's most likely alone, with no way out. This may work to my advantage. If Stella's trapped here with me, I can convince her to be with me. She can see for herself how sorry I am and choose to stay.

I trudge through the snow, up to the dark house. After a few knocks and no answer, I let myself in with the spare key Constance gave me. We never explicitly told our parents what happened between us. My dad connected the dots, but I'm not sure if Constance knows. They definitely noticed the shift between us, but never asked about it. Sometimes I wonder if she gave me the spare when I moved up here so I'd be here if Stella ever came back.

At first, I assume she's not here. The lights are off, and nothing seems out of place. After taking my coat and boots off, I hear the faint sounds of voices. One of them is a male voice. I make my way to the back of the first floor to the living room and see Stella sitting on a couch under a blanket.

"What do you mean you're alone?!" an angry Italian voice shouts at her. "How can you be so stupid to drive in the snow to a cabin in the woods?"

"Calm down, you sound dramatic as fuck right now, Val," she hedges.

It's that guy from the car. I don't like the way that he's talking to her, or that he's wasting my time with her. I cross the room and rip the phone out of her hand.

"What the fuck? How did you know I was here?" she shrieks. "Give me my phone back."

His bewildered face comes into focus on FaceTime, and I see a very surprised, angry man sitting somewhere outside. I smile to myself, knowing that today he'll lose any chance he'll ever have with my girl. We're not leaving this cabin until she's mine again.

"Not sorry to cut this short. You're not to call Stella Rose again or have any contact with her outside the parameters of her employment." I hang up the call, then turn off her phone. She won't need it for a while anyway.

I walk over to the light switch, wincing when I turn it on and find out the power is already out. As I try to remember where we keep the emergency kit with the candles, Stella rushes toward the front door. I scoop her up and throw her over my shoulder. She's not getting away from me–she can't anyway. There's no way she can drive in this storm.

"Put me down!" she screams. Her body is so cold, even with the blanket. I'm relieved I finally found her.

"No, baby girl. This ends now. We're hashing this out and getting back together again." I carry her up the stairs, to our bedroom. I'm not a romantic guy, but it seems right to fix us in the place where we fell apart.

"We'd have to break up in the first place to get back together again." Her comment reminds me of what I said to her six years ago.

We'd have to be together to break up.

I was such an asshole. If I could go back in time and tell my younger self to handle things differently, I would. But I can't undo this or avoid it any longer. The only way to fix this is to go through it and heal the wounds I caused us both.

I place her on the floor, immediately holding her so she can't get away. I let her thrash, claw, and scream all sorts of colorful phrases at me.

"Let me go! I hate you so much that if you were on fire, I wouldn't piss on you to put you out!" she yells as she beats her fists into my chest. Stella used to be so gentle...so easygoing and calm. She turned into a spitfire sometime in the last six years, and I love this version of her just as much.

"You can roast marshmallows over my corpse, baby girl," I promise. "But for now, I'll keep you close as long as it takes until you know I'm in this for the long haul. I'll do whatever it takes to fix this."

When she runs out of steam, I kick off my boots and bring us to the sitting area in the corner. I sit on the couch, arranging her so she's sitting on my thigh. She leans against me, placing her head on my shoulder.

"Do you really think I'd get involved with you again? As soon as I know my mom is on the mend, I'm leaving again," she informs me, like it's a foregone conclusion.

"Then I'll go with you. I'm not tied down to my cabin. I just built it here to feel close to you," I admit.

"Wait, that wooden box across the way is your house? You live there, like, full time?" she asks.

"Yes, that's my cabin. I tried to go to college and live the way I thought I should, but it all seemed so useless without you. I left my position at my dad's company, gave up my trust fund, and ended up building that *wooden box* with my own hands. Did you even keep tabs on me after you left?"

She shuffles around, lifting her head to look at me. "No. It hurt too much to think about you, and Woods Sr. and my mom knew enough not to bring you up. I moved on, and put you behind me."

That hurts. "I always kept a tab on you–even went out to visit you when you were doing a tour in London. I saw the itinerary online and tracked you down. My plan was to admit my undying love for you and bring you home. You were walking in Trafalgar Square with a smaller tour of about eight people, and I saw you from across the way. You looked so happy without me, like you had moved on. I ended up flying home that same day because I didn't want to ruin your life."

"That was a wise decision. I wouldn't have forgiven you then. I may not even forgive you now. And I was dating someone at the time anyway."

It pisses me off to hear her talk about other men. She should be with me... Even thinking about her with someone else makes me want to punch a hole through a wall. In an effort to calm down, I remind myself I'm the one who let her go. She had every right to try to find someone new.

"You're seeing someone now, it seems... Who's *Valentino*?"

"A very good friend and coworker. We travel together, eat pasta, watch old movies, and fuck each other's brains out. It's actually the perfect friendship." Her words lash me, and I grab her jaw, angling it so she can't look away from me.

"I don't want to hear about you fucking your friend. Do you fuck all your friends?!" I shout.

She ignores the question, hopping out of my lap and bolting to the upstairs bedroom. I'm hot on her heels the entire time. She tries to slam the door in the face, but I jam my hand between the door and frame right in time, prying it open before it can close. I stalk toward her, backing her up to the wall. My forearms cage her in on either side of her face, allowing me to lean in close.

"Answer me. Are you fucking anyone else?" Not knowing is driving me crazy, even though I have zero right to act this way.

She goes straight for my jugular. "If you didn't want me sleeping with people, then you shouldn't have left me! You shouldn't have paraded other women around in front of me like an asshole. You broke my heart so badly that I don't even want to have a relationship. I prefer keeping men at a distance, because if I don't fall in love, I can't get hurt," she cries.

"I regret my actions, and I wish I could take them back, but I had solid reasons," I tell her. "Your grandmother was trying to take your father's company and assets from your mom. She had a decent enough reason that it got tied up in the courts. My dad married your mom so she'd have the power of the Woods name behind her. They asked me not to tell you, because they didn't want you to stress."

She lets my words sink in. "I'll have a conversation with big Woods another time. What I need to know now is why you didn't tell me? Why did you feel the need to break any kind of relationship we had beyond repair?"

I take a deep breath, trying to gather my thoughts so I made sense. Looking back on my decisions, they seem so idiotic.

"I thought the scandal of a relationship between us would ruin your future. Men get away with shit, but you would have been branded *the whore who fucks her stepbrother*. The press is a nightmare, Stella, and I didn't want you to get dragged through the mud or blackballed. I wanted you to be able to find a man who could openly love you and give you everything I thought I couldn't at the time.

Destroying our relationship beyond repair is the only way I ensured I could stay away from you. I loved you so much, I made you hate me for your own good. But now I know better... I didn't have to give you up. I should have included you in the decision."

"Yeah. You should have. I loved you so much... losing you made me lose faith in love and in myself. If my best friend didn't love me, who would? I didn't feel like I was worth being loved."

I slant my lips over hers. At first, she resists, tries to push me away. Then she fists the front of my flannel. No matter how much she says she hates me, I know my Stell Bell still wants me deep down. We kiss until we need to come up for air. I press against her until there's no space between us. Taking her ear lobe between my teeth, I lightly nip it, feeling her shiver.

"I've loved you since I was too young to know what love was. I still love you," I whisper in her ear.

I lead her to the bed and we sit down. Taking her hand, I tell her something I've never told her before.

"Do you remember when we were four? Our moms took us to the circus, and there were clowns?" She nods, scrunching her face in disgust. "You cried, and I hugged you for the rest of the show. When we got home, my mom told me how I did a good job comforting you. She said I was a great friend."

"You were..." she trails off. "I loved your hugs."

"I told my mom and dad that day over dinner that I was going to marry you the next day and make you Mrs. Theo Woods, the Second of Maine. I thought that's how wives worked. My mom told me as long as you agreed and I treated you right, we could get married when we were adults."

"Sometimes we make crazy plans as children that don't always come true." Stella dips her head, taking a long look at the hardwood floor beneath us. "I dreamed that you would propose to me at a little cafe in Paris and then we'd have our two kids and a white picket fence."

"Baby girl, mark my words. I will do anything it takes to get you back. I don't care if I have to pick up and follow you around the world. I'll beg. I'll lock you in this cabin until you see sense. I'm never letting you go again. I want to marry you and give you a family, or no family, if you've changed your mind. I don't care what we do, but I need you."

Stella moves to sit on my lap, facing me, straddling my legs. She takes my face in her hands and runs her fingers through my beard. "We've both changed so much. How do you know we'll still work as friends, let alone be able to love each other?"

I grab her hips, rocking her back and forth so she can feel me beneath her.

"Give me a chance and let me show you," I say, leaning back until I'm flat on the bed.

"I'm not having sex with you."

I pull her down until she's lying next to me. She instinctively curls into my side and buries her head into my armpit.

"I don't expect you to, although if you change your mind, I'm down. You want to know if we can still love each other. I started to love you when we were friends, so let's be friends first. We move at your pace."

She wraps her arm over me, squeezing me tight. "Okay. Let's see if we can be friends."

EPILOGUE

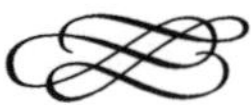

STELLA

Three Years Later

I walk into our cottage by the sea, leaving my sandy flip flops by the door. Theo and I are renting a house in Mykonos, right on the waterfront. He said he'll be home from his meeting soon, so I wait for him on the daybed in the back of the house. It has a beautiful view of the sea and the occasional bird or two that flies overhead. I take a picture of the sunset and sparkling sea before me, and remember how Theo loves to take photos of landscapes. And of me, when I let him.

I never went back to my job at EuroTrot. I stayed in Maine with Theo for a whole year. We lived in our neighboring cabins and spent every day rebuilding the bond we had. Parts of it were like riding a bike—I could never forget how protective, loving, and funny he was. Other parts, like his possessiveness and dislike of boundaries, took some getting used to. After seven months, our friendship turned into a relationship. He hates when I say he's my boyfriend because "that term sounds too juvenile for how I feel about you."

During our year in Maine, I wrote a business plan so I could open my own tour company, Far Away. We're currently scouting out tour locations in Greece. Theo is at a meeting with a national hotel chain here to see if we could hammer out a discount deal. I skipped that meeting, much more interested in sampling some of the local eateries. They say food is the most important part of any vacation.

I feel a hand slide over my breast, and a heavy weight settles on top of me. Opening my eyes, I see Theo smiling down at me. "Wake up, Sleepy-Stell. Guess who made a deal?"

"You did?!"

"Yes, I did. I got us discounts on a mix of four and five star hotels in Athens, Mykonos, Santorini, and Antiparos. How do you plan on thanking me?"

"Hmmm," I pretend to think about it, but we both know how.

I tap his side and he flips us over so I'm on top of him. The day bed is housed inside a cabana-like structure, and Theo must have closed it before he woke me up. We're shielded from prying eyes. I move down, so I'm straddling his legs, and unzip his fly. Pushing his pants and boxer briefs down, I lick my lips as his hard length pops free. I take the head in my mouth, swirling my tongue around before sucking it at an agonizingly slow pace. I tease him, taking him deeper and retreating again. He may be wearing tailored dress pants and a button up shirt, but my man will always be a burly, sexy lumberjack at heart. He proves it to me when he thrusts into my mouth, almost making me gag. Our eyes meet, and I swoon at the smoldering intensity of his green eyes. The passion behind them melts my heart every time.

Theo runs his fingers through my hair, gently pulling me off. "Lay down, babe." We switch places, and he loses his pants. He kneels between my spread thighs and flips my skirt up, ripping my lace panties off. He runs his fingers through my wetness, smirking to himself. "You're already wet for me."

"Yes, so go ahead. Fuck me, *please*," I whine. "I love you, don't make me wait."

Theo enjoys hearing me express my love for him. When we

rekindled our romance, I didn't say it to him until ten months in. I never stopped loving him, even when we were apart, but I wanted to make sure he was going to stick around.

"I'll always love you, Stella Rose."

He sinks into me, stretching and filling me until all I feel is him. He leans down, balancing on his forearms and caging me in so all I see is his face inches from mine. He kisses me, moving in slow, measured thrusts that make my toes curl. Sometimes we have rough, explosive sex, but this is all consuming. It's everything. Our souls are tangled in each other, and I never want it to end.

"Thank you for making my dreams come true," I rasp as a tear falls down my cheek.

"I told you, baby girl, I would do anything for you."

He kisses down my neck, across my chest. He must feel my pleasure rising inside me, because he kneels up, lifts my leg over his shoulder and he drives into me faster. His other hand pinches my clit, and I detonate. He follows me over the edge, then cuddles me into his side. He reaches down near his pants pocket, but I can't see what he's doing.

"Remember when we were in the cabin during that snowstorm?" he hesitantly asks.

"Yeah, we were snowed in for four days." Those were the roughest four days I'd ever spent with Theo. We did a lot of soul searching and tackled some hard truths. But putting in the work made us stronger in the end.

"I told you that story about our moms taking us to the circus..."

"Yeah. One day I'd like to visit a circus again and recreate the pictures we have from our childhood. We can give them to my mom as a Christmas gift or something."

"Whatever you want. I have a gift for you." He shows me a small, Santorini-blue ring box. He opens it, showing me a marquise cut diamond ring. It has a halo of diamonds around it and is set in white gold.

I gasp, speechless. It's so beautiful.

"I bought this our second day here at a local jeweler when you took a nap. Stella Rose Cunningham, have I proven to you that we can be more? That I'll treat you right and give you everything you've always wanted?"

I hug him, squishing the ring box between us. "Yes. A thousand times over, yes. You teach me daily what it means to truly love someone, to be the 'more' your other half deserves."

We kiss, and he smooths my hair away from my face. He takes my hand and places the ring on my finger. "Will you become Mrs. Theo Woods, The Second of Maine?"

"The Third. I'll be Mrs. Theo Woods, The Third of Maine because my mom also married a Theo Woods," I deadpan before breaking out into a fit of cackling laughter.

He sighs, rolling his eyes. "Why would you bring that up right now, while we're naked in bed?"

"Because I love busting your balls," I retort without missing a beat.

"As long as you massage them better afterward, bust them whenever you want," he growls, pulling me on top of him and taking off my tank top. "You can start now."

The End...*for now.*

Keep your eyes open for an expanded version of this story in 2024.

ABOUT M. BONNET

M. Bonnet is a woman on a literary rampage. She wanted to see more female characters like herself–curvy, hilarious, sassy, strong, and slightly off kilter. If you want chaos, curves, and collateral damage, check her out. She writes both contemporary MF and paranormal why choose.

Add her on Instagram and Tik Tok.

Join her readers group.

Sign up for her newsletter.

Check out her other works.

Made in the USA
Middletown, DE
14 September 2023

38301425R00361